Furco's Deluxe Sportfishing Boat Dropped Anchor . . .

While the old man talked, Furco concentrated on the breeze blowing up from the south.

"You, you're vital . . . the whole operation nationwide," Grisanti said. "Why you? Because you're smart. And why you think," Grisanti went on, "we been given this deal and not all the somebodies that wanted?

"Because"—three fingers came down on Furco's wrist—"we're clean, Luke." With the other hand he pulled one finger back. "We don't do no sharking," Grisanti shouted, his eyes boring into Furco so he couldn't look away. "Two—no dope. And, three—no women."

Furco looked down at the hand. He did not like to be touched. More, he did not like to be grilled.

"What is it wid you and this"—Grisanti's hand waved—"bitch." Furco couldn't help himself. He felt his ears pull back and a flush rising to his face. He turned his head away.

"Luck-y," Grisanti howled. "It's like that, is it? *Marron'*.

"Women are a dime a dozen, Lucky. Even the lookers. But let me remind you, case you forgot, this is business. Big business. Maybe bigger than you know. You get things straight with that Toni broad, one way or the other. For keeps . . ."

NEON CAESAR

MARK McGARRITY

POCKET BOOKS

New York   London   Toronto   Sydney   Tokyo

An *Original* Publication of POCKET BOOKS

 POCKET BOOKS, a division of Simon & Schuster Inc.
1230 Avenue of the Americas, New York, NY 10020

ISBN: 0-671-66197-3

First Pocket Books printing December 1989

10 9 8 7 6 5 4 3 2 1

For all the good women of the Old Main.

And the bad.

PART
I

1

It had begun earlier that night—or, rather, morning—as she spooled through the register tape looking for false rings and freebies. If she was to be stolen from, it would be out in the open where others would know. She glanced at the four men in the corner booth.

She was a handsome woman of early middle age, tallish with a narrow waist and good shoulders that looked as if they'd been angled out too sharp, like in dress ads in the paper. But it was more the way she carried herself that snagged eyes: dipping the left shoulder when she walked, like a boxer tensing a hook, or propping her elbows behind her on a counter so the flare of her upper body could be studied.

She wore a sequined gown on the Friday night in question. Bottle green and pinned with a gold brooch, it clung only to the clean edges of those shoulders and on most other women would have slipped off.

There were men in the kitchen, the dining room, and the two bars of the large and popular roadside restaurant half-way between Philly and A.C. who would have liked that. They could imagine how the rack of her shoulders, cool in the hollows, would make her breasts seem heavy, like the softest, warmest weights. Certainly they made her tanned back, which the dress nearly exposed, more seductively curved and her stomach seem flat.

3

And yet for all her allure, there was a certain caution in the woman. Maybe it had something to do with her eyes which were dark and had deepened with age, or her hair that was turning gray and she did nothing about. Or perhaps it was her smile that raised high, definite cheekbones and seemed to say that in her thirty-eight years she had seen maybe too much of the life she was now leading.

Like the register tape that had several items missing and the voice of her chef, who had joined her there.

"You think maybe they keep records a' these things? You think maybe they say: It's the middle of May and guys, it's time. Oh, yeah? All right—we always do this the middle of May. Let's do it now.

"Or you think maybe it's taxes, or them getting back what they think is a bigger percentage on this place?" His voice was a low, angry rasp meant to be heard by nobody but her. There were people all up and down the bar now at closing. He was speaking into her ear, trying to keep her from doing something dumb. "Or the FICA or unemployment comp or the insurance—shit, the insurance—coming due? Not these humps. Logic? Them *think?* Nah, they just act. The hit. The vendetta. You got, they want. And that Furco, he's the worst of them all. A viper. A snake.

"Toni—" Solieri reached for her hand, which had snatched up a drinks tab "—how many years we been together?" He drew her into him, speaking so his breath—spiced with Sen-Sen or cloves or something from the kitchen—fuzzed in her ear. They were thigh to thigh. "Ten years? Twelve? Do something for me, please. I beg yuh. Really. Get outta this shit. Forget that tab. What's a few drinks? And forget them and forget us and forget about Jack and that briefcase."

It was down in the shadows by their ankles.

"You don't have to do that for them or nobody. Really. You're still young. You'll always be beautiful, and you go that way about you, you know you do. You'll be all right. You need money? I got money. What I need money for? Far as I know, it's only because of you I got what I got.

"But dump—" He tugged on her arm, and she glanced up at him. His face was red and wrinkled, like a piece of suede that had been tried out slowly in the hard heat of kitchens

4

"—dump the whole goddamn works and take Tina and split. Puerto Rico, the islands, Florida—anyplace you can." He too now glanced at the corner booth. "But get out now. For me."

Muñoz, her maître d', who now appeared at her other elbow, disagreed. In a whisper he said, "Yeah, chure, spleet—but nod tonight. Take that theeng, do what they want so they like it and don' care. Then later maybe—couple days, next week—you just gone and nobody know where.

"But please, Toni, tonight—" He shook his head. "Furco—I wait on him. I know. He's wild, dangerous. On some kinda tear. And you, me, Solly—we work too hard to get blown outta here. Or worse. You know him."

Yes, and better than either of them, which was why it had to be now. To his face. It was one thing to be "partners" and have to work off debt and not just at the restaurant, quite another when they took—no, *stole*—a night's receipts that they'd done nothing themselves to make. And another still when they stole a whole *week's* receipts on the scam of a phony robbery, so they'd get paid double with the insurance.

With the warm spring weather it had been their best six days for months. Toni had first-quarter bills still to pay—utilities, purveyors, the insurance that with the liquor liability was insane. And she was damned if they'd make her dip into her own meager savings to keep afloat the restaurant that she and her husband, Jack, had started five years earlier. It was the savings she'd put by as escape money, in case the whole mess became worse than it already was.

"Think of Tina," Muñoz said.

She was, she told herself, especially of Tina. What kind of mother could she be if she didn't respect herself? It had come down to that.

She had found no Strega or Galliano charges on the register tape, and she pulled her arm away. She slid the card into the register and punched in three rounds for $31 with tax. She dropped it in the check slot for the corner booth.

Turning, she smiled professionally, her hands moving to her sequined thighs. "Excuse me," she said overloud and overbright to a clutch of drinkers who, deep in conversation, had turned their backs to the bar. "I'd like to buy you a drink. Can you tell me what it is you're drinking?" She reached for some glasses, and two old men—regulars—traded glances.

For beyond adjusting a fork or rearranging some flowers "the Tone," as they called her, touched nothing—no checks, no money, not a napkin, a reservation chit, or a corkscrew. She was the girl—or, rather, very much the woman—for whom the party (held nightly until two-thirty) was being thrown, and every paying customer was treated as her invited guest. The illusion, she had found, helped her patrons relax, knowing they themselves would not be made the center of attention and it would be okay to stare at the hostess.

And they did, especially when she came around the bar and, breaking another of her rules, sat and drank with them.

Said the smallest of the four men in the corner booth, "Whuz she doin' now?" His name was Mazullo, and his old man was a wheel from farther north on the Shore. He'd been put down here in A.C. to learn the ropes under the Griz who was a friend of the family and Furco's boss.

"Drinks," said one of the two others, who were all pumped up from years of weight lifting and provided ready muscle. Literally.

"Now? Why? Fewer here the better. I thought we tol' Nicky." Mazullo looked over at the bartender and then glanced at the other man in the booth, who had placed himself where he could watch Toni Spina and view the bar.

Yeah, Furco had told Nicky, and he had told her, too. But there she was shoving his face in it again, like she knew she could get away with it, though he'd never let on how he felt. They'd come down to it, one of these days, and he'd ream her ass good. He wondered how much she thought he could or would take. Or was there something else to it?

Like what? he asked himself. He was trying to keep it all clear. The whole picture.

At forty-four, Lucca Furco was still lean and athletic, and he took pride in looking sharp. Today it was a double-breasted blazer with contrasting pleated beige slacks and a quiet rep tie the same blue as the jacket. He kept his dark hair, which was graying, swept back along the sides, and his tassel loafers polished to a sheen that wasn't too bright. Furco liked everything just a little understated. There was no edge in attracting attention.

"You shoulda never let her stay," Mazullo went on. "You shoulda fuckin' broke her fuckin' head. First off. Then, she still wanted in, hey—" He hunched soft, rounded shoulders and inserted a finger between his collarless shirt and neck where his hair—whole black, oily tangles of it—curled onto his back. In a kind of disgust, he turned his head to the wall. His skin was sallow and looked flabby. His eyes were soft and liquid. A nostril twitched.

Furco waited what seemed like an hour for Mazullo to look at him again. Mazullo whose old man had gone over Furco's head to Grisanti to place him in the "dry," which was what they called the money-laundering operation that Furco ran. "Sure, he's young, but he'll learn," the Griz had told Furco. "If he don't, what's it to us? The old man'll pick him up in a coupla years anyways, and meanwhile we done an important guy a favor." If the punk wasn't already dead by then, Furco had thought even then.

Punks. Furco had been dealing with punks all his life, and he could pick them out by sight. Quicker by smell. They were all flash clothes and big mouths, but they stank of fear, and, old man or no old man, there was a smell off Dino Mazullo you could touch.

"You callin' the shots here?" Furco asked.

Mazullo didn't say no, he said, "It's just—"

"You know how something like this should go down?"

Mazullo again hunched his shoulders, as if to say, who don't? They were orders they had gotten direct from the Griz, who had gotten them from higher up. He'd been told to turn up the heat on her. Push her to the max. Make her think she'd never get out from under them. There was something she was being set up for, or so Mazullo's old man thought. Dino had heard it from him.

"You done this before with—" Furco flicked out a hand "—a woman like that? You know, an older, successful woman. A woman who's got—" again the hand "—four, five hundred witnesses here every night. Lawyers, cops, judges, influential people. You used to dealing with somebody like that?"

7

Mazullo made a point of looking at the other two before turning back. "Ain't sayin' that. Me? I'm used to dealing with bitches, is all."

Even hearing Mazullo speak of her like that set Furco off. "She a bitch?"

"She is to you."

"What's that mean?"

Mazullo's big, soft eyes widened. He even jacked up his voice like there was no respect. "Means she knows you'll take shit. Her shit. Show me you won't."

Blood surged past Furco's collar. It filled his head and pounded in his temples, and he had to fight to keep his hands from shooting across the table and crushing the cocky little fuck right there.

"Hey," Mazullo went on with a smirk, "it ain't me, it's her. She's the one's got your stones, 'member?"

Trying not to laugh, the others turned away.

But Furco held it. He had to. He hadn't gotten where he was by being stupid. His time would come, and, if he was lucky, the little suck would self-destruct. He was like a time bomb, ready to go off.

And then they were hearing a siren, and the dome beacon of a cruiser splashed the windows with bloody light.

"Which one's the manager?" asked a uniformed cop with wide, padded shoulders. "I been tol' there's been a robbery here."

Heads turned to Toni. She only looked at him. The Borghese was at that moment as quiet as she had ever known it. In the distance they could hear other sirens approaching.

The cop's head rolled, impatient. He tried to keep himself from looking toward the corner booth.

Finishing her drink, she stood and faced him. "I'm food and beverage. Theft is over there." She turned her chin to the corner booth.

Some of the drinkers began laughing as she returned to the back of the bar. There she snatched up the large valise from the floor and slammed it down on a beer cooler. Thumbing open the snaps, she popped the lid and revealed stacked rows of one-hundred-dollar bills.

A woman raised a hand to her mouth. Men began to lift themselves off their bar stools to gape.

Straightening up, Toni glared defiantly at the corner booth. "Is it all here, *Mr.* Furco?" Her eyes couldn't find Furco. "Got anything to add?" And when she heard nothing, she shouted, "Shall I go now? Or you want to wait for an official tally?" She meant the cop.

But she felt something hard on her wrist, and Furco was suddenly beside her with his back to the bar, pulling down on her arm so their shoulders touched. His right eye met her left. "Don't fuck with me," he said in a small voice that, she guessed, only she could hear. "Don't. *Please.*"

It wasn't the threat but the plea that frightened her. He wasn't bluffing, and she had heard the stories about who he was and how he'd arrived there. He'd kill her, if he had to.

Still meeting her gaze, he released her wrist.

Her step faltered as she moved toward the valise. She was shaking now, and she closed the lid and walked down the length of the bar, half-hoping some other cop would stop her on her way to her car.

"Who's the fuckin' beef?" the cop asked Furco when they'd reached the corner booth. "You oughta do somethin' about huh. Way she's acting, she could blow the whole thing." Their heads turned to Toni as she crossed the dining room toward the foyer and the door.

Said Mazullo, turning his calf eyes on Furco, "All we need is a word."

It took Furco a moment to think. Considering who Mazullo was and how he talked, Furco had best cover his ass in some way. "Tail her. Discreetly." His eyes swung to Mazullo's. "You know what that means, Dino?"

"Us, too?" one of the other two asked.

Furco turned his head to the glass blocks of the wall, through which lights from the cars in the parking lot were shining like little stars.

The three men left.

The cop slid into the booth.

2

Out in the parking lot, her courage returned. In the glare of police headlights she tossed the valise on the roof of her Seville, while she searched through her purse for her keys.

A cop got out and ambled over, his hand on his holster, looking around. "Anything wrong, Toni?" It was Mickle-savage, the sergeant who for a case of Grandad kept an eye on the place, or so he said.

"Oh, no—" she was still rummaging through her purse, and her anger made her voice husky, out of breath "—nothing. Not a thing, Sergeant. Everything's just as it should be." Twisting her head to him, she looked up into his eyes, and he glanced away, out into the night.

So, she thought, he was in on it, too. They probably all were. How much grease could Furco be spreading around? The "robbery" and his money-laundering operation, for which Toni had had to work now for more than two years, couldn't be all of it. Maybe he was into dope. Or women. Maybe he was running a book. She could sting him there.

She thought of her debt and Jack and how she'd gotten involved with Furco. But her hand came up with her keys, and she unlocked the door. "And how's by you? Enjoying the spring? Or don't you get out much? Never know what you'll see." She snatched the valise from the roof and held it in front of her so that it caught the full light from his cruiser, where some other man was sitting.

10

"I'm okay." His eyes now returned, reassessing her in the manner of a veteran cop—her bare arms, her evening dress, the fact that she wasn't wearing a coat. The eyes fell to the valise, then canted off again. No question, he knew. None whatsoever.

"Aren't you going to ask me where I'm going so early, Sergeant?" She opened the door. "Or what's in this case?" She waved it. "Mr. Furco claims there's been a robbery in there." She flicked her head toward the restaurant and with her free hand pushed back the lock of silvery hair that had fallen in front of one eye.

His eyes again lighted on the valise, then rose to her chest, checking her out.

"It could be that I'm the thief. Greedy. For insurance purposes. You know, double-dipping. Double receipts. Know who insures us? No—you couldn't know *that*. The pension fund of the Hotel and Casino Workers Union. Furco's or Grisanti's or Mazullo's union. One or another of those *gentlemen*.

"Think of it. We had a big week—banquets, a graduation, two weddings. It came to nearly $80,000 gross." She raised her chin and stared at him, waiting. "Why don't you meet me down the road? We'll stage our own little fiction with my half of the take. Fifty-fifty with my $35,000.

"The rest of it?" Toni hefted the valise with both hands, raising it into the direct beam from the police car. "Well, it's what I do for fun on weekends. Laundry. Imagine, a woman like me who was never near a tub in my life. But it's inviolable, as we both know. *Verboten*—or, rather, *proibito*, to keep the whole thing properly ethnic." Her eyes met his once more. "Can I tell you something you probably don't know?"

Micklesavage sighed, but she had his interest.

"A million in hundreds weighs sixty-two point five pounds. How much you think this is?" With both hands and using the strength of her shoulders, she chucked the valise at his chest.

He caught it and shook his head, then handed it back to her.

"What—you some sort of goon? Some bozo? Can it be you're on the take?" When he didn't answer, she added,

"Or you just scared?" Like the rest of us, she thought. But he knew that, too.

She jerked the valise by one handle and tried to toss it into the car. It hit the steering wheel and bounced off the seat onto the floor. She got in and pulled on the door.

But the cop was holding it. "Easy, Toni. Go easy," he said in a soothing voice. "We've known each other a long time. Them? They can only hurt themselves with this shit. There's only so much people will take." He jerked up a thumb, as though to indicate higher authorities.

She tried to pull the door closed, but he held it. "Remember what happened to Jack. Think of your daughter."

Was that another threat, or was she just getting paranoid? It was hard to tell sides when even uniforms didn't matter.

Tugging with all her might, she closed the door and let out a cry of frustration. And through tears that spangled the headlights and warped the shapes of cars passing on the highway, she turned the Caddy toward the dim glow she could see in the distance to the east.

Atlantic City. Toni Spina had been born and raised there. During summers when she was in college, she had worked in its casinos. She had met her husband in one, and later together they had "recreated" there. That was Jack's word for the activity that had so changed their lives, not always for the worse.

Now, however, she stopped only once before getting on with the "work" that even in her abjection she knew was more important than any she performed at the Borghese. In the parking deck of Harrah's Marina, she pulled up to a pay phone and called her home in Cherry Hill.

"Who's zis?" asked the woman who had functioned as the only mother Toni had ever known. "Toni ain' home."

"Ma—it's me, Toni." Her own mother had died at her birth.

There was a pause, then, "Why you not back? Iz late."

Toni could picture her mother-in-law as she always was, up every night until she returned. Since her husband's death nearly two decades before, Gabriela Spina—called Ma now by the two remaining people who really knew her—had worn black housedresses, black stockings and shoes, and a black, cable-knit cardigan. Like Jack's had been, her hair was still a lustrous platinum color. Cut short, it was combed back in the tight finger waves that had been popular in the Naples of her youth.

She was a pretty woman, and her skin was golden and supple. She wore rimless glasses with gold bows, and she now lived only for her granddaughter, Jack and Toni's child. In her hair was always a barrette, which was also gold and the one relic of a former vanity.

"Tina sleeping?"

"Sure—how come you no' home?"

Toni glanced up at the velour of the headliner, knowing the old woman would make it difficult. Across from the parking deck, three older men had hoisted themselves from the darkness of a stretch limo and now turned toward some stylish black women who were leaving the casino. One man, his face livid and his suit coat open, reached for his belt and in trying to hike his trousers over his belly uttered some drunken, manly growl. The effort made him stagger back.

"Asshole," said one of the women, twisting her head so that her dreadlocks spanked her shoulders.

"It's Friday, and I've got work again. Like I do every week." For 143 weeks, she did not think she should add. There were enough of them who were counting.

"Why?"

"Because I *have* to, Ma. Let's not get into this again. It's work and it's late and I'm tired."

"What kind of work?"

"Work work—the kind that pays the bills," Toni said sternly, her temper squalling.

"With men?"

The Old World again. It was all she could think, when for the past nearly three years Toni had in fact been as faithful to her own missing husband as Maria Francesca had been to hers for the eighteen years since his death. And to think that the old woman could have lived in this country for—how long had it been, nearly a half century?—and not understand that prostitution wasn't the only way out of debt for a woman. Or, at least, not the kind of prostitution that she imagined.

"Ma—I don't want to discuss it."

"How long?" There was a smug tone to that, as though she had confirmed her suspicions.

"The weekend. Like always. I'll be back Monday morning. Look—the number is in the book. In red on the first page. The Claridge." She waited, then said, "Are you still there?"

She had to wait some more.

At the entrance to the casino, two of the men had pulled the third back. "Bitch!" he shouted after the black women, who were now laughing, the voices clear and bell-like in the concrete garage. "Cunt!" They ignored him and stepped toward another limo with shaded windows that gleamed like onyx in the marquee lights. A chauffeur opened the door, and they eased themselves into the wide, empty car. Escort girls. Hookers with a difference. They hustled only "whales," the high rollers who were flown in with thousands to gamble and were therefore "comped"—compensated, or given free of charge—everything they needed but luck.

"How we get food?"

"Ma—there's plenty of food in the fridge, and you know it. If you run out, there's some in the freezer. If you run out of that or you just don't feel like cooking, call the place. Solly will send some out to you. You just tell him what you want. Anything."

"How Tin' getta school, if you not back?"

Her mother-in-law no longer left the house, but Toni would be back early Monday morning. She'd make sure of it. "I'll be there, but if I'm not, have Tina go next door. She's a big girl now, and you can watch her from the window. Jane'll take her down to the stop."

"She not. She *bambina*. And Jane—"

"Ma—not now, please. I have to hang up. You—" Be good? No. Take care? No again, for of course she would. "—give my love to Tina. Bye."

In a remote corner of the parking deck that still caught light from the Harrah's marquee, Toni dumped the stacks of money onto the mat of the floor and, removing the belly band from each bundle, counted the cash. After years of daily register tallies, her hands snapped through the bills—hundreds on top with mainly twenties below, rumpled and hand-worn from surreptitious, deathly street deals, she did not doubt—and she gave herself over to the rhythm of her count. When it came to cash, costly lessons had taught her to trust nobody, especially those whose money it was. And since they would hold *her* accountable for *their* total, she would make her own.

Her task completed and the sum noted in the diary that she kept in her purse, she removed a stack of manila envelopes from the valise and stuffed each with varying amounts up to $10,000. There were twelve envelopes. Tomorrow a messenger would bring her another valise with twelve more, and on Sunday the same yet again.

There had been a time when any dollar amount could be laundered through a casino, but a few years back the IRS had made all sums over $10,000 reportable. For a time certain casinos continued to break the law, but they got hit hard and nearly lost their gaming licenses. It was then that men like Furco and his boss, Grisanti, had organized their teams of "mules" who schlepped the "wash" or "dry" (the terms were used interchangeably) through the city's growing multiple of casinos.

It was piecework, but it was safe. With 30 million visitors running some $3 billion through the resort every year, the authorities would find it all but impossible to develop a case against anybody but an individual mule and his or her bundle on any given run. As a precaution, Furco had established in the names of his primary runners bank accounts sizable enough to justify their gambling activity. In Toni's case, with the Borghese in her name, such a device was not necessary, which was more to her shame, she thought.

She made sure nobody was around before sliding out again and carrying all but one bundle to the back of the car, where for safety she arranged them neatly in the spare-tire well. Replacing the lid and the carpet, she closed and locked the trunk lid, put the remaining bundle back in the valise, then drove the Seville back down the ramps and parked it in a prepaid slot near the attendant's office.

He opened the door for her, saying, "Evening, miss. Pleasure to see you again. Ain't you cold with no coat?"

It was only then that Toni realized that she was feeling the cold and in her anger and haste had left the overnight bag that she used on these weekends back at the restaurant. It could be cold in spring on the boardwalk, and she would need her coat. She shrugged and remarked, "Hot-blooded woman—what can I say?" not really thinking about her words but knowing she felt different—still angry, yes, but reckless, too, as if nothing could possibly be worth what she was now doing.

It was a dangerous mood. She had felt like that before, and it had never worked out well. "And I assume your place is heated." She meant the casino across the entrance road.

The old black man laughed. "It's that, all right. Sizzlin'."

Toni had almost forgotten, and she reached inside her purse and handed him the card. It read, "L. Furco," and nothing else. She hoped it meant some money to the old fellow, though she doubted it. It was like Furco's own, self-given key to the city, and as much as said that wherever Furco or his people went they went free. Or else.

He only slipped the card in his pocket, then said, "Say—you Sam's girl?"

She started at the mention of her father. He still lived and worked on St. Charles Place, though she preferred not to visit him at such times. "Yes." She smiled more fully now, studying his face, which she had been seeing on nights like this and now recognized from long ago. "Didn't you used to come to my father's Friday nights?"

"*Used* to?" he asked, smiling. "Still do. Heck, I just come from his place."

Founded as a resort, A.C. had been virtually an open city for the fifty years before the casinos arrived and gambling had been winked at by the authorities. Nearly every block had had its numbers grocery, nearly every neighborhood its back-room game.

"Hope you won. You're—?"

"Billy. Billy Miller."

Toni had gone to school with several Miller children, but she couldn't now remember their names.

"You're Toni, right? Sam keeps sayin' we should all come out and see you. Hammonton, ain't it? A restaurant. The big one there on the side of the road just up from the Ramada. The—"

"Borghese."

Chilled now, Toni tried to turn away.

"Sure is a mouthful. Where'd you get that name any-how?"

"My husband. Listen, Billy, I—"

"Yes, ma'am—you better get yourself inside." His eyes fell to the valise.

"See you in a bit," she said.

At the door to the casino, she turned back to see the old man staring down at Furco's card, and she had to force herself to move toward reception.

There she registered as Toni Spina, and established an $8,500 credit, which was enough to be comped a room. On Saturday she would re-register as Antonina Alexandra Spina, her full name, and on Sunday as A. A. Sammasian, her maiden name. Each time she would pay in some amount slightly less than $10,000 from the further satchels, and she would gamble a little in each casino, just to maintain the ruse. In such a way she alone would process around $350,000 over the three-day period, with the laundered funds being wired or mailed to one of a set of banks that she would be given instructions to name.

When a bellhop tried to carry her valise, she smiled and held up a hand. "Do I look that old?"

In the room, she removed a small notebook from her purse and picked up the phone. Calling each of the dozen other casinos, she made room reservations in her three names. Once she was on the computer, signing in over the next two days would be easier.

Back down in the parking deck, she said to Billy Miller, "Lucca Furco comes into my restaurant. He told me to give you that, you know, whenever— Is he being good to you?"

"Yes, ma'am," he replied too readily. "Mr. F., he never forgets."

"Well, in case he does, I appreciate your looking after me all these months." She held out her hand, and, when he didn't reach for it, she slipped the bill concealed by her fingers in his pocket.

"I can't take this," he complained. Pulling it out and turning it over, as if to check its authenticity.

"Why not?"

" 'Cause I've knowed you too long."

"I thought we just met."

But driving toward Trump's Castle, the next casino, Toni blushed with shame to think of what she had become and for whom. Where would it end? She rubbed her fingers together. They felt sticky from the blood money she had counted, though, of course, she didn't really know that, did she?"

She knew.

But *had* she actually lied to the old man? When an hour later she pulled into the Resorts International parking garage, she'd decided that she had. It had been her intention—whatever her words—to cover what she was doing, though he doubtless knew.

At the kiosk, she handed the Resorts man another little card and told him that she would return in the morning. She snatched up the valise. She would buy herself a jacket in one of the casino shops that were open all night and complete the drops on foot.

By sunup, her mood had eased somewhat, or at least she hoped it had, and with the new jacket pulled over her shoulders, Toni Spina walked south on the boardwalk, the valise becoming lighter with each casino stop. The onshore breeze was blustery and cold, but the sun on her face was pleasant, and she let her mind run free.

She thought of the ocean, her youth, the roof of her house in Cherry Hill, which was leaking and needed attention, her age, which she was beginning to feel. She looked down, and one of her earliest memories came back to her: of the sun on the bleached pine of the boardwalk and how in certain light, like now, it barely glowed with a rainbow sheen.

Once, barely able to walk and holding her father's hand, she had stooped to touch the colors, which vanished in her shadow. Again and again she'd tried to touch the rainbow and had spent the day on her knees tracing the herringbone pattern of the boards while her father talked to friends or drank coffee in the deep shade of a boardwalk bar or played cards on a picnic bench above her, his voice warm and confident and reassuring. She could still smell his cigar, the beer drying in the bottoms of paper cups, the sweetness of the hot sap in the boards, the iodine tang of the sea. She could still feel that sun.

And although she had tried to prevent it, the carny delights of the boardwalk with its forbidden foods and games of chance had crept into their lives. Steeplechase Pier had loomed large in what she viewed as her subversion. There she and her brother had spent Sundays splashing in the surf that broke against its even then old wooden pilings. On the way home with an hour left and a dollar apiece, they had plied the dodgems or shoved pennies into the machine games in the arcade. And when the gates rattled shut and they found themselves suddenly famished, home and their kitchen and the prospect of having to prepare a meal became a trial that nobody, especially her father, wished to endure.

Mortified with guilt, averting his dapper, mustachioed face so no fellow Jew might see him, Ibrihim Sammasian (Abe or Sam to his many friends) had waited while Toni and Jim ("You're in America now. I give you American names.") gorged on chili dogs with onions and mustard, funnel cakes, cotton candy, heroes dripping with hot sausage and greasy peppers. Still later in the evening ("We can't go home now. The neighbors'll see us. We'll wait till they're in bed.") they had played games of chance. In booths on the boardwalk, Toni had tossed balls at bottles, darts at balloons, had even fired guns at targets, and filled her bedroom with a collection of gruesome stuffed animals and kewpie dolls that had been the envy of all her friends.

Toni had learned other, better lessons from her father, but she had wondered now, as she glanced beyond the boardwalk glitz at a street of squat row houses and sagging commercial buildings, who had chosen whom: her father the city, or the city her father? For from her first trip away, Toni had realized that Atlantic City had the definite look of a place that just wasn't willing to sweat for a buck. It took life on a shake/roll, always looking for a quick score on a scam, and her father—God bless him—had interpreted the coming of casinos to the city as a direct sign that he had lived a good life: cards, stocks, real estate, women ("Does she or don't she, and you must *prove* it!"), fishing, horses, numbers, bingo, sweepstakes tickets, lotteries—he would bet on anything. But always and ever, it had been dice that had capti-vated him.

On Fridays, payday in the Atlantic City of her youth, her dark and still handsome father had arranged at the back of his tailor shop bolts of felt that formed a kind of craps table that could be taken down with a flick of his wrist. Smoking was prohibited, as was drinking, swearing, and any type of credit. It was a game for purists, from which, of course, children had also been excluded. It had made the game all the more alluring.

So that when, as was inevitable for two children of a widower who spent most of his life in his shop, he found them playing with his dice, he decided to expand their curriculum. Having been a teacher before emigrating from Romania, he told them, "School is good. It's necessary and broadens you. But what I show you here is vital. It's life. It can also be a weakness, a curse, but handled right—" he had glanced up at the light through the transom over the door "—*Sh'ma Yisroel,* it's sweet and can bring a spice and vibrancy to your life." He had then repeated the Biblical quote, "Be ye therefore wise as serpents but gentle as doves."

And thus in the back room leaning over the green felt, he had made them take pencils and note pads and log all scores in series of 144 rolls, over and over again, until it became obvious how many times the various numbers of the thirty-six possible combinations came up: sevens, sixes, and eights the most; next nines and fours; then tens, threes, and elevens; and finally snake eyes and boxcars. It also ex-plained why proposition bets—that a number or combination of numbers would or would not appear during a specified series of passes—were sucker shots and not worth the gamble.

"So, what's the point of it all?" Again his dark eyes had flashed. "*Streaks,*" he fairly shouted. "Rolls, tears, runs—call them what you will—but you know from your records there, they happen. Will you throw that seven or, if not, will you make your point and crap out? Three, four, five times running you can score. You saw on your chart that in 144 rolls the eight should come up twenty times, but when *will* it?

"I once saw a man make seventeen straight passes and then predict that on the eighteenth he'd fail. It was a proposition, incidentally, that your father could not resist. And I'm here to tell you—" his fingers had crimped toward the ceiling "—it was sublime. A revelation. A moment when things came together.

"You laugh?" His eyes had flickered down at them, but Toni had known even then that her father was baring himself. "You say, not probable? Impossible?" He had then stepped to the open door and pointed into the street. It was summer, and passersby, having heard his dramatic tones, had stopped to stare. "Isn't the world, the universe, life itself an improbability from all we can know? But *impossible?*"

"But how will we know when it's a streak?" they had asked.

"It can't be known, only felt. It's a thing that either strikes you or it don't. A premonition, or the way things are going. An . . . atmosphere. The hour, the day, the person, but something *must* strike you, and you must know it for what it is.

"If it don't, don't gamble. And if it does—" Abe Sammasian had then raised his tanned face to the ceiling and laughed in a way that Toni was never to hear again and now thought of as cruel "—don't gamble. *Much.*"

So it was that as usual on a Friday night, Toni—having completed her first pass through the casinos—should have felt tired, exhausted, but no longer did.

It was as if week after week her body kept playing a practical joke on her and, knowing that she would have to be ready to deal with another valise in only four or five quick hours, decided to keep her wide awake nearly until the time the messenger knocked on the door of her comped room at the Claridge, her favorite hotel. For only then would the exhaustion set in, just when she'd have to begin the trek from reception desk to reception desk.

Then, she had been told, she should gamble: "Make a show. Play the queen. Lose maybe two hundred per package, three at the outside, but no more. If you win, you make up what you lost. If you win big, it's yours. But I don't have to tell *you*—don't try."

21

Those had been Furco's words and unfair. Even then she hadn't cared for the flint in his eye and the way he had looked at her, sidelong and assessing. It was as though there were something about her that bothered him and that neither of them understood.

The deal of how and how long it would take her to work out from under the debt? Perhaps. And again its stigma encroached upon her mood, filling her mind with darkness, making her feel hopeless and spent. Then there had been the phony heist, which just added salt to the wound.

Ordering a Fernet Branca in a bar of the Trump Plaza, she thought of her husband and how hard they had worked to make the Borghese a success. And she thought of the tragedy of . . . expectations crushed, she decided, not wanting to consider the totality of their ruin. She ordered a second drink, which she sipped.

Until blood throbbed in her temples, and suddenly she found herself on her feet, disoriented by the rows of tiny lights and walls of mirrors and gaming tables that had been placed at various levels to confound perspective and make the immense void of the darkened gaming room seem unreal and out of time. A trap.

And, yes, her step faltered at first, and she could not quickly find the carpeted ramps that led up to the tables. Soon, however, she found herself stalking games, testing her luck at blackjack—two cards here, three there; a score, a loss, another small score—until within an hour or two she lost the requisite $200. Tired now, she turned to locate an exit and some way out of the deep maze. She would catch a taxi back to the Claridge. She would sleep until well past noon, and the new valise could wait until then.

But it was then she heard a kind of roaring, punctuated by shouts and cheers, from an area that was set off from the general gambling floor by a long, sloping ramp. A casino employee with a laminated picture ID clipped to his uniform vest was standing before the chrome stanchions of a rope gate.

"The game has a minimum, ma'am," he announced when Toni approached him.

Never before, not in her—how many now?—ten years of frequenting or working in or near casinos had she known a craps game to be removed from the gambling floor like this and monitored. She wondered if it was even legal or, rather, would be acceptable to the state gambling control commission when, as was inevitable, it was reported. "How much?" she asked.

"One hundred dollars," the man said with a curt, dismissive smile.

Toni opened her cupped hands and fanned a stack of fifty-dollar chips. Slipping the rope from its hook, the man stepped aside, and she advanced upon a smoky table that was packed with people who were betting heavily. Chips were stacked on every rail, and nowhere more than before a wide black man to her immediate right, who was wearing a rumpled blue waiter's tux with a frilly lavender shirt. The collar was open, and his bow tie was clipped to the tip of one corner.

Picking up the dice as another stack of chips was pushed his way, he turned to her and, although he was a huge person, smiled in a shy way that she found engaging. "How you doin' tonight, girl?" he asked in a low, familiar tone, his eyes running down her sequined gown and returning to her face.

"Not as well as you." She glanced at his stack of chips.

She had seen him before often on these weekends. For—how long was it now?—six months, seven perhaps, he had passed her on the boardwalk or had been gambling at a table nearby and once had even sat on a stool at a counter near the booth where she'd been having coffee.

It was there that they had struck up a conversation, after his head had swung suddenly as though looking at somebody passing by the windows on the boardwalk and he had seen her. He had smiled at her, that same shy smile, and nodded and turned away. Then, after a while, he'd turned back and asked, "Don't I know you from someplace?" in the way of gamblers who concentrate so totally on their game that they hardly notice things or people around them. "You come in the Trop? To eat, I mean. I'm a waiter there." He had motioned to his serving tux. "I try to remember all my covers, but we do volume there, and . . ."

It had gone on like that for a few minutes, Toni saying that she too was in the restaurant business and he pretending he'd heard of the Borghese, though he added that he was from Las Vegas and had been in A.C. less than a year.

"Got tired of the desert."

"Not the tables?" she had asked.

His smile was big then. "That's right. That's it," he'd said. "You and me, we *gamble* together. Now I remember," and from that time they had waved when they'd seen each other. On another occasion, when she had just needed some air and had taken a break on a bench outside the Tower, he had eased himself so soundlessly onto the other end that she was rather startled when she noticed him there.

"I'm keeping a log of how many hours I spend in restaurants and casinos," he had said. "That way when I retire or just get lazy, whichever comes first, I'll have me a pension. I'll start this big lawsuit against the tobacco companies or the air-conditioner companies or the casinos—" he held up a tan palm "—*no* restaurants, don't worry—about their bad air and this here emphysema or asthma or bronchitis or cough I'll make damn sure I got. And then you can find me in—"

He'd paused, and Toni had supplied, "Monaco or Curaçao or—"

"You got it. The Bahamas. Someplace I can get a little table action and still not lose my air-conditioner pension. De-troit, probably. An insurance man won't go near that place."

They had laughed and talked for a little while longer, and he had left.

But now the action was on him, and somebody yelled, "C'mon, man—roll 'em. Keep 'em rollin'," and the stickman echoed the call.

"When you hot, you hot," two white men behind them sang together without completing the other half of the lyric.

"Could you be Lady Luck?" he asked her in the same quiet voice in which he'd spoken to her on the bench, as if they were the only two standing there at the table. In his palm the white-pipped red dice looked like two bloody eyes.

Pushing her own small stack forward so as not to jinx his luck, Toni said, "Let's hope I'm early."

Immediately hands from the sides and in back of them followed her lead, and, as if to kiss the dice or warm them with his breath, the man raised his fist to his mouth. Straining beneath the synthetic material of the tux, the muscles of his forearm cocked once, twice, and then he cast the dice from his palm as though chucking something worthless away.

The red cubes skittered across the table and bounced off the rail, one spinning briefly on a corner until it fell in a single pip to match a six that was already down.

"A natural!" somebody shouted.

"Lady *Luck!*" the man said in an intense but quiet voice that was audible in spite of the roar from the crowd around the table. His left arm seized Toni by the waist and pulled her into him. Smiling fully now, he leaned toward her and bussed her cheek. Against her like that, he felt huge and as hard as granite, and, as he pulled back his head though still against her, his eyes met hers with a force that Toni found dizzying.

"Bastard's hot," yelled one of the men behind them. "Sombitch can roll. And roll. And roll." He started to laugh, harder as the stickman pushed back his pile of winnings. "How many times that been?"

"Don't ask!" somebody else cautioned. "You'll jinx—"

"Four times."

Yet another person mumbled something, then added, "Thing like this could make you believe in integration."

But the man and she were still staring at each other, smiling, studying features—his round and glistening and friendly—and then returning with the same heady force to each other's eyes.

And she thought for a moment she knew him, and not just as somebody she had gambled with. Had she met him in school or, later, at Trenton State where she had studied to be a teacher? Like here in A.C., many of her friends at college had been black. She couldn't get over the feeling that somewhere, someplace, she had met him before.

Or had Jack or her father or some other man smiled like that—a smile of recognition, as though, without words, he knew her and she him? Looking into his dark eyes, which shimmered in the spotlights that had been rigged to illluminate the table, she was sure something like that had happened, perhaps in a dream.

And here now, standing with him hip to hip, his one arm wrapping her waist so that his hand rested hot on her stomach, as though stroking it, she felt like they had been together forever or that the moment was out of time—an hour, two, four, a week, part of her life. His smile, when he won, was huge. And suddenly she realized her forehead was damp, her ears were fuzzed. People passed before her in the smoke of the table as through a distant haze. She tried to remember how many drinks she had had. Two. Three?

But as the dice boat was passed to him, time seemed to make up for the lapse with a suddenness that was complete. As though drugged or stunned or being led, but willingly, she followed his lead, pushing out all the chips in front of her and wishing she had more. She felt light-headed and dizzy, but euphoric.

The dice then appeared in his hand, which he raised to his lips, kissing them. Turning to her, he then offered her his palm, and she, too, kissed them. In raising her face, her eyes again met his, and suddenly her lips were on his and their bodies together. The crowd cheered, and she could feel his other arm cock once, twice, and a third time, as he cast the dice from them.

"Eleven!" the crowd roared.

Breaking from him, Toni thought she might topple over. But he held her, and the crowd cried out again and again, as in a kind of ritual he first kissed the dice, made her kiss them, too, and then his lips scorched hers. Only then did he cast the dice. Against his body, her legs trembled.

And he was a smart bettor, working grinds with free odds on both pass and come and placing bets on six and eight. But it did not seem to matter what they called: proposition bets, "hard-way" bets, hops, horns; they were streaking, and both of them knew it.

"Press it," he said, when he had wildly called an eight and they had recklessly backed it with everything. "Press it again," he repeated, meaning to leave the bet and its winnings on the same number. They won once more.

And it was either then or during some other roll deep into the run that, after they had kissed, she did something that she had never done to any other man—Jack, her husband, included—in public. Standing there, surrounded by people who were concentrating on their bets and the tumbling dice, Toni reached into the shadows of the rib-high craps table and took hold of him.

She squeezed him and ran her thumb over the top of the wider, softer part. Flushed, the blood pounding in her temples, nearly faint now, she scratched her nails across the slick material of the tuxedo trousers, tickling him, coaxing him, trying to get him to turn to her. She then reached yet lower and hefted him in the palm of her hand, again squeezing him, but gently.

Why? She did not know.

Did she want him? Yes.

No.

She did not know.

And when on the next roll he turned to her, his hand was quaking—she could feel it—as he raised the dice to her lips. As he lowered his head to hers, their eyes met with all the force of freight trains colliding. Her tongue darted into his mouth. He responded. She was his, if he wanted her.

Breaking from him, she found herself suddenly out of breath. The green felt of the table, its gold lines and chips, swam before her eyes.

It was after that roll that he said, "I pass. Take me down."

The others at the table cried out, but the man smilingly insisted. "I know when to quit."

"Can we get you a drink?" a pit boss asked, suddenly at their side and wanting *his* money back. His way.

"Don't drink."

"A meal? A room? Everybody here's having so much fun."

"Nobody more than me," the man said jocularly, though not taking his eyes off the stickman, who was stacking his chips.

"But, sir—where's your sense of fun?"

It was then that the man turned to the pit boss, his smile falling. "Anybody ever tell you you try too hard?" he said in a low, soft voice that tilted back the pit boss's head.

Yet his first smile returned when he swung back to his chips. "Is this sport?" he asked the stickman to his immediate right.

"Yes, sir," the stickman answered, eyeing the eight stacks of hundred-dollar chips. "It's sport."

The man handed him a chip. "Sport?" he asked the boxman and the dice-dealer on the other side of the table.

Smiling, they chorused, "Sport!" and off the wide, flat thumbnail of his right hand he flipped the same to each.

Scooping up the tray with his chips, he did not once glance at Toni, only turned and pushed past the pit boss and was gone.

Suddenly chagrined and exhausted, Toni did not know what to do or think.

"Great roll," said the pit boss, who now took the place by her side. "Two off the house record. Obviously you know who he is."

How *obviously*, she wondered, flashing him a smile and trying to clear her head.

"Would you have his name and address?" the young man went on, removing a pen and note pad from a pocket. "We'd like at least to comp him a weekend." She could feel his eyes move down her body. "Or two." He then glanced at the stacks of chips before her. "You must be parched. Can I get you a drink?"

Would she have gone with him? It rather frightened her to think that she would have. Given all the problems Jack had had and what she'd had to deal with after he vanished, it had actually been years since she'd been with a man. She was, after all, a wife and a mother. She owned a business, or at least part of one, and people knew who she was. She would not allow herself to pick up a strange man in a casino.

Yet, trying to concentrate on the stacking of her chips across the table, she could still feel him in the palm of her hand, rigid but soft between her fingers and thumb.

Then the prospect of the two days to come and the necessity of having to return to the Borghese on Tuesday occurred to her like a great, vague unpleasantness that she thought she'd do almost anything to avoid. Raising the hand, she looked down into it and made a fist.

"Or a meal," said the pit boss, who was still with her. "Look—I'm only doing my job."

The best that you can, Toni thought, which wasn't much. Looking past him, she thought she could see the broad blue swath of the man's back in front of a cash cage, and she realized that she had not felt like that (hot, trembling, capable of anything) in years. And the feeling had been a rush. Undeniably good.

But capable of what, exactly? Her mind then flooded with images of something breathless, frantic, and even violent in a dark room. And then he was black, which added to the allure. Her father had always warned her against blacks. Like the table in front of her, it had become something that Toni always secretly wanted, if perhaps for a complex of other reasons too entwined to unravel.

"Actually, I'm more tired than famished or parched," she said to the pit boss, still staring down at her crimped fist. Having herself once worked for tips, she then tossed down on the table three hundred-dollar chips.

"Hear, hear!" said one. " 'At's a lady," said another.

"Where're you staying? May I comp you a room?" the boy went on. "Our floor show is unbeatable. Tonight we'll have—"

"Maybe some other time. I'm already staying here," she said, picking up her chips and moving by him.

But after she had cashed out and had swung her head to find an exit, she caught sight of the man climbing some stairs toward a cocktail lounge that seemed to be suspended in air above the gaming floor. On the top stair, he turned and looked directly at her, as though he had known exactly where she was.

Out on the boardwalk, she thought at first she would hike her skirt above her knees and run as fast as she could into the stiff breeze that was blowing in from the northeast. Soon she would be at the Claridge and her room and her own bed.

Instead, she turned around and stepped back into the casino. She was, she decided, more parched than tired. And famished. In her own way, she was famished.

She took an empty seat beside him at the bar and waved off the bartender who asked her if she wanted a drink. She then waited until they were alone.

"What happened down there at the table. I mean us, not the gambling. It was—" Again she waited, and in the mirror in back of the bar his eyes replied that it had been like that for him, too. He looked back down at his drink.

"Look—" she went on, not knowing the words to use but understanding even in her need that she had to be honest and brutally so. Her life was so . . . circumscribed that it couldn't tolerate another complication. "I don't know how you feel about it, but I want you—" she raised a hand "—for tonight but not—" her wrist turned.

He seemed to smirk, but he then smiled and turned his head to her. "Was it *you* who walked away? Or me?"

Then, suddenly, she was nervous. She fumbled with her jacket and tried to pay for his drink. She told him that it had to be the Claridge. "I might get a phone call," she said, not exactly lying.

In the taxi she did not actually shiver, but every once in a while her body seemed to jump, and the realization that all the emotions that for years now she had been stuffing down and denying and telling herself that she was too old for or didn't deserve or could no longer afford on any basis, would now suddenly be released nearly proved too much for her to control.

In the corner of a crowded casino hotel elevator, she reached behind her and again filled her hands with him, kneading him, clawing her nails up his thighs so that, when the door opened and they found themselves in the hallway, she could hardly walk. And the light had gone dim, colorless, and grainy.

And like one drunk or ill—she had to think about breathing—she staggered down the hallway, and at the door her teeth jumped for his tongue. His hand then pulled down the top of her sequined dress and the other lifted or drew or pulled her into the room, so that what happened against the other side of the door—she felt the cold metal on her bare back—was like combat: she slight and white and him a huge presence, filling her, crushing her. A man, after all that time.

Yet she won there, locking him with her thighs, refusing to let him go, and again on the edge of the bed with—it seemed to her—him desperate, pounding into her, the muscles of his back slick now from his exertion, the ridged crests of his buttocks forcing her palms apart after each thrust.

Only later—after she had answered the knock at the door and, taking the new satchel, thrown it into the back of the closet—with her swaying above him or, still later—after she had made the deliveries and returned to the room to find him still there—staring at the reflected fuzz of neon lights on the ceiling while he kept closing her eyes for her with each long, slow movement, had he his moments. She felt him throb and throb again and again, until he diminished and lay still.

Still later at the tables, as she lost and lost, she asked herself if she was *rebelling*—a word that she despised—against her father, who would have told her in great detail why she was losing: tired, distracted, reaching for WIN money, which he had taught her was half of anything she had won and should above all be saved; even asking, *begging* had been more like it, for markers that she couldn't afford.

Or was it the fact that her father had denied her a black friend when she had been old enough to think of him in other ways? Yes.

No.

She didn't know, only that life at the moment seemed to be nothing more than chance, and that room at the Claridge a necessary refuge.

At intervals only a few words were exchanged—"What's your name, anyhow?" he asked. "Coffee? A drink? Some breakfast?"

She had only smiled or reached for him or closed her eyes.

Until the knock came on the door of the room two days later and much before the time for the Sunday delivery. Toni sat up in bed and placed a finger to her lips. Who except Furco or somebody who worked for him could know she was there? Her mother-in-law. Could something have happened to Tina? Flushing with worry and guilt, she reached for the robe she had bought earlier in the day.

Leaving the night latch in place, she opened the door to find a short, stocky man dressed in a chauffeur's uniform. His feet were slightly spread, his black-gloved hands clasped in front of him. There was a cap on his head. "Ms. Spina?" he asked.

She nodded.

"Mr. H. Bruce Payson would like to see you. It's checked out with Mr. Grisanti and Mr. Furco. Mr. Payson cleared it with them."

The gloves moved, and like a magic trick a card appeared. The chauffeur had a wide, sallow face that looked almost oriental. A sharp widow's peak was showing beneath the brim of the cap. He extended the card toward the gap in the door.

"But I don't know this man," she said, taking it.

"I've been instructed to tell you that Mr. Payson will make you an offer that will end all of this."

"All of what?" She wondered if he could see into the room, and how much.

"The weekends. The casinos. He'd like to meet with you and talk to you personally there." He nodded toward the card. "In New York. Beekman Place. If you don't like the offer, I'll bring you right back here. To your car, the Caddy that's parked at Resorts. Or here." The man glanced over her shoulder into the room. "Anywhere you say."

She narrowed the gap through which they were speaking. Did they know about her car because she'd been followed, or because she'd made it a habit, always parking there?

"No more valises," the chauffeur went on, seeing her hesitate. "No more Furcos. Mr. Payson told me to tell you that. No more little 'robberies.' Mr. Payson told me to tell you that, too."

And maybe no more me, she thought, searching the chauffeur's eyes. He looked contained, reserved, considered. The type. Exactly.

But turning back to glance at what was now an empty, rumpled bed, she almost wished for that. And then, if they wanted her, she wasn't hard to find. "May I call this number?" She meant the telephone number on the card.

"Mr. Payson is expecting your call. I'll wait for you in the lobby."

The chauffeur touched the brim of his cap, then turned and walked slowly down the hallway.

Toni closed the door.

He was Lucca by birth, Luke in the world, and Lucky to his friends.

And three days after Toni Spina's summons to New York, he was sitting in one of two command chairs in the cockpit at the stern of his sportfishing boat. It was anchored in a ragged line with dozens of others on the Reef, a formation of shoals twenty-seven miles off the Atlantic City beach-front.

Given the distance offshore, none of the boats was small. But Furco's *Bark-a-Roll*—a loaded, 78-foot Huckins Fair-way Flyer with a cruising speed in excess of forty knots, a climate-controlled cabin for all-weather operation, and re-mote TV scanners with monitors even in the fishing cock-pit—was obviously the flagship of the fleet, and Furco was taking pride in the fact.

He had a Campari and soda in the glass well on the right armrest of the chair, and a thin, dark cigar between two fingers of his left hand. But Furco hardly drew on either. Nor was it with any anticipation that, along with the older man in the other chair who was also dressed in spanking whites, he was now waiting for the tide to turn.

Instead, he concentrated on the day that was unusually hot, maybe the last of what Furco thought of as high spring. While the man sitting beside him spoke, the boat slowly swung around on its anchor, heading up into the current that now began to flow in from the east. At the same time a brisk breeze from the south sprang up. It was cool and chilled the well-bronzed skin of Furco's face and hands whenever a cloud passed by the sun.

The sensation was pleasant, like a hot-towel-and-alcohol massage, and soothed him. Not so the stink. Already chum lines of old, chopped mackerel in fish oil were sluicing coppery through the sparkling, green tide wake there at the stern. Seagulls were spiraling down into the slick, their cries mingling with the squeals from the girl behind him and the wind in his ears. It made him miss most of what Grisanti had been sent to say.

That too was good. Furco had thought it might be coming, right down to the few words that because of the breeze that roared in his ears he could now catch. But of the three who'd been with him that night, who was the rat? The Bear, or Mazullo—Dino he was called—though Furco believed he knew which one had talked.

"... you, you're vital ... the whole operation, nationwide ... and why *you* and not ... ?" Grisanti's eyes, which were dark and quick and hidden in fleshy, pouchlike sacks, now shied behind Furco in the direction of the girl's nervous laughter. "Because you're smart. And you got a way wit' you." The wind rumbled in his ears, and Grisanti's hand reached across the space between them, as if it would touch Furco's wrist. It did not.

Swinging his head toward him, Furco instead watched the mate. He was lowering over the side a brimming bucket of chum, and Furco's eyes followed every sway, the *Bark* being for him almost a sacred thing. It was his retreat, his own little world where he alone was captain, the one thing he could point to and say that for all the shit he had done and had had to put up with—well, at least there was that.

A guy whose simplicity sometimes made him feel dumb, Furco often thought that, if life had a purpose, it was the way he felt on the deck of that boat he'd had customized for him and the dream he had of it. And fishing with Grisanti—who had not really been invited—was nowhere in that picture.

The lecture, which Furco continued to hear intermittently, went on: "So why us? Why we been given the dry and not all the somebodies that wanted. . . . Because we got . . . and the stiffs? Sure, *sure,* we got stiffs, who don't? Because . . ." As he kept speaking, Grisanti's eyes flickered back toward the cabin and the girl whose voice came to them from time to time. He then leaned closer, his face rounded and soft, all creases and folds like some kind of lizard, and raised the right hand that he talked with. "Nah. None of that.

"Because, *because*—" three fingers came down on Furco's wrist "—we're clean, Luke." The fingers had thick, graying hair, like steely fur, right down to the nails. With the other hand, he pulled one finger back. "We don't do no sharking," Grisanti as much as shouted, his eyes—as understanding as Furco's brutal father's had been—boring into him so he couldn't look away. "Two—no dope. And, three—no women."

Furco looked down at the hand. He did not like to be touched. More, he did not like to be grilled, and suddenly the wind either died or he could hear everything, even—he believed—Grisanti's breathing.

"What is it wid you and this—" the hand waved, and the eyes caught Furco's again "—gash?"

Furco couldn't help himself. He could feel his ears pull back and a flush rising to his face. He turned his head away. Avoiding the slick, black puddle in the bucket between them, he instead looked down into the tide wake.

"Luck-y," Grisanti practically howled. "It's like that, is it? *Marron',*" he laughed, and tried to twist around to see if the woman's voice, which came to them again, meant that the others had heard.

The mate then called from the flying bridge above the cabin, " 'Kay, Cap. I got 'em on the finder. Big school about forty feet. The chum is bringing them up." From some other boats cheering could now be heard, but Grisanti would not let him off.

"Jesus. Haitch. *Christ!*" he roared. "He got it bad," he sang in a rich baritone that surprised Furco, "and that ain't good." Leaning away, assessing Furco, Grisanti wrinkled his forehead and asked, "How olda you anyhow, Luck?"

Rhymes with fuck, Furco thought. At the moment he thought he could kill the old cocksucker, and maybe he

35

would—busting his rocks because he knew he could get away with it. Maybe Grisanti knew too much. Maybe after all these years he was too sure of himself.

"Not old enough, I can see," he went on, still chuckling. "A *woman,* Lucky? What's a *woman?* What she do for you you can't for yourself, 'sides slip your fazzong somewhere the sun don't shine? And if they couldn't or wouldn't, you think we'd have 'em around? Nah," he scoffed. "Nevah. There'd be a bounty on 'em, just like . . . just like on rattlers. You ever meet one you could hang out with? Bad company. The worst. They know nothin' about the world.

"And a dime a fuckin' dozen, Luke. Even the lookers. Take 'em to dinner, take 'em to bed. Feed 'em and fuck 'em. Works every time—big, small, tall, short. Blondes, redheads, brunettes. There ain't one—my mothah, your mothah, my wife, your wife—don't want to make it with—" the hand shot out and waved at the horizon "—a big buncha baboons. Whores, is all, when they ain't kept in line."

But when Furco failed to look up, the hand came down on his thigh. "So—so what? So—you like one more than the others. You think she's the sun and the moon, and there's this somethin' to the way she talks or walks or smiles. It gives you a charge. But whuz she got? Two arms, two legs. Some teeth. Hair, tits, the works like the others. And this one—I checked her out—not bad, but she's got a problem, and I don't have to tell *you* what *that* is.

"Hey—" now that he had caught Furco's eyes, Grisanti winked "—and she ain't even young, like—" He tried to twist around and look toward the salon. "What you think they're doin' with that tomatah in there?

"And look, Luke," he pleaded, "I been there before. You, too. Your wife."

Furco tried not to look one way or the other. He had married his wife because his father had told him it was smart and then gave him a direct order. It had made Grisanti something like his uncle-in-law, if there was such a thing.

"Boys, Luke—*boys* fall in whatever the fuck you got for this broad." The hand was now firmly on Furco's knee. "Men—men don't let that shit bothah them, at least not so much they screw up business. And let me remind you, case you forgot, this is business. Big business. Bigger maybe than you know."

That got Furco. He looked up.

"You know Cheech?"

Sure, Furco knew him. Cheech was the nickname they had hung on the power behind the power, Sal Infantino's money guy who they said made a whole bunch for them legal through investments, banks, and whatnot, more than any hustle in the street.

Sal had given him some other handle, something they could use through a wiretap, but it didn't stick. Instead, some old Moustache Pete, jealous of Sal, sure, but also of what the guy could do, started calling him Cheech. It referred to *cece,* or garbanzo beans, and meant that no matter how much he brought down, he could never command their respect as a man. Simply put, the Cheech had never cracked an egg.

Furco had met him only once, during the Statue of Liberty celebration in July of '86, and he liked his style. It was low-key. The lowest. After speaking for a while and making them feel at home on his boat—some slick sailboat that looked like a needle in the water—he had just shut up and listened the afternoon long, while, like magic, most of the others drank and spilled their guts. It had been as though he was pumping them, each in his turn. And when they were about to leave, he had taken Grisanti and him aside and given them the chance to do something for him personal as a favor. "A long shot. Something that might do us a lot of good, but most likely will come to nothing." And then, when Grisanti had gone below for his jacket, he had added to Furco, "Luke—I understand you're a sailor." When Furco had nodded, he added, "Steady as she goes. It might seem a long passage, but your day will come. Count on it."

And Furco had, at least so far as thinking that the Cheech was somebody he could appeal to, if anything happened, or if he wanted to move out on his own. He had even gone to someplace like Harvard and was both a lawyer and a CPA. A week later, Furco had received a gift from the Cheech in the mail. A box of thin dark cigars, one of which he now held in his hand. It had gone out.

"He tapped her. The Cheech," Grisanti said, and Furco's eyes met his with force.

Grisanti laughed again and shook his head. Hump, Grisanti thought. Like a kid with his first hard-on. Lead him around by the nose or, better, the dick. "Sure—right there in the casino. Had somebody tell huh, hey, I like what you're doin' fuh me. Maybe you can do a little more. Brought her right into the city and laid it on huh."

He waited, watching Furco's eyes that were some strange, light shade of gray search his, and he decided to string him along. "You think I lie? Me lie to you, Luck? Hey, my friend, if you don't believe me, you can ask for yourself. Call, why don't you? Maybe he'll put her on. You can ask her if she's having fun." Grisanti motioned to all the electronic stuff, the TVs and whatnot, that had been built into the transom of the boat. "If you don't have his number, hell, I do." Grisanti made a pretense of reaching for his wallet, though having the man's private number was beyond him. Only wheels with clout or those whose money the Cheech controlled directly had it, and Grisanti, while no slouch with a buck, was far from that category. In a way, he and Furco only worked for the guy.

Grisanti now waited while it dawned on Furco what he had meant by "tapped," and thought to himself: Shit—guys like Furco, guys like that fuckin' Cheech—they're our future? It was at moments like this he was glad he'd never had any sons.

When finally Furco blinked, he went on with the pitch. "And you, Luke. Christ, you got balls. Plomstahs! How you handled them punks Southside Philly? Why you think we dropped this gig on you and not somebody of the everybody elses who wanted it? You're lucky, you're on a roll. Don't fuck things up.

"And where's the need?" The hand now shook Furco's leg. "What—you want a place to suck some drinks? Drink here. What's wrong with here? Or, hell, drink in a casino where it's free.

"You wanna eat? I make you a promise. Anytime you get hungry, you want something to eat, you just want to sit down and take a load off, I—" the hand came up and smacked Grisanti's own chest "—me, the Mick, I grab the tab, no problem.'' Again he paused, waiting for some response from Furco. Was the fucker even alive? What good was life if you couldn't laugh and shout and bust balls and fuck around?

"You doubt me? You think I can't afford it?" The hand came back down on Furco's knee, and Grisanti turned his head, as though speaking to some witness. "The fucker's doubting me when—fuckin' A—I'm so flush I could buy maybe the ass end of this tub with a balloon mortgage at prime." He squeezed the knee, which prompted Furco to make a conciliatory gesture. In addition to the dry and his other action, Grisanti had inherited a meat-packing business which, because of his contacts, now distributed nationwide. He had more money and power than Furco probably would ever see.

Furco closed his eyes. He nodded.

"But, Lucca—no more candy-ass there at the Borghese. I want you to get things straight with that Toni broad. For keeps. One way or the other, if only to get things straight with—" He motioned his head to the salon behind them, meaning Mazullo and the two others Furco was supposed to be running as part of the dry.

Yet again Grisanti waited, watching a muscle twitch on the side of Furco's lean jaw, knowing he had nailed him there. It was one thing to be weak private, another to let the people you controlled in on that weakness so that they lost respect. And when Furco didn't raise his eyes, he added, "And for fuck's sake, do it and be done. With force, once and for all so people know.

"And finally, no more shit with the police. They're greedy bastards. Pricks. They get a hint we got a problem, we're weak, they'll suck us dry.

"Now—" Grisanti reached into his windbreaker and came out with two little cards, which Furco looked down at; from the other boats the shouts were continuing, and he could now feel somebody behind him. "—you're smarting, I can tell. You're burnt. You think maybe we're not 'uman, and we don't understand? But years—mark my words—years from now you might be talkin' just what I'm talkin' here, and I want you should remember how it went down.

"These here—" He waved the cards, then glanced up at

39

Mazullo, who had remained a step back from the chairs, wanting to say something but waiting to be asked. His soft lips were pulled back in a kind of smile, though his eyes were watchful. "—these here we picked up for you from the Nugget and Harrah's. Some big spade got on a roll, and she tapped," Grisanti held the word just long enough to let Furco know, "his luck for a time. Broads." He shook his head. "Maybe it's the lever you need, maybe not."

Furco looked away, if only to keep himself together. Out at the other boats, bluefish were biting.

"Any case, you're to know this—" Grisanti waited until Furco's eyes rose to him; he was serious now. It was the message he'd been sent to say. "—you're too valuable, what you do, for any . . . distraction on the side. What we got in the dry is the kinda thing we always wanted. It's maybe the best thing we run onto here in A.C., and we won't have it fucked up. You unhappy with that?" The eyes bulged. "You tell me, cuz if you are—hey, somethin' can be arranged." The eyes flicked up at Mazullo, who was still standing behind them.

"But how it comes down is you gotta cool this thing with this beef, one way or another. Get me? If you're goin' to own the joint, own it. If not, get out. So, we *give* you these—" he offered Furco the cards in a way that made him reach "—cuz we wanna show you we value who you are and what you do for us. We show by this we got respec' for your feelin's. It happens. It's happened to us all. It can be the best thing. Or the worst.

"Now—what I just say?" Grisanti demanded, not releasing the cards.

Furco glanced up at him. Could there be *more?*

"You know—what I'm talkin' here." Grisanti now leaned away, as though sizing him up. "The point."

"Dino," one of the others called. "C'mon—she's going down. *Now.*" Mazullo shifted his feet impatiently and glanced back at the cabin.

Furco stared down at Grisanti's thumb on the cards. It was covering the print. His face was flushed, his forehead sweating. He hadn't felt so total since those two weeks in Philly, though there, too, he had contained his rage and chosen his shots. He had iced one punk so perfectly they thought at first he had died of natural causes, until they found the pick hole right at the top of his head. "The beef," Furco murmured.

"I can't *hear* you." On the cards, Grisanti's thumbnail was white.

"The beef," Furco shouted at the rail. "The fuckin' *beef,* Griz. I got it. Awright?"

"Guys," said Mazullo, breaking in, "that one." He jerked a thumb at the salon. "We stuffed her nose fulla coke. Says she wants to pull a train."

"No shit?" Grisanti released the cards. "Really?" The hand came up again but with the palm open in a gesture of wonder or—was it?—fright.

Mazullo raised the side of his upper lip. He snorted. "Bimbo. They're back there pokin' her now. Says she don't care how many or what. You check her out? Fuckin' Miss fuckin' America." Ringlets of shiny black curls had spilled onto his forehead. He was dressed in some baggy outfit with shoulder pads, like somebody out of "Miami Vice."

"Where?" Grisanti asked.

"Back in the boat. You comin'?"

Grisanti glanced at Furco. The hand was still in the air. "Me? At my age?"

"Sure. Why not? Give her a jump. We all will." Mazullo glanced at Furco. In his eyes was a challenge.

Said Grisanti, "You gotta be kidding. Who you think I am anyways—Mighty Joe Young?" The hand came down, dipping into the plastic tub between the two chairs, and snatched up a slick, black river eel that wriggled and squirmed, bending back trying to clamp its soft mouth on Grisanti's hand.

"Five minutes in saltwater, she'll turn white. Blond," he explained about the eel, suddenly changing the subject. "Blues won't keep their jaws off huh."

"Dino!" somebody called. "She says she *needs* you."

Furco looked down at the cards. Markers they were, from A. A. Spina to the two casinos. The first was for $6,220 and the other for $11,000 even. Not a lot, but enough for a woman with debts.

"Says won't be no five minutes today," the voice went on

from the direction of the cabin. "Says she wants to ball 'til she's sore. Says we won't have enough to give huh."

Furco reached for the television monitor that had been built into the transom and snapped it on, dialing the channel selector that could surveil every part of the boat's interior until he found the girl and the two other young men.

"Whuz zat?" Grisanti asked, eel and line in one hand, pole in the other. Squinting, he peered down at the small screen that was protected by an antiglare mesh, as Furco rose to leave.

A drinks girl from a casino. They had her on the big, circular berth in the master cabin, on hands and knees, her big, powder-white ass in the air. They'd taken off only her panties and pulled down her top, so the thigh-length silver stockings she wore at work still sheathed her legs, like shimmering pirate's boots.

A blonde, her tits were firm and nipples neat—how old could she be? Furco wondered—and her whole body was juddering with their effort.

Having only unzipped his fly, Joe, the Bear—immense and swarthy, he had his hands on his hips like he wouldn't even touch her—was getting her from behind, and she had taken Tiny, another big man, in her mouth. Like snap-the-whip, they were flailing her between them.

"Holy shit," Grisanti roared, the eel squirming in his hands. "This bawge is great!"

Furco punched the button once, twice, and again. And, like the security monitors in the casinos, each snap pulled in the focus until her face filled the screen. About the same age as two of Furco's four daughters, she had a pert little nose and rosebud lips. Her eyes seemed closed until Furco punched the button again.

They were blue with tiny flecks of gray, which from either the dope or her ecstasy or both had formed bright pinwheels around pupils that were hardly there at all. And was she smiling? Furco wondered. It appeared so. Gone. Her lips taut and her cheeks straining to keep it in her mouth.

"See!" Grisanti shouted. "See what I was telling yuh? Take a whack at her myself. Latah."

The afternoon long, from the vantage of the flying bridge, Furco watched Grisanti fish. As the bluefish hit and hit and hit again, the cockpit became cluttered with black tangles of dead or discarded eels. The stern ran red with the blood of the fish that the mate gaffed and hauled aboard. Twisting around from a big catch that nearly leapt back over the rail and in an agony of death danced toward the salon, Grisanti threw Furco the bird. "A shawk! Like a fuckin' shawk, fuh crissakes. I tell you, Luke, you got it made heah."

Furco only looked away, touching the markers in his shirt pocket, trying to keep clear the picture he had of the boat and what she could mean to him.

The decks could always be washed, the slime scrubbed off. He had been thinking of changing the master cabin anyway, before he brought her aboard.

4

Mazullo the younger's phone call had come late Saturday night to his townhouse on Beekman Place, but H. Bruce Payson had still been up. Sitting in the arc of the three Georgian windows that looked out into his lighted back garden, he had been immersed in what he thought of as his profession. Unlike the other data that his small staff logged to disk, Payson's almost nightly, three-decade-long excursion into the world of printed matter provided him an overview that no binary decision-making system could hope to emulate, and at such times "being informed," as he termed it, induced in him a trancelike state.

Unaided, it seemed, pages turned before his eyes, and a rhythmical counterpoint was established between the slight swaying of his ladder-back rocker and the progress of his eyes through a specific piece. When it was completed, he would hold his worn BVLGARI lighter to the end of a Cosimo de Medici panatela, which he was seldom without, take a few puffs, reach to the table for something else, and the process would begin again. Payson took no notes. He saved nothing. And only hours later, when the area around the rocker was mounded with reports, periodicals, letters, memos, and newspapers, would he seem to surface, mentally climbing up through all that he had scanned to squint at the clock or stretch or yawn or—as on Saturday night—to pick up the phone.

"Cheech?"

"Que?" he asked, his mind still functioning in the language of the newspaper he had been reading.

"Dino M. here—we met once on your boat during the Liberty celebration. I'm the Maz's kid, guy heads the pension fund. He gave me your number, said if it was important you wouldn't mind. I took the chance."

Who? Payson thought. And what? He had last been reading reports and newspapers from Brazil, where the money that he directed was heavily exposed, and his mind was equating the odd, nasal gutteralisms that he was hearing on the telephone with Brazilian Portuguese.

"We got a problem at the Borghese. Furco don't know I'm doin' this, but I'm thinkin' of us all. Know what I mean?" There was a pause, and then he asked, "Cheech?"

"Yes?" Payson managed.

"It's with the beef, Toni—she runs fuh Fuhco. A mule. She made a scene at the joint last night, and he done nothin' about it. Let her mouth in front of . . . I dunno, a couple hundred people. Then later here, too, with some coon at the Trump. It's like she's tryin' to blow it, and Fuhco, he . . .."

As the caller spoke on, Payson was put in mind of first attempts to learn a difficult foreign language. One caught a word here and another there, and out of habit he now set his mind to the task of deciphering the message. And to consider, he thought—snapping the BVLGARI and drawing deeply on the cigar—that the squalid Brooklyn of his childhood might as easily have forced him, too, into the box from which the caller was now raising his complaint. One person, a nun, had saved Payson with a few kind words and a volume by Tully. But after painful lessons as an undergraduate when he still called himself dePasquale, he had chosen to nurture, rather than deny, his background, and he now savored even his nickname.

Thus it was with a kind of condescending delight that he now followed the vocal eccentricities of the caller, who was, nonetheless, a rat and untrustworthy. Payson wondered how old Mazullo was. His tone was overemphatic and the timbre of his voice oscillated between adolescent extremes. He could at least assume Mazullo was untrustworthy until the young Italian completed what he wished to say.

"Dean?" Payson then asked, remembering the file that he kept on everybody with whom he was associated in a professional way.

"Dino," he corrected.

Ah, yes, Payson thought: a callow youth. Like so many others of his generation, the young man had rejected the anglicization that his father had learned was often necessary, especially when dealing impersonally, say, over the telephone or in a simple business transaction.

"Dino—could you run through that for me again?"

As the boy—young man?—spoke, Payson reminded himself that it was the slime that nourished the roots that fed the trunk that grew the limbs, and so on. And how could he, who was involved with only the rarest of the flowers of that plant, object to any element of that growth? And then the process by which the Mazullos had chosen (or had been chosen) to become slime and Payson himself involved in what he euphemistically called horticulture, was still a matter of some wonder to him.

It was the mention of the woman, however, that interested Payson most, and he nearly congratulated himself that the seed that he had planted almost three years earlier was maturing just as he had decided to "go to market," as it were. Could he have planned it like that? Not really. Was he instead merely lucky? Well, after years of successful investing, Payson understood that the element of chance entered every transaction in some way or another.

Toni Spina was a case in point. Payson had been reading the New Jersey section of the *Sunday New York Times*—how long ago? Nearly five years now—when a photo of a wedding that had been attended by celebrities in Atlantic City caught his eye. Having a contact at the *Times*, he'd managed to get a copy of the original and immediately booked himself into the Claridge, where for a weekend he did nothing but haunt the Mayfair Room of the then newly reopened hotel-casino. Sitting at the bar or at a table and watching Toni Spina greet customers with a warmth and aplomb that was at no time unctuous, he had decided. The resemblance was so striking that the possibility existed.

And now, after three years of careful and—he hoped—

inconspicuous manipulation, could the opportunity have arrived as well? Payson thought so.

Thanking the young cretin on the phone, Payson hung up. In his upstairs dressing room, he took care not to wake the woman who was sleeping in a bedroom beyond another door. Selecting a topcoat, he descended the stairs and opened the door to a small anteroom near the main entrance on the street floor, where Dom slept, though it could hardly be called sleeping.

He found him, as always it seemed to Payson, positioned on a high Japanese bed, the internal stove of which Dom stoked during cold afternoons. It was a ritual that delighted Payson and tanged the air of Beekman Place with the smoke of kindling cedar. Dom slept with every window open three inches so that he could monitor passersby and traffic in the street. Or so Payson assumed.

There in the dark with his back against a windowless wall, and facing the door, he was sitting in a lotuslike position but with both arms folded beneath the plackets of an oriental dressing gown. His eyes were open. They were dark and clear.

Payson, a tall man in early middle age and with a full head of silver hair that had been allowed to curl at the nape of his neck, approached him. In spite of what on first glance appeared to be an obvious age difference, Dom and he had grown up together in a dim alley off Brooklyn's Atlantic Avenue. And there from the first day that Payson had known him, Dom had evidenced a natural predilection for the process of instilling death.

First it had been rats. Rocks, slingshots, pellet guns, guns provided by the neighborhood *capo di regime,* who was fascinated by Dom's precocity—it didn't seem to matter what weapon was employed, Dom always quickly became adept at any manipulation that killed. Cats and stray dogs came next, and not, it had seemed to Payson even then, for sport or cruel fun, but rather to hone techniques. While others played sports or chased girls or, like Payson himself, took small jobs and haunted libraries, Dom became a hunter and fisherman of some reknown. He filled his narrow bedroom off a dark hall with cased rifles and knives and the shafts and oiled reels of fishing poles that he strung in neat rows along the ceiling. But not a single trophy. It wasn't the *fact* of having killed that attracted him. It was the *act* of inducing death, the method of killing.

When, later, Dom discovered the martial arts, he'd abandoned himself to those several disciplines: boxing, wrestling, judo, karate. He was soon expert in them all. In the marines, he became a trip-wire specialist. Airdropped at night into hostile territory, he had alone, living off the land, acted as point spotter along the Ho Chi Minh Trail for fourteen months. He was awarded the Bronze Star, the Vietnamese Cross, and a host of army commendations.

Of his brothers who had shared that cramped tenement bedroom with Dom, one had gone on to become a musician and the other a baker. Their father had been a brickmason, when he worked; their mother—after they had grown— opened one of the first beauty parlors in their neighborhood. They were all creative people in their several ways. How, then, to explain Dom, except that his *diamon* drove him to be creatively destructive. A nice inversion, Payson had long thought.

Taking a dog-eared photograph from his wallet, he handed it to Dom. "I'd like to speak to this woman. She's presently registered at all the Atlantic City casino-hotels, but I believe—"

"The Claridge," Dom said. He had, of course, remembered. If eyes were windows to the soul, then Dom's central self was inscrutable. Payson wondered if he knew himself. More to the point, however, was how well he knew Payson, given what would transpire.

Closing the front door of the townhouse behind him, Payson stepped toward the east, where from the vantage of the heights on Sutton Place he could look out over the FDR Drive at the East River. Somehow the troubled waters rushing south from Hell Gate always managed to call him.

On Sunday evening, a day later, Payson met Toni Spina at the door of the Beekman Place townhouse and was again amazed at her resemblance to his companion, Giancarla, who was upstairs. He was tempted to call her down and introduce her to the woman, but that would ruin everything they had planned.

Through the half-glasses that he sometimes wore when his eyes were very tired, Payson now studied the definite structure of her long face, and then his eyes swept the rake of her shoulders, her narrow waist, the flare of her hips, which a half-jacket and taupe slacks made more obvious. Her nose was perhaps a little more thinly bridged, he concluded, and her body, while femininely full, was almost mannish in the power it suggested. But, except for those few details and their eyes, the similarity between the two women was so striking that now knowing it might be done filled Payson with an inner joy and—was it?—a fright that he had not felt in years and now found bracing.

"Why—Ms. Spina," he said, "I must apologize for having interrupted your weekend, but it's time we talked. Come in, come in." With a newspaper in his other hand, Payson waved to the flight of stairs that led up into the building. But when she did not move, he explained, "I'm H. Bruce Payson. Lucca Furco and his minions 'work' for me, if you can call it that. I'd like to discuss with you the possibility of ending your indebtedness to us in a much more pleasant manner than your weekly excursions to Atlantic City. If you're not interested, you need only say so and Dom will take you back. It would please me greatly, however, if you would hear me out." Removing the half-glasses, he treated her to the sincerity of his light blue eyes.

Hers, which were brown with hazel highlights, had tracked his every gesture for false moves, flaws, any uncertainty, and now they unabashedly scanned the white, ox-ford-cloth shirt that had been fitted to his once ruler-straight shoulders, his gray slacks, the Moroccan-leather belt that looped a trim waist, and finally the handmade loafers to match. She then turned her head and surveyed the tasteful accoutrements of the hall: a Braque painting, an eighteenth-century secretaire that functioned as Dom's desk, the glistening parquet flooring, the architect-designed light fixture.

All the while, Payson admired her cool. She was facing him squarely, one hand clasping the elbow of the other arm, her back straight, her head erect so that she appeared to be staring down her long, Roman nose at *him* who had *her* so much in the palm of his hand. She then turned and looked directly at Dom, who was standing stolidly before the door.

"A friend," Payson said. He paused, then added, "Until otherwise instructed, Dom will protect you with his life."

She blinked. Payson could not keep himself from admiring the containment of her shape, as she climbed the stairs in front of him, and the swing of her easy, big-shouldered gait, as she moved into the foyer.

In the study, he seated her in one of the two ladder-back rockers that had been positioned near the Georgian windows overlooking the lighted garden. He offered her coffee, tea. "A drink?" She would need some softening up.

But she only shook her head, her eyes seeming to say, You think me that much a fool? We have business. Please proceed.

Then words would have to suffice, Payson decided, pushing a computer keyboard on the table out of the way so he could set down an ashtray. He took the other chair and arranged its pillow so it would catch him in the small of his chair-abused back.

And they could not come to the point directly; she must be reminded of her past, he decided.

Twining his fingers in back of his head, Payson rocked some and listened to the chimes of the church in the next street ring in the hour. Ten o'clock. As good a time as any for histrionics, he judged.

He then waited further, his eyes lost in the walnut mortises of the groin-vaulted ceiling, though thinking was not necessary, until he deemed the mood established: of quiet reflection. *A la recherche du temps perdu* for a former teacher of modern languages, he thought, wondering if she still spoke the French that she had taught for several years after college. What was it one of her professors had said of her skills: ". . . a 'scholastic' fluency in French and nearly the same in Italian. Her German is passable, as is her Spanish." All courtesy, Payson did not doubt, of her cosmopolitan father, who had done as much academically for her brother and her as any tailor could.

"So," he said, turning his eyes to her, "Antonina Alexandra Spina. Born seven, twenty-two, forty-nine at the Lying-In Hospital, Philadelphia, to Ibrihim 'Abe' or 'Sam' Sammasian and Giovanna Maria Cutone, who died at your birth. Your parents had been married seven years.

"Your mother was the daughter of one Giovanni Cutone, a professor of music at Penn, who objected strenuously to an alliance with a scarcely employed Romanian tailor who at that time barely spoke the language and was also a Jew. But love and your father, it seems, won out. Your brother, Jim, who is a lawyer now in Long Branch, was their first child, born on September 2, 1941. I suppose you remember your parents' wedding date?"

Toni did not, her father never having mentioned it.

"March seventeenth of the same year. Saint Patrick's Day, as luck would have it, though I mention these facts not to inform."

But to instruct, she thought. And the lesson? That her brother had been conceived out of wedlock, and that for Payson knowledge was very much power, from which there could be no refuge. Should you sting him, he would know where you were and seek you out. Toni had been threatened like that before by experts, but never so elliptically. It was nearly enough to make her smile.

And as the man spoke on, recounting details of her early life and schooling that were either forgotten or unknown to her, she pulled her eyes from his. Scanning the rows of books stacked to the ceiling, the piles of newspapers and magazines, the file cabinets that she could see down a short flight of stairs in a room that seemed to extend under the lighted garden, she wondered just who he was. One of the "New Dons," as the newspapers called them, adept at converting fresh cash into seemingly honest profits? It would mesh with the laundering scheme, since there would necessarily have to be some other steps: someplace to hide the new money, somebody who would know how to make it grow.

Until she heard her husband's name mentioned, and she swung her head back.

". . . met in a casino, didn't you? Caesars, where you were working as a boxman on your summer vacation from teaching high school French in Toms River." Payson made a moue, asking, "Box person?"

Toni only watched him, waiting for the other shoe to fall.

"Tall and blond and tanned," Payson continued, "Jack worked just across the Claridge esplanade at Harrah's, and you made a handsome couple. The handsomest in the city, some said. And so talented at your profession that, when the Claridge reopened, they made you an offer. A package deal, so to speak, generous enough for you to quit your teaching career and induce Jack to leave Harrah's. They made him gaming manager and put you in charge of the restaurants, and suddenly you found yourselves making the kind of money that you deserved.

"It was then that, pooling your capital and mortgaging yourselves to the earlobes, you bought Marimar, a great Iberian pile right on the beach on Ventnor that some Mafioso had erected in the twenties and that was then falling down. Together you restored the house, working crazy hours and partying there with your friends whenever you could.

"And you had friends, too many perhaps. Individually, each of you had a certain appeal, a presence, a magnetism, an—" Payson waved a hand "—*élan,* if you will. But together? Everybody wanted to know you. And when, finally, you decided to get married, even the governor showed up. Sure, it was two weeks before an election, and he had been invited by the Claridge, which was only using you two to front a stodgy place that would really never make it big. But the coup was that Old Blue Eyes was in town.

"He said from the stage of the Nugget that he couldn't do an encore because he had a wedding to catch. 'You hear about it?' he asked the audience. 'Toni and Jack over at the Claridge. Nice kids. You know, the big, blond guy who runs the place and that luscious doll who manages the Mayfair Room. They're finally doing the decent thing and tying the knot. I gotta hurry. Maybe I can talk them out of it.' His entourage arrived with limos brimming with champagne and another band that jammed until noon of the next day. You were in all the papers."

Time, Toni thought. How fast it had gone. She could remember now even the aroma of the tea roses, a tall trellis full of them, that had grown up the side of Marimar. Jack and she had not been able to bring themselves to cut it back, and for May and June of three all-too-short years it had filled the terrace and lawn with a perfume so heady that from the beach you didn't have to see which house was theirs. They would lunch with friends on the terrace until it was time to go to work. There were always bright, gay, and successful people around them. And opportunities. And as if on a kind of streak there for a while, the world had seemed to unfold for them, petal by petal. Jack soon became chief of operations of the Claridge. Her restaurants thrived. With profit sharing and two good investments, they'd quickly paid off Miramar and begun building a bank account.

And more than their evident success—as the man Payson kept speaking, Toni turned her head and looked out into the early spring bowers of the lighted garden—they had been successful together, joyous in each other's company, wanting to do everything together, and nothing had seemed impossible. They had been so young and vital then. Their horizons had been as limitless as the ocean that they'd watched from their terrace.

Until Toni herself had made a change. *For the better*, she thought, twisting her head and looking away from the garden. "Why salaries," she asked Jack, "when we could be making profits?" They had already talked about it, and agreed: that if this country was set up for something, it was for owning your own business (or, rather, putting other people to work). Hadn't Jack once said, "Working for somebody else is a certain form of slavery?"

But when she had found the location and argued the price, and it was time for Jack to come in and do what he was best at—getting the last little bit and making the other party think they were doing the right thing—he had quailed. "It's Hammonton, not A.C.," he'd said. "There's no gambling in Hammonton. What will *I* do in your supper club? Work tables or the bar? Or the floor, glad-handing drunks and old ladies? That's not me. I'm gambling, it's all I know."

"But, Jack," she had pleaded, "it's our chance to score big, I can feel it. You know how it goes. People really want to get out of town for dinner. By the time they come to eat, they're tired of the casinos. Everybody'll come out and see us, and you can learn the business. You'll be good at it—the books, ordering, hiring and firing. There's a whole other world to a restaurant that you just don't see."

And don't want to see, was his answer, though he had not put it so bluntly. "Look, Tone, my salary's good. It'll help you get over the hump. But I'm gambling. It's all I know."

And not well enough, as it turned out. After she opened, they hardly saw each other and then only at odd hours, usually when Jack was in the casino or just getting off. Exhausted, hardly able to speak, Toni just did not want to go home right away, or so she said. And easy, like that, like it was no big thing and just something that people in their circumstances did, they themselves began gambling, though they knew it was wrong.

Had the urge been in reality something dark and sinister? Toni asked herself, and not for the first time. A way of trying to deny by disaster the new life that both hated but Toni could not abandon? Thinking momentarily of the two days just past and then forcing herself to put them out of her mind, she now decided it was.

"When was it," Payson, the man who said he could relieve her of at least the monetary burden of that night, was now saying, "the twenty-first of July, a day before your thirty-fifth birthday."

Which they had been celebrating, since the twenty-second was a Saturday and with her advertised special, "Shore Dinners," packing the place, Toni had had to work. Drinks and champagne and a surprise birthday party with just their closest friends, and then down to the tables at the Tropicana. Some blackjack, a little craps, roulette, and finally baccarat, where at first Toni, sitting alongside Jack, lost while Jack won. The stakes were high, running close to $2,000 a hand, and she should have quit then when she knew she was running sour. But their winnings kept pace with their losses until Jack was beeped back to the Claridge for an emergency that proved to be nothing.

While he was gone, Toni—too tired, really, to concentrate and lingering only because the others in their party wanted to stay—dropped $12,000. Not a whole bunch, but enough, with the Borghese mortgage and a young child, to make Jack want to get clear upon his return. What had been his words? "You get some sleep, Tone, while I even up. I'll be home before you know it." He'd been drinking, she could tell, but she did not know how much, and when she rolled over well past noon to turn off the alarm, she thought he had merely gotten up before her. When by five in the afternoon he still hadn't returned, she'd dressed and gone looking for him, first at the Claridge and then—half-knowing that the worst had finally happened—at the Tropicana, where she found him in the same chair, his tux a mess, a day's growth of beard on his face, and Lucca Furco standing behind him. A vulture.

It wasn't the first time she had seen Furco, since he often dined at the Borghese, but it was the first time he had looked at her like that. Like how? Possessively. As though it would only be a matter of time.

And Jack saw it, too. He'd looked away, and—was it—from then on that he never again looked at her directly? Yes, she now decided, and she should have known. Immediately. Right there at the table.

Instead, she had said, "Jack, cash in and come home."

He shook his head. "Not while I'm winning." In front of him were stacks of chips, bought—she would later learn—by Furco. It was, she at first believed, the first lie he had ever told her, though she later knew differently.

"But your job—don't you have to be at work sometime tonight?"

"I'll call in sick."

Gaming managers did not get sick. Or, rather, they did not *call* in sick, like some shift worker. It had been an admission, but she had not been sharp or savvy or attentive enough to know it at the time.

"*You*—call in sick? Well, it must be good." She had again glanced down at the chips. "I'd appreciate your checking in later, when you get home. I've got to rush."

And if only he had admitted the loss then, they might have made it up. Or if he had told her, "Look, I've been gambling on my own for months, and I've lost. We're hundreds of big ones down already, and I don't know what to do." But that wasn't Jack. Jack had never really lost before in his life, ever, not in school or in sports or in his jobs or with women, and the admission would have been a denial of all that he believed he was: strong, prudent, a good husband, provider, and friend. And more, a good father to his eighteen-month-old daughter, whom he seemed to love more than anybody in the world, even more than Toni.

But time went by. Two months. Five, while he drank, and went out with other women, Toni later heard. He wrecked two cars, but didn't hurt himself. Then he lost his job, and one day crashed through the barrier and plunged into the icy race at Absecon Point. It was November and frigid, and they found the car in seventy-five feet of water, a quarter mile off the end of the breakwater. But no Jack.

Toni had spent the next three weeks, and then every Tuesday and Wednesday she could spare, canvassing beach residents north and south of the point, speaking to the few fishermen who were out that week, visiting morgues as far away as Delaware and Long Island on the advice of the police who were handling the case. They said it might have been some drug deal that had gone sour, hinting that Jack had been into that, too.

"I'm a little vague about what actually happened to your husband," Payson now said, taking his hands from behind his head and reaching for the keyboard by his feet. "Do you know?"

Still she only stared at him, while he punched the keys and glanced at a monitor that had been positioned so as to be viewed only from his rocker. She had not come there to tell him anything. She was there to listen.

"Strange that he was never found. I have only the date . . ." His voice trailed off, and again his eyes, which were the color of light through deep ice, met hers. "November 11, 1986."

He struck a key and kept his finger on it until the monitor swung around so Toni could see it, too. The entry under her husband's name listed all the particulars of his life in a kind of curriculum vitae. There was a list of names of women. And then a list of addresses at which they had lived.

"The body was never found?" Payson asked.

Toni looked away.

One address was in Florida, another in Texas, a third in Georgia.

Payson keyed off the screen. "Enter Lucca Furco. With the vigorish, Jack's total loss came to nearly a half million dollars, though you negotiated it down. I know Furco. What could you have said to make him discount the vig?"

That she couldn't and wouldn't pay it, she thought, her mind on the computer screen. That she'd simply walk away. That they could do to her whatever they'd done to Jack, but without her they'd never run the Borghese so it'd make a buck, or at least the bucks she was making. And Furco was sharp enough to understand that.

Who could those women have been? And how long had they known Jack? Worse still, had he known them all through their marriage? How much of a fool had she really been for him? She thought she had recognized one of the names—some woman who had been at their wedding—and she wished she had caught at least one name and address.

"And so you began running off a $340,000 debt at—" Payson glanced up at her, but she knew he knew, and she was not about to mouth the sum of her abjection: $2,000 a week *plus* the real vigorish, which was the cut—currently 59 percent—that Furco, who was anything but a fool, took from her profits. And for the first time in two days she thought of the little heist at the restaurant that would effectively put almost $30,000 extra in his or Grisanti's or a cut in all of their pockets.

She also thought with shame of the markers she had taken in Caesars and the Nugget, so as not to dip into the money she'd been sent to clean. Furco's money, which was really hers. Mortified now—to have been so stupid and so used by Jack and now by Furco and this man—she turned her head aside.

Then there had been the man, the other one. The black man who said his name was Colin Ross. Yes, she had needed him, desperately, and he had been good to her. But out of what deprivation had she been driven to an interlude like that, and then to the wild, crazy gambling afterwards? Had her life been so barren over the past two years that now, suddenly, the inner Toni was losing control? And was any kind of reward, even down to the Borghese itself, which she had promised herself she'd hold onto, worth that?

Why hadn't she been willing to date other men after Jack? Why hadn't she kept telling herself that gambling had never been good for her, not ever? She didn't know. More, she didn't want to know, not while this man before her was talking escape.

"Which leaves about $200,000 outstanding," he said. "I figure that out at two-plus years of further weekend service."

At last they were coming to the deal.

Toni searched for a cigarette in her purse. It was another thing that had happened to her after Jack's disappearance, yet another abuse that through force of long habit she now put out of her mind. Long ago she had decided that some things weren't worth dwelling upon. People weren't perfect. She had not expected perfection from Jack; it was the totality of a person's life that mattered. She could remember her father telling harrowing stories of what amounted to a pogrom in Romania after the First World War. They only mattered after. After you had gotten through.

Payson reached his lighter toward her, and their eyes met as she pulled in the smoke.

Yes, he thought: having been tried through a penance that would have broken most men, she had proved that she possessed the requisite *virtu* to carry it off. She would not wilt at customs or the desks of international banks. Her hands would not shake or her eyes dart to doors or windows, and Payson wondered if she could throw a punch or fire a weapon. And in bed? How was she there, and what was the difference, woman to woman? As far as he could know from her file, she'd been chaste since her husband's disappearance, and he could imagine that in the way she comported herself—regally, almost—she frightened most men. And then she'd been busy, the last few years.

Which would continue, he thought, smiling. "Thirds," he said. "We'd like you to go on three trips for us of about a week apiece, and after that you're free. By that I mean no more debt, no more—how shall I phrase it as indelicately as they deserve?—" Payson held the lighter to the snubby end of his Cosimo de Medici and breathed out the smoke "—goons. The ones in the corner booth of your bar. They and I will drop out of your life for good. You'll also get paid, and well. And finally, when it's all over, I'll return the title deed to the place itself."

She did not even blink, and Payson decided upon the tack to take with her: honesty, as complete as necessary to control her. She would respond to no less.

Ten seconds went by. Twenty, eye to eye.

There was a soft rap on the door, and Dom stepped in. He

moved toward Payson, placed an envelope on the card table by the rocker, and left.

Thirty—an eternity in a situation like that, especially when staring at a face that, it seemed, he had been seeing for years. Was her mouth perhaps too wide and her lips too full? Well, she was after all the bigger woman, and the nostrils of her long nose arced back in a graceful curve that would best be seen in smile, he imagined. Her eyes were flecked with so much hazel they were nearly dark ruby in color, like a good claret or a mature port.

"Well?" he demanded, almost giddy to have broken first. She'd be superb for what he intended.

"Trips?" she asked.

"Yes—to foreign parts."

"Carrying what?"

"Nothing but yourself."

"And there. What do I do there?"

He wondered why she seemed to have no trace of a Jersey accent, or, rather, of the last Jersey accent that he had heard: Mazullo. Dean, the Maz's kid. He would have to deal with him or, rather, the father. And soon.

"Nothing illegal. You'll merely establish some banking agreements in your own married name." He reached down to the floor and removed another Cosimo de Medici from an ebony humidor that was sitting there. Breathing out the rich, blue smoke, he said, "As you doubtless have guessed, we launder money. We also shelter and invest money and provide—" he swirled his hand before slipping the lighter back into his trouser pocket "—mechanisms whereby persons who are making too much money can enjoy the fruits of their enterprises without having to pay a government or go to jail."

With the cigar right in the middle of his mouth, he twined his hands behind his head. He stared up at the ceiling. If she could just bring it off, it would be everything to him: the bonus that he so richly deserved, retirement, and victory over the *scarafaggi* whom he had suffered these many years. In a way Giancarla was right: it was time to put all that by him and seek new challenges and other acquaintances.

But she was wrong, too. It was *the* challenge, the ultimate, as far as he was concerned, and not merely because it would make for a life on the grandest scale. All his concentration, his knowledge, skill, and experience, would have to be brought to bear, for later any detail, even the smallest, might bring them down on him. Later. They would have to vanish without a trace, leaving only—

"You yourself," he went on, "are only one of a small army of runners, and the casino end of it is just part of our operation, rather less important—I might add—since the government required that all cash transactions over $10,000 be reported.

"But we have other means of purifying the funds that come our way: legitimate, cash businesses, the gross receipts of which can be inflated. We have other businesses with 'ghost' employees who nonetheless pay taxes. We have banks here and there who either need funds or whose employees are underpaid or both. We have shell corporations that on paper conduct huge retail trades that are exempted from scrutiny, pension funds into which members long deceased contribute weekly, insurance companies, credit unions—I could go on.

"Suffice it to say that the business is big. There's a Justice Department report that says over $100 billion must be laundered in this country every year. My guess is lower, but not by much.

"It's one thing, however, to wash out a million here in a casino or a couple hundred million in a bank or brokerage house, but then what? Any interest-bearing account or deposit over $10,000 invites the scrutiny of the IRS. The answer? Banks in countries that look the other way: Panama, Grand Cayman Island, the Netherlands Antilles, Switzerland, Liechtenstein, San Marino, and Monaco. The longer and more intricate the paper trail, the better. Such institutions, however, usually require a human being—somebody to log in the credit and shake hands."

Toni thought for a moment. The only advantage of the restaurant business was the possibility of enjoying tax-free cash profits on a daily basis, and the last thing she wanted was to invite the scrutiny of the IRS. "And I? How could I help you?"

"Essentially by transferring money from one pocket to

another. Of course, neither the pockets nor the money will be yours, beyond the fact that your debt will be—'' Payson searched for a fitting term ''—amortized.'' He smiled. He rather liked his choice of words.

Which meant essentially that he would get her services for nothing. For the vigorish, which had doubled the money that Jack had lost every two weeks. Only the initial loss, $48,000, had been covered out of Furco's—or had it really been this man's?—pocket (to think of pockets), but that had been merely another financial manipulation.

Which caused Toni to realize something else. ''That money—the 'pocket-to-pocket' money—must currently be in my name.''

Payson only smiled.

''Or can easily be placed in my name.''

He cocked his head.

She thought of how intricate and complex her involvement with them had actually been. Could she or Jack or Jack *and* she have been set up for just this purpose? Was that why Furco hardly ever left the Borghese—waiting, watching her, keeping her on ice until now?

Then why the phony heist? She didn't know. She was tired and her mind was fuzzy. And why her? How could they have known she would go along with them?

Payson answered the question, as though he could follow the train of her thoughts. ''Because of your commitments to your creation, the Borghese, and to your daughter and mother-in-law, we showed you the down side of your debt all those weekends in the casinos. This is the up side. And of all our runners, you are easily the most intelligent, literate, and lingual and most credibly the—'' his strange, blue eyes ran down her legs ''—sort of person who *would* be transferring such sums.

''And worry not about the IRS or any other governmental agency. All this is extraterritorial—beyond their jurisdiction or observation. As far as anybody will know, you're merely taking a short, foreign holiday with your duly licensed financial advisor.'' Elaborately Payson pointed to his own chest.

''And why all the money?'' he went on glibly. ''The sudden and swift canceling of your debt? Simply because we need you—a genuine American citizen with a traceable, verifiable past and the owner of a business that would generate—how shall I phrase it?—tax-free profits that you might want to divert to Panama and then redirect to the Netherlands Antilles to further confound the trail. That's where we'll be heading. Tomorrow, if you agree."

Again their eyes met.

"On succeeding occasions our destinations may be different. But this can be no partial commitment. It must be all or nothing. Either you agree or you refuse. In either case, I ask for complete and utter confidentiality. Nothing of what I have just said can leave this room. If ever I were to learn that you'd mentioned to anybody—here I'm thinking even of, say, your mother-in-law or your daughter, Tina—the smallest detail of our junkets, I would be overcome, *consumed* with—" dramatically he waved a hand "—and so forth. I'm not very good at threats.

"But believe me, beyond your promise and my insistence upon absolute secrecy—" he paused until they again had eye contact "—nothing more will be required of you but a few signatures, for which you will be well paid. And nothing whatsoever will come back to haunt you. Like H&R Block, the tax people, I guarantee it. If anything does, I'll personally pay the loss, and that's a promise."

Once more she turned to the lighted garden. Too much had been going on in her life for too long, and what had happened to her over the weekend had to stop. She was spiraling down, she could feel it, and that was no good. Could this be a way out?

She thought of Lucca Furco and his shabby little theft. Why did she keep focusing on him? As her father had always said, you cause your own problems, nobody else.

Her father: a poor little back-street Romanian tailor in a tawdry wreck of a town. Well, not exactly poor, but was she feeling sorry for herself? As she had also been taught, it was the worst mistake, the one that denied what was best about being human. Which was?

Said Payson, "Think of it this way. Since we need a real, *live* human being and the money is in your name, that alone will ensure your protection. We will, of course, need you again—" he held up a hand "—every once in a very great while for transfers or deposits, but all of that can be handled by signature and post and will require nothing more than dinner and a pen.

"Look—we'll handle it like a vacation. Better, an enforced rest for medical reasons. I'll have a doctor call Furco, and *he* can tell your staff."

Toni now studied Payson: the light blue eyes, the slightly wrinkled, tanned skin that had been cared for, she could tell, with emollients, good food, plenty of exercise and rest. How old could he be? Forty-five? Fifty-five? Sixty? He had the long, thin nose and chiseled features that went with the name and the address. Obviously an intelligent man—how had he become involved with people like Furco and the others? It was equally obvious that he did not feel himself a part of them. Could it be money alone? People were always surprising her.

And more to the point, could she trust him? No. Did she want to trust him? No again. But had she any choice? Not really, if she wanted to preserve a modicum of self-respect. Maybe, when it was all over, she'd sell out and take Tina and her mother-in-law someplace where she'd have a choice.

"How much money are we talking about?"

Payson only shook his head.

Obviously too much to talk about, which meant danger. How much could any life be worth when compared to the obscene sums that he was clearly talking about? Why else would he take the risk of making her privy to his operation?

Toni stubbed out the cigarette in the ashtray near the rocker. "I want the names of the women on that computer. And the addresses in Florida, Texas, and Georgia."

Payson cocked his head, considering, then said, "When we're through. I don't want you distracted by any inessential issue. You know, it rather interests me that you care, your husband having been—how shall I put it?—a womanizer."

Toni could not help it. Blood rushed to her temples. They throbbed. She reached for another cigarette, but the package was empty. She turned to the windows and the garden. It was as though no aspect of her life was untouched; all her hopes and dreams and ambitions from Jack and her marriage through her business and her present life had been despoiled, even her memories of their life together. All she had left, really, was her daughter, his child, whom she would kill for if need be.

"When do I start?"

"Right away. I mean, in seven hours. Until then, you can get some rest here or upstairs, if you like. Dom will take you to a room. If you prefer some other arrangement, we can get you a hotel room, either here in Manhattan or out at Kennedy. Your succeeding assignment will be in two weeks. And the final trip a month from then."

"When will I be paid?"

Payson smiled. "First installment in advance?" he asked. Opening a drawer in a library table, he withdrew a checkbook. "How do you feel now?"

"Dirty. And—" *Used,* she nearly added, glancing down at the pleated silk blouse and taupe slacks that she had worn, off and on, since changing out of her work dress sometime in the afternoon of the day before.

"Not to worry," said Payson, draping the check on her knee. "I've provided for that contingency as well. You'll find complete changes of clothes in your size upstairs. You can lay out what you think you'll need for, say, four days in a tropical climate. I'll be accompanying you, and let me warn you: I dine well and formally. Dom will pack your bag."

She stared down at the figure that had been written in a strange, backhand script: $75,000, drawn on the account of Beekman Research Associates at the Bank of New York and signed by H. Bruce Payson.

"Why be niggardly?" he said. "Those who carry millions should certainly have thousands in reward. Would you like to go upstairs?"

As she straightened up, their faces nearly met. Had he been that sure of her? she asked herself. Could it be that she was an open book to everybody but herself? Or just stupid? Why was it that she hadn't even suspected Jack until after he'd messed up? "May I make a phone call?"

"Of course—here," he pointed to a phone, "or there," meaning upstairs.

A few minutes later, sitting on a bed in a darkened room from which she could see a corner of the lighted garden, Toni wondered what she could tell her mother-in-law that she'd accept. Nothing, she decided, which was what she'd tell her.

In the study, Payson opened the note that Dom had left him. It said, "I didn't see him, but I'm almost sure there was a man with her in that room in the Nugget."

Payson raised an eyebrow. Well—perhaps their trips might be more interesting than he'd first thought. He speculated about her taste in men: tall and blond and broad, like Jack?

And how well would the clothes upstairs fit her? Sinking back into the rocker, he believed he would very much like to watch her dress. Or, better, watch the two women—Giancarla and the woman who looked so much like her—dress each other. She was also upstairs, but had been instructed to stay out of sight.

Concentration, he reminded himself. And decorum. There would be time enough for all that. After.

PART
II

5

By Friday afternoon of the following week, Toni Spina still had not returned to the Borghese in Hammonton, and Max Solieri, her chef, was more than a little worried.

Sure, the Tone had taken a few days off before—Hialeah, the Derby, she had even once flown up to Saratoga for Race Week—but she'd always called in religiously, wanting to know everything about the joint, even down to fresh flowers: what kind were they and had they been placed on the tables? "Check for me please, Solly," she would say. He'd hold his hand over the phone and count to thirty. Every day about four-thirty, she would call in. Now it was four-thirty, and no call. The excuse Furco had given, that she had a "condition that needs attention," Solieri didn't buy. What kind of condition could keep her from a phone?

So he had taken to strolling through the dining rooms during off hours, just to keep an eye on the place. And now he caught sight of Furco, sitting in the same corner with the same three other punks, and this offended Solieri's sense of justice and darkened his mood. Just who the fuck *were* they, they thought they could sit around, leaching the profits, while others worked? He'd heard they had slapped some monster vigorish on some debt that Toni or Jack had run up. They were killers and they thought that gave them the right. Who they were and how they acted, even down to the wise-guy swagger they seemed to have been born with, was everything Solieri considered old-world and dark and un-American. Their presence burned. It galled, there where he and all the others, who were working hard to make something good, could see. His breath came hard.

Bumping back through the swinging doors, he suddenly stopped. Was she dead? It was the first time he had let himself think of it in a while, and the question could not be denied. Could Furco have done Toni, like he'd done Jack? After the phony heist and Toni's outburst, there was the possibility. Furco was the worst—a tarantula, some quick fucking spider in a shadowed web, just ready to spring—and the word was he took no shit.

"Where's he from? Originally," the sous chef now asked him.

In the manner of work conversations that can last an hour, a week, a career, they had been discussing him for the past several days. "Margate City, after his father hit it big. Before that, I don't know. The father got his start as a pugknuckle pimp. Then rolled on from there."

"Whazzat?"

They began moving down two long tables laden with shelled, fourteen-count shrimp, which, steamed and served with cocktail sauce, would be placed—one apiece—in front of every customer who took a seat in the restaurant. Explained the Tone when they'd first opened after Solieri asked her if she was trying to give the joint away, "Not at all, Solly. Just the opposite. It's a taste, and what's a taste? Usually enough to make a person say, why go someplace else? I'm hungry. I must eat, and here the food is good." Then, the shrimp itself suggested big-ticket entrees. "If we're good enough," she had added, "we'll make it up on the tab. Nobody minds paying a little more for a *good* meal." Which Solieri now agreed with perfectly.

He glanced at the clock over the swinging doors. Almost a quarter to five. She hadn't missed a Friday pep talk in the almost five years they'd been open.

Pivoting, Solieri moved to the other table, which was lined with jumbo, nine-count shrimp. "Means he was into porn before porn pictures."

Like gray waves from the bow of a boat, shrimp meat scudded back from his blade, exposing long black seams that he plucked out and wiped on a side towel. He would then immerse the jumbos in a marinade of olive oil, vinegar, garlic, pepper, chili powder, salt, basil, and chopped, fresh mint, which had just come out this time of year and was still delicate in flavor. Solieri would then broil them for Sunday brunch, at which he always took pride in serving something different.

"We can't do too good a job," the Tone was always saying, and it was worth it, the extra. When once in a very long while on one of his rare Mondays off, he took the wife out to dinner someplace nice, he had only to say, "Max Solieri," when the hostess asked his name. "From the Borghese?" He'd only smile. The chef at the place would then jump through hoops, trying to show his stuff. Solieri knew he had the right kind of rep. People respected him for what he did, and a lot of that was because of Toni Spina.

"How you mean, porn with no pics? Thought one meant the other." Philly was a compact, sallow man with a Pancho Villa moustache thick as a shoe brush. The man knew his food and didn't complain, but Solieri could never remember his name, only where he was from. Like everything else in the kitchen, that too had been made to conform to his purpose.

"Invasion of privacy. Rubes, mostly." Through with the shrimp now, Solieri—like a diver rising from the depths—straightened up and stretched, as he did several times a day. He blinked his pale eyes, scanning his domain. Waitresses were now assembling in the serving area near the door. Again he glanced at the clock. Ten of five.

He turned to the kettles of soups he had bubbling on a range, and Philly, like a partner in a special dance, now followed him. Using towels on the handles, they hefted one of four kettles of soup off a range, and began scuttling it across the floor toward the serving tables. The gaggle of waitresses broke before them.

Solieri continued his explanation to Philly: "Some big farm boy from Pennsy. Muscles. The works. Hey, buddy, wanna rip off a piece? Gee, I don't know—my wife or my mother or my girlfriend's back at the shack. Come on, you'll be in and out quick. Girls. No women. She'll love it. 'Specially from a buck like you. Tell ya what—you here on your

71

own or you part of a group? Which of course Furco's old man already knew.

"Oh, no—I'm here with the Kay a' Cee from Germany Flats or the Sons of Poland or some It'lo-American Society from North Philly. That right? You don't say. I got a cousin from—he'd mention the town just over the line. I'm gonna give you guys something to talk about, you'll see. One I have in mind looks like—" they turned and, carrying the empty kettle, walked back through the waitresses, who, though deep in their own talk, again stepped away without looking at them directly "—Lana Turner, or Rita Hayworth."

"Who they? Lookers?"

"Bombshells. Stacked. Stop traffic out on the Pike." With his chin Solieri gestured toward the front of the joint, meaning the White Horse Pike that ran past it.

They reached for another kettle.

"Then, while Furco was setting the kid up, he'd have guys in cigar stores, on street corners, and in joints selling tickets a buck a crack. Peep show," he said through his teeth. At the serving table again, they lifted the kettle of oxtail soup and, as carefully, poured it into another of the deep wells. Suddenly their foreheads were blistered with sweat.

"Weirdos, I'd say. Or guys who were weirdos and didn't know it, then. Then some other guys who liked guys or little girls. She'd be young, lemme tell ya, somebody Furco, the old man, was just breaking in. And there they'd be in the middla this room, going at it. She'd say things like—" Solieri waited until they were well past the waitresses; in falsetto he then went on, "—'I just *love* your *cock*. I want you to come and come,' and a' course, he just—"

"Came and came and came," Philly supplied, laughing, raising his head to the pots and pans over the sink in his approximation of a stretch.

"Kid. All pumped up. And old Furco? Instead of just ten bucks for a hump, he'd get maybe a couple hundred with all the little holes drilled into the walls and whatever else he'd pull out of the rube, after he sold him the roll of film he'd say he took of him. Then, maybe a little snake oil for the clap he'd tell him he may have picked up from the broad.

He'd leave the poor suck with socks and shorts. Fleeced. Plucked dry.''

They went for the fourth soup, which was, as always, French onion.

"Later, of course, Fur, as they called him—no, no, you gotta get this right. Follow me—'' Solieri turned to Philly and said, "Fuh, as in *huh*,'' which was his native Jersey City for *her*.

Turning his head so as not to insult Solieri, Philly said, "Oh, yeah—*huh*,'' and laughed volubly. For the first few weeks at the Borghese, he had understood only half of what Solieri had said.

"You got it. Fuh. He was one of the first to get into dope for the girls, which was cheaper than paying them and lucrative in its own right with the big black population A.C. had even then. Then the home movie end of the business. He'd get some—'' Solieri glanced at Philly, never having decided what the man's racial background was; some sort of Spic or Arab, he assumed ''—nigger to bang the broad. Schwanz a yard long. Guy'd go through gyrations, slamming it into her like he scoffed a boatload of rubber bananas. She'd roll her eyes and claw at everything in sight.''

Over the kettle they swapped glances.

"Niggers here then?'' Philly asked, averting his eyes.

"Oh, yeah. Niggers been here since the eighteen-eighties or -nineties. Place was pricey then. Mansions with chauffeurs and servants. The works. They called the place the 'Queen of Resorts.' But when the money pulled out, the coloreds stayed, and anything you did to them was okay with the heat, just so long as they had a piece of it. Place was wide open. A pesthole.''

Finished with the soups, they broke from each other, moving in opposite directions around to their respective areas of the serving tables. Behind them were grills, ranges, ovens, and banks of eye-level broilers and microwaves, which Solieri hated but found useful to heat things up. It was another way of cooking, quicker, not better.

Both then washed off their shrimp knives and replaced them in their respective sheaths. Solieri's knife case contained an even dozen specialized blades, which he now raised himself on tiptoes to place on top of the walk-in where he kept his wallet, his work schedules, and his calendar.

"But this one. The guy in the corner booth?" Philly kept his particulars in a locked box under a prep table. He had learned long ago that where your tools were concerned, you trusted nobody.

"Him?" A wiry man with a gaunt, red face, Solieri layered his hands on a cutting table, as though resting them. He crossed his ankles and looked away. He was fifty-two now, and had spent most of his life in the white porcelain and quarry-tile confines of kitchens. Speculating about the world, which he seldom got to see, was important to him. It was as though he was always shocked to realize how crummy things really were, and he was consoled only by the possibility that his musings might be fantasy.

"All that dough from the broads and dope—hey, it made them respectable, what else? Like I said, the father knocked down a half dozen shacks somewhere in Margate and put up a big, gaudy pile with statues and shit on the lawn—you know the kind. And it made them smart, all that money. Lawyers, doctors, they even sent one of them to business school, so he could learn how to make money the right way, like normal people.

"But Lucca?" Solieri jerked his chin at the door. "It's like he come outta nowhere. I don't even know where he fits in the family or his background. Education and stuff.

"First I heard he was kind of a runner for Grisanti. Banks. Politicians. Cops. He smoothed things out. Then he made a smart marriage to the daughter of some Philly don, kept himself out of jail, and here he is." Our boss, Solieri did not add. It was the kind of thing, said loosely, that could get a person killed.

Yet again he thought of Toni. He knocked back his high hat and glanced out through the plate slots at the clock and the waitresses.

"Coffee, Sol?" one now asked. "Philly?"

"You tryin' to make points with us, Dolores?" Solieri asked without looking at her. Reaching behind him, he untied his apron and replaced it with a fresh one.

Philly now did the same.

"Get you nothin' but a veal française."

74

Philly began to laugh. His laugh was deep, earthy, and prurient. His dark eyes flashed. "Sauce. Lotsa sauce!" he roared, so that nearly everybody else smiled.

But when his laughter stopped, the kitchen was suddenly quiet. Some were glancing at the clock. They could hear the ice-maker spitting new cubes into its bin and the sounds of some other people approaching the door from the dining room.

"Could that be her?" Philly asked Solieri in an undertone.

It was the question that was on everybody's mind, most having worked at the Borghese steadily since it opened. Yeah, the work was hard and the sidework (all the polishing and cleaning) phenomenal, but the tips were good—*better* than in A.C.—and the place was always shaped up and made you feel proud to work there. Then, mortgages, car payments, school tuitions, marriages, and families were riding on the dough that was taken home, and for a week now the uncertainty of where Toni was and what might happen to the place had worried everybody.

Solieri only folded his arms across his chest.

Philly leaned back against a counter.

Slowly, hesitantly, the door opened, and they saw first only a hand with long, lacquered nails on the edge of the door, then the sharp angle of a bare shoulder, as she turned and said something to somebody behind her. Finally, her face appeared, her dark eyes quickly surveying the group, which now, as one, smiled at her.

"Oh, well—you're all here. Hi," she said almost diffidently, as though meeting a large group of strangers.

Drawing herself up to her full height, which only seemed great because of the dress of red crushed silk that sheathed her like a body stocking to midcalf, where it flowed out in a scalloped flounce, she backed open the door to let a tea wagon pass. Covered by a tablecloth, it was being pushed by one of the hostesses. Though young and blond with regular features and a good build, the girl appeared insubstantial and fey beside the mature beauty of the darker woman. And with one hand on the door and her back arched to permit the passage of the wagon, the Tone was standing in profile, her curves and the rake of her deeply tanned shoulders obvious.

As though nervous, she touched a hand to her graying hair, gathered in a graceful sweep, which was also new, at the back of her head, and smiled. Against the olive tones of her long face, her teeth and the whites of her hazel eyes were in brilliant contrast. She stepped into the kitchen and closed the door behind her. Taking another step forward, she moved her hands to her thighs and looked down at them, as if collecting her thoughts before she would speak.

"Wait a minute. Ho! Just what you think this is?" Solieri said. Pushing himself off the counter with his hands still folded across his chest, he began walking through the women, who again made way for him. "Who you think we are that you can waltz in here at—" his hand shot out "—five o'clock a week later, after no calls, nothing, no word about where you been and how you are and what you want done with this place, 'cept for the word of some—" again the hand went up "—some—" yet again "—mobster?"

Heads went back. People looked at each other quickly before turning away.

Solieri's face was red now; he knew he had made a mistake. People talked. One way or another, it would get back to the man. "Where you been?" he demanded.

Plainly embarrassed, again touching a hand to the back of her hair, Toni said, "Well, I—"

"And *how* you been?" He cut her off, wanting now just to end what had begun as a rough expression of affection, visceral and undeniable, but was now clearly distressing to both of them.

Her eyes rose to meet his, and she was touched at how serious he was. "All right, I guess."

"Nothing serious?"

Curving her shoulders, she shook her head.

"You sure?"

Again she nodded and smiled fully, seeing him raise his arms and walk toward her.

"Tone," he said, picking her off the floor and swinging her around. "Don't you evah, *evah,* leave us again like that, without a word about where you are and how long you're staying and what we should do. And phones—weren't there no phones at this place?'' He held her away from him.

When their eyes met, he saw it was something she just did not want to discuss. "We're glad to have you back," he went on. "But remember—next time, you can call collect." He kissed both of her cheeks, and let her down.

"Now—" he waved a hand "—on with the show." As he moved away from her, elbows struck elbows, as not a few of the waiting personnel noticed that Solly's eyes were filled with tears.

Back behind the slots he said to Philly, "Fuck it—I'm just a big bag a' shit." Turning his back to the group, he blotted his eyes.

Worse, thought Philly, a big bag of fired shit. Or much worse, a big bag of fired, dead shit, and he wondered if he himself would go, too. Or would they offer him Solieri's job?

Suddenly his life was filled with details he just didn't want to know, and anyways, the boss had begun talking, and the way she looked he could watch her for days.

"Well, it's apparent that you all know I've been away for a while," she was saying. "I was—" she glanced off, up at the ceiling "—exhausted, I guess, and I needed a rest. In the next few months I might take a few more weeks off, and I've asked Sandy to set up a vacations schedule for those of you who want to take one." She turned to the blonde, who was the assistant dining room manager and was watching her with sparkling, admiring eyes. "We all need rest. Working around here for years at a time could drive anybody a little crazy."

The others smiled.

"Now—" with her hands on her thighs, she again looked down, curving her shoulders so that the strapless, dark red dress opened up and presented a mounded and tanned gulf that Philly thought was maybe wide and soft enough to dive into "—you've probably heard that we've got a gang coming tonight, and . . ."

And, you know, her face wasn't really pretty, he decided. With her nose that was long and thin on the bridge and slightly crooked and her high cheekbones, she was good-looking, all right, but in a strong way that—with her wide mouth and all those teeth—showed up best when she smiled. Then, her upper lip was a little too big or stuck out too far or something, and gave her this little lisp that was nice.

". . . some parties," she was saying. "A big sit-down dinner in the Pine Barrens Room. And then we've got reservations for 652, as of the moment I passed by the desk."

A few of the waitresses grinned. More shifted their feet and glanced at the clock.

"Now, in addition to the soups, of which I'm sure you're aware, Solly's got as specials shad and shad roe combo plates or either/or. He's got—" her head and eyes flicked up "—medallions of veal chervil with lime sauce, poached halibut steaks with saffron caviar sauce . . ."

And the way she now pressed down on her hands, firming first her biceps and then, as she breathed in, her upper body, made her look like somebody on stage, like she was about to break into song. Philly wondered if she, you know, *knew* how she wanted to look and that's what she was giving them, or was just being herself naturally with no put-ons. Beauty, he had learned from experience, *was* only skin deep, but there was something about the slope of her chest and the hollows of her neck and the little golden knobs on the ends of her shoulders that'd probably turn any guy on.

Only twenty-eight himself, he didn't even mind her gray hair that she wouldn't touch up or the wrinkles that you could sometimes see when the light was right. And he thought how good she was at what she did a miracle: knowing everything about the joint right down to what they would be serving even when she was away. Far as he knew, him and Solly had been the only two to talk it over. "This place wired," he whispered to Solieri, "or she got a crystal ball?"

". . . rack of spring lamb Bretonne. That's with the white pea beans and tomatoes. And finally, you can tell the vampires, at least a few of whom will be sitting at your tables tonight, ladies, that we've even got Texas ribs. That's the special, prime ribs that've been cut from mastodons. How many do we have, Solly?"

Having now gathered himself, Solieri only closed his eyes and nodded. With him it was a matter of pride that he never ran out of anything; it kept operating expenses somewhat higher, but it was worth the price. *Nobody* went away from *his* tables disappointed.

"Enough, he says. Well—" she held out her hands, as though examining her nails, before letting her arms swing by her sides "—I'm talking to you like this now because I want you to forget that number." She leaned her head toward the 1,418 marked out in plastic tags over the swinging doors to the dining rooms. It was their dinner max, done on a day two years before during the hottest two weeks on record. The special had been "Clambakes," which were served buffet-style and were easy for the staff.

"I want you to do nothing different from what you do so well every night. What's a number? Something more important than offering the wine list and selling our soups and appetizers with the decorum with which you work those tables every night? Or mentioning, if you're asked, that all our vegetables are fresh and steamed to order, our breads and desserts homemade from scratch right here on the premises?

"Yes—" she nodded once and blinked "—we'll probably have to hustle more tonight than on other nights. It'll be worth it, I'm sure, but remember this—making some people wait with a drink in a lounge or the bar is preferable to rushing others through their meal for a new cover. We'll treat every table like we always do—like it's our last—and I don't mean just using the crumber and keeping the ashtrays clean and the water glasses filled.

"I mean our smiles, our greetings, and how we finish their meal. First impressions and last. It's word of mouth that's gotten us where we are and will keep us there. Just as soon as the party in the Barrens Room is over, I've arranged for a band to play there with complimentary cognacs for everyone and Macanudos for the men.

"But let me say this—" her expression suddenly changed, becoming more serious, Solieri judged, her dark eyes meeting theirs "—none of the Borghese's success, the fact that we're probably going to break that number not just tonight but on nights in the future, would be possible without you." Suddenly glassy, her eyes searched through the gathered staff. "Being away for a while gave me a chance to understand this. I've worked with some good crews in my time, but none as good as you. You're the best. Professionals. Every last one of you, and there's the difference.''

It was a difficult moment: the statement of what many of them already knew but seldom, if ever, allowed themselves to think, and more forceful because she had said it. Yeah, Solieri thought, they were pretty good, but the best he had ever worked with? Maybe, he decided, but they would soon see, wouldn't they? Every night was the test.

"Oh, and one thing more," she went on. "Those men in the corner booth of the bar? They're not mobsters. No." She shook her head. "They're gangsters, and one of these days—soon, you'll see—they'll just vanish, faster than you can say Al Capone. And that's a promise. Me to you."

The others laughed, and only Solieri raised an eyebrow. It was then that the swinging door opened a little, and a bit more, a small hand grasping the edge. Ringlets of dark brown hair appeared and eyes an unlikely pure blue in color and bright with youth and good health. "Mommy—we have *customers*," Tina said officiously, and the others began to laugh.

"Now," she insisted.

"Wait," said Toni, moving toward the tea wagon as the others began to leave. "I've got something for you. And what's customers anyhow? They'll appreciate us more if we make them wait, right?" She drew back the tablecloth to reveal a wagon brimming with individual orchid corsages for the women and carnation boutonnieres for the men.

"Tina—can you help me with these?" The aroma of the flowers spread through the kitchen as the plastic was removed from the packages. "I think there's one here for you."

Her eyes filling with the spectacle of the flowers, Tina toddled forward to help.

Said Philly, shaking his head, "Man—ain't she somethin'? She plays us like a pianola. That number? We'll knock it by ten o'clock. I mean—" there was a cast to his eyes as he watched her pinning the corsages on the waitresses "—she's maybe the best-lookin', best-actin' *lady* I ever seen."

A few moments before, Solieri would have agreed. Sure, he was touched she'd backed his error with the gangster bit.

And, sure, he'd never once heard her promise nothing that didn't come to pass.

But could she be serious?

He probably knew the Furcos of this world better than her, and you got nothing for nothing from none of them. If you had nothing to begin with—hey, worse off for you. They'd take what they wanted out of your skin. And Solieri, whose life of hard work had been dedicated to serving a small constellation of persons, of whom Toni Spina was probably the brightest star, was again plunged into a kind of funk.

How? he thought. What did she promise them? What were they making her do?

6

She was doing nothing at the moment that she did not want to do. For the restaurant was, after all, her creation, and since her talk in the kitchen, it had been spinning like a well-oiled machine at the peak of its power.

There had been no chatter among the staff, no gossiping, no kidding. Nobody was stopping in the service area beyond the second set of swinging doors for a coffee or a smoke, which marked even busy nights. And, keeping half an eye on certain key tables, she could tell that service was not merely crisp, it was snappy.

More, Toni was appreciating the special ambience of the night: how newcomers were noticing first the appurtenances of the place, then its cleanliness, the smiles of the staff, and perhaps even having a drink or two with the complimentary shrimp before opening the menu. Their eyes ran across the page to the prices, which were not low. They either caught a glimpse of a passing entree or glanced toward another table.

It was then that what she thought of as the "click," which sometimes she believed she could almost hear, occurred: that moment when the menu was lowered to the table or a smile began or fingers were twined. It was as though they said, "Why not? This place won't disappoint me. Tonight I'll forget about the cost and have a good time." One man was saying to a large table, obviously a family, "Kids—go ahead—have the lobster. Stuffed. The last one I had here was outta sight. On me. Waitress? The check—" A finger then punched a proud chest. "And some wine, some Spuma. Keep it flowing, all around." Clicks were going off everywhere, which Toni knew all too well did not often happen even in the best restaurants.

"What you gonna do with all your money, Tone—move to Florida?" It was, of course, what the elderly man and woman in the bar booth were about to do. They had been steady customers nearly from day one.

"No—Monte Carlo's more to my taste," she blurted out, realizing too late that Furco in the corner booth might be able to hear her. "How are your dinners tonight?"

"If it wasn't good, would we tell you?"

"If you didn't, I wouldn't allow you back."

"You know—" as though blessing the crowd, the man waved a fork at the dining room that they could see through a Tuscan arch "—maybe half these people are here because of us. I missed my calling. I shoulda gone into advertising."

"Or restaurants," Toni said, having had the same conversation, or one like it, with countless people dozens of times before. It was a variation on the saw that success has a thousand mothers. "And his reward?" she now asked the man's wife.

"Him? He keeps telling me he's too old for that sort of thing."

Pushing himself back in the booth, the man said, "What—no twist, no beans?" He meant pony glasses of Sambuca with twists of lemon rind and two coffee beans in the bottom. As Toni now remembered, it was their favorite after-dinner drink.

She shook her head, allowing her eyes to scan nearby tables and to watch a waitress who was serving entrees. "Tonight it's 'Make-Believe Ballroom Time,' " she said, alluding to a radio show from New York that was popular with many of the senior citizens who frequented the Borghese. "That means a Macanudo to keep the young girls away, some Rémy Martin for your heart, and a little light stepping in the Barrens Room, *if* you think you can handle it." Now remembering that the man had been a successful lawyer in Cherry Hill, she added, "Please sign the hold-harmless agreement before you go in. My liability rates are high enough as it is.''

The man started laughing so hard he had to raise his napkin to his mouth. "When's this all begin?" he managed.

"In about twenty minutes. Don't let the threat ruin your meal."

"You gonna be there?"

"I'm probably the only one here who knows CPR," she said, though it was her own pulse that had risen.

It was the moment she had been dreading, and, turning now to Furco, she noted how carefully his dark hair had been clipped, how finely tailored was the cut of his gray linen suit. It was handmade, she could tell, having helped her father in his tailor shop. Like his pearl gray tie, his shirt was silk. With sharp but even features, he was actually a handsome man.

But why had he chosen to occupy an entire booth when they had customers waiting right out the door? As the controlling partner who had proved time and again his own greed, what could he be thinking of? And the contrast between him and everybody else in the place—could he have realized that?

Sure—she thought as she nodded once and said, "Mr. Furco"—how could he have missed it? He was the only person in the place at a table who wasn't having something to eat. Then why? Ego? Perhaps, though in no way was he a flamboyant character for his type. It was then that her two years of having carefully observed him coalesced for Toni. Furco's need, she decided, was to have others observe the power that he enjoyed, *there* in the Borghese. But why? "May I interest you in a seat at the bar?" she asked, wondering further—to what end?

Now allowing himself to look at her directly for the first time, Furco could hardly control himself. For the half hour she had been in the lounge, it had been like she was taunting him, using that red dress, the tan, her moves, and the way she swung her shoulders, working the crowd, gliding slow, booth to booth. He'd been trying to figure it out, what she touched in him.

He thought, as he'd thought before, that maybe one time

he had dreamed her or seen somebody like her in a movie, or even that she reminded him of the way he thought his mother might've looked when she was younger, which was difficult for him to admit.

He had made her being away and him not seeing her for a week a kind of personal test of how much who she was and the way she looked meant to him. But when she'd appeared in the archway in that dress, having to lean against a table as a waitress with a tray went by, it was like she had reached right inside him, grabbed, and begun twisting, and, like Grisanti had said, he had nobody but himself to blame.

"How was your trip?" he asked.

She blinked. Payson had told her to say nothing to anybody.

"Where'd you go?" Furco let his eyes slide from her face to the hollows of her wide shoulders and then to her upper chest. "South, I can see."

Toni only looked away.

"Panama, I'd say. And then I hear they got some great beaches on Grand Cayman Island."

Toni tried to keep her eyes from giving her away. Panama was right. Having registered at a hotel as one Giancarla Marchetti, she'd nevertheless banked as A. A. Spina, withdrawing all funds in the list of accounts that Payson had given her and transferring them by wire to another bank on St. Maarten in the Netherlands Antilles. There—signing into yet another hotel as Giancarla Marchetti while conducting business in her own name—she'd completed some other set of manipulations, keeping her eyes straight ahead of her, as Payson, who remained by her side throughout, requested.

He'd then suggested that they relax a bit. "Why hurry back? I don't think I've seen the sun since September." Courtly throughout the stay, he took her to wide, empty beaches during the day and crowded nightspots and casinos in the evening, always introducing her to the several acquaintances he'd met as Giancarla Marchetti.

"Aruba?" Furco guessed again.

She held his gaze.

"Curaçao?"

She waited, wondering if it was a test. Or could it be that

he himself did not know? Watching him now as his slight smile fell, she thought the latter.

"Sit down," he said.

She tilted her head. "I beg your pardon." Smiling at him like she smiled at any cover.

She had changed her hair, piled it up on top, neat but loose, too. Nice, he thought, imagining how it would look on a pillow. But where the fuck had she been? The guy—Cheech—had it all over him. He might have sent her to the moon, for all Furco would ever know. And why? To do what?

"I said, sit down."

"What?"

Furco's hand jumped from the glass. He pointed to the booth's empty seat opposite him. His fingers snapped and, like lightning flashing, their eyes met for several moments that seemed to Furco an eternity. He thought of how it had started for him, the thing with her.

Slow. Not right away. Yeah, he had known who she was, all right, everybody in A.C. did after a while. She had an old Mercedes convertible, canary yellow with wire wheels, she used to tool around in. But after she'd made the Mayfair Room hands-down the best place in the area to eat, she turned into a kind of princess. People who worked in the city bowed to her, they scraped, and not because she insisted or nothing. She just was who she was—better, is all, and they knew it.

Owners and stars—Frankie Valli, Gabe Kaplan, even the Chairman—wanted to be seen with her. In nightclubs she always got to sit at a headliner's table or up front, and not because of Jack, like some people thought. When Furco first took notice of her and met Jack, he'd thought: woman like that needs a front man, some big stiff to walk her around, open doors, get her a seat, take her to dinner, that sort of thing.

Tall and blond, Jack had shoulders a yard either side and teeth like the grille of a fifties Buick. He looked like he'd just climbed off a surfboard, and just as dumb. And from his hey-buddy handshake to the way his eyes couldn't stay on his cards but kept jumping to the shoe, impatient, like wanting to know what he'd be dealt next, it was plain the man could never take care of somebody like her. Way it worked out, Jack, who'd never had nothing, couldn't even handle the little that then came his way—booze, gambling, women, drugs. Asshole just never knew when he'd had enough. Now, staring into her eyes that seemed to be dancing with some knowledge of how Furco himself didn't measure up, he wondered if she'd make any guy into a Jack. He'd heard of broads like that, and in a way his wife was one.

The night Furco and she had opened the wedding presents, he'd poked her there in the wrappers. Then she'd asked, "Is there anything more?" meaning more gifts. It was all downhill from that moment on. Next day she went shopping, and now Furco couldn't think of her without her arms full of bags and boxes of expensive shit that crammed all the closets and spare rooms of the house until every once in a while she just gave it all away.

The cost? At first it had bothered him, but to keep the picture clear, like he always tried to do, she had brought him his main chance through her father and her family. Then, she was the mother of his children, and, like most of the other men he respected, Furco divided his world into three parts: his family, which was primary; his associates, who could be dangerous; and everything else, which was there for the taking, if you were strong.

Problem was, a few years ago, like a whammy, his wife's question—the one she'd asked on their wedding night—rose up and blindsided Furco. Suddenly, all the "pop," as he called it, that he used to get from little things like food and a nice sunset and a walk on the beach had gone out of his life. Even the joy he'd once got from his kids, whom he would die for and had killed for, was drained from him. Far as he was concerned, they were spoiled, like their mother, and every day they just seemed to look so much like her that he even once wondered if he had anything much to do with being their old man besides paying the bills.

For a while there, he'd put it down to his age, which was forty, or the dry, which kept laundering money like a machine, day in and day out, and no longer challenged him. All it required was being there, changing runners regularly, and making sure he wasn't being cheated. But the fact was he had nothing—or *felt* nothing for what he did—except maybe his boat, and even that wasn't complete. It just seemed he had nothing he liked to do, nothing else he wanted to own or be.

And she was different—Toni—and not just in how she treated the husband, there at the end. Anybody else would have dumped him first chance, after he got in deep and lost his job and lushed out. Not Toni, leaving the joint to run him around; taking his abuse in public when he was stiff; paying and paying and paying, even for his broads, as it turned out. "Oh, Jack," Furco had once heard her say when she was trying to load all 250 pounds of drunk into her car, "when are you going to shape up?" like it was something a guy like him, who had bent and broken, could do.

Then there was the way she handled people right through that trouble: smiling, knowing everybody's first name and what was going on with them, coming on warm but straight. Even with him. In those first few weeks, it had been that difference that bugged him, and then, suddenly he didn't mind at all.

"I said, sit down. I want to talk to you," Furco now said.

With a kind of admiration he watched her wait for him to reveal more of what he wanted. Like all strong people, she was first a watcher, a conciliator, who only acted when she was sure of the results. And he now told himself it had been her caution and tact that had first turned him on.

Seeing her suddenly smile, he changed his mind. No, there was *nothing* about her that he didn't find interesting. He could watch her for hours, days, years. He kept seeing her beside him on the *Bark-a-Roll*. But thinking, why him? And why her? And why now at this time in his life? It made Furco's anger surge.

Her dark eyes searched his face and, not finding what they were looking for, glanced away through the archway into the crowded dining room. Turning back to him, they sparkled. She had her hands on her biceps, defensive. "You know I'm manager here, and this is no usual busy night."

Furco couldn't help himself. Knowing it was wrong, he still blurted out, "And you know who I am, and I want you to sit down." She *was* different, he told himself, and he had to *treat* her different, but she had to stop breaking his stones.

He wondered if maybe he really didn't want to make out with her, maybe he really wanted things ugly. Furco could make it that way. He knew at least that much about himself.

But the way she smiled again and cocked her head before replying made him *know* what she could mean to him. "Could I interest you in some light patter and some—" one hand flicked off her forearm toward his glass "—Galliano in, say, twenty-five minutes? We have a big sit-down dinner finishing up in the Barrens Room, and I—"

Staring down at the empty glass, Furco shook his head. *"Now,"* he nearly shouted.

People in nearby booths looked over; at the bar, heads turned to them.

"Why *now?*" she demanded back.

"Because *I*—" he punched his chest "—*say* now."

"But now is inconvenient for me, for the Borghese, and for you, too, if you'll think about it." She smiled again, her hands still in place. "You know, sometimes I get the feeling that you really don't want this restaurant to succeed. How many other nights have you just sat here, watching things? Yes, I agree, we should have a chat, but why tonight of all nights?"

Toni again looked away, her eyes by habit falling to the tables and trays around her. She had let Furco distract her, and she was struggling to keep her mind on the rhythm of the restaurant. "I'll be back shortly. You just sit tight. It would be better to meet in the bar, though. Paying customers could use this booth." She turned and raised a hand to the bartender, who had been hired by Furco and was now watching them. She pointed to Furco's glass and started to walk away.

Furco's hand shot out and grabbed her wrist. Hard.

She stopped, turned only her head, and looked down at his hand. "Take your hand off my arm."

"Sit down," he said through his teeth.

"Take your hand off my arm." Her eyes, darting to his face, now seared him.

At the bar, two regulars had twisted around on their stools. One had placed a foot on the floor. The old man in the next booth stood up, napkin in hand. "Something wrong, Toni?"

"I don't think so." Her eyes, collecting Furco's again, dropped to the hand.

Snorting once, laughing a little, he shook his head and released her. "*Marron*—you tick me off."

But she did not move away. Instead, she waved thanks to the man in the booth, and stepped closer to Furco's table. She eased herself down onto the seat opposite him, the silk of her dress whistling over the Naugahyde. Their knees bumped.

She folded her hands before her, and when at length he said nothing, she reached two fingers across the table and touched his wrist. "You were saying?"

Again with a headshake and a laugh, Furco glanced up at her. "You're something, you know that? Really." His half-smile was wan, and his eyes searched her face, though he couldn't keep himself from thinking about their knees beneath the table. Would they touch again? What would it be like, really, to get into her? Would it cure him? He breathed out and decided to make one last stab. "You know, there's not a broad in maybe the entire world I'd let treat me like this."

A hand came up to her chest, as though to say, Me, a *broad?*

"You know what I mean. And look—" His smile was now full. Furco himself knew how to turn it on, when he wanted. He'd give her one last chance. "—I tell myself it's me, that somehow, somewhere back there I offended this beautiful person. Me? What do I know? I've made a career of offending people, but this one?" Furco shook his head. "Nah—not her, because she's special."

Toni smiled.

"Really." Furco chanced it and reached two of his own fingers over to touch her wrist. Beneath the table his knee again touched hers and he almost jumped, like some kid all goofed up, silly. But he knew this—he hadn't felt so up in a long time, and with her the "pop" could be put back in his life. "I don't think there's nothin', you know, you could do—change a light bulb or maybe sweep the floor—that you wouldn't do with—" he waved a hand "—class. And then the way you look, the way you carry yourself—" He thought for a moment he was going too far. "I'm just trying to say

I'm an admirer of yours. Really," he insisted, "and maybe I should've told you before."

"Then you're my business partner, right?" he blundered on, feeling sweat beginning to bead on his forehead. It was something, the way he felt about her. "That alone—" Pushing off against the table, he firmed his upper body so she could see he, too, was put together good and had kept himself in shape. In his time, beautiful women *had* loved Lucca Furco, and he was determined she would, too. "—would make you special." He winked.

She smiled.

He hurried on. "So, look—this is a nice place, you do a good job here. I myself want to continue but, you know, on a different footing. And to show you just how much I value you and the—" he glanced at the bar; there was some huge spade sitting there, and Furco didn't care for niggers, 'specially in any place he had anything to do with "—partnership and to make things *different,* like I said, between us—" he waited until their eyes met "—I got a coupla little somethings for you.

"First, you know last Friday night? What happened? The little *loss* we suffered, here at the joint?" Furco waited, trying to read her eyes that were boring into his, holding his gaze, but she gave him nothing. Not even a blink to say she understood what he meant. "That bothered you, I could tell. So, as long as we're together, you and me, I make you a promise—no more Friday nights or nothing like it. Evah again. All right?"

Two smile lines appeared at the corners of her mouth.

Heady now, the room almost spinning for him, Furco blundered right on, the line just spilling out of him, unplanned, "You're saying to yourself, 'Easy to say, but where's the backer? What's he got to *prove* it,' right? Two little things I picked up in the city, just for you, so you know how much I care."

Toni was disturbed by his effusiveness, wondering what it could mean. And then she was confused by what he meant. City? New York? Or Philly, which was closer? Until he drew out the long, thick slips—perforated segments on card stock, like claim checks ripped from the bottoms of two cards. She had seen her signature on such things before.

Furco slid them across the table, waiting—he told himself—to see how she'd react. And when, staring down at them, her eyelids did not flicker, he added, "You know—from Caesars and Harrah's. The othah night—$17,220."

He ripped them in two, dropping the four pieces between them. "That's partners. Me and you."

Her eyes rose to him and searched his face.

"One condition."

She blinked.

"You let me take you to dinner. Anyplace you want. Say, Monday—the day you sort of take off, right? See, I know more about you than you think."

But it was like she didn't even have to consider it, Furco was later to muse; like she had these certain conditions or situations or words that she just never let work on her, no matter the cost.

Her fingers came out and folded down over the back of his hand. They were cool and dry. "I appreciate the gesture, Lucca—may I call you that? Really." Her eyes now gathered and held his; it was like they'd been seized. "And I won't forget it. Ever. But understand this in the spirit it's said: I played, I pay.

"Now—if you'll excuse me for just a moment, I'll be right back." Pushing off against his hand in a way that Furco interpreted as a squeeze, Toni rose from the booth and turned.

Walking directly to the bar, she could almost feel the eyes of the others, and she stared straight ahead. "Nicky," she said to the bartender, "would you hand me my purse? It's in the drawer below the register."

And it was only when she turned that Toni became aware of the man beside her—wide and dark and wearing a blue waiter's tux with a ruffled cravat.

"Mrs. Spina," he said.

Toni stopped.

"Colin Ross. We met in A.C. You said stop by about maybe my working for you."

Stunned, Toni looked down at her right hand, which was now wrapped in his. With his other hand he held out her card, the one that she had left on the nightstand before she had left the room. The little that they had spoken, she had told him that she, too, was in the restaurant business. She had mentioned the Borghese, but she would never have insulted him by offering him employment. The card had been an afterthought.

"Yes," she now said, blushing more deeply to have been forced to endorse the falsehood there where she insisted upon such exactitude from others. "Oh, yes—could you wait here a moment?" No, that was wrong. How could she possibly speak to him there? "I'll have a booth for you in a moment," which was even worse. He had not come there to dine. "You must try our food." She could say that he had waited on her, and, impressed by his professionalism, she had suggested that he come and work for her. He had seemed reluctant, and she was trying to win him over.

Almost dizzy now, she turned from him and took a faltering step toward Furco's booth, flaying herself with thoughts of how it had been with Ross. Good. Very good. Too good, perhaps. And wrong, of that—having seen him again and knowing it would continue—she was sure.

For after Jack she had struggled to keep things simple and together, and now suddenly the pace had quickened and the variables increased: her daughter, her mother-in-law, the restaurant, its debt, Payson who could bail her out, Furco who as much as owned her but now wanted—what? Something more? And the man, Colin Ross. And he wanted—?

Asking Furco for a pen, she was handed a designer model that complemented his gray linen suit and the silvering waves of his carefully cut hair.

In her hand, the pen shook.

"Like I said, you don't have to do this, Toni." He was tentative with her name, trying it and liking its sound, she could tell. "We're partners, right? Maybe someday you can do the same for me."

Did she see him smirk? She thought she did, and she was tempted to write the check for $92,000, which with the sum from Payson and her modest savings she could just swing, and tell him that in a short time he'd be all paid off. But she resisted the temptation. Never trump without backers, her father had told her, and then Payson had said it was between him and her only. *Omertà*. It was something even Furco could understand.

And he took the check, positioning it on the table squarely in front of him. "Whatever you want. You're the boss."

"Now, about this 'date,' " Toni said, wondering where the sureness of her voice, her control were coming from. From her father's advice never to telegraph her feelings, never to display anything but the utter confidence that she was surely in command? Or from her years as a restauratrice, during which she had dealt with every sort of person? Or the realization, which now jolted her suddenly, that Furco—whose dark eyes were searching her hair, her face, her neck—felt differently about her than she about him?

Others had been attracted to her, especially after Jack, and they had wanted to kiss or touch her or take her out. But this was—she glanced up at the creases around the corners of his eyes, which were smiling—different, and it rather disturbed her to decide without having to think that she should press the advantage. Why?

"I can't think of two other people who more desperately need to know each other than you and I, Lucca," she said, glancing at the bar and the broad, tuxedoed back of the man, who was not—thank God—conversing with the bartender. "But I don't go on 'dates' or 'go to dinner,' if we understand each other perfectly, either on my day off or otherwise. Is that understood?"

Furco blinked. If anything his smile became fuller. Everything he'd heard, she didn't fool around, this broad, even when the husband had been at his worst, shacking up with everybody he could. Essentially a conservative guy, Furco liked that. It made her almost virginal but better, since it was a matter of choice. The way she used her body—Furco had an idea she'd be good in the sack.

And then, if she could be loyal to a deadbeat and a drunk, how about to somebody who would show her every day, in everything he did, that he was strong and could take care of her? Not for the first time, he thought what she did here couldn't be easy. Maybe she wanted a rest? Maybe she'd like to become a real woman—all the way—and be taken care of?

Like Grisanti had said, he had it bad, but it was looking better now.

She went on, "So, if we can call it something else and . . ." She began to smile.

Furco smiled as well. ". . . do something different," he supplied. "How about the casinos?" With a finger he swirled her check at her so it lapped over the back of her hand. "With me I know your luck'll change. Guaranteed."

Her eyes widened. Had he, after all, a sense of humor? she wondered. "Are you making fun of me?"

"I wouldn't dare. Sailing? Boating?" Furco as much as held his breath. Was there a chance he could get her out on his boat?

"Do you have a boat?"

"Me? A boat? Nah—I don't have no boat. I got a *vessel.*"

"From which a woman might drop a line?"

His smile began to diminish. "How you mean?"

She gestured with her hands as though casting a rod. It was something she used to do regularly with her father.

"Fishing?"

"I haven't gone out for blues in years. They're running, aren't they?"

Fishing? Furco had only used the *Bark-a-Roll* once for fishing—with Grisanti—which was enough for a lifetime. But Furco forced himself. He jacked up his smile. "Sure. Sure, Toni—I got a cap'n knows just where they are." And just maybe, he thought—but he wouldn't let his fantasies get out of control. Not yet. He had too much riding on the possibility to let himself dream.

"Monday, then?" she asked.

"*Monday?* Monday's a whole three days away."

"But *we* have to work until then. Here at *our* business."

Furco raised both hands. "But, Tone—what I think, what I'm trying to tell you, you work too hard. No vacations, no rest. How 'bout tomorrow noon I pick you up at Harrah's dock and have you back by five?"

"But we'll hardly get out before you'll have to bring me back," she complained. "And I have my daughter. I absolutely refuse to squander the time I've set aside for Tina."

Furco saw his opening, a way of changing how she thought about him so far. "So bring her along, too. And the old lady. I hear you take care of her. That's nice. When was the last time she had an airing?"

Toni again smiled. That confirmed it—he *did* have a sense of humor, and if only she could better her relations with him, things would be so much easier for her on a daily basis. "You like children, Lucca?"

"Love 'em."

"And difficult old Italian ladies?"

"You think I haven't had to put up with them before?" He paused, watching the way her lips, which were wide and full, pulled back over those teeth that were so big and perfect they looked almost fake, and he concluded, "So—it's on. Monday morning around—"

"Ten," she said. "No, ten-thirty." She'd have to call the school and make an excuse for Tina, and then getting her mother-in-law into the car would be a chore.

Added Furco, "And it's *not* a date. Never with you."

When she laughed and turned her head to look at the bar, Furco almost shook his own hand. It was the key, he decided, to winning her: to be light, to make sure they had fun.

She began to leave the booth, the bodice of her evening dress opening into Furco's eyes as she leaned over. "Incidentally, Lucca—aren't you married?"

Their knees were touching. He tried to smile. "Aren't you?"

"I hope you'll remember it."

Furco tugged his eyes from her cleavage. His head turned to the bar. "Who's the splib?"

"The what?"

"The splib. The nigger. It's something we said in 'Nam."

"You were in Vietnam?"

"Course. Wasn't everybody?" he said proudly. "What's he want?"

"A job, he said. He's a waiter." Toni stared appreciatively at the broad stretch of Ross's back. "I hear he's good."

Furco shook his head, but then looked away without saying anything. There was a cast to his eyes that she had seen before, a glaze that made them seem shallow, like hard, black agates.

"You have a problem with blacks, Lucca?"

"Me?" Furco leaned back in the booth and touched the tips of his fingers to his chest. "No problem. None. They're

people, like all of us, and deserve whatever they can get."
He paused, wondering if he should chance it and deciding he
should. There were things about him that he just couldn't
hide, and with her he suspected it was better not to try. "I
just don't like 'em around, is all. It's bad for business, bad
for . . ." His voice trailed off. "That surprise you?"

It didn't, but she wondered how she could get along with
him on any level. Even bluefishing.

7

At the bar Ross handed her a completed application, which she now scanned. "Yes, well—is it Colin? That's an English name. Is it not?" she said in a stultified tone that made her blush and glance at the bartender to see if he was listening. Furco's man in more ways than one, he was staring at Ross with that same glaze in his eyes. "As you can see, we're rather busy tonight, but—" turning to the booths, she was relieved to see that none was available "—if you'll just follow me, we can speak in my office."

Work stopped momentarily as they passed through the kitchen, and Solieri's eyes followed them to the stairs. In the office downstairs, she did not pause to close the door behind them, but instead moved directly to her desk chair and indicated a seat on the other side of the desk.

He said, "Look—I didn't want to embarrass you like this. And don't think that I'm actually looking for a job. I just thought—"

She glanced up from the application, which she now placed on the desk, and their eyes met with all the force of that first time at the craps table. And it occurred to her how in the hotel room she at first didn't think she could fit the whole head of his penis into her mouth. It had made her lips feel like they'd split at the corners, and she thought she'd gag. But she'd held it, until—

And she almost asked him now to close the door so she

could sweep all the papers and the adding machine and the computer terminal right off the desk and— She hadn't done something like that since she was just out of college and Jack and she had first met. Once they'd made it in the shadows at the bottom of a Claridge stairwell, and in a broom closet down the hall from her office, and in a walk-in freezer in the cellar of the restaurant she was managing, where his cock, as he called it, felt so warm that at first she thought he was burning her.

But here now, like this, with Ross having declared in public that he was applying for a position in her restaurant, any indiscretion would violate every rule that she had ever established for herself or her employees in the workplace. And in a distant tone that did not at all reflect her true feelings, she asked, "You thought what?"

She scanned the breadth of his shoulders and the way the material of the cheap service tux was stretched taut over the muscles of his arms. He was a man of medium height and so dark of hue that his features, which were rounded and smooth, seemed almost to shine, like some hard dark wood. In the way that compacted size suggests strength, he was a handsome man. His forehead was broad, his nose a wide knob, and his chin so deeply dimpled it looked cleft. But it was his smile that now attracted her most, as it had that night in the casino. It was big and warm and it came right at you, as now, when, to cover his obvious embarrassment, he said, "If I thought it'd be like this . . ."

But there was steel there, too, she remembered from the way he'd brushed off the pit boss at the casino that night, and how he'd handled her later: making her perform again and again, even when she was tired and wanted to sleep, working her into a state until *she* goaded *him* to continue when he obviously couldn't, as if he had been afraid that their one time together would be their last. And here he was again.

"Thought that maybe you'd like to see me again, the way I'd like to see you," he said. "I don't think I've thought of anything else for days."

Again their eyes met, and the rush of knowing it would happen again and maybe right there and then pulsed through her. As though suddenly cold, she grasped her elbows and shivered, but she could feel dampness on her upper lip, her forehead. "When and where?" she asked, though she was hoping he wouldn't say now.

His smile fell, and his eyes flashed at the open door. But he said, "Motel, hotel is out, 'specially—"

Around here, she completed mentally, given her business and their difference in color.

"But where I live"—he pointed to the application—"is way out of the way, with a long drive leading to the house. You know Maxwell?"

It was about ten miles from the Borghese and completely surrounded by the Pine Barrens, where she had ridden horses as a young girl. Ironically, it was also where she'd lost her virginity, she remembered with a slight smile forming at the corners of her mouth. He had been a riding instructor, a Princeton undergraduate whom she dated until he got too serious and asked her to marry him. Even then she'd known what she wanted from men—until Jack.

Dismissing thoughts of how he had used her, she now concentrated on Ross, who had picked up the application and turned it over to write directions on the back. "You can't miss the place. It's the only house for miles." Finishing with a small map, he placed the pen on the desk and glanced up at her. "Tonight?" He stood.

She curved her shoulders. "I don't know." She raised a hand to indicate the restaurant upstairs, and her eyes then fell to his waist, and lower. He was aroused, too, and her eyes traced the outline of his penis in the leg of his trousers; then her gaze rose to his face. It wasn't love, as it had been with Jack. It was sex, but it was hot, perhaps hotter, and he wanted her, too.

"It don't matter, the time. I ain't married. No girlfriend. No—"

"Could you close that door?" she asked in a small voice that sounded to her disembodied, as though uttered by somebody else.

"What's that?" he asked.

Her eyes met his. Her heart was beating so fast she was actually breathless. It was going to happen, there on the desk or the carpet or the couch. There was a small changing room with a shower behind her. She would have him fuck her there in her clothes closet over and over again. No. She would have to go back upstairs soon, since people knew they were down there.

She would have him fuck her quickly, and later— She placed the application with the directions to his house in the top drawer of her desk.

He was smiling now, and he cocked his head. "Really?"

"Close the door," she now ordered. "And push the button. Make sure it's locked."

"You sure about this?" He laughed, but he turned and pushed the door closed, his thumb depressing the lock.

When he turned back, he found that she had unzipped the sides of the strapless, red, crushed-silk evening gown, so that when she stood and reached for him it fell to her hips. "Back there, through that door," she said into his ear, one hand grasping the taut muscles of his neck, the other reaching below for his fly.

She did not wear pantyhose, which she found hot and confining, and when with one motion of both hands he tugged up the skirt of the gown and exposed only garters and briefs, he pulled them aside and was in her before they got to the door.

There in the shadows of the changing room they blundered through a rack of hanging gowns, which fell, and in the darkness of one corner on a kind of bed of silk and costly fabric, she arched her back to meet and grind on each thrust, making him probe her as deeply as he could until she came with a suddenness that made her want to call out.

But she held it, her mouth wrapping, her tongue skewering one of his ears until the throbbing of his cock diminished. Pulling away from him quickly, so that he flinched and caught his breath, she said, "I must get back upstairs. And you, too. Do you mind going out the way you came in, so people can see you?"

"What about later?" he asked, looming over her, the girth of his body silhouetted against the light from the office. He had taken her breasts in his hands, and his thumbs were flicking over her nipples.

"I'll have to see. And really . . ."

* * *

Mazullo the elder had wanted his kids to have a more usual name and had even once asked his lawyer about changing it to Massey. The lawyer, who was then defending him against charges of aggravated assault and manslaughter, had said, "Don't bother me with that shit. You want a name change, go to Hollywood, become an actor."

Dean Mazullo, his son, who had been sitting at the bar of the Borghese for about two hours, was of the same opinion. The movie *The Godfather* was the single most important cultural experience of his youth, and Sonny Corleone—as played by James Caan—was his hero. True, young Mazullo didn't have Caan's shoulders or his height or his looks, but with practice he'd gotten the ramrod swagger down pat and he wore suspenders and a shoulder holster when he could. Then he took to calling himself Dino, which served two purposes.

First, it pissed off his old man, who had turned into a colorless business type and never did nothing no more without lawyers and consultations. Second, it was what Mazullo thought of as a macho name. It made people know he was Italian and maybe think Mob, which he was proud of.

With Joe "The Bear" Scarpone and "Tiny" Rik Falci, who were like-minded, he'd been up at the track at Monmouth. They had a kind of meet planned with some snatch for around two o'clock in A.C., but between times Mazullo had insisted they check in at the Borghese. He'd decided to go for Furco and Furco's dry, which was something sweet, and it interested him what was going down between Furco and the woman.

In spite of the tailor-made suits, the health club tan, the boat, and the 735-i, Furco was to Mazullo's way of thinking just another nothing asshole who didn't deserve what he had. He was quiet, like a kind of fucking banker, and, in spite of the stories Mazullo'd heard about Furco being an iceman, the thing he had for this older broad, who was really just a bitch, showed he was weak.

But when the big coon came back out of the kitchen, walking quickly past the bar and toward the foyer and the door, it hit Mazullo. "Ain't he the one from the Trump? You know, the night she blew the wad? The one with the shake-and-kiss routine?"

"The one *what?*"

"The coon, the nigger."

Falci turned the trunk of his body, which was outsized from weight lifting, toward the foyer, where Ross could be seen trying to move himself through the line that had gathered there. "All I remember is the dude was big and a nigger. And he's got botha them."

Said Scarpone through an ice cube, "And that fuckin' smile—all teeth and lips and shit."

"Nicky!" Falci shouted, calling for another round.

Scarpone continued, "So she likes coons. It's cheaper than gambling. Fuh huh." He then flicked his eyes at Mazullo to catch his reaction.

By far the smallest of the three, Mazullo had nonetheless run things at least since high school, and if he'd learned anything since, it was never to break anybody's stones, even a waste like Furco, for nothing.

But he couldn't help thinking: so, she likes coons and maybe not Furco. Or—if Furco got lucky—Furco *and* coons, which would be even worse for Furco. He'd go crazy. Batshit. "What you think about that?" he asked nobody in particular. "Her and maybe that nigger."

"Cock-a-doodle-do," said Falci, glancing at Furco, who was still in the booth, eating now.

So meet or no meet, Mazullo, Falci, and Scarpone were still in a car at the Borghese when, well after 3 A.M., Toni Spina locked the front door behind her cleaning crew and walked toward her Caddy.

Said Mazullo, "Look at the way she moves. Them shoulders. The way she carries herself. Don't she look like a guy?"

Said Scarpone to Falci, "Thought he had a thing fuh Furco. Now he's got a thing fuh huh. Maybe he just got a thing fuh guys."

Said Mazullo, "Hey, she's old, but I'd poke her. You?"

"Not when we got them bimbos waitin'." Scarpone checked his watch. "Almost a couple hours late already." He pulled a joint from the lapel pocket of his sport coat and twined the ends. "What we doin' here anyhow—private eye? Maybe we should've been cops."

And when Toni arrived at a Ramada Inn, where on weekends she shared a suite of rooms with her daughter and mother-in-law so she would not have to drive the thirty-five miles to Cherry Hill every night, Scarpone said, "See—she's a saint. She don't fool around with nobody. She's over it. You know—change of life."

"Yeah," Falci agreed, wanting only to get the hell out of there and back to A.C.

"Nah," said Mazullo. "Her? She's action whether she knows it or not. Furco ain't no fool."

"See?" Falci said to Scarpone. "See what I'm sayin'? She bit the Fur, man, and she's bit the Maz, too. Good. And the nicest part is nobody's gettin' nothin'. She's leading both of them around by their dicks, and they're lovin' it."

Mazullo just watched her climbing the stairs to her rooms, the tight red skirt of her evening gown making her body sway. He'd read someplace in one of those soldier-of-fortune magazines or maybe in *Playboy* or *Penthouse* that you had to know your enemy to fuck him over. And, yeah, he could see the attraction and feel with his nuts how Furco would want to *do* her good. Fact was, she seemed to Mazullo even stronger—no, not stronger—but, you know, more *there* than Furco himself. And Furco was enough *there* for Mazullo to want to be Furco. He wondered what it would be like to be there with her, too, though he reminded himself that she was the key. He'd get Furco through her, he thought, and then—later, if he still felt like it—Mazullo could always get her.

"We'll just wait here a bit. See if she stays put."

"Oh, man!" Scarpone wailed at the dashboard of Mazullo's Trans-Am. "At this hour? Why?"

"Because we got business, is why," said Mazullo. "And I don't wanna hear no shit."

Inside the motel suite, Toni's mother-in-law met her at the door. "Jane call," she said in her broken English. "She say yeah, okay, nex' weekend she sit with Tina and me. Whaz wrong with me? I too old? And who Jane to us? Where you?"

"Oh, Ma—not now, please. I'm beat, and I need a shower." And a drink, she thought. Earlier in the day she had phoned her next-door neighbor, who, with three young children and a husband who was a teacher, needed the money. Payson had said Toni would be gone for three days.

And not even pausing to scan the old woman's accusatory stare, the way she checked Toni head to foot as though inspecting a child, she passed into her bedroom, where she kicked off her shoes and quickly slipped out of the red gown and her underwear.

"Where you, this time?" her mother-in-law demanded, following Toni right into the bathroom, the shoes and underwear now in her hands. "Why you think I no care for Tina? Tina my— And what you do?" She shook the shoes at her.

"Ma—please. *Frenarsi tu. Piensa di Tina,"* she implored, using the Italian she had learned in college. Wrenching on the water, she thought of what she would have to do for Payson on the following weekend, and of her nondate with Furco on Monday. And she thought of her debt and the markers and finally of the man, Colin Ross.

In the shower, the pulse of the massage shower-head beat on her upturned face and head, drowning out the voice of the old woman. And suddenly, as she increased the heat and worked the soap over her body, she thought again of the hours she had spent with him in the dark hotel room. Had it been a kind of escape? Yes, definitely.

When she had awakened, she'd found she could not move. He had pinned her legs and arms and entered her again, but he lay still. At first she found it pleasurable, warm and crushed like that, until she discovered she could touch nothing with her fingers or her toes. She could not move her ankles. And she panicked, not knowing him or what he really wanted or what he would do.

"Colin," she'd called out. "Colin!" But each time she said his name she slipped on him, and the pleasure of his probing the very back of her vagina, of his grasping her to him as though he was trying to make them one, of his holding her so still like they were dead, was too great to be denied. "Colin," she called out. "Colin, Colin, Colin—"

And, while the old woman now actually banged on the glass door of the stall as though she would follow Toni right in there, the knowledge that the man was only a few miles away rose up from the drain where the soapsuds were sluicing away and invested her. She had not had enough of him, there in her clothes closet. She needed more, and now.

"Jews," her father had once said to her when they were discussing Israel, "don't trust life. How can they? Look at Israel, where it is. Surrounded. Its huge debt. Its belligerence and greed." On demand, he had been sending a brother a check monthly. "And why? We're afraid . . . to win." Toni twisted off the water.

Said Gabriela, who was still standing there when Toni opened the shower stall door, "So—what you gonna do?"

"Tonight, Ma?" she asked, reaching for a towel and moving past her. "Tonight I think I'll go over to the health club." It was up the road several miles.

"Now?" the old woman asked.

"*Si. Ora,*" she replied, hating to have to lie. At the closet she reached for a bright red turtleneck, a black leather skirt and jacket, red lacy stockings, and high heels.

And her gym bag.

Out in the Trans-Am after their third and final joint was gone, Falci had said to Mazullo, "I'm not gonna say this again, Dino. You had your play here. It's ovah. Tiny and me, we want them bimbos. Un'erstan'?"

Mazullo got the message. His two large friends could only be pushed so far, and, a conciliator only when the situation demanded, he reached for the keys.

But back at the Borghese, where the others had left their cars, he changed his mind. Hey, he could always get laid, and he was remembering how the bitch, Toni, had been at that craps table with that coon, the way she'd leaned into him when they kissed. The way her face got flushed, like earlier that night at the bar just talking to him. And the way they'd hurried through the bar toward the kitchen. What he want, anyways? Waiter? Nah—Furco would never allow it. He hated niggers.

"You guys go on without me. You handle that quiff, if you can."

"Whatta you mean, *without you?* What you got goin' you don't want us around?"

Pushing Scarpone away from the Trans-Am, Falci said, "He got nothin' goin' but a hard-on. For her. For him. If he gets anything tonight, it'll be with his hand."

But nearing the Ramada from the west on the White Horse Pike, Mazullo got lucky. There in the parking lot maybe 200, 300 yards in front of him he saw the lights of her Caddy switch on, and he slowed nearly to a crawl until the double bars of the Seville taillights pulled out in front of him. They made following her a breeze.

She stopped once at an all-night convenience store where she bought some cigarettes and beer, and, seeing how she was dressed all in black with big gold earrings and red stockings, Mazullo was sure. She was up to something. Even her step, which was quick now, gave it away. She didn't look up once, and back in the Caddy she floored it, not off to A.C. or—in the other direction—Philly, like Mazullo would have thought, but across the pike and down some dark back road into Hammonton.

Mazullo waited until he couldn't see red no more and then goosed the powerful Trans-Am, soon getting back up to speed and catching sight of her again. They went this way and that, quick though, like she knew where she was going. And maybe seven or eight minutes later he saw her brake lights go on, and she turned down a dirt road.

Pulling to the shoulder, Mazullo doused his lights and waited until the double bars of the taillights were gone in the pines that began growing around there and stretched off for miles and miles into the Barrens. But when he flicked them back on and eased forward, he found only a new mailbox that said ROSS in reflector letters and a long, sandy drive that curved off into the trees. No house, no nothing else but a rusted-out refrigerator and a heap of old boards where some old house had been. But the driveway, like the mailbox, looked new and freshly graded, and there were other tire tracks impressed in the soft Barrens sand.

And suddenly Mazullo was caught between knowing—no, not *knowing*—*feeling* with his nuts he was right and the uncertainty that he couldn't know for sure without parking the car someplace safe and sneaking in there to look for himself.

Maybe it was the fucking hammer he could pound into

Furco's fucking brain, but the problem was maybe the fucking coon had a fucking dog or some other fucking niggers with him, and, hey, Mazullo was alone. Wouldn't that be something, though? A bunch of niggers taking turns on her. But the fact was—and Mazullo now faced it—he hadn't done nothing for years without Tiny and the Bear. It was why they were a team, and he should never've let them leave like that when he was feeling so right about the bitch.

Well, he'd just have to wait. Turning to glance one more time down the drive before pulling away to find someplace to conceal himself, Mazullo reached for his crotch. If he was right, hey, he wouldn't wait until he'd whacked out Furco. No, he'd do her good, just like them niggers were, *before* Furco. Who could she go to, who could she tell, Mazullo knowing what he knew about her?

In the pocket of his sport shirt that was printed with palm fronds and a red-slash design, he found his last joint. He twisted the ends tight, then powered up the window for all the contact he could get. Striking his lighter and holding it to the end, he wondered too late if there might be anybody around. Fuck it, he thought. Who gives a shit? Couple of weeks he'd have the whole A.C. dry—the operation end—in his back pocket, and he'd tell the rest of the world to go screw.

At first the house seemed dark to Toni, until she flicked off the lights to the car. But she found the front door open, and she traced a glow back through two other rooms to a bedroom where the man was reading in a large, round bed. He had on a shiny blue warm-up robe, like the kind a boxer or wrestler would wear, and wire-rimmed spectacles that seemed so . . . disjunctive on his large, round face that she stopped and examined the rest of the room.

On one wall was a garish rendering of a tiger in fuzzy velvet. The background was purple. On another were crossed spears balanced by two African initiation masks. There were books, mostly paperbacks, everywhere, it seemed, and in the background classical music was playing. Brahms, she guessed.

He lowered the book, and she moved toward him.

"What are you reading?"

"Just something to improve myself." He closed the book and set it on the nightstand, but she picked it up.

It was a new paperback copy of the Swiss dramatist Friedrich Dürrenmatt's play *The Physicist,* which Toni herself had once struggled through while in college. Surprised that he—waiter and gambler and what else she couldn't guess—would be interested in something so unusual, she asked, "You read German, Colin?"

"I try. I picked up a little German when I was over there in the service. Had a friend who got me into the literature. She sent me that." He meant the book.

"Is that the woman there?" Toni pointed the book to a framed photograph of a blond woman on the dresser in the corner of the bedroom.

"No—that's a woman from Las Vegas."

"Do you correspond with her as well?"

Ross glanced at the picture and hesitated before replying, as though debating what he should say. "I suppose there'd be something strange about a person our age who didn't have a history."

But a history of what, Toni wondered, white women? Was he working out some problem? Had he singled her out because she was white?

No, of course not. He hadn't *singled* her out at all. It had been she who had discovered him at the craps table after all those many months of a nodding acquaintance. She could have stood someplace else at the table, and it had been she who had chosen—after having decided otherwise—to join him at that bar.

And finally, what if he had? She herself hadn't arrived there in his house for history, and if he was a "user" of white women, what of it? Surely she had a use for him, not a little of which had to do with the fact that he was black. "Did you think I'd come?"

He smiled. "I was hoping. Couldn't sleep, thinking about you and that closet. You know, in your office with you all dressed up and looking like the lady. That was—" he closed his eyes and made a small sound of pleasure "—but too quick. Me, I like weekends or weeks or—"

With both hands she reached down and lifted the spectacles off his face. They were old, an antique of sorts, like the type John Lennon had worn.

Breathless again, her heart pounding in her chest, she then reached for the belt of the robe and untied the knot. Drawing back the plackets of the robe, she gazed down on him. His body, like some massive idol, made the bed look small.

But she could not keep herself from wondering just who he was beyond waiter, gambler, devotee of German literature, womanizer, and now—she supposed—her lover.

Out in the Trans-Am, which was concealed behind a clump of low pines, Mazullo fell asleep, and he was still out at dawn when the Seville swung onto the tar road and swept off in a hush toward the south and Hammonton. Nor did he hear the other car that had followed the Seville and him there. All night long with all four windows open three inches, the driver had maintained his vigil. He gave the Caddy a good two-minute lead and then eased out onto the otherwise deserted road. He had an idea that Toni Spina would now need sleep.

In fact, Mazullo—socked by a late, heavy meal, the drinks, and the weed he'd smoked—woke up only when the spring sun was well overhead. And Ross, leaving around ten, slowed the LeSabre Grand National he drove to make a mental note of the make and type of car and the almost logo of its vanity plate. MAZU, it read in block capitals.

It was the first time Ross had seen a car parked out there like that in the eight months that he'd been living there. And then, keeping track of details was very much Ross's stock in trade, and not just in his role as a waiter.

PART
III

8

It was a bright spring morning by the time Lucca Furco and his mate left the dock of the old summer house he owned on the Mullica River twenty miles northwest of A.C. The sky was perfect and just the shade of early spring blue that looked green over the ocean and pale yellow over the land. The yellow was the same color as the boughs of the willows on the riverbank, Furco noted, and, pulling off his sunglasses to make sure he was right, he let the sun warm his whole face.

He was on the flying bridge, where he took the helm, and he turned to watch squadrons of gulls wheeling down into the Brigantine National Wildlife Refuge, a protected marshland that was draining now at low tide. In the inlets and creeks, kids were already fishing for snapper blues, and Furco slowed the seventy-eight feet of the Fairway Flyer to the regulation twelve knots so he wouldn't upset their skiffs and whalers.

In his time, Furco himself had fished every cove along the Mullica and Brigantine Bay. He had crabbed and purse-seined and trolled for whole days at a time, until it came to him once that to kill anything that didn't threaten you personally was wrong. He'd been out fishing with his brother when he hooked a huge striped bass that took all afternoon to bring aboard.

But when at last they got it aboard, it filled their little boat with so much silvery, writhing life that Furco couldn't bring himself to knock it dead. After the hours they had spent, each on an end of the line, they had formed something like friendship but better, and the plea in the large eye—as bright and as brown as his own—could not be denied.

Over his brother's shouts and curses, Furco bundled the fish in his arms and, surprised at how warm it felt, slipped it over the side. They watched while it bellied up and then swam a bit and finally disappeared in a flash, diving down into the black bay water. Said his brother, "I'll never go fishing with you again." Which was all right by Furco. He himself had never fished again.

She was waiting on Harrah's dock. Scanning the shore through binoculars, Furco half-hoped she wouldn't show up, but she was already there, standing by her Seville, tall and angular with all the graying, reddish-brown hair being riffled by the breeze. He hadn't told her from which direction he'd be coming, and, as she turned now this way and that, Furco got a look at her from a couple of angles. Yeah, he said to himself. Yeah.

One thing she knew was how to dress for what she had, and she was wearing a white turtleneck sweater and a snug bomber jacket that nipped her waist right where the sweater flared over her hips. Her slacks were also white, and her deck boots were of a piece with the jacket—leather with furry tops. She was dressed for the weather, and Furco was willing to bet that if it turned warmer, she'd be ready for that, too. She was something rare—a broad you could depend on.

And now, seeing him approaching, she put a hand to her eyes and squinted up—it seemed to Furco through the 9X power binoculars—into his face. He blasted his air horn twice, and she smiled. The doors of the car opened, and her kid and what looked like a waiter got out. It was Muñoz, the Spic maître d' from the joint. He went around back and boosted a big cooler from the trunk.

And Furco watched with pleasure the effect the yacht had on the three on the dock, as he headed up into the swift outgoing tide and even with a contrary wind eased the big boat into the dock.

And what she said when she carried her daughter aboard and ducked in out of the breeze—"Oh, Lucca—your boat. I had no idea. I didn't realize you'd have a galley"—made Furco preen. She glanced down at the hamper that Muñoz now placed in the cabin before returning to the car for the old lady, and finished, "—and I had Solly pack us . . ." It was music to his ears.

She took a few steps past him. "She's so sleek and"—she stepped forward so she could see into the salon, which he'd just got done up for he didn't want to think about how much—"stylish and sumptuous. Really elegant." Her eyes met his, as though wanting him to know she meant it. "You've met Tina before." She set her daughter down between them. "This is Mr. Furco, Tina."

"Luke," said Furco, easing down on his haunches and holding out his hand. "I think we've met a few times, but a shake wouldn't hurt now, would it?"

The kid, who looked more like her father but pretty just the same, obviously didn't want to shake, and she looked up at her mother, as if for approval.

"If you don't want to shake, I can understand that," Furco went on. "Ladies don't have to shake. In fact, maybe it's better we don't."

The child studied his face, then asked, "Why better?"

"Because, if you do, maybe we'll become friends, and you won't like that. You don't like being friends with people, do you?"

The smile began at the corners of her mouth, and her eyes moved from Furco's face to his hand and back to his face. Even this young, she had her mother's cool, and Furco wondered if it was something that could be bred. None of his kids had his caution or his daring. They all acted like their mother, like everything should be given to them because they were special or that was just how things went.

Again the little girl glanced up at her mother.

"You can shake Lucca's hand and be friends if you want. It's up to you."

The small hand came up, and Furco took it.

"I'm Luke Furco, who are you?"

"Tina Spina." She smiled shyly. "What would it take to make *your* name rhyme?"

"Gee, I don't know. I never thought about it." Squatting down as he was, Furco's eyes swept up past the broad bow of her mother's chest and they exchanged glances. "I guess I'd either be Lurco Furco or Lurk the Furk," he said spontaneously, and he laughed along when she cried, *"Lurk the Furk.* That's the silliest name ever."

The old woman only said, *"Molto piacere, signore. Io sono la signora Spina. Gabriela."* She took what looked like needlework into the salon.

And so the afternoon progressed, with Furco scoring one little point after another, he hoped. First there was the boat itself. She liked nice things—he knew that much about her—and he showed her around, with her and the kid oohing and aahing at the cabins, the controls, even the engine room, which she insisted on seeing.

Finally she said, "You know—I was brought up right over there." They were in the galley, and she turned to point out a window toward the city beyond the docks and rubble that had once been the old part of town before urban "renewal." Furco's old man had made a bundle on that. "And I love the ocean. I guess I've always really wanted a boat, but, Lucca"—she turned on him a smile so bright it almost made him flinch—"I thought you were joking or just fooling when you described her as a vessel. But you're right. She's immense. How many feet?"

"Seventy-eight," Furco said proudly.

"And you call her?"

Knowing they were pressed for time, the mate had shoved off, and, easing the throttle forward, swung the boat away from the dock in a wide arc, then headed toward the concrete pylons of the Brigantine Bridge and the ocean beyond.

"Bark-a-Roll."

"What's it mean?" Tina asked.

"She's into names today," her mother said. She had bent to open the oven door of the Garland range that Furco had specially ordered for the boat. He had never seen her in slacks before, but he liked what he saw. Straightening up, she added, "It's a kind of song boatmen sing in Venice in Italy while they're poling people down the canals. You remember, Tina, we saw pictures of that in the book you have about different parts of the world.''

Furco didn't want to add that spelled his way it meant the shout uttered when throwing craps.

"Are you from Italy?'' the little girl asked him.

"In a way. I'm from Ventnor.''

Her mother actually broke out laughing, her right hand coming down on Furco's shoulder, which she squeezed. "You really do have a sense of humor. I only wish I had known that earlier.''

Better now than never, Furco thought. Being, you know, *light* had its advantages, and there would come a time, Furco told himself, when he would press them.

Now even the weather was backing his play. When they got out to the Reef and anchored among the other boats gathered there, the wind suddenly faired out to a steady, gentle breeze, and then died altogether. Over the radio, Lou, the mate, learned that the blues weren't running yet, so he got out bottom-fishing rigs and set Tina in a command chair at the stern, where she pulled in the first fish that she had ever caught.

"But, Mommy, it's so flat. It only has a face on one side, and it's . . . ugly.''

The mate laid the fish on top of the ice chest, and it began flapping wildly.

"But you eat fish like that all the time,'' Toni said.

There was a pause while Tina again stared down at the fish and touched a finger to its brown, speckled back. "I do?''

"What's your favorite fish to eat?''

"Sole. That's not a sole. Sole is white.''

The mate turned the fish over so that its white side was showing.

"That's a flounder,'' Toni explained, "which is a first cousin to a sole, and many times when you thought you were eating sole, you were actually eating flounder. Usually we can only get sole frozen, but flounder is almost always fresh, which makes it taste better.''

Again there was a pause during which the three adults, the sun now beating strongly on their backs, looked down on the rainbow sheen in Tina's auburn curls as she considered her fish. Furco even chanced reaching out to touch a lock.

Squinting up at her mother, Tina asked, "Can we put it back in the ocean before it dies?"

The mate began to chuckle. "Excuse me," he said. Looking away at the other boats, he added, "I beg your pardon."

Furco touched his arm to tell him it was okay. He was in a good mood, the best. Here even the kid had his approach to fishing.

Toni explained, "That's not the purpose of fishing, Tina. We catch fish to eat. Do you think Lucca has all this equipment just to throw the fish he catches back? Tell you what—we'll take your fish and all the others you catch back to Solly and Philly at the restaurant, and they'll make them taste better than sole. What you don't want yourself, we'll sell and make money."

The sun felt so good that Furco decided to take off his jacket, which he did, and then helped Toni out of hers, his nostrils flaring to catch the scent of whatever perfume it was she always wore that made him think of gold and evening gowns and piano music and the flash of her dark eyes.

Hell—the hook was in and set deep. He had to work something out with her definite, or work himself free.

"I'll make money?" Tina asked.

Furco's eyes met Toni's, and he had to wrench them away. He started laughing and he didn't know why. He felt like a jerk, but a happy jerk. He hadn't felt so good or free or easy in a long time, and he decided that what he'd thought, the little dream he'd had about her and the boat, was bingo; right on the money. Fuck, they were a match, all right.

Said Toni, "Well—sure you'll make money. At least, you'll make your share, and I'll see you get it *after* your expenses. You know expenses, Tina?"

The child thought for a while. "You mean, like bills?" She had often helped Toni pay bills: watching her write out checks, helping her put them in envelopes, and punching them through the mailing machine.

"That's right. The costs of doing business. In this operation you'll have to pay Lucca for the use of his boat and Lou for helping you bring them in and then me and Lucca for whatever prep and serving expenses we'll have at the restaurant.''

It was a nice touch, Furco decided, including him like that, and it made him think about how good she could be for him on a permanent basis. No bimbo, she had class and knew how to handle herself. What's more, she would know how to deal with his associates, the big wheels who mattered. Why else would Payson have brought her to New York, like Grisanti had told him the week before?

Pushing those thoughts out of his mind, Furco raised the fur collar of her jacket to his nose and breathed in her perfume, the scent of her skin and hair. Christ—that was dumb, but at this point he really didn't care.

Was he in love? he dared to ask himself. He didn't like the word, but whatever it was, it was hot, and he felt it totally, in every part of him. He could go on being with and looking at her forever.

"How much money?" the girl asked.

"It depends on how many fish you catch, and what we can get for them."

"How about this one—what can we get for it?"

"Broiled flounder? Nine ninety-five. Figure two dollars to Lucca, one to Lou, three dollars to the restaurant. That makes how many dollars?"

After a pause, Tina said, "Six."

"Very good. Now, if the price is nine ninety-five, what's your profit?"

"You mean, what's left?"

While she worked out her take on the fish, Furco saw the tip of her fishing rod bob, and Lou smiled, turning to them.

Furco put a finger to his lips.

"Three dollars and ninety-five cents for me?" She squinted up at her mother.

"Oh, you're good. Very good. We'll make a business-woman of you yet. But remember, only *if* we sell them. Now, shall we keep your flounder or throw it back?"

The decision wasn't easy, and Furco turned to see if Lou had set out the chaise lounges on the afterdeck, as Furco had earlier requested. The guy was good, and he didn't talk or ask questions.

And when the little girl finally decided to keep the fish and then pulled in a second and another after that and another and Toni said she had thought the day would warm up and she had brought her bathing suit and would he mind . . . Furco felt a bliss that he had not known in years.

The bathing suit was white, and Furco imagined that she'd been wearing it right under the slacks and sweater, since she returned so fast to the lounge chair beside him. Not wanting to get caught staring, he nonetheless noticed that, maybe because of her tan, her skin looked supple and fine, maybe not as smooth as somebody younger, but the way it wrinkled in tight folds on her thigh when she cocked one leg told him, yeah, she had aged well and would continue to age well. And when she asked him if he'd like a little wine and something to eat, Furco only smiled and closed his eyes. In his mind he still saw that little green line, the one on the horizon out to sea where they could go and . . .

When she returned with a tray, Furco noticed how the heads of guys cruising by in other boats turned to them. Furco knew what they were thinking: look at that guy—not young, not old, big boat, knockout wife and cute little daughter, mate and all. He's got the world by the balls.

And maybe she was thinking that, too, because after they'd been in the lounge chairs for a while, she said, "You know, Lucca—I envy you your boat and your . . . life."

He turned his head to try to read her eyes, but they were concealed behind sunglasses. "What about my life? Maybe you don't know my life." And the things I done and had to do, he did not add.

"The—" she let her head fall back into the cushions of the chair, and she said to the sky, "—power. Or, at least, the illusion of power that you convey. I suppose we all have to report to somebody. Ultimately."

"You mean Payson?" Furco now felt the first twinge of the threat somebody like Payson could pose. He could see how she'd go for a guy like him, all them degrees and shit, and he still wanted to know what she was doing for him. "Nah—he's just a guy, an advisor who does some stuff for us. Don't get me wrong, he's important, but he's no real part of our operation." Furco drew in a deep breath and held it for thirty seconds before letting it out. It calmed him. Anger had always been with Furco a thing that, when he let it loose, he almost never could get back on his own. It was the reason he always tried to keep himself so much in control. He couldn't let himself go, like other people.

So he said, "You think I chose this? What I am?" He wanted to show her he thought about things and was, you know, kind of "deep," like the Cheech probably was. "Nah—I got born and brought up, like you, like everybody. My old man was a gangster, like you tol' everybody in the kitchen the other night." When her head turned to him, he smiled. "No problem. The truth—it's not something I worry about.

"Yours? He was a tailor. *Is* a tailor, from what I know. And that's why you became a restaurant owner and me a gangster. Your father taught you what most people think is right and wrong. He also taught you to make things. My father taught me nothing but to be who I was and not worry about nothing I do short of getting caught. He also taught me why make things when you can get other people to make them for you? Only suckers make things. I'm not trying to insult you, but I think you respect the truth, too." Furco let that sink in. He wanted her to know that between them there should be only honesty. He wouldn't have it any other way.

There was a line of gulls working the rip about a quarter mile off the stern, and already a number of boats had weighed anchor and were making for the spot.

"He was wrong. Or, let me say that different—now I know he was wrong. But at forty-seven when everything's set and it's too late.

"And me with my kids? I don't think I did even as good a job, except that none of them will ever be a gangster. Tell you the truth, they're grown, but I don't know what they'd do without me. The gangster."

Said Toni, looking out at her daughter, whom the mate was helping reel in the fishing line, "It's tough on kids, these days. So much has changed."

"You mean, like right and wrong?"

She again turned her head to him. "Yeah—it sometimes gets so I don't know myself. The difference between what we were taught and how all that . . ." She paused, searching for a phrase, and Furco's eyes followed the smooth line of her body down to her legs, which were long and slightly bowed. She was wearing white pointed shoes with low heels. ". . . works out in life. Not often but, you know, once in a while I find myself doing things that afterward I think are pointless or stupid or self-destructive."

Furco thought he knew what she was referring to: the gambling and maybe even Jack, though at least that had produced the restaurant and the kid, who was a little doll. Said Furco, "As long as you don't hurt nobody else—hey, where's the problem?" He hunched his shoulders. "Myself, I'm thinking of getting out of all of this—" he kept himself from saying "shit" "—I mean, not the boat, but the . . ."

Toni thought she knew what he meant; but how? She had heard there was no quitting what he was into. "But you're still a young man, Lucca. What would you do?"

Furco was pleased that she was taking an interest in him. He wasn't used to speaking about himself, much less his finances, but he said, "I been putting a little something aside, now and then. And I'd find something—" Legit? No, that wasn't the word. "—fun to do. Like you, I like business."

When her head went back a little, he went on quickly, "No, really. Something—how do I say this and not sound insincere—legitimate and, you know, worthwhile in the big sense."

"Certainly you're not thinking of becoming a priest."

"Me? Wouldn't I make a great priest? 'Hey, buddy—I give you a week to clean up your act. If you don't, I'll be by to see you.' And *collections?*"

Both of them started laughing, and Furco couldn't help himself. He howled. He hadn't laughed like that in years.

When he got himself together, he said, "No, but to tell you the truth, I was thinking of going into the restaurant business."

"As second choice after the priesthood?"

"No, really. Honestly. Something like your place, and let's clear the air about that. It's yours. I only went along with this thing to begin with because I was tol' to. I understand I'll be out of it before long, too."

Told by whom? Toni wondered. Payson? Who else, given what she was now doing for him. And what was that? She didn't know, really, beyond what Payson himself had told her—transferring funds and changing ownership. She had checked with a local banking friend as completely as she could without arousing suspicion; she herself could be questioned only on the transactions and not the dollar amounts, and she could always either deny her involvement or say she had broken no laws and would reveal nothing. Sure, she'd probably get audited year after year, but almost anything was worth climbing out from underneath the debt and the "debt-service," as she saw it, that she had had to endure every weekend.

And then Furco was implying that Jack and she had been set up. By whom? Payson himself? She wondered, given what Furco had said about him. And so far in advance? She really didn't know Furco well enough to ask him, but she couldn't help herself. Too much of her life had been displaced, disrupted, destroyed. She was thinking of the feelings she'd had about who she was and what she could do when she was first married—all that optimism and joy, which was the biggest loss. She thought of how her relationships with other people, men in particular, had deteriorated.

"Why?" she demanded.

"Why what?"

"Why was I set up?"

Furco hunched his shoulders. Suddenly he had lost control of the conversation, and he didn't know where he'd gone wrong, except getting so personal. But, hell, that was the point of it, no? "There's only so much somebody can be set up. Guy like Jack—hey, he set himself up."

"But *why?* I mean, why the setup? Did you do it on orders, or was it something that just occurred to you, like . . . an opportunity?"

Furco thought, One look at you, babe, and your lunchbag husband with his blond hair and two yards of chest and Boy Scout smile— But it hadn't been like that. It had been orders, plain and simple, and direct from Brooklyn. Said Sal, the Babe, that Fourth of July on Payson's boat, "We been talkin', Cheech and me, and we want her involved in the dry. We don't care what it takes. If her husband gets in the way—" The big guy had looked at Grisanti and smiled. Payson had gone below for a camera to take some shots of the tall ships that were passing them at the time.

That was before Furco had seen who she was and watched her moves and got to know her. Things had then changed for him, though, of course, he had no choice but to play out the hand he'd been palmed.

He hunched his shoulders. "Far as I remember, *Jack* came to *me*. And knowing you like I do now, can I tell you how I feel about it honestly?" He had his hand out, but she only stared down at it appraisingly.

"I think it was right because it got you away from that—" he almost said "fuckin' "—lush and loser, Jack, who was—"

Her hands went up to her ears. "Please. I don't want to hear it." Like that, her tits were squeezed together, and the way she seemed almost cringing and helpless appealed to Furco, but he went on, knowing it had to be said, if he was to have any chance with her.

He took her wrist, which he found surprisingly thin, and pulled a hand down. "Look—it's gotta be said." He swung his legs over and moved up in the lounge chair so he could face her. "Whatta we got back there?" He pointed to the west and the land, only a thin brown line of which could be seen at the very edge of the horizon. "A jungle? Maybe not with the vines and trees and actual panthers and quicksand and piranhas, but a jungle with all sorts of other traps and snakes. And I'm not gonna kid yuh that sometimes I'm not one of them. Sometimes almost everybody is. You gotta be. Why? Because if there's one lesson out there, it's everybody's gotta take care a' themselves. If you don't, nobody else will, and the people who really run things in this country have set things up for themselves and their kind. And they don't give two—"

Furco looked away. He had nearly said "shits," but he was hot now and believed what he was saying implicitly. It had been the central operating principle of his life and was the only reason he was still alive and, in what he considered a small way, successful.

"—cents if you or me or anybody like us lives or dies. And that goes for the big guys in Washington or Wall Street or the other big guys on Mulberry and Mott streets or Anselmo Avenue, Brooklyn. It means people like us have gotta be even stronger. You show you're weak, you mark yourself, and the—" Furco looked out over the stern. The *Bark-a-Roll* was the only boat still anchored there. Shouts and cheering could now be heard from the others that had followed the gulls. "—sharks start circling. I know that sounds—"

"Trite," she suggested.

He guessed that's what he meant. "Like a—"

"Cliché."

"Yeah, that too. But—"

"But what you're telling me," she interrupted again, "is that so far you're a *lucky* shark." She had flicked her sunglasses down on the bridge of her nose and was considering him.

Furco removed his own; bad as the subject was, it was time for him to make his play. "I won't kid you about that either. I'm sorry—really, *truly*—if I hurt you or caused you any"—it wasn't the right word, and he was messing things up, but he said it anyways—"grief. But how else would I have got to know you, and now I do I—" Easy, easy now; she wasn't anybody he could rush. "Lemme just say just bein' with you here, like this, or back at the joint, gives me a charge." He held up a palm. "Scout's honor. Really. No more. Just that. You bein' here."

As she continued to appraise him, her eyes searching his face, Furco tried a slight smile. But she didn't respond, and even looked away and shook her head.

And then from the bridge, the mate asked, "We go over there, Cap? Radio says they're pullin' 'em in. Blues and big ones. One boat's already got a dozen."

Furco glanced at the hopeful, expectant look on the little girl's face and nodded. A few moments later they were away.

After that all of them were down in the stern, with Tina strapped into a command chair and Toni pulling in one flapping, gaffed-bloody bluefish after another, Lou stepping on each fresh catch with a rubber boot to wriggle free the hook, which popped out of the fish with a sucking sound. He then baited the hook, which was tossed back.

The sun had grown hot now, and the water was roiling with an enormous school of menhaden, some of which every now and then broke the surface, leaping in silvery arcs to escape the ravenous blues that were feeding on them.

Through the school the hooked blues surged and sounded, bending the light-action graphite poles nearly in half.

Soon the cockpit was deep in scaly bodies, the blueness of which quickly paled to gray as the fish expired. And there was blood everywhere, it seemed: on the mate's boots and jeans, the gunwales and coaming, on Furco's whites, and even spattered in a kind of fine spray that glistened like flecks of ruby in the sun across Toni's tanned skin, her arms, and the stark white of the bikini.

And yet the little girl kept crying out, "I got another, Mommy. *Another*. A big one!" almost the moment that the hook hit the water.

Her eyes bright, a tight, close-lipped smile making dimples that Furco had never before seen, Toni turned back to Furco and glanced down at his empty hands. In profile like that with her torso twisted and her shoulders and neck muscles taut, she looked like some big *beautiful* bird of prey, Furco mused, at once turned on and turned off by her obvious . . . *physicalness,* he decided. It fit in with the way she walked, swinging her shoulders, and her moves that were all one thing. But there was something else there, too, that he didn't want to name, until he was sure it turned him on. And he wasn't.

"Don't you fish?" she asked.

"Sure. All the time, but you have your fun. I'll get the insta-freezer. You ever see one of them things?"

"No—we'll clean them first. We've nearly got enough for a dinner special here, and I serve fresh fish, not frozen."

"Clean?" Tina asked.

"Yes—that's part of it, too, little one," her mother explained. "What you catch, you must use. Otherwise, it's just cruelty and waste. And to use these fish the way we planned at the restaurant, we've got to clean them out."

"Then I'll get the knives and the aprons and stuff," said Furco. Somehow everything wasn't going just right anymore, but he wasn't sure it was going bad either, and he needed a break to think things out.

In the main salon, he found the old lady at a window, smiling down at the scene. Turning shining eyes on him, she said, *"Il mare. Che bello! Tanta ricchezza, tanta abbondanza."*

126

Furco didn't speak Italian, but he got the point that she was having a good time. And it was only when he had carried out the cutting boards and filleting knives, the waxed paper and white cardboard boxes that had been printed with *Bark-a-Roll*'s compass rose, that he got a clear view of the real Toni Spina—the one he'd been seeing all along but not really *seeing*—and not the one he had created in his mind.

Now wearing the turtleneck sweater but not the slacks, she strapped on a bib apron and positioned herself in front of the waist-high cockpit and reached for a fish. And with her daughter on the stairs where she could see, she began explaining the different methods of cleaning—gutting for oven baking or roasting *en papillote,* filleting for broiling or frying—all the while working on one fish after another, her body on her long legs rocking, her shoulders swaying almost rhythmically, the knife blade flashing in the sun so fast that even Lou, who was an expert at it, stopped to admire her work.

"Beg pardon, ma'am, but it looks like you done this before."

Almost as though startled, she looked up from her work. "What? Oh, yes—I'd say that. Do you know the Borghese in Hammonton? When we first opened I could only afford a chef and a pearl diver in the back of the house. I had to do the prep work myself. Mornings. Then I changed into my hostess garb for lunch, and back again to get ready for dinner. We bought our fish fresh and whole. Still do."

"You get out that way much?" Her eyes flashed up at Lou while she kept working.

"Course."

"Then you stop in and see us. You've certainly made a hit with my daughter today."

That was nice. Furco liked that. She knew how to get along with people. It was how she'd taken a nothing joint in a nowhere location and built it into maybe the best restaurant on the shore. And he decided he liked the way she now looked in them white bikini briefs and low heels.

But the impression she now gave Furco was the same he sometimes got an inkling of at the restaurant but had never before figured out: that the way she looked—how she was always touching herself like to be sure—was a surprise to her, too. And, like some pro ballplayer who took his body and build for granted, she thought more about what she did and how she did it—her professionalism—than the way she looked. And yet for all that, she couldn't deny that body. She was a very physical person.

A half hour later as they were headed back and him and the old lady and kid were having coffee and hot chocolate in the salon and Lou was at the wheel, Furco honestly wondered *without any other thought but that* if there were enough towels in the head where Toni was showering. After knocking, he stepped into the master cabin.

She was standing by a mirror drying her hair with only a towel wrapped around her.

"I just thought maybe there weren't—"

"I found them."

Their eyes met for a long moment, before she said, "I haven't had fun like this for too long, Lucca. Could we do it again?" in such a way that Furco heard *maybe* loud enough to make his day.

"Sure, Toni. Of course. You name the time and place. There's a big terry robe in that locker and infrared—" He flipped a switch before reaching for the handle of the door through which he had entered. "It's on a timer and'll turn itself out." Furco stepped out of the cabin and closed the door.

Later at the Seville when she was about to leave, she said, "Would you like a ride to your car? The BMW. I saw it parked at the restaurant this morning."

He shook his head. "I'll take the boat back."

"Isn't that what a mate is for?"

"Yeah, but—" leaning toward the window, he had been looking off toward A.C. so she could catch his face in profile in the twilight "—I'm a little messy. I'll have to change. And anyways—" he turned his head to her "—I thought we were closed. Don't you ever take time off?"

"*La bella figura*," she replied, changing the subject. "How ethnic of you, Lucca. But I must say you always look well-turned-out and . . ." She searched for a term. ". . . sharp."

Added the old lady, "*Ah, sì, signore—Lei e molto gentile. Mille grazie, signore.*"

Asked the little girl, leaning across her mother to look up at him, "Is your name Lucca or Luke?"

Furco shook his head. "Far as I can remember, it's Lurk the Furk."

They all laughed, and then Furco felt her mother's hand on his. "See you tomorrow."

Oh, yeah—he'd see her tomorrow and tomorrows to come. And he'd think of a way to get them out of the traps they were in. Both of them.

They'd then go someplace, he didn't know where, where they could live nice and relaxed like human beings—Italy, since she spoke Italian and things there just naturally appealed to him. The old lady would like that, too. Or Greece, where he'd been once and enjoyed it. Or Spain. He liked what he knew about Spain: the rolling open plains, the orange groves near the sea around Granada. He'd never been there.

He looked to the east where the sky now at twilight was deep purple flecked with lilac-colored clouds. Right at the horizon there was a thin band of green. And, walking back to the boat, he thought, *there,* there's where we'll go, if only in our minds. Furco knew one thing about himself: he could dream, but he was basically a realist.

9

"See? What I tell you?" Mazullo shouted when the black LeSabre Grand National with the sun-shield windows pulled up to the mailbox. They were parked near the driveway in Maxwell that he had been staking out since he learned that Colin Ross, a waiter at the Trop, lived there. The hand that was pulling out a couple days' worth of mail was wide and black, the wrist thick and banded by a gold watch that sparkled in the twilight. The cuff of the lavender shirt was frilly. The sleeve of the coat was blue.

Explained Mazullo, "First I couldn't find who owned the place, which was all I had to go on. County Clerk's Office in Burlington was closed and, hey, I wasn't goin' to no police in case we get into it with the guy." Hyperlike, he flashed his eyes across the front seat at the Bear. "You know?" he asked Tiny, who was in the backseat. After a whole weekend running the nigger down, Mazullo was wired. He wanted action, but, like always, he needed the others. He wouldn't do nothing without them.

"Same thing with the post office," he went on. "I got this idea. Why don't I call a real estate office? Say I'm interested in someplace like that place and why not that place? You know them real estate assholes. They do anything to make a sale. And they got ways a' finding out things I don't.

"Guy goes—'I can find out who owns the place and make an offer if you want, Mr. Spina.' " Mazullo again turned back to Falci, his eyes shining, the corners of his soft mouth wrinkling in smile so it was hard for him to speak. "See—ain't it beautiful? I was at the joint at the time. I figure if I was the husband, I'd be a little pissed my wife was getting pooned by some—" He let his driving glove say what he felt. He smacked it down on the steering wheel. "I'd be burnt." The glove fell again. "Scorched." And again.

The window of the Grand National slid back up, but the car didn't pull off down the driveway. It stayed there for a while before disappearing down the driveway, like the guy was checking out his mail, even though he had to know the Trans-Am was there and they were watching him. Mazullo hadn't taken much care to conceal it this time. He wanted the fuck to know he was gonna fuckin' pay.

And her. She'd pay twice: once for herself and again for Furco.

"Turns out his name is Colin Ross. Like that? *Colin* Ross, like some sort of goddamn gentleman or something. Been living here for a few months. Came from Vegas, where he was a waiter, too. The Trop. Got into a jam, and they gave him a job out here instead. Gambler pretty heavy, but he paid for the house in—listen to this—cash. And never guess his strong suit." Mazullo paused. "It's what got him into trouble out there and what's got him into trouble—and lemme tell you, he's got *big* trouble—here." Mazullo waited, glancing in the rearview mirror, where he saw Falci shake his head and look away. Said Scarpone, "White women." His dark eyebrows, which were heavy like some video star made up to look mean, were hooding his eyes so Mazullo couldn't see them.

Said Falci, "So the hump likes to hump white women. Jus' long as he don't hump *our* white women, who cares? And I thought what we after is Furco. Let *him* take care of this dude if he wants to. Why us?"

"You chicken?" Mazullo asked.

Falci again looked out the window and smiled. He shook his head. " 'Member them coons up in Asbury Park, 'member? Shit—" From the back they heard the slide of an automatic and its action engaging. In the rearview mirror, Mazullo watched Falci raise the army-issue .45—his "pocket howitzer," he called it—to his eye and sight in the back of

Scarpone's head. Falci was huge. He was blond with short wiry hair that bristled and white, pinky skin. To Mazullo he had always looked like a big prickly porker. A fuckin' hog who couldn't always be controlled, like Scarpone.

"Yeah, but we're talkin' *this* nigger here. How'd you like your sister gettin' stuck by some spade? And a fuckin' waiter. All frilly shirt and shit."

Falci looked out the open window and sighted on something else with the automatic.

"Hey, Tiny," Mazullo complained. "What if a cop went by? He have us up on a bullshit charge. Only assholes get the slam for shit like that."

Falci turned the gun and pointed it at Mazullo's face in the mirror. "Ain't got no sister."

"But what if you did?"

"Hey—I wouldn't be fuckin' her. And who she fucked be her fuckin' business, wouldn't it?"

The Bear's hands fell so hard on the dashboard that Mazullo jumped, the adrenaline pulsing through him. *"Nigger!"* Scarpone roared, his sallow, tanned face getting instantly red the way it had for an entire game at a time on the football field when they were in high school. At five-eleven and 242 pounds, he'd been an animal, All-State with offers from colleges. "That fuckin' nigger thinks he can get away with that shit heah—*he-ah!*—" he stabbed a finger at the drive shaft "—where *we* live? Ne-vah! They wouldn't take shit like that out in Vegas. We don't take shit like that here!"

Scarpone swung his head around on Falci. "You wit' us, Tiny? 'Cause if you ain't, get the fuck out. *Now!*"

Falci was maybe six-two or so and big from steroids and weights. But although they'd never gotten into it, Mazullo knew Falci could never get up the way Scarpone was up now, and Falci secretly feared the smaller man when he got that way. Falci had played ball, too, but he was never All-State.

He now glanced down at the barrel of the gun and then up at Scarpone's flushed face. His smile was thin and forced. "I'm here, ain't I? I'm along for the ride."

You better fuckin' believe you are, thought Mazullo, firing up the Trans-Am and with short, quick bursts of the engine popping them across the road and down the driveway.

132

The house was about a quarter mile from the road, and, picking out the lights through the pines, Mazullo checked to make sure the Grand National was the only car there.

"What's the drill?" Falci asked.

Mazullo only looked away. He ran things, and he had long ago learned never to discuss how.

"What if there's more than just one of 'em?"

"How many would it take to make you shit your pants, Rik?" Scarpone asked.

From the pouch under the seat Mazullo pulled a Walther PPK and a Mauser machine pistol, a kind of antique, which he handed to Scarpone. It had a twelve-inch barrel and a four-inch suppressor. Mazullo loved guns. He had begun his collection on his twelfth birthday.

"Motherfuckin' coon," Scarpone said to himself, screwing down the suppressor.

The last thing they wanted was to kill the nigger, but what they needed for Furco was some kind of proof—a picture, a note or letter, even just an admission that she'd been there and he'd been boning her. Furco would believe Scarpone. He was so dumb he never lied, ever, not even when it got him in trouble.

At the house Mazullo wheeled the Trans-Am around so the sleek nose was pointed toward the driveway, just in case. The house was a kind of bungalow with a veranda on three sides. There was a front door and another on the end of the porch where they were parked. A light was on, and the guy opened the door and stood behind a rusted screen as Mazullo got out.

"Help you?" he asked.

"If that's your car, you sure can. That your car?"

Ross now opened the screen and stepped out, not closing the door behind him. At the mailbox at the beginning of the driveway he had made a quick call on the cellular telephone in the Grand National, and then another from the house. There he had quickly doffed the tux jacket for a bulky, dark gray crewneck sweater that would make him appear round and soft and vulnerable.

"I said, that your car?" Mazullo again demanded, sizing him up. Ross wasn't tall but he was big, sort of like Scarpone but broader and wider and older. There was gray on the

133

sides of his head; and his eyes, which now followed Scarpone and Falci as they pulled themselves out of the low Trans-Am, were wary.

He then took a step toward Mazullo, who backed away off the steps, and began moving toward the car. He wasn't about to get into it himself. That's what the other two were for, and if they couldn't handle him, Mazullo would have to get himself a couple other assholes who could.

But suddenly the guy, quick for his size, was down the stairs and by his side, his hand up under Mazullo's arm, his face in his ear. "We got a problem? You tell me 'bout our problem. You got a mouth? Use it, motherfucker. Talk to me. Talk. Keep talking." His eyes were popped white, the features of his dark face hard, taut—ready, Mazullo only now realized. Too late.

Ross had his own idea how to handle a situation like this. The thing was to act wild, different, funny, disturbed, anything to distract them, and then, like in the rugby matches Ross had played through college and then on the club level in law school and for almost ten years after for Old Blue in New York, he would make as much contact with them as possible. That way they'd have less opportunity to use whatever weapons they were carrying. That way they'd have to deal with him one-on-one, if kept in close.

"C'mon, you little fuck. Speak. We gotta problem?"

Mazullo was barely able to talk from the pressure the guy was putting on his arm. It was like pain but it wasn't pain, and it was almost lifting him right off his feet. The only good part was they were moving right toward the other two. "My car," he managed. "You park at the Trop. You—" He sucked in some breath; now it was pain and excruciating; he felt his eyeballs flicker back into his head. It felt like the guy was taking his whole fucking shoulder off. "You noodged me. My car—it cost a bundle. You ins—" He couldn't finish.

"I *what* you, you little asshole?" the guy said in his ear. "What kinda word is that? Me, insured? Sure I'm insured. You know who insures me? You know?" He increased the pressure on the arm, and Mazullo squealed, "No!"

"The fuckin' Mafia, that's who. Ain't it a gas? Like the bumper stickers you see on cars. You know the cars? Cars punks drive, punks like you." Ross knew all of their first names, last names, and nicknames. He had studied their faces, read their sheets.

They were on the far side of the Trans-Am, and Ross even now let one of them get behind him. It wouldn't matter, long as he had hold of "Dino," as Dean liked to be called.

Said Scarpone, taking a step toward them, "What he sayin' to you? He hurtin' you, Dino?"

Said Falci, "Hey, nigger—get your fuckin' hands off him."

But Ross had Mazullo between them, and he now bent the two of them at the waist, ostensibly to examine the side of the car. "Here," he asked. "Is here where I 'noodged' Toni Spina?"

Scarpone and Falci had started for them, but Ross, whipping his head to them, said, "Hey—wait. Know what? He's right. I noodged him. Dented the hell out of the side of this car." Grabbing Mazullo by his long, curly hair, Ross smashed his head into the Trans-Am, the sheet metal of which gave off a roaring, hollow sound. Once. Twice.

By the third blow Mazullo had gone limp in Ross's hands, and Falci had jumped him, grabbing his arms and trying to pull them back.

Scuttling, as though to gather momentum, Scarpone launched a punch that Ross, falling to one knee, slipped; then he snapped himself back up to butt his head under Scarpone's chin with all he had.

There was a sideways slip to Scarpone's jaw and an ugly crunching sound. "Shit!" he roared, a hand moving to his mouth. "My teeth." He spat something out. "My fuckin' *teeth*." He spat again. "I'll kill the fuckin' nigger!"

But Ross, again bending at the waist and twisting as though to shake Falci off, made him plant his legs wide. It was then that Ross's right heel snapped up and sank deep into Falci's crotch.

Falci uttered what sounded to Ross like a kind of sigh, and his arms first flinched and then seemed to spasm and finally slid down Ross's body as Scarpone, enraged, began wading in, his arms flailing.

Hell, thought Ross—ducking one punch and taking another off the side of his head—were these the button men of the new Mob? What playground did Luke Furco get these yum-yums off of? Mazullo he could understand, because of his father, but these other two? Beef alone never cut it.

Bobbing down, Ross heard two other punches fly by his ears, and he grabbed Scarpone by the front of his shirt and pulled him in. He then launched a punch from down by his ankles that whistled up the front of Scarpone's body and caught him under the chin.

When you came down to it, littlish quick guys who could handle their fists and maybe a knife and for sure a rod were worth a weight room of pumped-up assholes. Furco himself was an example.

Chopping another punch down into Scarpone's nose, which folded under his knuckles, Ross decided that Furco couldn't know about this. It wasn't his style, which was sneaky. If Furco had wanted him, Ross wouldn't have seen him coming, especially way out here in the woods.

But still Scarpone did not go down, and out of the corner of his eye Ross could see Falci pulling at something near his belt. Still flailing and blinded now, his face bleeding from the mouth and a nostril that was split right up to the eye, it seemed, Scarpone staggered forward, tripping over Mazullo so that Ross had only to jerk a knee into his stomach and backhand the side of his head to make him go down.

Spinning around, Ross again kicked out and caught Falci's hand, which was holding something large and black that exploded, bucking a slug through the door of the Trans-Am. Another kick clipped him just behind the ear and caromed his head, like a billiard ball, off the car. And again. Now sitting on the ground near Mazullo, Falci's body slowly bent forward until his head was nearly resting on his knees.

He coughed. It was wet. He coughed again and then, falling onto his side, began to vomit.

Pizza, Ross decided, snatching up the .45. No wonder the hump was fat. He then relieved Mazullo of his piece and Scarpone, who was out and a mess, of his. Back in the sixties when Ross began his involvement with guns, Walthers and Mausers had been the preferred weapons of the radical chic. Now they were being used by the Mafia, and he considered the process by which anything fashionable was eventually made available to the masses—or, here, asses—for a buck. Later he'd check, but he was willing to bet these particular pieces weren't even originals. Clones, mock-ups, look-alikes, there were thousands of them out there, and most of them junk.

Said Mazullo, "You fuckin' nigger, you're dead fuckin' nigger meat. Know that?"

"You think?" Ross started back toward the house. "How you gonna make that happen? Who you gonna get? Lucca Furco? I bet he'll be proud of you today. You gonna tell him or shall I?" They weren't finished with him yet, he figured, but for the next exchange he'd have to be equipped.

Opening the screen door, Ross chucked the three handguns onto a nearby couch and reached for the short-barreled, pump-action riot gun that earlier, before the Trans-Am had appeared in the driveway, he had positioned there.

Turning back, he saw that Mazullo had gotten to his feet and had walked himself around the car to the driver's side door, which he had opened. He was now reaching down under the seat.

Ross moved quickly and quietly back down the stairs. At the car he said, "You just don't learn, do you, Dino?" and jacked the shotgun right up Mazullo's ass so he shrieked like a girl before launching himself across the bucket seats, his face slamming into the other door.

Ross jabbed him again and again. "Know what this is? Guess. What you think it is?" Ross found the Velcro-sealed pouch that contained a .22 Ruger magnum, a kind of assassination weapon, and a Baretta automatic of the same caliber. It was something meant to be carried in a pocket or a woman's purse.

Button men? Ross chuckled. No, just assholes. On weapons charges alone they could spend the best part of their lives in Rahway. New Jersey had maybe the toughest gun laws in the country. But *what* lives? Ross had an idea that, given a chance, they'd take care of themselves, one way or another.

"Shotgun," he said. "Birdshot and lead. It'll take you a good twenty minutes to bleed to death. If you live, you'll need exploratory surgery to get it all out. If you survive that, you'll probably die even slower of lead poisoning. Ain't no way they'll ever get all of it out.

"Like that, you little asshole?" Putting his arm into it, Ross rammed the shotgun upward, skewering the barrel.

Mazullo wailed. He screamed, "Nigger. You fuckin' nigger!"

It took him and Falci ten minutes to load Scarpone back into the car. Scarpone's nose was broken and some of his teeth, but he came around again and tried to find Ross and go after him. Falci held him back. "He's got a shotgun. He'll kill you. There's always later." Falci's eyes shot toward the porch where Ross was standing, his legs crossed, the shotgun resting in his folded arms.

When finally Mazullo started the Trans-Am and turned on the lights, Ross again moved down the stairs and positioned himself beside the car. He could not be sure that he had relieved them of all their weapons, and he wanted to be where he could see them inside the car.

Suddenly Mazullo goosed the car forward and, swinging the wheel, tried to catch Ross with a fender.

In stepping aside, Ross merely raised the shotgun slightly and squeezed off a shell. The blast was deafening. It shattered the Trans-Am's plastic grille and punched through the radiator, spewing water over the hood.

But Mazullo didn't stop. Skidding, swerving in the soft sand, the car lurched off down the driveway and through the trees.

Well, Ross thought, he'd been made, but as what? Nigger? Nigger lover? *Rather*—he almost chuckled—the nigger who was the lover of a very special white woman and who might also be the heat, the way he handled himself. Could the three of them put that much together? Possibly. At least they now had some idea he might be more than a humble waiter.

It would be something else, though, if it got back to somebody with brains, like Furco or Grisanti or the elder Mazullo or the big guy from Brooklyn—Infantino—who controlled things. Maybe even the guy who was called Cheech. But Ross doubted it. He couldn't picture any one of the three owning up to a beating, least of all Mazullo, though he didn't doubt they'd be back.

It'd be something low-down and dirty. Something from a distance, a rifle or a bomb. Or he'd send somebody else on contract, somebody who knew what he was doing. That would be Mazullo's speed, and for speed he was all they had.

Picking up the ejected shell, Ross made straight for the house. If he didn't call back soon, there'd be an all-points issued on the Trans-Am and in short order a team surrounding the house. And having spent the past few years in a government office cubicle, he rather appreciated his present assignment and hoped it would last.

10

As Toni pulled into the parking lot of the restaurant, she didn't see the low, swept-wing car that she knew all too well until she was nearly upon it. They had pulled it in past the cedar-board blind that concealed the dumpster and so close to the delivery stairs that it was nearly blocking her way to the kitchen.

What could they want at this hour with the Borghese closed? she wondered. They never had actual business here, and Lucca would have mentioned something. She scanned the rest of the large parking lot for his car but saw only Solieri's Town Car and Philly's battered Camaro. They would be completing their prep work for the week to come.

What was that smell? Fire? She closed her car door and took a few quick steps toward the restaurant, which was showing only one light over the back door and another from the small square window in the door itself.

She slowed. It wasn't actual fire, it was more—turning her head to one side as she approached the low car, she tried to peer within—like the smell of scorched metal or some automotive or industrial effluent. Until she was nearly alongside the car and she heard it hissing and pinging and caught the acrid reek of burnt coolant and plastic and rubber, and suddenly the passenger door swung open and blocked her way to the stairs.

At first she didn't know what she was seeing, or, rather,

who. As though drunk or drugged or—no, beaten—he now raised his head to her in a series of slight jerks, his dark hair wet with blood, both eyes puffy red and almost closed, a nostril split deep into his face, and his mouth a kind of bloody gash in which his two front teeth were the merest of stubs right on the line of his gum.

There was a small plastic package on the dashboard and another on the console between the two front seats. Both had been opened and were fuzzed with white powder.

Bending her head, Toni looked deeper into the car at the driver, whose snarl she recognized though his face was bruised and puffy. "Dean—is that you? What happened here? What—" She again looked down at the young man in the passenger seat.

"Nothin' you can't fix," a voice said from the backseat, and then a hand jumped out from the shadows and pulled her roughly into the car.

She smacked her temple hard on the door frame and twisted her ankle, and only when she found herself sprawled across their laps did she realize that one of them—the one who was so horribly disfigured, Scarpone, she thought his name was—was bare from the waist down, his trousers bunched at his feet.

But she had no time to complete the thought and understand totally what was happening to her, for with six hands—the third man, Falci, squatting down over the drive shaft in back—they began rolling her over and over, like a kind of log or cylinder in their laps, tearing, ripping at her clothes, feeling her, slapping her, giving her pokes and probes that made her jump, the little one, Mazullo, saying, "Nigger lady. We hear you good. Roll huh! Roll 'uh ovah! You give it good. Roll huh! Roll 'uh ovah!"

And she was tossed roughly around on her stomach, her back, her stomach again and again, the waist- and legbands of the bikini she was wearing under her slacks digging into her flesh before the fabric tore, and one of them cheered. Toni felt something hot that stung her back and then felt wet working its way up her spine. Only when it tugged at the collar of the sheepskin jacket she was wearing, rending it in two, did it occur to her—turning to see the blade of some large hunting knife, the kind used for skinning game—that

141

she had been cut and that they, the three of them, had done this before.

Pushing herself up with her elbows she screamed, "Solly!" out the open driver's-side window and pulled up with all her strength on the horn lever, until Mazullo with the hand that held the heavy knife chopped its butt down on her neck. Behind her eyes she saw a great burst of white light that muted to yellow then yellow fringed with vermilion laced with royal blue that turned to lilac and mauve and deep purple and finally black.

Something that smelled like medicine—no, adhesive tape—was then shoved over her mouth, and one of them had her by the nipples and was squeezing as hard as he could. She shrieked, or tried to, the sound stifled in the back of her throat.

"Don't P.O. on us, momma. Don't P.O. We wants you to groove on us, momma. Deep, where you lives," Mazullo was saying into her ear.

"Ready, Bear?" And then to Falci, his tone suddenly intimate and mock tender, "Look at that Bear. You think he ready for this nigger momma? You think he gonna teach her what dick is all about?"

As if speaking admiringly of a lover, his voice soft and deep, his tongue thickened, Falci said, "Bear can take shit, have his bell rung and still come up hard. Looka that shaft. Where you think he got hung like that?"

"It's the nigger in him, right, Bear?"

But it was like the Bear was in a kind of trance or the coke had been too much on top of the beating he had taken. All he could say through his broken teeth was, "Come sit on me, momma. Come sit. Come sit on me, momma. Come sit," while he worked a hand that he had shaped into a taut fist up and down his prick.

"And we gonna watch while that nigger *does* her *good.* Ready now, alley-oop. Hey, look at them tits. We oughta bring her down ta Furco's boat. Make a video. He'd like that."

Toni, still stunned from the blow and whatever had happened to her back, again felt the hands on her, and trying to struggle free, she again struck her head on the headliner of the low car. But somebody—Scarpone, the man in front—

forcing her wrists down to her waist, pressed in and raised her over him. And from behind the seat she felt somebody else seize her ankles and draw them roughly into the back of the car.

"Looka them tits, man. Suck 'em up, Bear. Go on, suck 'em up."

As though something light and insubstantial, she was then rocked from side to side, and she opened her eyes to see her nipples being played into the puffed and bloody mouth of the man—Scarpone—below her.

Again she tried to scream, but Mazullo raised the knife to her throat. "You know snuff? Bear likes a snuff. You wouldn't be his first."

In the kitchen of the Borghese where he had been prepping entrees for Tuesday, Max Solieri looked up from his work when he thought he heard his name shouted.

But from where? He was the only one there except for Philly, who had gone downstairs to the storage walk-in for another side of veal. All the equipment in the kitchen was running: compressors, exhaust fans, the ice machines, salad coolers, pie cases, and ice-cream chests. Only the dishwasher was down.

But when he heard the car horn blow, weak, one of the new, muted jobs like they had in New York, he wiped the blade of his filleting knife on a side towel and moved toward the little square window in the heavy metal door.

Toni had called a half hour before, saying she was coming in to do the books and had a whole bunch of fresh-caught bluefish for him, and he was expecting her.

At the window, which was steamy, Solieri glanced out and saw—or thought he saw—only the car of the three scumbags who were usually sitting with Furco in the corner booth of the barroom. Didn't they know by now the place was closed Mondays? And why park there behind the blind near the dumpster?

Solieri was walking back to the prep table where the fourteen-count shrimp were spread out like an array of gray letter Cs when he thought, anything they were up to couldn't be good, not at the back of *his* joint when it was closed. And he then realized he had seen something more.

A shoe. A woman's shoe, it had looked like, and then some other things, like trash he had first thought, but which could also be—

At the window, Solieri wiped a hand across the glass and squinted. He couldn't see into the car itself, because of the dark-tinted screen, but it definitely was a woman's shoe, a kind of white shoe with a low heel that he'd seen before. And women's clothes ripped to hell were all over the place—his hand reached for the key he'd put in the back door after she had called—and a furry hunk of collar from a bomber jacket.

Christ—he'd seen that before.

And then the door kept swinging open, and he saw, in the second it was wide, skin. Flesh. A shoulder and the flash of something shiny being held to her neck. Mazullo—the kid—was beyond her, and the squat wide one under her.

"Toni!" he roared and, fumbling with the key, wrenched open the door that snapped in its stop and nearly whipped back on him as he lunged out onto the loading platform, the filleting knife that he'd had in his hand up. Ready.

Dom couldn't figure it out and didn't know what was wrong. From a room in Harrah's he had watched the boat, Furco's *Bark-a-Roll*, dock and let her and the old lady and kid off.

By the time the mate had loaded the trunk of her Seville and Furco and she had spoken, Dom was already in the stretch limo and up the ramp and waiting by the casino entrance to see the Caddy move off in the rearview mirror. In and around A.C. there were so many limos people didn't even see them anymore.

At the Ramada in Hammonton just down the road from her restaurant, where she would drop off the old lady and kid, Dom drove right by and pulled into a gas station where he'd made arrangements a week or so earlier when Bruce told him to watch her close. There he dumped the limo and his chauffeur's jacket and cap for a khaki golfer's hat and matching raincoat and a used tan Cressida with a big "P.G.A. Member" emblem on the back window and an "I'd Rather Be Swinging" sticker on the bumper that pictured a guy teeing off. Its registration was Ohio—white plates with green letters—and different enough from the sky blue and cream of the Jersey-registered limo and the big, battered Caprice he kept next to it in back of the filling station.

But here at the restaurant, he'd watched her park the Seville and walk off toward the rear entrance maybe three, four minutes ago. The stairs were concealed by a wooden fence, but when the door finally opened, it wasn't the broad who appeared in the cone of light but some guy. The chef. Bruce had instructed Dom that she was extremely important to them: "I can't tell you how yet, but she's probably the most necessary person we'll be dealing with for the rest of our business lives." Dom had made it a point to know everything he could about her. What was important *to her*. And who, right down to what they drove. And besides the Seville, in the lot there was only the second chef's beat-up Camaro and the chef's Town Car.

And he, the chef, had something shiny in his hand that in the split second Dom saw him on the platform outside the kitchen door looked like a shiv or a short, narrow-bladed knife, the way he carried it. And what else Bruce had said came back to Dom: "We've got to keep her close. If anything happens to her we'll have to start again, right from the beginning. That could take three or four years."

Too long for Dom. He was out of the car and moving toward them. He didn't care who saw.

Jumping right off the loading platform, Solieri staggered against the Trans-Am, righted himself, and pulled back the passenger door, and what he saw he could not at first believe and for a moment it stopped him.

There was Toni—*his* Toni, the Tone, the Lady herself— nude. With her arms pinned by her sides, she had been raised over Scarpone. There was a big band of adhesive tape over her mouth, and her eyes, which now turned to him, were glassy and frightened and pleading and distant. Somebody in back—the bloated one, Falci—was holding her ankles. Scarpone was all bloody and had his eyes closed and was humming and mumbling, a bubble of blood and saliva having formed at the corner of his mouth, tossing her up and down.

Said Mazullo in the driver's seat, "Hey, Solly—you

145

wanna piece? I bet you always wanted to fuck huh. Now's your chance. Bear says she's prime."

It was then that all the years of having hated THEM and who THEY were and what THEY stood for and what THEY were now doing to the only other person in the world he loved besides his wife overwhelmed Solieri, and in a blind fury he reacted.

When the bastard tossed Toni up, Solieri leaned into the car and slapped his left hand under her shoulder, holding her up, off of him, and with his right hand—the one that grasped the filleting knife—he swiped below Toni, low.

At first the bastard made no sound. He even stopped humming and mumbling. His eyes opened, as wide as the swelling would allow. And he then uttered a shriek that froze Mazullo and the other one in the back. But Solieri didn't stop.

With the knife he again swiped, down the shoulder and forearm of Scarpone, there in the front seat, and across the back of the hand, the veins and tendons of which popped, of the other one—the blond, Falci—who was holding her legs.

Roaring now, Scarpone tossed Toni away from him, out the door past Solieri, and tried to get out of the car, his stomach now a mass of blood that was spurting from his crotch.

Solieri, pushing Toni away from the car, used his foot to slam the door closed—it caught, it locked—on Scarpone's hand. He heard the shriek again, and through the window, which was open, he saw Scarpone's eyes flicker up into his head, before his shriek turned to a scream that continued.

But Solieri wasn't through with them yet, and pushing Toni, who had gotten unsteadily to her feet, toward the back of the car and the parking lot—"Go. Run! Call the cops!"— Solieri rushed around the car. He would kill one of them. Mazullo, the little snakey cocksucker. Scum from scum. He would slice him up like a butterflied fillet.

He grabbed the driver's side door and pulled it open, but Mazullo was waiting for him. Lunging across the steering wheel, Mazullo popped the large skinning knife up to the hilt, right through Solieri's chest so that it pierced his back and came out shiny through his white cotton work shirt. And Mazullo—surprised at how easily the blade had gone

146

through the guy, like through a pumpkin—was equally surprised at how smoothly it came out.

But the guy, who was dead—he had to be—didn't go down right away. He just dropped the knife and stood there frozen, his eyes light blue and bugged and staring at him, while Scarpone's and now Falci's cries became whimpers and the woman, Toni, screamed, "Solly! Oh, Solly!" Snatching up the little knife, now she tried to come at Mazullo.

But there was somebody else out there, Mazullo could see out of the corners of his eyes. Some guy who, using a tan raincoat, wrapped the broad in it and said, "Get into my car. The Toyota. I'll take care of this," in a quiet way Mazullo didn't like.

Mazullo then tried to start up the Trans-Am, which coughed and sputtered but finally caught. He rammed it into reverse, goosing it backward and nearly catching the woman, who was running barefoot across the parking lot toward her own car. Throwing it into first, Mazullo tried for her again but missed. And he thought for a moment maybe he'd just wait for her to get in and he'd jump in with her and get the fuck out of there in a car that would take him where he'd have to go to get clear of this thing.

But he couldn't leave Scarpone and Falci. They knew too much and could put him there. Then, Scarpone's cousin was a doctor, and if he could just make Little Egg Harbor— And finally, the guy—he'd seen him somewhere before. He'd never get the other two out of the Trans-Am and into the Seville in time.

But Toni ran right by the Toyota and, tossing the knife that she still held in her right hand across the seat, jumped into her own Seville, flicking the switch to lock all four doors. She wasn't going anywhere with anybody who had anything to do with what had happened out in that parking lot.

Pulling out the reserve key she kept in a magnetized tin under the dash, she started the Caddy and swept out of the parking lot, turning out onto the White Horse Pike in the direction opposite the other car.

But where to go? The Ramada for clothes? Yes.

No. Hadn't they tried to kill her, slowly, like animals, a

pack of jackals, playing a death game with her. And the other one, Dom, whom she recognized as Payson's driver—had he told her to get into his car because he was there to make sure of the kill? Where had he come from, and why?

No, not the Ramada. Tina was there, and Ma. And she could see the lights of A.C. in front of her. Her back had now begun hurting, galling her deeply like no other hurt she had ever felt. She'd need a doctor but not a hospital. No, no hospital. Somehow, she'd have to get herself together and get her child and her mother-in-law and get the hell out of this place.

She'd just leave the whole place to Furco and flee. She'd change her name, get a job doing something else. Anything. Even teaching again.

Tears gushed from her eyes and splotched the backs of her hands. She couldn't see and thought of pulling over, but she drove on.

Blood was pooling at the base of her spine.

Through the square window in the kitchen door, Philly had watched them murder Solieri. And he was so stunned by the sight that he couldn't move away, even when the man—the stocky one who had wrapped Toni in the coat and was now wearing only a white shirt and bow tie—returned with his car and carried poor Solly toward the open trunk.

And only when the man closed the lid and got in the car and drove off did Philly realize that the door was still unlocked, and he had pissed in his pants. The urine had filled his shoes, which squished when he moved, and stung his thighs.

Locking the door and turning to the empty kitchen, he asked himself what he should do. The prep tables behind him were covered with shrimp ready to be cleaned, and of course he had the side of veal to bone out. That would take him most of the rest of the night, *after* he got himself cleaned up and together.

He'd have to then catch some sleep so he could fill in for Solly at lunch—

"*Solly!*" he called out, his voice ringing in the large empty pots that were hung on the walls. "They *keeled* you! I can't fuckin' believe it."

And he walked right down the stairs to the office. Furco's number would be in the dial book, the one Toni—"And Toni!"—kept on her desk. He didn't know what they done to her, but it wasn't good.

If they thought they could just do that to people like them two, just think what they'd do to somebody like him. Philly had been born in this country, but he was too well acquainted with the Honduran history of his family to think that he was more than simply expendable, and he wouldn't do nothing without the personal okay of Mr. Lucca Furco.

"Who—?" Furco asked from the Brigantine condo he'd bought after having moved out of his wife's house in Longport three years before.

"Philly. The sous chef from the joint. The Borghese. I'm sorry to disturb you, Mr. Furco, and I wouldn't but something terrible has happened down here, and I thought you should know. You know Solly? And Toni?" Philly now began to cry uncontrollably, and it happened again. The piss.

"*Toni?* What happened to Toni?" Furco waited and finally demanded, "Pull yourself together, for crissakes, and tell me what happened to Toni!"

11

It was her father's question exactly. He had raised a hand to her face to pick at the adhesive material that had stuck to her skin like a white moustache.

After parking her Seville in the alley behind his tailor shop off Pacific Avenue, Toni had had to bang with the heel of her fist to raise her father, whom she could see through the iron bars that striped the back-door window. He was reading in a wingback chair in the pattern room where he did most of his tailoring.

But it was warm in the shop. And the familiar smells of mothballs and bolts of wool and silk and linen and cotton and the light machine oil that every day he applied to his ancient Singers, his steamers and stitching machines, made her feel at least welcome, if not comfortable.

"Rape," she said. In her shame—why *shame?* She had nothing to be ashamed about—she could not look at her father directly, and turning her back to him, she dropped the coat from her shoulders to show him her wound. "And murder."

"Oh, Toni! You?"

"Raped. But Max, my chef—"

"Solieri? Murdered?" Her father's thin face was incredulous, his moustache wrapping the corners of his mouth. His dark eyes were wide; the hand on her shoulder, which now

directed her into the beam of an overhead light, was shaking.
"But who?"

Who do you think? she nearly asked. But she had never
spoken to him of her troubles before, beyond announcing
once, after he had inquired some time after the accident in
which Jack vanished, that her husband had left her. Her
father had then waited for an explanation, but, when none
was forthcoming, he had asked no more, and she had been
grateful for his tact.

Yes, she now decided, she *was* guilty for not having taken
Solieri's advice and walked away from the Borghese and her
involvement with—"Wise guys," she now said. It was the
phrase her father had always used for gangsters.

"But—do you know them?"

"Too well, which is why I'm here, Pop, and not at a
hospital or calling the police."

Pulling the coat farther down her back, he said, "My God,
Toni—you're hurt. This is deep. I'm calling Freddie." He
meant the doctor she'd had as a child, who had been and
still was one of her father's closest friends and who lived in
the next block. Long retired, he was one of the regulars at
the tailor shop.

"It's why I'm here." She thought she should call the
motel to see if her daughter and mother-in-law were all right.
But why wouldn't they be? Solly had gotten to at least two
of the three in the car, and they would be trying to find their
own medical attention now.

"But first I must shower," she said. "And get into some
warm clothes." Suddenly she had begun to shake uncontrollably, and she wondered if she was in shock.

The doctor was dismayed that "something like this could
happen to a lady like you here in Atlantic City. It shows how
deep we've sunk since—" Since gambling was legalized, he
meant. And after he had left, Toni borrowed a cigarette from
her father and tried to ease herself into the wingback chair.
She felt exhausted utterly, but she knew the pain would not
allow her to sleep, and she had refused the narcotics that the
doctor had offered her. She had to think and act quickly, if
she were to extricate herself and her daughter and mother-
in-law from the mess she had gotten them into.

"Help me with this, Pop," she said, exhaling the smoke

and trying to keep out of her mind the image of Solly standing there dead with the huge, ugly knife plunged through his heart, yet his eyes wide open. "What would you do . . ." and she explained her predicament from the beginning, telling him now why Jack had disappeared and about the restaurant and the debt and the debt-service, right on up through what she knew and suspected of Payson's involvement in her entrapment and what presently she had done and perhaps might continue to do for him. She finished with what had happened that night.

Her father's long, sallow face, which she had always thought of as handsome and dapper, was drawn. As she spoke, he had removed a pipe from the rack on the mantel of the fireplace into which a gas heater had been set, and now the air was scented with the rich, blue smoke of the black Sobranie pipe mixture that he had smoked since she could first remember.

Sitting back in one of the other soft chairs that made the large workroom look small, he took the pipe from his mouth and looked down into the bowl. A wisp of smoke curled from his nostrils, which, like her own, were large but delicately shaped, arcing back as though fluted. He was a man of moderate habits and good judgment, and she valued his opinion. More to the point, he, like every other businessperson in Atlantic City, had had to live with the Mob and corruption.

"Well—you've been set up, but *why?* For your restaurant?" He canted his head to one side and looked off through the smoke. He was wearing a brown cardigan over a starched white shirt with a bow tie to match even now, at night. She could not remember having seen him here in his shop without some sort of neckwear—a regular tie or a cravat—and she could remember his saying, "It's a habit, but it's an attitude also. Pressed, cleaned, and starched. It's important always to look your best." It reminded her of Lucca Furco. She also then thought of the other three. And Solly. Her eyes blurred.

"Maybe they want a big, legitimate operation like yours. You know, for the cash flow. But I'm thinking it's something else that has to do with this Payson. He's big-time. What would he want with a restaurant here in Jersey or anyplace for that matter? If your impressions about him are right—the Beekman Place house, what he's told you already about his operation, the movement of money, and the two names, one of them your own—" He shook his head. "I don't like that. I don't like that one bit.

"And you know what I like even less?"

She waited while he relit the pipe.

"Him telling you anything at all. Sure, he wants your cooperation and he knows he'll get it more easily if he squares with you. But is he telling you everything? People usually do, one way or another, if you listen close."

Toni thought back, trying to replay in her mind everything that Payson had said to her. Had she listened to him? Totally, with all the attention she could muster, but she could not come up with even the smallest revelation of intent beyond what he had said: they were moving the money for security and investment purposes.

Her father stabbed the air with the bit of his pipe. "And *your* name. Why would he want your name on those accounts? Because, like he said, *you're* just the sort of person who *would* be squirreling away tax-free profits in tax havens like that?" He tilted his head to the side for a moment, considering. "Maybe, but what amounts?"

Toni did not know. As instructed, she had kept her eyes straight ahead and off the documents she had signed. Payson had watched her very closely on that: sitting by her side and turned so that he could watch her face.

"This Payson—" her father again shook his head "—we just don't know enough about him. Did he order this thing? Solly and what they did—no—why? Could he be doing this thing—the transfer of money, the new accounts—on his own?" Her father shook his head one more time. "There'd be no point. They'd kill him.

"You sure we shouldn't take you to a hospital?"

Toni said no again.

"We don't know enough about him. Just who he is. What he's doing." He waited for a while, pulling on the pipe, then asked, "So—what are your plans? What will you do?"

Toni shook her head. She was still too close to what had happened and could think only of Solly. And then her back was hurting now, reminding her of how narrowly she had escaped.

"Leave everything and take off?" He waited, then said, "It'd be a shame to have to give up all that you've worked so hard to make—out there in Hammonton. But it's not like you can't begin again. You're young and beautiful and intelligent—" he looked up at her and managed a thin smile "—and, you know, it's not as though I haven't made a dollar here. It'll be yours and Jim's soon anyway, and I've read it's better to get rid of it before—"

Solly's advice, almost right down to the words. Toni shook her head. "I've got some money, remember?" She had the check from Payson, and just leaving her piece of the restaurant to Furco or Payson or whoever ran things among them would more than satisfy her debt.

But instead she said, "It's been years now since Jack left, and what would you say if I told you I have a black boyfriend?"

Her father glanced toward the front hall and the direction in which the doctor, who was black, had left. "Is that what it was all about? Tonight?"

She shook her head. "Not all of it, I don't think."

His eyebrows had come up, his forehead was wrinkled. He spoke down at his pipe. "I suppose you're old enough, and it's your business. A few years ago I would've said something different. But most of my friends—and I mean *friends*—are, too. And I don't see why you can't have yours."

Toni nodded, thanking him for what, she knew, was a major concession. It was one thing for him to have black friends, but quite another for his daughter to have a black *boyfriend,* with all that might mean, real or imagined.

But she raised her head and watched her father turn and try to look in back of his chair. For she, too, now felt something in the room that was different. Not noise or a movement or a change in atmosphere, but rather a presence. And looking up and off to one side toward the back door, she was startled to see Dom, Payson's chauffeur, standing there.

"What?" her father demanded, beginning to pull himself out of the chair. "Who are you? How did you get in?"

Said Dom to Toni, "I brought you a dress and some clothes. I thought—" He glanced down at the dark dress that she was now wearing. It had been her mother's.

"Is this one of them?" her father went on, nearly out of the chair now.

Staying him with a hand, Toni said, "Not one of *them*." It occurred to her that, if he had gotten the green suit for her, he had also come across Tina and Ma.

As though reading her thoughts, he said, "Your daughter and mother-in-law are okay. I brought them back to Cherry Hill. Jane is with them now.

"There's been a change in plans." He glanced at her father, then decided to continue. "What was planned for the weekend Mr. P. says we'll do tomorrow or the next day. He tol' me to bring you back."

When she still didn't move, he added, "I took care of the details. There's nothin' to worry about, at least for a while."

"But Solly had a wife," Toni objected. Dom said nothing and only stood there in his chauffeur's uniform, the green dress over one arm. "And what about his—" She couldn't say "killers"; she couldn't bring herself to it.

The man blinked. "It was a mistake. Theirs. And they'll be taken care of."

"By you?"

He hunched his shoulders. "Maybe I won't have to."

"Why? What do you mean?" The police? she wondered. No. He wouldn't have called the police.

He pulled back the cuff of the sleeve over which the dress was draped and glanced at his wristwatch. "Mr. P. wants you on a plane in three hours. He's made the reservation."

Said her father, "I hope you're not considering—"

"He said, give you this." From an interior pocket he drew an envelope. In it was a cashier's check for another trip: $75,000.

She placed it on the table beside her, and again the man anticipated what she wanted and handed her a pen. She endorsed the check and handed it to her father. "You take care of this, Pop, and if anything—"

"I'll call Jim," her father said, glancing at Dom. "But don't, Toni. You don't have to. Like we said, forget the restaurant. Forget everything—"

But already she had begun trying to maneuver herself out of the soft, deep chair. The stitching in her back was taut and the slightest movement painful.

Had she any choice? They knew where her daughter and mother-in-law were, and look how fast they had found her.

Dom moved forward to help, but she ignored his hand.

PART
IV

12

With its wide, open porches on the ground floor and screened balconies that looked out in every direction from the upper two stories, there was the look of class to Lucca Furco's Longport house. When he'd first seen it, he'd thought of spending lazy summer afternoons out on those porches in white ducks and a Brooks Brothers shirt, sitting in a tall rocker reading something like the *New Yorker* or the *Wall Street Journal* and sipping tea.

He'd tried it once, but it didn't feel right. Inside the house his wife had been bitching about this and that, and then every time a car came by he'd hoped it wasn't somebody he knew who could see him.

But today he hardly glanced at its tall hedges and the curvy drive that forked off to the back door. He stopped the pearl gray 735-i and got out without switching off the engine or closing the door. He was only there to pick up some stuff. He wasn't staying long.

The back door was not just open, it was standing open. How many times had he told his old lady about that; and the thought of it just sent him higher. Cops come, door is open. Assholes take a picture of it and walk in. In court they say, it was a hot day, door was open, I don't know why. We walked in, ain't it so? They got witnesses, pictures.

He found her in the dining room at the head of the long oval table that once had been filled with kids and was now covered with a lace tablecloth from Verona—the real one, not the one near Montclair—that had cost him a fortune. She was dressed in a silver silk housecoat with an ermine collar and had on her head a platinum-colored wig he'd just got the bill for on his gold card. Real human hair styled by Elizabeth Arden, which he didn't mind—the mother of his kids should look nice, as long as she was carrying his name— but eleven hundred bucks? He wondered what it was going to cost him every time she put it in the box and sent it up to New York for a perm.

Before her was the crystal, plate, and silver service that he also recognized from last Christmas's bills and a chafing dish that could serve maybe thirty. Candles were lit. She reached for the lid and lifted it, looking up. "I thought when you called maybe you'd want to have breakfast with me." Her voice was maybe lower than his from all the butts she smoked. Her eyes were pouched with satchels of flesh. "You ain't been home in four and a half weeks."

Home? He hadn't been living there for three and a half years.

The eyes themselves were brown and murky, and he wondered if she'd been boozing again. They were reading his face. "What'sa matter?" she asked, and they read some more. They had known each other since they were kids and had even gotten married then. Both nineteen and him in the army.

He shoved aside the chair in front of the place that had been set for him and walked toward the long, wainscoted hall and the stairs that led to the rock-wall cellar.

"Oh, no, Lucca. Not that again. Please. For—" she almost said "me," he thought "—the kids. What if you should—"

Get your name in the paper? Front page or—not quite as bad—the obits. One of their kids was studying to be a doctor. Of philosophy. Another was married to a real doctor, but that only gave her the license to be a bigger bitch than her mother. The third and fourth were in college: Bowdoin so far up in Maine that Furco hardly ever saw her, which was good, and Brandeis with all the Jews.

Hey, he thought, Toni was a Jew, or at least a partial Jew. *Toni.*

Furco shoved the wine barrels out of the way, one after another, so that they rumbled across the concrete and banged into the wall and each other, sounding like the distant guns Furco had heard from the mountains when they'd been patrolling the border in Vietnam.

"Las' time—"

She was drunk.

"Las' time you nearly got yourself killed."

Furco reached down to the bottom of the wall where he'd had the Tuscan stonemason conceal the wedge. The guy had been right from the old country and planned to go back, was why Furco employed him, and he told how he'd built plenty of them during the war to keep valuables and guns from the Germans.

It was beautiful, really, like some work of art, and now using both hands and all he had on the stone surface, he managed to lift it slightly but just enough. Like magic, a kind of low door opened. It was something out of *The Count of Monte Cristo,* and he imagined it wouldn't keep out a real search team with, say, a dog. But when Grisanti and the others had been out boozing and balling chicks, he'd gotten ahold of the mason guy, who'd owed him, and they'd put it in together. Having now really to tug to pull it back, he also imagined there'd come a day when he'd be too old or weak to get in, but by then—

"Las' time you almost went to jail, you bastard. That's what you are, a *bas-tard!* Our kids, they're clean. They want none of your *shit,* Lucca. None of it."

Ducking in, Furco ran his hand along the wall until he found the light, the wires of which they'd encased in the wall itself so no smart-ass Fed could trace them.

And about the kids—sure they'd taught them well, him and Carmella. He'd taught them to respect themselves and work hard and remember that what goes around comes around, so don't step on nobody unless you plan to forget them. Or worse. She'd taught them to hate him for the lesson. The kid at Bowdoin wouldn't even answer his calls, but she cashed his checks.

"Television, radio. The papers. The court. People stopped speaking to me. We had to move, change schools, you bastard, and all because of your *temp-ah!*"

He'd heard it all before. It was the reason she said she drank. And he now heard the cellar door slam and knew right where she was headed—to the crystal decanter on the sideboard right behind where she'd been sitting when he walked in.

Furco turned to what the small room contained: racks of old wine that once, when he'd been into fine wine, he'd collected and now merely gathered dust.

Then there was the file of records Furco kept just for himself to make sure Grisanti and Mazullo senior weren't stealing from him, though they knew what would happen if they did. Luke Furco took no shit, it was as simple as that. You fucked with him, he'd whack you out or you him. And, after Vietnam and the war in South Philly, what still scared the shit out of anybody who'd thought of it was that it didn't seem to matter to him which way it came down. Having nothing he valued to lose, Furco was fearless. Absolutely without caution, until now.

Maybe he had something to lose, he thought, reaching for the first weapon he saw, a case that contained a Smith & Wesson Model 41, a kind of target pistol with a seven-inch barrel that could be fitted with a silencer. Just maybe. And maybe they had found what it was and stung him. He added his pick and a double-sided straight razor that could open and lock with a flick of the wrist, and a throwing knife with another double-sided blade long enough to be used as a thrusting and cutting weapon, too. But he also had a surprise for them. While Grisanti and Mazullo's old man had been out "cabareting," as they called it, Furco had been practicing with every weapon he owned and working out with some martial-arts guys: Furco had never had time for the high life and all that shit. And it—the sting—would only make him more ruthless, he could feel it in his chest and heart. Absolutely without fucking pity.

Those bimbos. Those big, pumped-up pussies and that little rat-fuck Mazullo. Furco could feel his ears pull back and his nostrils flex just to think of them, and he turned suddenly and whipped the throwing knife underhand out the low door. Without even being able to see the cellar stairs, he heard the satisfying thunk of the blade sinking into the wood. He couldn't count the hours it had taken to learn that. It hadn't been fun, it had just been necessary. He'd known that someday it would again come down to this, and he was ready. Out in the car he had a Saturn 2-22 that could fire up to 3,000 rimfire rounds per minute and a Benelli M1 S-90 automatic shotgun stoked with 500-grain rifled slugs that were accurate at thirty yards and could pierce steel plate.

Furco had learned well the major lesson of Vietnam, which was firepower. When it came down to trading shots at close quarters, you just had to have it, and to ice a guy Furco preferred "up close and personal," like they used to say on TV. If you didn't want to see a guy die, why kill him? Furco had to feel that strong.

Up in the kitchen he found Carmella at the sink, staring out the window at the long lawn and the pines at the back of the lot. He knew without having to look that there was a drink in the well in front of her. He could smell it. Bourbon, something cheap—Early Times or Jim Beam, he decided, dialing Grisanti.

The phone answered on the first ring. "Freddo?" a hyped voice asked. It was Grisanti wanting to know if it was Freddo Mazullo, Dean's old man, on the line, and Furco wondered what was up.

"Nah—it's me," said Furco, offhand like a normal call.

"Where the fuck you been? I been callin' you everywhere. Know that pickup we got today at Newark?"

Grisanti meant the airport. Furco waited.

"I can't make it. Could you—?"

"Course." If he was going to do this thing, he'd have to show everybody he kept the operation going while he did it. The minute his son was gone, Freddo would demand a sitdown, and Furco would have to prove that while Freddo's son Dean or Dino or whatever the little cockbite wanted to be called and his friends were out raping and murdering Furco's people, Furco took care of business *before* settling the account. "Anytime. What you got?" He wanted to know what was keeping Grisanti from making the pickup. Grisanti made all big pickups in their operation; he insisted upon it.

There was a pause. "Can't say."

That meant a meet. It also meant Mazullo senior would be there.

"Where?" Furco chanced, knowing Grisanti wouldn't

answer, but maybe he'd get a handle on where the little bastard was. Eventually Dean would make contact with his old man, if only for money, and Furco wanted to be there. Where better than after a meet someplace out of the way that had already been secured by the big guy from Brooklyn?

"You wouldn't believe it if I tol' you. Shit—you think Alfie's is bad? Christ—I been tol' wear long johns."

Furco's mind raced through the possibilities: Alfie's was one of Grisanti's meat-packing facilities, but it wouldn't be there. Long-johns meant someplace cold. The roof of a building? No. Why? What was coming down he didn't know about?

Then, they'd had plenty of cover Fourth of July Centennial. Cops couldn't get near or even see them with all the boats passing by.

"Hey, Luck—I gotta split. Where you be later, the club?" Grisanti meant the Borghese. He didn't know what had happened; there wasn't a hint in his voice.

"See you there?" Furco asked.

"A date, sweetheart."

Turning from the telephone, he found Carmella facing him. She had the housecoat open and except for panties the same silver silk as the coat she was naked. The aureoles of her nipples were large and dark brown, the color of coffee. "When was the last time we made love, Lucca?" Her eyes were streaming with tears. "I thought this morning maybe you'd make love to me one more time. Any way you want."

Furco turned and walked out to the waiting BMW. She wouldn't want the way he would want this morning, and Furco hadn't made *love* to anybody, not even her, for about as long as he could remember.

13

Even as a child Payson had despised New Jersey. Here in spring his father, a stonemason, had brought his brothers and him to work on the gaudy beachfront piles that were being erected by asphalt or numbers or garbage-dump tycoons. Having been taken out of school, where he shone and which was his love, Payson had spent long days laboring outside in the frigid breezes off the ocean, only to collapse exhausted into a cold bed in one of a series of tarpaper shacks where they—then *paesans* in every sense—had been quartered.

True, their large family had needed the money, even at the expense of his education, but when one day a packer of sausage meats, who also ran a book and a stable of women, yelled up to Payson's father, "Hey, Giusepp', come down here and help my wife with the groceries," Payson had made two vows.

For Carlo dePasquale had been an honest, hardworking, and powerfully built man who had taken pride in his occupation; and looking down for a moment before he descended the scaffold, it had been as though he had implored his large, stone-hardened hands not to do the damage of which they were capable. He had then turned to his youngest son, as though for a reason to forbear, and, saying nothing, had complied with the man's wishes.

But to that son the lesson was plain: never to find himself

in such a position, and to remember that, as things turned back on themselves, his time would come.

And it had.

From afar now for two days, Payson had been viewing the interspersed clusters of wharves, boardwalks, houses, and water tanks that were the seaside communities of the Jersey Shore. Aboard his yacht, a sixty-seven-foot Herreschoff yawl that had been built in '28 and restored by him lovingly and at great expense in '82, Payson had motored away from his mooring at Shelter Island, through the Hell Gate into the East River, and past his residence on Beekman Place. Once having cleared Liberty Island in the upper bay, he raised sail. Following a moderate southwesterly wind, he'd rounded Sandy Hook and wing-on-wing glided along the 40.8 nautical miles that would take him nearly to the southernmost tip of Island Beach State Park.

It was a fifteen-mile stretch of barrier island that had been conserved as a natural area and even—Payson had read—enjoyed an ecology unlike any other in the state, including a species of plant and two of lichen that were found nowhere else. Of more interest to him, however, was the fact that access could be gained only along the beach, which because of winter storm damage had been closed, and by a single road that was monitored by a guardhouse. And for two days now, the park superintendent, who was a nephew of a friend of Grisanti, had denied all cars but the four that Payson could now see through binoculars scattered in a parking lot about a mile or so from Barnegat Inlet.

Activating the automatic sailing device, Payson went below. There in the master cabin of the yawl, he removed the windbreaker that he had been wearing since sunup and donned oilskins, the visored hood of which could be pulled forward to nearly conceal his face. The laces of his storm boots, however, he did not tie closed. Instead he removed the 4.5" TEC-38 from the waterproof pouch fixed to the lining. It was a kind of modern derringer with a nylon grip and a smooth, hammerless action that wouldn't snag in the lining of his boot. He swung its twin barrels to the left and made sure that the sea air hadn't corroded its two shiny .38-special rounds.

How many of them would there be? he again asked himself. Five for sure, and then maybe one guard apiece. But, then, it wouldn't be Payson whom they didn't trust, but each other.

Up on deck and within several hundred yards of the beach and the parking lot, Payson swung the wheel and headed the graceful yacht into the wind, the mainsail fluttering and then snapping in the breeze. It was another brilliant spring day out to sea, Payson noted as he rolled the sail, binding it loosely with a Gloucester loop which could be loosened with a tug. Over the land, however, a troubled sky was being driven clear by the breeze that had freshened since dawn. In all, it was a dramatic skyscape, he decided, and well suited to the meet that he had called for, here where there would be no witnesses.

Puffs of low, purplish clouds were scudding under banks of buff thunderheads, and over near Philadelphia to the west it looked like it was raining. A pathetic fallacy with nature mourning? He wondered who beyond a wife or an immediate family member or some bimbo would mourn their passing. "He had a nice smile," Payson remembered having heard the wife of a murdered don say at his funeral. Perhaps, but Payson had only ever seen the man snarl. And then, he had been a saint compared to the men he could now see lumbering between the dunes toward the beach and the water.

Pushing the dinghy away from the yacht, Payson rowed several strokes into the wind and then, turning to the stubby mast, raised the small sail. As he pushed the tiller to starboard, the dinghy caught the breeze and heeled over.

Was he rationalizing now? he asked himself. Trying to make it all seem right, when by any standard the death of—Payson now counted them—nine men was wrong?

Or was it?

Payson hiked his weight over the gunwale and glanced toward the shore.

In a purposeless universe, the event could be loaded with no moral opprobrium whatsoever. It just was, or, he corrected himself, would be.

If all went according to plan.

On shore, Frank Grisanti turned to Fred Mazullo, who, dressed in topcoat and fedora and wing-tipped bluchers like he was going to some four-course fucking lunch, was slipping all over the place in the deep, soft sand. And he was sweating, even though the breeze was so stiff and cold off the ocean that Grisanti's hand moved to his throat to button the collar of his windbreaker. Underneath, Grisanti himself was wearing a cashmere V-neck sweater—canary yellow to match his slacks and the knit cap with the fuzzy white pom-pom peak. On his feet were a pair of high-top Adidas sneakers, him having dressed for the occasion. The beach.

"I don' know," he said to nobody in particular, the pouchy folds of his tanned face narrowing as he squinted one direction down the wide, empty shoreline and then, turning his head to the south, the other. "This ain' my style. How much we talk here, freezin' our nuts off like this? Him? Look at the bastard." He wagged a hand at Payson in the dinghy, which was plunging through the heavy chop. "Looks like Christopher fuckin' Columbus, don' he? Or somebody like that."

Said Sal "The Babe" Infantino, a fat old man who was wearing a beige raincoat and a porkpie hat and had a long cigar positioned in the middle of his mouth, "You read the papers? You watch television or hear the radio?" He was puffing, out of breath. He removed the cigar and coughed. "Guy's hangout, guy's house, guy's fuckin' car even rolling down the pike ain't safe. You look around."

He stopped to wave the cigar and to rest, it appeared to Grisanti, who, fifteen years younger, would not mind in the least stepping into the old man's shoes. Infantino had a big, open face and a ready smile, and he had gotten where he was, which was the top, not by murder and moving in on other guys' action but by being careful and doing favors. There wasn't a connected guy nationwide who didn't respect him—or owe him, which was more important.

Then, in addition to the construction racket he had run out of Brooklyn for years, Infantino had a legitimate business hauling trash in the five boroughs and out on the Island. Grisanti respected that. His own family was still in the meat-packing business—pepperoni, salami, bologna, and all the luncheon meats.

Nevertheless, whenever the Griz heard or read of a big construction job going down in the city, which was nearly every day, it seemed, he couldn't help figuring the 2 percent vig for "labor peace," as Infantino put it. "I'm a peacemaker," he had once heard the man say. "And I'm pissed one of you guys ain't put me in for the prize. You know, the one with the 400K ticket that the dynamite maker from Sweden financed? You know—Nobel was his name." Everybody had laughed. The Babe was known for his sense of humor as well as for his clout.

He had thick arching eyebrows, like they were put on with mascara, and he used them to effect, as now in saying to Grisanti, "Nobody here. Nobody to pick us off 'cept maybe an airplane, and if one comes by, don't look up."

A couple of the others chuckled.

"That guy—"

"Payson," one of the two men Infantino had brought, and who now flanked him, supplied.

"Nah, nah—" the old man waved the name off "—you think I don't know him? DePasqual'. Fuckin' *dePasqual*'s his name. His old man and me go back, or—hey—we *went* back, before he went down, God rest his soul."

Infantino paused and again looked out at the dinghy that was nearly surfing in now on the breakers of an incoming tide. "I put that kid through fuckin' Harvard, if you wanna know the truth." He darted the cigar at the small boat and continued walking. "Henrico. And he's smart. Top of his class. Could have been anything he wanted, but he chose to make *us*—his people—money. He didn't forget, not like some. He only uses that name for business. And if he says it's here we meet, it's out *here,* and I hope none of youse tol' nobody we're here. 'Cause if you did and you put me in stir at my age, I'll probably hate you for the three months it takes me to kick off. Then again, I just might have your balls cut off, broiled, and fed to the gulls à la mode. And I don' mean the ones for hire, either."

Again the others laughed. Infantino was well liked, but they got the point.

Infantino looked up at a gull gliding by in the wind. "Yeah—out here with the birds and the ducks and the wind and the fuckin' cold. I ain't been so cold since I got shot and your old man thought I was dead and dragged me into one of his meat lockers to preserve me for my family." He turned and smiled at Grisanti. It was generally a true story, except that Grisanti's father had helped him into the locker to hide him from the police, who were swarming all over the place.

"And what's wrong with you, anyways?" Infantino asked Grisanti. "You still holdin' that 'Cheech' shit against this guy? Guys who started that 'Cheech' shit, where they?" Infantino puffed on the cigar and sent a blast of smoke into the face of Grisanti, who was a step behind him out of respect. "In the can. All of them. Why? Because they're dumb. They wanna talk in some nightclub or grocery store or some fuckin' Jaguar you could spot a state away.

"And anyway—" at the ebb line of the last high tide he stopped and held out his hand to Grisanti, pulling him closer "—where you get them fuckin' duds, Frankie? You look like you gonna retire to Florida. Someplace where the breakers ain't too high. Geez, you know if somebody said your name was Schwartz, I'd believe it." The others had begun laughing now, and, turning to them, Infantino added, "Don't he look more like a kike than anybody you ever seen?"

But Payson's dinghy was on the final wave now, and, dousing sail and pulling up the short centerboard, he waited until the wave broke and then deftly hopped out. In a foot or so of boil, he took hold of a handle that had been fixed to the prow of the small boat and hauled it toward the men. Two, who were much younger and obviously attending the other seven, moved forward to help him, but Payson raised a palm and stayed them. He did not want the boat so far up the beach that it would take much time to get it back in. As it was, he'd have to struggle to buck it back through that tide, and he'd have little time. Yes, the place was isolated, but the sooner he was away from it the better. You could never tell who was around, and the yacht—he glanced back out at it to make sure the anchor was holding in the sandy bottom there near the beach—was conspicuous.

"Chi-chi-beaner!" Infantino said, holding out his arms and drawing Payson into him. "How the fuck are you?"

"Babe—the fuck I am how." It was the rejoinder, a kind of verbal tautology, that had passed as their greeting since the night that Infantino had met Payson in Grand Central after his first semester at Harvard. In his fat hand Infantino

170

had held Payson's grades. "What's this four-oh shit? What happened to the other ninety-six?" But his pride had been evident in his smile. As it was now, as he held Payson back and looked into his eyes.

Said Payson, "What about this place, Babe, brisk enough for you?"

"Ain't Palm Beach, but I ain't Betty Hutton neither. And they tell me she died broke, which we been guessin' is why you brought us here."

Payson's eyes widened. Could they know?

But Infantino went right on, "Tell us how the fuck is our money and make it quick. These guys here are candy and are freezin' their asses off. What you got?"

Thankful that the old man had decided to lead things and rush them along, Payson smiled and held his gaze and then turned to the other men, shaking their hands and saying their names. He held Grisanti's a little longer, saying, " 'Specially good to see you, Griz. How's the family?"

But he put it to them quickly, his spiel, turning his back to the breeze and anybody who might appear in the parking lot or along the beach to the northeast. He wanted them lined up like that, with their backs to the south, as he and Dom had planned. With his eyes on the sky beyond the Barnegat Lighthouse, which was no more than a mile away across the inlet behind them, he said it plain and in their words, so he could get Infantino and himself away from them quickly. Already he could hear the rhythmical beat of the rotors off in the distance, and there was no predicting when a pleasure boat might approach or leave the inlet. Granted, it was early in the season, but Dom would have to keep low enough never to appear on radar, and more than one pass might invite unwanted attention.

As it was, he would have to lift the old chopper over the tumbledown barn, in which it had been stored and the trees surrounding the Pine Barrens farmhouse that Payson had bought in the name of a friend of a friend—how many?—five or six years earlier. About a year later, he'd acquired the helicopter at a government surplus auction and had it retrofitted with its original Vietnam armaments and maintained by a service buddy of Dom's, who had recently passed away.

But in spite of the circuitous route they had chosen, Dom was sure to be seen and heard by scores of people in this, the most populous state in the nation. Also, the authorities would certainly attempt to ascertain its flight path from the farm to its ditching point, once the caliber of the major weapon and the angle at which it had been employed were discovered. Payson had marked the spot earlier in the day as he was sailing south. It was a "hole," a 200-meter depression in the continental shelf about five miles to the northeast of Barnegat Inlet.

Said Payson, "The RICO commission has taken many of our key personnel. And maybe you've heard, like I have, that they're going to try for our money. The talks with the Antilles and the Cayman Islands that the federal government began in '85 are about to be concluded, and my contact tells me it doesn't look good for anybody sheltering tax-free dollars in those places. As we know, Switzerland went down as a haven in '86 with their reporting of the Marcos billions. It's only a matter of time before they begin reporting, say—" Payson waved a hand "—terrorist money or drug money or Mafia—" he nearly shouted "—money. In the present political environment, we can't be too careful. And I don't have to tell you how much is at stake."

Millions, their eyes read. They were watching Payson closely. The beat of the rotors was louder now, and one of the men turned and looked behind him, off at the Barnegat Lighthouse, which now that the edge of the storm front had passed was silhouetted against the sparkling blue sky.

"Added to that, we've got the DEA and FBI and other federal and state people on us. They all want to make a splash, and they smell blood. That's why I asked you to meet me here, of all places, where we can be sure we're alone and unobserved. That's why I'm telling you now that already I've had to move some of our money, and I want your permission to move the rest. I've got a plan, which I'll outline to Babe here, if you're for moving it. He can then tell you, if he so chooses. But the fewer who know the details, the better, just in case you say no and sometime in the future we want to come back with it. I've taken precautions that if anything should happen to me, nothing will be lost. Babe knows about those precautions already."

Infantino nodded and drew on his cigar. He, too, began to turn to the noise of the helicopter, which was, Payson estimated, now maybe six or seven miles away. He had to hurry.

"If you don't or won't or can't—" he raised a hand "—that's your decision. But I can't guarantee all of the funds. For sure we'll lose all the new stuff, and by that I mean anything later than '84."

Some of the men grumbled and looked down at their shoes. Said Mazullo, "Christ—before '84 my guys didn't have squat. I mean, nothin' like we got today."

Said another man, "But *where,* if not any of the places you just said? I mean, where else is there? In general. I don't want to know the particulars."

"Well—?" Payson asked, referring the decision to divulge even that much information to Infantino, who nodded. "We're going to keep half of it in Switzerland and the other half—just to be safe—in little San Marino."

"Where's that?" another asked.

"It's in Italy, actually, about thirty miles west of Rimini. Like the Papal States, it's an independent nation, and the oldest republic in Europe. We own a bank there, and San Marino's laws don't require us to divulge share- or account-holders. I can report that our bank is doing very well, very well indeed." All of what Payson had just represented to them was the truth, which was easiest to tell, because in a very few minutes it wouldn't matter what he had told them. He kept his eyes on the horizon to the southeast.

"But *Switzerland?* I thought you said after Marcos that place wasn't safe. And what about that Levine guy from Wall Street? They busted his ass but good, and he had all his stuff in Switzerland."

"And Duvalier, the dictator's son from Haiti. They got nailed, the both of them," another added. "This guy don't think we read the papers."

Payson raised a hand. "You weren't listening closely. I said it wasn't safe for terrorist money or drug money or Mafia money, but consider this. First, by the time our money gets there, it's no longer identifiable as crime money. That's why you pay me.

"Second, the Swiss economic miracle—a history of un-

173

broken prosperity unequaled by any nation in the world—was begun during the French revolution when emigrés discovered that Swiss bankers would accept and shield their deposits from any external inquiry. At the present time, the world has more than $500 billion lodged in the banks of a country the size of the state of Maine, and Swiss bankers, afraid that their reputation for confidentiality and discretion has been tarnished, have gotten a Catch-22 passed into law. It makes the kind of investigation that a RICO commission or the DEA would launch dependent upon just the information that only Swiss banks themselves would have and would never reveal: deposit dates, denominations and amounts, withdrawal activity.

"And finally—say all of our money was in none of our names."

"What?" Fred Mazullo asked. "That don't make sense. If it's not in our names, how we get it out?"

"Through an intermediary. Somebody who's utterly clean, somebody who would very probably have a good, if limited, use for a Swiss bank account. Somebody in a legitimate cash business who over the years might have taken some tax-free profits that a Swiss bank could shield."

"The broad? The one from the restaurant?" Grisanti asked. "Compared to our action, that's only a piss-ass place."

Payson nodded. "Just the person. And the smaller her operation, the better. The less chance she'll be singled out for scrutiny here. Over there, dollar amounts mean the same as they mean here—the more the merrier. Swiss bankers are businessmen. They're not performing a public service, they're out to make profits. Marcos and Duvalier were political cases and made international headlines. Switzerland is a functioning democracy, and the Swiss people won't tolerate despots secreting blood money in Swiss banks. Levine? In that case, the U.S. government had a handle. The Swiss invest here. They've made and will continue to make billions on Wall Street, and they couldn't let a little snake like him get in their way. Pressure was brought to bear.

"But, look—" If only as a kind of courtesy, Payson had to get Infantino away from the others. Getting himself away, however, was another imperative altogether, and for the first time in recent memory tendrils of fear coursed through his body.

Over their shoulders to the south he could now actually see the helicopter imposed like a kind of dark, mechanical spider on the horizon of a postcard-perfect beachscape. "—we don't or we won't have money in Wall Street, and we're despots only in our own houses and to those who get in our way. I was educated in Switzerland, I presently own a chalet outside Bern; for thirty years I've been mediating between here and there, and I've developed the best contacts in the most discreet banking house in that country. To put it bluntly, they'll guard our dough like it's their own, and on the amounts we've got to put away they're presently paying 9.5 percent tax-free in a currency that's been solid for 400 years.

"Try—" Payson glanced up at the helicopter; four miles or three and closing "—just try to get that anywhere else in the world.

"Babe?" Payson now asked Infantino, taking a step away from the others and waiting that so the older man would follow him.

Said Infantino, moving forward, "Don't none of you guys slip out for a smash while I check this out."

A few of them laughed, but already his two guards had turned to the helicopter, which, having rounded the lighthouse and cleared the granite breakwaters on either bank of the inlet, now dipped radically down in the nose so that the tips of its landing gear nearly touched the sand and its tail and tail rotor could be seen against the sky. And there it seemed to hesitate for a moment, as if sighting on them.

But then, as Payson kept drawing Infantino away, it sprang forward, the throb of the main rotor so loud now it seemed to be coming right out of the sand.

"Aw, Christ," one of the men said, "don't tell me we're gonna be busted."

Said another, "Nah—that's just some asshole from the National Guard playing soldier."

Infantino's two keepers had both drawn weapons, but before they could turn and plant themselves, tiny bursts of flame, like the signal of some baleful code, were seen to

175

issue from the nose of the copter, and they heard the thwack of something soft and hollow, like a melon being struck by a large, dense stone. The chest of one of the men—his tan windbreaker flapping—was driven back from him, so that, when his corpse flopped on the sand, it was yards distant, his head skidding under his severed back.

Fred Mazullo, turning to run, found that he couldn't. Looking down, he discovered that his right foot was still facing in the other direction, the femur of the leg having been shortened at the knee. But before he could fall, a 20mm round struck him directly, removing his jaw, a cheekbone, and most of the back of his head.

Two others were strewn in bits across the sand, like paper scattering before a strong wind, and the other four lit out—two toward the water, two across the soft sand toward the dunes and the cars beyond.

Standing beside Infantino, who after the first deafening report of the weapons had not moved even so much as to pull the cigar from his mouth, Payson watched as the Iroquois banked to the left and swung back on the two men, one of whom had just gained the top of a dune. Pulling back the slide of his automatic, the bodyguard turned to Payson and Infantino, as if seeking permission for what he would do, and shouted something like "aid" or "laid" but that was most probably "Babe!" before pivoting in a crouch and with both hands aiming at the gunship.

But like an explosive mine had burst around him, fire from the gunship flowered the dune with sprays of fine sand that were blown away in the rotor blast, like puffs of silver smoke. Until a round, bucking through the top of his head, pinned him, like a supplicating effigy, to the top of the dune.

The other man, Grisanti, was cowering face down in the sand. Considering all the yellow he was wearing and the white pom-pom on his knitted cap, he looked like some large, plump Easter favor—a marshmallow chick—that had been concealed there on the flank of the dune. And he just lay there shaking, crying while the spray from the nose gun walked down the dune and bathed him in a hail of fire. It riddled his body, making it jump and hop. Something on him was flammable—his jacket or sweater, or perhaps he was carrying a flask—and now ignited, the rotor blast quickly fanning the flames into a dark, smudgy fire.

Turning to the two men who had tried to flee into the ocean, Dom from his Olympian height looked down on Payson and Infantino as he passed, his face—cloaked in dark aviator glasses—impassive. The helicopter kicked up a cloud of sand, and Payson turned his head back only after the helicopter had passed beyond them and cut down from afar, as in a kind of distant target practice, the one who had fled up the beach, and then turned to the other man, who was trying to hide by submerging himself in the water.

The guns roiled the water red, and then, as in an intricate dance that began and ended with a single simple step, the gunship paused, raised its tail, and beat directly out to sea. According to plan, Dom, still at wave-top level, would trace a complex, evasive path for two full hours, thereby confusing any attempt to track the helicopter and availing Payson of the necessary time to reach the "hole" where it would be ditched.

Turning away from the helicopter and the ruin of the men on the beach, Infantino discovered that Payson was now holding the TEC derringer.

He sighed and shook his head, the cigar still in the middle of his mouth. "Why not me, like that?"

Payson hunched his shoulders. He really didn't know, except that he suspected that he owed the old man at least that much. No, that was wrong. He owed the old man nothing. He had never asked him for a thing. Everything that had been done for Payson had been voluntary and had given Infantino himself pleasure.

"Because my wife would prefer an open casket?" Their eyes met, and Infantino began to smile, then laugh, his dark eyebrows arching like the wings of a bird. "That's good," he said through his laughter. "I like that. I like that a lot."

A crow, Payson thought. A big, intelligent, raucous raven.

Infantino's face grew red, and tears formed in his eyes. Of joy or of fear? Was the laughter merely a defense mechanism, Payson wondered, a way of distancing himself from the horror of contemplating his own death?

No, he decided. Not once while the helicopter was above them had he tried to run or seek cover. And the laughter now made all that Payson had done and was about to do seem rather banal.

"Well," Infantino went on, after he stopped laughing, "at least it's you, and not some—" He did not complete the thought. He removed the cigar from his mouth. "And what you gonna do, anyways? Run things?" He shook his head. "You and Giancarla? Even as a little girl, she was ashamed of everything about me but my money." Infantino shook his head. He began laughing again, but quietly, wryly. He looked down at the cigar. "Who'd a thunk it?" It had gone out, and he considered the ash. "Imagine—at this moment, of all times. It used to be—" He didn't complete that thought, either. "Hard to get a good smoke nowadays."

Payson raised the TEC and put two quick slugs in Infantino's temple. The holes were dark, almost black, but quickly filled with the brightest blood.

Walking toward the dinghy and scanning the carnage on the beach, he couldn't keep himself from thinking that the man had fallen, as he had lived, proud as a statue.

But Payson had more on his mind than the dead. After ditching the helicopter, they would sail back to New York. There he would drop off Dom, who would take the first plane to Bern. Payson himself would return the yacht to its mooring and drive back to the house in Beekman Place, where he would complete the legal arrangements that would tie off every loose end.

With those details in place and Giancarla gone as well, he, too, would then vanish. For good, by plan.

14

Toni awoke to the aroma of hot, dark coffee with scalded milk. A tray had been placed on the nightstand by her bed. Because of her back, she had had to sleep on her stomach, and her head was turned the other way.

Besides the coffee, the tray would contain a small, wrapped basket of fresh-baked and still hot croissants and brioches and a dish of whipped sweet butter. There would also be a large glass of freshly squeezed orange juice, as she had requested, and a small vase with a single rose and a sprig of fern. Across the bedroom and through the door to the sitting room of the suite, the full bouquet of fresh flowers would soon be replaced. That was if the Schweizerhof in Bern ran true to form.

It was Toni's third morning there, and she waited until the lock on the door to the hall clicked a fourth time before pushing herself off the soft mattress and carefully turning her back into the pillows that had been propped against the headboard. Only then did she open her eyes. For the tastefully decorated suite with its deep drapes and stuffed chairs and sofas, its French windows, paintings, and lithographs of the city and the Bernese Oberland, had soothed her from the moment that she had entered it. And in spite of the hotel doctor's repeated suggestions that she get some air, Toni had remained where she was. He had arrived at her room shortly after she had gotten there, and had looked in on her daily since, sent, she believed, by Payson.

The care was reassuring, and she had given herself over to recovering at least some of her . . . was it dignity? Yes, but her pride, too. R&R, she had made herself think, with the emphasis very much on the first, though she had made repeated phone calls: to her mother-in-law and daughter, who were still at the house of her next-door neighbor, Jane. To Muñoz, her maître d', who needed the direction of an owner who was not Lucca Furco. To Philly, who had been struggling in the kitchen and was buoyed by her encouragement and help.

Philly had said, "But, Ms. Spina—I don't mind the work, the work I can handle. The hours." There was a pause and, lowering his voice, he went on in a rush. "But lemme tell ya, I'm scared. Really scared. The way they— I got to the back door just as—

"And what's what? Those guys, them big two, the gorillas—they work for Furco or what? I saw . . . Solly." His voice broke for a moment. "But when Furco, when I tol' him—who else could I call?—he like blew up, wanted to know everything. And the few times he been here, he's like a wil' man. He wantsa know were you here? Anybody hear anythin' from you? Nobody hear nothin' 'til—"

"And you've still heard nothing, Philly," Toni had said. "Make me that promise. Just shake your head, if he asks, and go on with your work. What about Solly?"

Another pause. "What about him?"

"Any news—in the papers? Have the police been around?"

"No, ma'am. Nothin'. Nobody. His wife calls. She wantsa know where he's at. Muñoz says *we* wanna know where he's at. Ain't here at work. Maybe he's into the booze. Tell him to call here the minute he gets home. But, you know, Muñoz don't know. He just—"

"Suspects," Toni completed. She knew Muñoz well. He was street-smart and careful, and he wouldn't hesitate to pull out if he thought he was in any danger. And without Solly and her *and* Muñoz, they might as well put the key in the door and turn out the lights. "Who does know?"

"Just me and you and Furco, who tol' me shut up totally.

Nothing, not a word. Then there's the guy, the dark-haired guy who took Solly, after, and the guys that done it. And . . . that's it, I guess."

It put another light on things—that Furco, like Dom and Payson, had not known of or sanctioned what had happened to her and Solly. It meant the other three—Mazullo, Scarpone, and Falci—had been acting on their own. Why? What they had said, simple prejudice? Or as a challenge to Furco? There was that in everything young Mazullo had ever done or said in her presence. And, as she understood it, his father was a Mob person himself.

"On the phone first time Furco says, and you excuse me, 'The little bastard! The little bastard!' over and over again. Then later the nex' morning, he says, 'You tell me if any of them come around,' and he gives me some numbers to call."

"May I have them, please?" One thing she knew about Lucca Furco: he would do her a favor, if she asked. And, given her own situation here in Switzerland with her daughter and mother-in-law in Cherry Hill, she might need him. She had heard a lifetime of stories about one boss challenging another or some punk gunning his way into higher ranks. Raids. Hits. Rubouts. How had she gotten herself involved with such people? Jack.

No, not Jack. *She* had gotten *herself* involved with Jack, and the rest was history. But for the first time ever she was glad that she knew Lucca Furco, and that they were in some way associated.

While Philly was gone getting the numbers, Toni forced herself to think of how the kitchen would continue without Solieri's direction and planning. After she'd copied the phone numbers into her address book, she asked, "So, how are you doing there in the kitchen?"

"Okay. Not great like . . . but not bad either. Guy came around, guy you interviewed for a job. Black guy. Waiter. Said he don't want to get stuck back here, but he done it before and could help out."

"Colin Ross?"

"Yeah, Colin. That's his name. Big guy. Good so far. Fast on the grill."

"Put him on."

"Yeah?"

181

"Yes, Philly—put him on, please."

"Anythin' you say, Ms. Spina. Hang on. I got him cleanin' the walk-in."

Said Ross after what seemed like an interminable wait, "Miz Spina?"

"Colin—what are you doing there?"

He hesitated for a moment in which Toni could hear kitchen sounds that only further reminded her of Solly and what had happened. She should have realized how obvious Ross and she must have been, how somebody like Mazullo and the others would have been watching and would have known. And to have been so selfish, to have thought only of her own desires and not how other people might be hurt . . .

No. She had been debating it for the three days since it had happened, and she had decided that she would not burden herself with that guilt. There had been no way she could have anticipated what had occurred, and how could she possibly take responsibility for the actions of people like that?

"Well, you want a story or you want honest?"

"Honest, of course."

He sighed, and then his voice, too, went lower. "Some young guys came by my place couple, three nights ago."

"Three of them in a low, two-door car?"

"Un-hunh."

"And you—?"

"Me? Me, nothin'. They tried to get rough, and I had to deal with that."

She remembered how the car, Mazullo's, had smelled and looked and her first glimpse of the one in the front seat, Scarpone, the one who had raped her—his teeth and nose broken, his eyes nearly swollen shut—though in effect all three of them had raped her.

And she judged that regardless of the chance of scandal, it was best that Colin Ross was there. "Can you take care of the place while I'm away, Colin?"

Did he laugh? She thought he did. "You mean, cookin'? Hey, I can cook but not like Philly. That man's a pro, and he don't do nothin' that ain't right. Las' night he like as worked my—"

"No, not cooking. I mean the three men. And Lucca

Furco. He's—'' she rejected *unpredictable* and *prejudiced* and *vindictive* and settled for ''—volatile. You can never tell with him. And he's not like those other three.''

"Punks," Ross said. "Big, dirty, dangerous punks. Can I ask you something?"

"Of course."

"Who this Luke Furco? He the guy who makes out like he owns the place? And why they following you around, anyhow? They said they followed you to the casino that night. And they must've followed you out to my place."

When she said nothing, he said, "Guess I can't ask you that. Answer me this, then—why you want me to take care of this place? What's goin' down that I should know?"

And when she still said nothing, he kept on, "Where you at, anyhow? This long distance? Sounds like you're speaking through a tunnel."

The spate of questions like this on the phone surprised her. Aside from their *physical* intimacy, he hardly knew her. They had spoken little, and she had been careful not to reveal any details that might further compromise her life. And why, after saying that he would never embarrass her and that he had only applied for a job as a ruse to see her again, had he suddenly again appeared at the Borghese in her absence—to *protect* her?

It also seemed rather farfetched that he would choose to plummet from professional waiter to food prep, even if just for a while. A good waiter could make a couple hundred dollars a day, a kitchen man sixty. And how had he, one man, dealt so easily and brutally with Mazullo and the others?

She thought then of the craps game, the one at the Trump Plaza where she had met him and how, contrary to all the rules, the table had been cordoned off. And his winning. The way suddenly he had won and turned to her. *Had* she been set up twice, once by Payson and Furco and another time only a few weeks ago by Ross and whoever he represented?

How could they know she would be there? It occurred to her for the first time that she hadn't really varied her routine, casino to casino, during all the time that she had been running for Furco. There had been no real need to. As far as she'd been told, she had been doing nothing actually illegal, since the money could very well be—and was on that night— her own, and all sums under $10,000 were not recorded and reported to the IRS.

How could they have known she would gamble and that her game of choice would be craps? Sure—if they had followed her at all, they would have known that she did gamble every week and always at the Plaza and never anything but a little twenty-one just to test her luck for craps.

The whole thing could have been a setup. Then, during the game when she got there, they could have switched in tops, which was the practice of having the stickman switch in dice that would roll only those numbers that would have kept Ross winning without arousing suspicion. Usually a stickman tried to keep a shooter from winning, but with a full set of shaved or loaded tops, a skilled "mechanic"—as a professional boardman was called—could make a game go either way. Also, the table itself could have been confiscated from a "juice joint." Toni had seen one once. The dice had been molded around metal inserts on certain sides, such that when electromagnetic plates that had been built into the table under the felt were activated, the dice, even when stationary, could be made to hop to a seven or a twelve. When the juice was turned off, they behaved normally and would pass anything but an X-ray inspection or a weight test.

And finally she considered Colin Ross's use of ghettoese: improper verbs, double negatives, and incorrect pronunciations from a man who donned granny glasses to read Friedrich Dürrenmatt *auf Deutsch?*

It struck her then that Colin Ross knew very well who Lucca Furco was. "Look, Colin, it's probably too late and the wrong way to ask this, but I have no choice now. Could you—no, no, let me rephrase that—*would* you look after the Borghese? I also have a daughter and mother-in-law at my home in Cherry Hill."

As though acknowledging that some sort of breakthrough had occurred, Ross waited before responding. When he spoke, his tone and even his accent were different. "You mean, with Jane. Well, it's not as though I have an army, but you relax, if that's possible. The place is in good hands. And your daughter. Let me ask you one more time, though—where are you?''

"I'm—" She thought of Dom, who could make himself ubiquitous, it seemed, and Payson, who had advised her that she should either accept or reject his proposal with no half measures. She knew these people. Even if the government did all it could for her, she would still have to leave the area and her business. And then there'd be the worry, daily. If Tina were late five minutes, she'd panic.

And then, had she any reason to doubt Payson? Unlike the man on the other end of the line, he had been nothing but honest with her, up front. What had happened with Mazullo and the others had been either spontaneous or something between them and Furco, she was now convinced. And how could Ross, whoever he was or was with, help her from Hammonton? "—I can't."

"Sure you can. All's I need is a city, an address. We got people all over the world."

"Who's we?"

It was his turn not to answer. Finally he said, "Well—you hurry back. You got my number?"

"Yes."

"Let me give you another where you can always reach me, one way or another."

After she jotted it into her address book, he said, "*Coraggio*, Antonina," and hung up.

Later, she was mulling this over, sipping her coffee, which had grown cold, when the phone rang again. It was Dom.

"Been making some calls?"

"Yes, to my daughter and my restaurant. I believe you know I'm in business."

"Mr. Payson will be arriving in an hour or so. He wants us to meet him in the—" he fumbled with a German word and added, "grill."

"You're here?" Toni asked.

But all Dom replied was, "Mr. Payson hopes you're feeling better. He'd appreciate it if you could be ready in forty-five minutes. You'll find everything you need in the closet in your room. If you need any help dressing, you can call for a maid."

As on the trip she had taken with Payson to Panama and St. Maarten, Toni discovered that the bags that had been packed for her were filled with only the most tasteful and costly original designs by couturiers like Christian Dior and Pierre Cardin, with a difference this time. Into the lining of each garment, even into linings of the handmade shoes that fit her nearly perfectly, had been sewn an identifying tag that had not been recently added.

Using the compact sewing kit given to her by her father years before, Toni discovered that the hand that had stitched the custom tailoring in one suit jacket was the same hand that had attached the name tag to the lining. As her father had told her, "For tailors, stitching is like handwriting or fingerprints. No two tailors stitch the same. It's a matter of coordination and personality, and once it's learned, it's like your signature."

All the tags read "Giancarla Marchetti" or simply "G. Marchetti," the name she had traveled under then and now.

A real person, this Giancarla Marchetti? At first she had thought not, the name being so unlikely and romantic-sounding, at least to her ear. But many of the clothes were just slightly out of date, and some bore unmistakable signs of having been worn before. Then, every pair of shoes in that closet had been constructed with an arch that was just slightly higher than Toni's and pressed against the bottom of her foot with each step. And whoever had worn them—Toni was now guessing Giancarla Marchetti herself—had a third toe that was just slightly shorter than hers. Whenever Toni took a long stride, pushing off on the ball of her foot, her toe, moving back, slid into the depression that the other woman's had made in the soft leather.

Hurrying now, Toni chose an exquisite silk marocain suit that had pleated pants and a jacket with short above-the-elbows sleeves. It fit snugly at the waist and took some doing to get on without pain. But it showed a broad swath of the nearly transparent silk georgette sleeveless top beneath and looked on her—Toni believed—quite nice. For lipstick she chose from an array of colors in the makeup case, which had also been provided, a color called champagne. The sprays and perfumes were all by Hermès.

In two leather bags from a furrier on the Rue de la Paix

she found a sur Bukhara broadtail coat with a sable scarf, and the most beautiful and lavish display of fur that she had ever seen. It was an ankle-length, natural Russian sable coat that sparkled like silver and rather complemented her hair, she judged.

But what could such a thing cost? Again she searched for a name tag. What point was Payson trying to make with it and the other things? That Giancarla Marchetti was an expensive and/or wealthy woman who thought nothing of keeping fifty- or sixty-thousand-dollar furs in a leather bag in a hotel closet to which maids and porters had access? Or that A. A. Spina, the woman who was "doing some banking," as he had put it when they had first spoken, was merely looking the part? Then why travel under one name and conduct business under another?

Obviously to leave a trail as one woman while obscuring the identity of the other. But again, why? To set Giancarla Marchetti up?

And how had they gotten her clothes? Robbery? Theft?

Anything was possible.

In a jewelry box she next discovered an incredible diamond-and-amethyst choker by Boucheron with a bracelet and ring that completed the set. The stone in the ring was almost garish. But whoever had chosen the piece had understood her coloring, and she could not keep herself from wondering if it had been purchased just for the purpose that they were about. How many women had silvering auburn hair and skin the color of her own? Few. None that she knew.

Pausing before the mirror to fit on gloves that she imagined were also colored "champagne," Toni glanced at the choker and wondered if it was a symbol. And of what?

Opening the door upon Dom, who was waiting in the hall, she had an idea.

He was dressed again in his gray chauffeur's uniform. "Afternoon, ma'am." He took the sable coat, which Toni had been unable to resist, from her and let her lead them to the shimmering, leaded-glass facade of the elevator.

There was artwork everywhere in the old hotel: religious figures carved in wood for which the Swiss were renowned, metalwork plates and pots in copper and brass, paintings by

Swiss masters, and great bowls and vases of fresh flowers. For a moment Toni allowed herself to appreciate the setting.

It was just three o'clock, and clocks were ringing throughout the hotel and the city.

Payson was seated at a low table near the horseshoe bar in the hotel's Schultheissenstube grill, reading, as ever. In his lap was a magazine. On the long, thin bridge of his nose was a pair of half-glasses. Though the bar area was crowded and noisy, he seemed absorbed.

He had his suit jacket draped over his shoulders, and he was wearing a maroon paisley ascot beneath a light pink silk shirt. Although the suit was gray, its weave contained strands of deep red that blended with the Moroccan leather of his shoes and made him look at first glance like a scholar or a professor or some slowly aging man of letters of moderate means who was rather lost there amidst the crystal and gleaming copper and wood of the bar.

Until Toni got closer. It was then that the care he took of himself and his appearance became obvious. The material of the suit was costly and his cuff links gold. As he turned a page, the silk of the shirt tugged at the well-defined line of a bicep, and the skin of his face was supple and tanned. And finally—she stopped before him, Dom a step behind—there was an air of unconcern about H. Bruce Payson, a certain distance, as though he had freed himself from most contingencies and now engaged life only through surrogates.

Like a well-dressed lackey, Toni now waited for him to acknowledge her presence, and it was obvious that the dramatic pause was consciously intended. For as though only just becoming aware of her, he slowly lowered the magazine and looked up, his unlikely blue eyes searching her face.

A full smile broke. "Ah—Giancarla," he said overloudly, standing. *"Come va?"* He was a tall, handsome man, and more heads turned to them. In English he added, "I hope your trip from New York was pleasant," when in point of fact it had been he who had just arrived from New York.

"Male? Well—perhaps we can remedy that. Shall we take a stroll? We can as easily walk to our appointment. Dom." Payson looked down at the sable coat, which the chauffeur

now raised and draped over Toni's shoulders. Dom then picked up Payson's bag.

Somebody behind her murmured something in French that ended in ". . . *magnifique*," and a waiter with a tray, stepping aside to let them pass, stared first at her face, then at the choker, and finally at the coat.

Out in the hall, Payson said, "Well—how *are* you? I hear you ran afoul of the *canaglia* there in South Jersey. But you're well." He glanced at her. They were walking his pace, which was quick. His legs were long and rangy and there was a boyish bounce to his step. "At least, you look smashing, and Dom tells me that the hotel doctor says there's no sign of infection. Are you enjoying yourself?"

The city was known for its arcades. The one they now began walking through was labeled Schweizerhof Passage in bold, backlit letters and had been constructed right through the hotel. Both sides were lined with specialty shops.

Payson stopped suddenly before one. "I hear you lost your watch in the fracas. There's no place like Bern to buy a good watch. Let's see if we can remedy your loss."

He directed her to the window, which was arrayed with watches. Inside Payson bid the clerk good day in German, and with the same charming insouciance scanned what was offered in the cases before them.

"Do you see anything you like?" he was asked.

"As a matter of fact, I don't," he said. "What I want is this." He slipped his own watch off his wrist and handed it to the woman. "But for a lady."

The woman turned her head to the side and clicked her tongue. "It would be in the safe. I'll get the owner."

He soon appeared, having to raise a watchmaker's monocle from in front of a lens of his regular eyeglasses to look at them. "Ah—Monsieur Sevrier. *Il y a longtemps.* How good to see you. How many years has it been?"

"Too long, Jurgen. How are your wife and family?"

"All grown now, I'm afraid."

"Afraid? I should think you'd say 'at last.' "

The man was balding, and what hair remained he combed back close to his head in the style that seemed the acceptable norm among middle-aged Swiss men. He removed his thick glasses and stared down at them. "No, Henri—it's like suddenly we're bereft, my wife and I. Hilda has moved to Basel. She's a dentist now. And Jurgen, our journalist, has opted for foreign parts—South Africa at one moment, the Lebanon at another—and without either of them home, our days are filled with nothing but worry. It's better never to have children in the first place." Without his glasses, the watchmaker's weak eyes squinted from Payson to Toni and back. "You give them so much, but they take so much more away when they leave."

Said Payson jocularly, "I'll take that advice," and, turning to Toni, he added, "You remember Jurgen Hummacher, don't you, dear?" And to Hummacher, "Jurgen—my wife."

"Of course, of course," said the watchmaker. "I believe I recognized you yesterday, or was it the day before, Madame Sevrier, when the doorman at the Schweizerhof was helping you out of a taxi. I hope you weren't ill?"

Toni only shook her head and tried to smile, wondering why suddenly she had changed from Giancarla Marchetti to Madame Henri Sevrier, or were they one and the same? And H. Bruce Payson—was that his name, or was he Sevrier?

The man soon located the requested watch. It was a platinum BVLGARI quartz wristwatch with a platinum-and-gold-weave band and gold bezel. The hours were marked in diamonds, and the face of the watch was a disk of sterling silver.

"I wonder if we could have it inscribed?" Payson asked.

"Yes. Certainly. Immediately, if you so wish."

"I do, Jurgen. How about something simple like, 'To Giancarla from Papa.'"

Hummacher looked perplexed. "Papa?" he asked.

Payson smiled. "It's a *nom d'affection.* Just between us."

While they waited, they perused the other items that the shop offered, Payson pointing out to Toni the differences in craftsmanship and quality of those things he recognized.

When Hummacher returned, Payson said, "Over the years I've discovered that this woman has a flaw."

"I can't imagine that," the watchmaker replied gallantly.

"She smokes. I wonder if we might have a lighter to match." Payson flashed his own lighter, and the man produced its slimmer counterpart.

"Are you in Konstanz now or Grindelwald?" he asked as they were leaving the shop.

"The latter. You can send the damage there."

And to Toni he said, when they had left the passage and stepped "outside" under a further line of arcades that canopied many of the walkways in the center of Bern, "Happy now?"

She could manage only a thin smile. Magnificent as the presents were, she wondered if he thought that in any way they might compensate for what had happened at the Borghese.

Yet again Payson or Sevrier or whatever his name was seemed to read her thoughts and, turning up another arcade that seemed to be leading them farther into the city, he took her by the arm. "So—it seems some explanation is in order."

Glancing up at his face, she noted that in spite of what must be significant jet lag his eyes were bright and there was color in his cheeks. He seemed exuberant or somehow energized. His grip on her arm was firm, and he was smiling slightly. And for the first time she wondered what it would be like really to be Mrs. H. Bruce Payson or Madame Sevrier. Here was a bright, intelligent, handsome, and, in his own way, sensitive man who was nothing if not capable. And wealthy.

But what else she could only guess.

15

Bern had long appealed to Payson, and he now enjoyed again prowling its damp, vaulted sidewalks as he had when a student more than thirty years before.

Having arrived here as a youth still smarting from the discord and confusion of his undergraduate career, he had been immediately soothed by the variety and medieval utility of the arcaded Bernese streets. Ambling out in almost any direction from the digs that he had shared with several other poor students, he had strolled in all seasons under the five miles of brick-and-sandstone arches that grace Bern's commercial center.

The Bernese, high to low, took time to stop and "jaw"— it was their own term—in their clear but vowelly German even with a student and an American at that with the unlikely name of dePasquale. Once he'd said it, he was usually asked, *"Parla italiano?"* and with a reply in kind he was then scrutinized even more closely and often introduced to some member of Bern's small but influential Italian community.

One Schwyzerdütsch-speaking man, whom Payson had met in a café, had even taken an afternoon off to drive the young law student out to the chalet of the chairman of a private Bern banking house whose own surname was simply Pasqual. Thus had begun a friendship that had lasted nearly thirty years and which Payson was about to renew.

True, the city itself—Payson now drew Toni to him before

stepping out of the arcade and crossing over to the Marktgasse—was one of the most quaint and well preserved in all of Europe, but the other benefits of living here attracted him equally. In spite of his trim shape, Payson enjoyed dining well, and the Bernese cuisine was international in the best sense. Then, the local wines were mild and fine and too special to have been discovered by the rest of the world, by which Payson meant America. And then, even the weather, which the arcades had been built to defeat, conspired to make Bern a special place. For within a radius of ten miles, Payson had often enjoyed a comfortable day's sail and swim in Lake Thun only to find himself skiing by moonlight through fresh powder snow on Kandersteg or Blümlisalp, two of the promontories that formed the great wall of the Alps not far from Bern to the south.

But it was when he'd learned the history of the city and become acquainted with the Bernese character that Payson decided there was more to be learned from the circumspect, confidential, and wise Bernese than from the international law he was studying at their university. For by their sheer calculating ability, by waiting and bargaining and purchasing, they had succeeded in making their modest city—packed as it was into a narrow isthmus on the Aare—both dominate Swiss politics and acquire a disproportionate share of the world's wealth.

In his own quiet, confident way, the poor law student had then begun developing the contacts with and knowledge of Swiss banking—its havens and opportunities for inconspicuous profit—that formed the basis of his career in New York. Not once, however, did he forget Bern, for it was here in the Bernese Oberland and not in the Midi or Monaco or La Spezia that Payson recreated at least once a year and planned what would now necessarily be a most reclusive early retirement.

Having traversed the length of the Marktgasse, another arcaded street that was lined—as the name suggested—with further shops, they now approached Bern's famous *Zeitglocken Turm* before which a crowd of tourists and children with nannies and young mothers had now gathered.

"How felicitous," said Payson to Toni. "Do you know of this thing? It's been the ultimate clock since 1530. There's

193

nothing like it in the entire world." He waited until her eyes looked up to meet his. They contained reddish highlights like the color of her hair.

Yes, he thought, she was more beautiful than Giancarla and even more elegant in the way that she carried herself. There was a certain self-possession, the very quality that had caused him to single her out and that he very much admired. And then, this woman was rangier, stronger, and certainly she had proven time and again that she could endure travails that would have incapacitated his companion. But, alas, the fact was that she was *not* Giancarla, and he would need only one woman to keep himself hidden.

Reaching for her wrist, ostensibly to check the time, he said, "Yes, exquisite. And I see we have a few minutes before the show begins." He meant the clockwork performance that accompanied the ringing of every hour. It was the reason that the crowd was gathering.

"Where to begin?" he asked rhetorically, easing them back against a column of an arcade. "With my sincerest apologies. Really." He lit a small, dark cigar. "What happened to your chef and you—" he shook his head, and suddenly the playful expression vanished from his face "—it's proof of who we are and what we're really about."

"We?"

"The people I represent. Our concerns are nothing like this." He swirled the cigar to indicate the square. "That clock tower was constructed in the tenth century, the clockworks themselves in 1530. It took order, centuries of it, to build and preserve this."

It was now a few minutes before four, and the crowd, consisting mostly of children, began cheering as the mechanical jester on the ancient mechanism began nodding its brazen head and ringing two small bells.

"And who is it exactly that you represent? What are their concerns?"

Payson breathed out blue cigar smoke. Leaning against the arcade in his gray chesterfield coat with one leg crossed over the other and the cigar held jauntily in a gloved hand, he seemed confident and fashionable.

The slight smile now returned, and, as with Infantino and the others, he thought, why not tell her at least some of the truth? What harm could it possibly bring? "Oh, disorder and darkness without a doubt, but that doesn't preclude my admiring all of this, does it? Eros and Thanatos, yin and yang, and all that claptrap. The literati would have us believe that creative and destructive forces are really just two sides of a coin."

From a small arch in the clock two bears now appeared. One was piping and the other drumming, leading a procession that included a horseman with a sword, a proud bear wearing a crown, and lesser bears each carrying a gun, sword, or spear.

"And you believe?"

Payson blew out some cigar smoke. "That chaos is the rule, and that what you see here—this city and country with its passion for peace and tranquillity and justice, with very little crime and high standards in everything from how they comport themselves in public to how neat the average"—he waved the cigar—"closet, is an anomaly. Nearly everywhere else, chaos reigns. Take your own Hammonton or A.C. and your 'partner'—can I use that term?—Luke Furco." His smile bared his teeth. "What do you think he's about at the present moment?"

Toni had not thought about it, but now that she did—

"Chaos. Lovely, bloody, destructive chaos, I should imagine, with Messrs. Mazullo, Scarpone, and Falci as the objects of his destructive impulses."

The bears had passed, and now a shiny cockerel began crowing and flapping its wings, after which a knight in golden armor at the top of the tower started hammering out the four strokes of the hour.

Presiding over all was the figure of Father Time. He was seated on a throne in the middle of the tower, holding a sword in one hand and an hourglass in the other.

Said Toni, "But since you admire what we're seeing, your own impulse obviously is to move from darkness to light, from chaos to order. Is it now your intention to purchase all of this with the fruits of chaos?" Payson said nothing, and Toni decided to continue. She hadn't come this far suddenly to be cautious. "It wouldn't surprise me one bit if Monsieur Sevrier establishes or has already established himself here."

Payson smiled and cocked his head. He threw down the cigar. She was quick, perhaps too quick, and there were still two days left. He would have to watch her, and he had had enough of the truth. "We should hurry. Our appointment is in fifteen minutes."

"Appointment?"

"Yes—at perhaps the most exclusive bank in the world." He took hold of her sable-wrapped arm and guided her through the disbursing crowd. "I won't tell you the names of the other depositors for fear you'll begin thinking too highly of yourself."

Toni thought it unlikely. She wasn't even wearing her own clothes.

The two elderly bankers were seated at a long, bare table in what at one time must have been the ballroom of one of the grand private residences of the city. Apart from two other empty chairs and a few smaller tables that had been positioned against the walls between tall French windows, the large room was otherwise devoid of furniture. As Toni and Payson approached the table, the sounds of their heels on the marble floor echoed, like reports from a gun.

Signor Pasqual and Herr Kreis stood. They were wearing wing collars, swallowtail coats, and morning pants. There was a folder in front of Pasqual along with a pen and an inkstand, the well of which was capped by a bronze eagle in flight. Set back from the street behind a formal garden, the house was quiet. Painted on the vaulted, baroque ceiling of the room was a celestial scene that detailed the delights of heaven, chief of which—it seemed to Toni—was nudity.

Payson spoke first, introducing her to Kreis, who, he explained, was the first actual Bernesian he had met when he was a student here, and then to Pasqual, who was the second. Kreis, slightly younger, questioned him about New York, where evidently they sometimes also met, and then, saying that he had a matter to take care of, left the room.

Pasqual's face was square, and he kept his hair, which was still largely dark brown, clipped in a kind of brush cut that made him look to Toni like a fifties tough whom time had otherwise ravaged. His sallow face was creased and lined, and one eye, which had been hazel, was glazed now with age and seemed blinded. A dark mustache, silvering at the tips, concealed teeth that Toni assumed were either bad or missing. With quaking hands he opened a file that appeared to be some sort of banking statement and stared down at it. Somewhere on the other side of the room and through the windows, songbirds were singing.

"So, Henrico—at last after how many years you bring us a client."

"Only thirty-five." Sitting close, Payson had crossed his legs toward Toni and was smiling. "I knew you'd wait, but I was merely preserving my emphasis."

"As I can see." Bending his good eye to the document in front of him, Pasqual scanned the first page and then the two that followed. "Remarkable." And after he had completed his perusal of the file, "Exceptional. And to think that it's not an old fossil, such as I, or a mature gentleman, as you, Henrico, who has amassed this fortune, but rather a beautiful young woman."

Ponderously returning the sheets to their original order, Pasqual looked up at her. "Well, Ms. Spina—life has been good to you. May I ask what your plans are for this money? Much as I would like it, I don't believe for a moment that you will leave much of it parked in our bank." As though in caress, his old hand, inspissated with knobby veins, passed over the agreement.

Said Toni, "Only to continue to allow life to be good to me."

Payson smiled.

"I mean, for investment purposes. Will you be seeking equity or income, or some combination of goals? As you obviously know, since you've decided to make us your depository, we provide investment counseling that has proved rather successful over the years. We charge a fee, of course, but only if we make you money over and above standard interest rates."

Said Payson, "I believe I've already dealt with that, Franco. Ms. Spina has asked me to act as her financial advisor, but since we plan to keep ourselves at least 20 percent liquid at all times, all of us will profit. For openers, we plan to take advantage of the present currency market, and you could surely help us with that. For a fee."

"Specifically?"

"Oh, Taiwan and Singapore dollars. The yen. The deutsche mark."

As they spoke, it struck Toni that the old man was either a consummate actor or that Payson had done such a thorough job of laundering the funds through so many intermediary countries and banks that it had lost every trace of its source.

When the conversation returned to the matter at hand, Pasqual asked Toni, "Then I suppose you know the procedure for deposits and withdrawals?"

Toni neither raised an eyebrow nor blinked, which the banker took for a yes, and turned back to the first page of the agreement. "Then shall we complete the registration process, after which I hope you'll join us for tea. We serve perhaps—"

"No, no, Franco. Thanks very much, but we must beg off. As it is, we're pressed for time. Unfortunately we have another engagement."

"More banking?"

"Don't tell me you're getting paranoid in your old age. And greedy."

"Of course not—I was *born* both of those things, as you well know, or you wouldn't be here."

They laughed, and the old eye again swept Toni before Pasqual said, "So—to proceed. I must ask for your signature, Ms. Spina, at every point at which you see—"

It was then that the door at the other end of the room opened, and a young man entered, walking quickly toward them.

Pasqual looked up.

"There is a telephone call from New York for Mr. Payson. The caller says it's urgent. An emergency."

"Who is it?"

"The lady would not give her name. She said you would know."

Payson's eyes moved from the servant to the documents on the table to Toni and then back to the young man. "Can't I take the call here?"

"I'm sorry, sir. The closest telephone is in the hall. Right near the door to this room."

Payson's head turned, as though to look behind him, but suddenly he seemed to regain his composure. He smiled. "It's probably my secretary. One person's definition of an emergency is another's of a challenge. She once called me in London when a copy machine broke down, but she's valuable in other ways."

The banker nodded and smiled, and Payson followed the man toward the hallway where the telephone was located. He left the door open. They heard him say, "Yes?" He listened, then, "I told you, no, you can't. You're to remain there . . . at your desk until I return. It's absolutely essential that there be no deviations."

In the reflection off the French window behind the banker, Toni could see Payson standing in the doorway while he spoke, watching them.

Said Pasqual to her, "Have you known Henrico for long?"

Meeting the old man's gaze, which, she suspected, saw more than his creased face and pleasant smile and one good eye would suggest, Toni wondered how she should answer. As Payson's minion, or as somebody who genuinely wanted to know more for only the best reason—her life? Obviously Pasqual had known Payson for some time, but equally obvious was his ignorance of what Payson was to her.

Still she said nothing; Payson was not a man who would give her a second chance.

"Not long, I gather. This—" with one hand he slid the banking agreement forward "—is an enormous amount of money, a fabulous sum. From what we know of you, you are neither a political person nor a criminal. We also understand, however, that your only known source of income is a rather large restaurant, but still, a restaurant. How you came by this money and whether all possible tax has been paid on it is no concern of ours. You are declaring yourself the true owner of this account, and we have in no way provided active assistance in the flight of capital, which is all our new law, the *convention de diligence,* requires. We are under no obligation to observe American laws, and unless the proper authorities there make the proper representations here naming you and this obscure little bank here in Bern, it's a matter between you, me, Signor Payson, and—'' Pasqual pointed to the ceiling and smiled benignly.

Toni let her eyes fall to the top sheet of the agreement. Her back was to Payson, who was still on the phone in the hall, but all she could read was what she guessed was the name of the bank, which was printed in bold type, and the account number, which had been completed with pen and ink:

Die Nydegg Finanz Gaselltschaft

Konto #: 371

Used to the many digits and computer codes of American banks, Toni wondered if there could only ever have been 371 depositors in the history of the bank, or did the figure refer to current accounts?

"What should concern us now, however, is the disposition of your assets." Pasqual's good eye flickered over Toni's shoulder toward the open doorway and the sound of Payson's voice. "Often it is better to get several opinions when one is investing her money.

"Suffice it to say that we are well experienced at this sort of thing, and Henrico can only be less so. Mind you, I admire him and value his friendship. But this is business, as you Americans say, and Henrico is a lawyer by training, I understand. Though we've tried, we've found it impossible to learn more about H. Bruce Payson. That *is* his current name, isn't it?"

Toni said nothing. She didn't nod, she didn't blink.

"Well—in matters as essential as one's financial well-being, one should seek out an investment specialist, wouldn't you think? Do you have my card?"

Payson now left the doorway, obviously to hang up the telephone.

Should she chance it? What was she risking if Payson discovered she had taken the old man's card? She could always say that she couldn't refuse, that he had handed it to her saying he wanted to have dinner: "I think he wanted . . ."

But how long would it take him to produce the card and slide it toward her?

She shook her head.

Slowly Pasqual leaned away from the exquisite Louis Quinze table that was patterned with inlaid gold and multicolored woods and opened the drawer. And it took forever, it seemed, for his fingers to produce not a wallet-sized business card but rather an engraved sheet the size of a note card that he pushed toward her, just as Payson entered the room and turned to close the door. His footsteps were rapid, and she could see in the reflection off the window that he was staring intently at them as he approached.

"Between us," the banker added, flicking the card with the nail of his middle finger so that it glided across the table and fell in her lap.

She placed her hands over it.

"So—what gives?" said Payson, standing over her and looking down at the table. With two fingers he moved the banking agreement back toward Pasqual, who asked, "May we proceed now?"

"Yes, definitely. Please excuse the interruption. I could see that you two were getting to know each other."

The banker waved a hand and looked toward the windows beyond which they could hear the songbirds warbling. "A beautiful woman. After all, Henrico, it's spring, is it not?"

Payson turned to reach for the arm of his chair and draw it yet closer, and Toni slipped the card up the left sleeve of the sable coat.

When she signed the banking agreement, she kept that arm beneath the table and her eyes straight ahead. Payson said they should read the fine print, and only after a pause did he allow her to write her name.

Before leaving, she asked to use the ladies' room, and there she wrote on the back of Pasqual's card the number 371, the way she had seen it on the bank document. She then folded and placed it under the flap of the leather case in which she kept her passport, the one that said she was Giancarla Marchetti.

At the Schweizerhof she discovered that Dom had packed their bags and checked them out.

"Where are we going?" she asked Payson.

"To my chalet. Or, rather, the chalet of Henri Sevrier, in Grindelwald. We'll rest a day there and see if you're up for a kind of climb and a long, cold hike, at the end of which I can promise you all the sun and warmth that you'll ever need. We've got one more deposit to make, and then the Borghese in Hammonton, New Jersey, is yours free and clear." He smiled. They were waiting for Dom to ease a long, black Mercedes past a queue of taxis in front of the hotel.

Once inside the car, though, he added, "This will be no usual fifty miles. Are we ready, Dom?"

"All set."

"Bags?"

"They're gone."

"Under what name?"

"Spina."

"Anybody see you?"

The chauffeur glanced in the mirror. *"Bruce,"* he admonished.

Payson held up a conciliating palm. "Just checking." He turned to Toni and smiled, but she couldn't help wondering at their relationship, his and Dom's.

But the Mercedes never left Bern. They passed complexes of Swiss federal government buildings, which Payson pointed out to Toni, and at least a half dozen times they crossed the Aare, passing over one picturesque bridge after another. "Sight-seeing," Payson said. But Dom drove at speed, running stoplights whenever he could and taking them down back streets and alleys that could scarcely accommodate the wide car.

They left it in a cul-de-sac that, surprisingly, was just around the corner from the Schweizerhof and the train station. There they took a local train to a charming town called Spiez on Lake Thun, where another, smaller car was waiting, and drove back through Bern to the town of Burgdorf on the Emme.

There they boarded another train that delivered them to Otten, and finally, traveling in separate compartments, yet another train that took them to Interlaken, where late at night in a parking lot several streets from the train station they again joined up at a Land Rover that Dom then drove

202

high into the mountains. At first light, which was a deep mauve blush to the east that Payson said promised fair weather, they arrived at the chalet.

Toni was too exhausted both mentally and physically for the breakfast that a servant, who referred to Payson as Monsieur Sevrier, prepared. Instead she went straight to a bed so deep in down that she thought she might smother.

16

By Friday afternoon, "Tiny" Rik Falci was feeling much better. The back of his right hand no longer hurt like hell, and the doctor—Dino's cousin in Philly—had told him that all the veins and tendons would heal, "if you keep that thing in the splint and don't move your fingers. *At all.*"

Falci was trying. In fact, he had dedicated the rest of the month and maybe a couple more to nothing else, since suddenly he couldn't get hold of Dino Mazullo in spite of what had happened to his old man and the others on the beach. Then, the doctor had rushed the Bear to the U. of Penn. Hospital in Philly. He had lost so much blood and was so messed up from coke and the beating the nigger had given them that he could've died of shock.

"*Should*'ve died," Dino had said the last time Falci saw him, which was a couple of days ago. They'd met in a little coffee shop in Manahawkin just about the time that Mazullo's old man must've been getting it, and Dino had made sure there was a clear run to the back door where he'd parked his mother's sky blue Camaro out of sight. He jumped every time the door opened and ordered nothing but coffee.

Falci ate for strength. His mother, who was Irish, had always told him when he got hurt: "Your body has to recover. You must give it the goodness it needs to repair itself," and he tucked away a plate of steak and eggs and

204

another of pancakes and sausage swimming in syrup while
Dino tore up Scarpone. "Asshole like that, letting that nigger
walk all ovah him. Christ—you think he coulda taken him.
Old man. Old! How old you think he was? Without the Bear
there, I bet you could of . . . you could of made your play
first."

Falci had looked away. He *had* been there, he had seen
Colin Ross in action, and he was glad it had been Scarpone
and not him who had taken it to the guy. Then, he had been
against the whole night from the start, what had happened.
Far as he could remember, both things—the nigger and the
woman—had been Mazullo's ideas, like the murder of the
chef, which at least he'd done himself. And his talk over
breakfast bothered Falci even more.

Sure, there were the police to worry about, but so far
nothing about the restaurant incident had hit the papers,
which was odd. Had the wide dude, the one in the tan coat
who seemed to be with the broad, had he taken care of it?
Why? Or maybe the police were keeping it quiet so they
could tag them easy? Any case, Falci wouldn't get a head-
ache over the story not showing up, but Luke Furco was a
whole other thing.

Falci knew Luke Furco, and with Scarpone out of commission and Mazullo's father and nearly every other guy
who had been somebody in South Jersey dead, Furco was
pretty much in the saddle, if he wanted to be, and it wasn't
like Furco to let slide anything like what had happened at
his restaurant, especially with a broad he had a thing for.

Worse still, could it have been Furco who'd whacked out
the big wheels there on the beach with some kind of plane
or chopper, they still didn't know which? One of the bodies—Grisanti's—was so screwed up the immediate family
couldn't make a positive ID. Mazullo's old man had been
almost decapitated. Some mother of a slug had taken out a
big piece of his neck, the back of his head, and his jaw, so
that what was left was just held on by skin. Falci had bought
all the papers—the locals and the ones from Philly and New
York.

When Dino and him had left the coffee shop, Falci had
asked, "So—where you goin'?"

"None of your fuckin' business."

"Hey—you know what you sound? You sound scared shitless, my friend."

"And you ain't?"

"Wasn't my idea to take it to that nigger. You fuck the broad? I know I didn't. And I didn't pop that chef with that skinning knife neither. Asshole thing to do. Where was the point, guy like that? You could've locked your door, rolled up the window." Falci shook his head.

"Hey—it's done, ain't it, and if you're getting any ideas, lemme remind you it wasn't the first for any of us, okay? You got that?"

Falci eyed Mazullo closely. Was he fucked up on something? Coke or speed? Or was he just fucked up in general?

"And you think that'll matter to him?" Mazullo went on. "You were there, is all he'll wanna know. You held her legs, I seem to remember. That's why your hand got hit."

Falci looked away, at his Gran Prix baking in the sun of the sandy parking lot behind the coffee shop. "I was hoping you forgot that." He thought for a moment it had come down to a him-or-me, and he should take the little bastard for a ride. One thing he knew about Mazullo, the guy was a coward and undependable in a spot, and now without his old man to prop him up? What if he delivered him to Furco? What would that get him?

But there had been too many in the coffee shop who'd seen them together, and Falci wasn't the sort of button man who could just whack a guy out because he knew it was better if he did.

No, Falci had to work himself up, get pissed off, make up some *reason* to waste a guy, and even then it was almost enough to make him puke. Truth was, he was really a pretty laid-back guy, and he'd been against sticking that restaurant broad from the moment Mazullo pulled out the coke to their stopping near the dumpster where she'd have to walk right by their car. When the thing got going, well—that was something else; and he thought he wanted to tell Luke Furco the first part, if he only could bring himself to call him up.

But the deeper truth, the one Falci knew but would never admit to himself, was that he was really as much of a coward as Mazullo, and then where he was now—on a piece of barren beach in Holgate where in high school they used to come to drink and party—there was no phone, and maybe Furco didn't know he had been with the other two. After all, he'd been in the backseat, and the Trans-Am had tinted windows. The broad? Maybe she went into shock after the blow Mazullo had given her.

Mazullo, Falci thought. Yeah—he should've saved Furco the trouble and made Mazullo the thing to get him back to the only kind of work he knew that wasn't work and paid good. There was still the possibility.

Pushing himself off the beach blanket with his one good hand, Falci paused a moment and looked in every direction. You could never tell with a sneaky suck like Furco, even though only a couple of guys would know he might be here. One of them was in the hospital and the other probably halfway to the moon.

It had turned hot, and the sun had lulled him and made him feel draggy and sweaty, and he thought he'd cool out in the water. He'd been in yesterday and the day before and had even tried jogging up one side of the beach and down to the point at Beach Haven Inlet. But it was boring and what was the point? He had the place to himself. There hadn't been nobody but a couple of surf casters for three whole days and now some big-ass sportfisherman maybe a half mile off the beach.

He picked the bikini bathing suit out of where it had stuck in the crack of his ass.

Shit—the water was colder than he remembered, but he strode purposely forward. It was in little things—like this, he decided—that a person got the mental toughness to be able to survive. Had it come to that? Thinking of what had happened to those guys on the beach, he guessed it had, and also that he'd try to get in touch with Furco that night. He'd give him the rest of the afternoon to cool out.

Furco—could he have done those guys on the beach? Nah. How? And why? It must have been some other guys at their level, or the Feds. They'd gone nuts, like there wasn't a fuckin' *Constitution*, in the past couple years. At least, Falci had heard Mazullo's old man say that.

Waiting until his body was totally immersed and tingling from the cold seawater, Falci eased onto his back and began floating. The surf was light and pleasant and—canceling all previous decisions—Falci decided he'd just get the fuck away from the entire fucking Mob. Soon as he got out of the water, he'd drive straight to Florida, where he had a friend, and he'd find a little nothing job and just exist, free from all this hassle. It wasn't worth it, all the stress.

Falci had always been a good floater, and the sun beating down on his bare belly, along with the waves that rocked him gently, nearly put him to sleep. When he opened his eyes he saw great bursts of summer-blue sky framed silvery by the surf-foam that clung to his eyebrows and eyelashes. The wave-water kept bubbling his ears, blocking out sound and making him believe that he was in his own world where nothing mattered but the water and the wind and the sun.

That was when he felt it. A stinging sensation that began at the top of his spine and continued right down his backbone to the band of his briefs. Falci tried to reach around and touch it, but he got a mouthful of seawater, and the feeling soon went away. And then the sun felt so good, he even began getting a little light-headed, like after a good hit of boo.

Until, opening his eyes, he saw how the sky looked— grainy, with millions of white swimming spots everywhere— and his arms, when he moved them, felt weak.

And then when he tried to touch bottom he found that he had drifted out farther than he wanted and—he cried out in horror—the water all around him was bright red, like with blood.

He started swimming madly, furiously, feeling nothing now but his hands and arms smashing the water, until he touched sand and scrambled up and began running up the beach, grabbing for his stuff—his shirt, the keys to the car, his beach bag that had in it the Ruger GP-100 that had never been registered and that he'd paid a yard for, and his money, $7,700 from the savings account he'd had since he began working at the Steeplechase Arcade when he was a kid.

But bending over, he saw the blood sliding greasy out the leghole of the bikini swim shorts, and he knew he had trouble. Whipping his good hand around, he flinched to feel the trough of the cut that, now he was aware of it, began to hurt like a hot poker pressed to the length of his back. Somehow he'd been cut all down the length of his back, the way Mazullo'd cut the broad with the skinning knife when he ripped off her bomber jacket. And, straightening up, he looked in every direction—up and down the beach, behind him, the water itself—to find Furco, but there was nobody. Only the boat.

Pivoting, Falci began running toward his car, which was parked deep in the dunes where it couldn't be seen from the road. But crazy. Everything seemed out of whack, and he kept stumbling and falling. He lost the shirt and then the gym bag with the Ruger. Fuck, he'd need that. He could see it in the deep dune sand behind him. But he just couldn't bring himself to go back. He had to concentrate on the keys and getting the hell out of there. If the guy could sting him like that when he was relaxing so he didn't even know—

Suddenly he was at the car and in it, and he had the key in the ignition. Nothing. Not even a click. He tried it again. Still nothing. Slapping both hands on the wheel, he cried out like a baby. He wailed. Tears popped from his eyes. He was gonna fuckin' bleed to fuckin' death out here all the fuck alone for that fuckin' little asshole Mazullo. Jesus, he should've iced him, like he'd thought.

"You tell me where he's at, you got a chance," a voice said from the backseat. He knew the voice, but the head and face in the rearview mirror made him jump. It was black-hooded with goggles—a wet suit. There was a Saturn 2-22 machine pistol in his hand. Only Furco carried one of them, and only on a hit.

"How'd you find me?"

"How you think?"

"Mazullo?"

The message had sat for two days on Furco's answering machine before he picked it up.

"The little rat bastard," said Falci.

Ace-ing a witness to murder, thought Furco. The easy way.

"Luke—look, I been wanting to call you. It wasn't me, honest. I was against it from the start. I told him no, it was wrong."

"But you was there."

"Not like you think. I didn't touch her."

209

"You do somethin' to stop him?" Pushing up the passenger seat, Furco pulled up the lock and opened the door.

"You know him and Scarpone. They get a thing in their heads—"

"He says you held her legs. He says you were next. He says you cut her bad, right up the back, and pinched her nipples, pinched them hard till she almost passed out."

"No. Not me. That was him, Mazullo, that little prick. He did it all. He stuck the chef."

With the Saturn aimed at Falci's face, Furco got out of the car and walked around the hood. He opened Falci's door. "Stick out your legs."

"No. Jesus! Lucca! We go back, you and me. Way back. I always done everything you wanted, you know that. To the letter. You ever complain about me? Shit, no. You told the Griz—I heard you—I got brains. Potential. And you know them. They're nuts—Scarpone and that fuck, he wants you bad. He thought he'd—"

"I know what he thought. Stick out your fuckin' legs or I'll blow your head off."

"What you want? Where they are? Scarpone—he's at the U. of Penn. Hospital. That's where they took him. Fifth floor. They got him under his mother's name."

Furco knew that. Mazullo had told him that, too. "And Mazullo?"

"I dunno. I had breakfast with him two—no—three days ago. He was scared shitless. You know, before his old man—" Falci tried to focus on Furco's eyes through the goggles, but he couldn't. Instead, he smiled. "You pull that off, Luke? Was that you?"

Furco touched his finger to the trigger of the Saturn, and in one second a burst of fifty rounds was jacked through its double barrels. The blast was deafening. Furco had aimed the gun at the back of the car, the windows; and the side of Falci's face, his hair, his neck, were spangled with tiny bits and slivers of glass.

He was crying again now. The cloud of gunsmoke made him cough and choke.

"I said, stick out your feet."

Slowly, bawling now, his huge body quaking, Falci turned himself so he could pull his legs from under the steering wheel. He knew he had shit his shorts but he didn't care, just so long as he didn't get blown apart, like his car was now, with the Saturn.

"You say, you tell me now I heard it all?"

"Yeah—everything. I don't know where the fucker is. Honest." He shook his head. "The bastard. He's the one you want."

"He told me you'd be here. Called up and left a message on the answering machine. You know him. Where you think he'd go?"

Falci shook his head. Even after all this time, he really didn't know Mazullo. Guy didn't really like nothing, he had no routines Falci knew of. Except the shit that now had got Falci dead. Mazullo loved that: hitting boardwalk spots, mom-and-pop operations where he could knock people around; banging broads, the bunch of them together; whupping niggers, or at least trying to. Chicken-shit drills and no more, and the shame was Falci had known it all along but done nothing that would've gotten him away and saved his own ass. "He's got a sister in Philly married to some kinda lawyer. They live on Rittenhouse Square, but he wouldn't go near her. He hates her."

"Scarpone's cousin fix you up? The doctor?" Furco jerked the barrel at the bandaged splint on his hand.

Falci nodded.

"What's Mazullo driving?"

"His mother's Camaro. Light blue. Maybe a '85. A '85, I think."

Furco paused, as if debating. "You hold her legs?"

Falci looked away, at the long road out of the dunes, which was how it would be. He knew Furco, and Furco knew he knew the risk.

Falci nodded, and Furco, producing some kind of blade like a straight-edge, in one deep swipe cut both of his Achilles tendons right down at the heel. They actually popped, which surprised Falci, and his calf muscles knotted up painfully.

"Luke—" Falci wailed after Furco, who turned and started through the deep sand toward the beach and his boat. "For crissakes, Luke, I tol' you what you wanted. Ain't it enough that I'll never be able to walk again? And the broad got away. Those fucks would've killed huh."

But Falci knew it was better this way, bleeding to death slow, than with the Saturn. And then, Furco was probably the last . . . you know, human being that he would ever see. He watched him reach down and pick up the gym bag and search through it until he came up with the Ruger GP-100. God, Falci had loved that gun. It was so big and strong, like nothing could ever happen to it. He now started crying, as the picture began to fade for him.

Still, he tried the horn. Nothing.

He swung his fucked legs into the car and closed the door. With all the windows gone, it was drafty in there, and he was cold.

17

Toni awoke to the strangest sensation. It felt as though somebody were drawing a feather down her spine. Pushing herself off the soft mattress, she twisted her body around.

Sometime during the night she had found all the goose down insufferably hot, and she had tossed the quilt off her back and onto the floor. She was still sleeping on her stomach, and the sheet was the next item jettisoned. The bed was so soft it just seemed to encase her in its folds. And now there was Payson, sitting on the edge of the bed.

She glanced at the door, which she thought she had locked. "Yes?" She then realized she was bare from the waist up; Payson's eyes had fallen to her breasts, which were still bruised.

"I just wanted to see." He tried to reach around her and again touch his fingertips to the bristly line of sutures that traced the length of her back, but she leaned away. "Still hurt?"

Drawing the sheet over her, Toni turned around. It did hurt, but she said, "Not much." She raised her wrist and was surprised by the time on her new BVLGARI wristwatch. It was seven o'clock in the *morning?* She glanced around the room, the windows of which were obscured by shutters.

"It's evening," Payson said, standing, "but I brought you a cup of coffee. We want to get an early start in the morning, and I thought, if you tried to sleep through, you'd probably wake up in the middle of the night and find yourself tired tomorrow.

"Then—perhaps you'd like to see the sunset. It's spectacular here in the Alps." He was dressed in a multicolored hand-knitted sweater with a turtleneck under it and knickers and knee socks and what looked like climbing boots.

"Have you been out already?"

"Yes, of course. Hours ago. Why do you ask?"

"No reason. It's just that I wanted to look around. I've never been in the Alps before."

"Then you must see this sunset. Just get dressed and come out. You can bathe or sauna or whatever later." At the door, he turned back. "Oh, incidentally—were you treated in a hospital for your wound? There in New Jersey before Dom found you at your father's house?"

Toni wondered, why the question, why now?

"I only ask because the wound looks to have been severe. And dangerous, so close to your spine. There's no risk of infection, I hope."

"I don't think so. A friend of my father, our family doctor, took care of it."

"There at your father's place in Atlantic City?"

She nodded. "And then the doctor at the Schweizerhof looked at it twice."

The sunset was indeed spectacular. A storm front was moving off to the west somewhere in France, and the sun seemed to be playing a kind of peekaboo through the clouds. At one moment it plunged the Alps into a kind of immemorial gloom, the tones funereal with the monoliths of the Wetterhorn and Eiger looking like crags on the face of a hostile planet, only to reappear suddenly as a blaze of magenta with fleecy columns towering into the stratosphere, where the sky was a clear pale blue.

They were sitting before wide glass windows that had been added to the third story of the chalet, and below them down a steep slope of mountain was a broad valley that was patched here and there with the green of new spring grass. Farther still were the silver plates of Lake Brienz and Lake Thun, which turned to fire whenever the sun broke through the clouds.

"Well?" Payson asked.

214

"Incredible. How did you ever find this place?"

"As you might have gathered, I went to law school here in Bern. And, of course, after Brooklyn, where I grew up, and Cambridge, where I was an undergraduate, this vista knocked me off my feet. It was love at first sight."

Standing, Toni walked toward the windows. She had again found clothes to fit her in the closet of the bedroom and now was dressed in slacks and a turtleneck sweater. "What are your plans, to retire here?"

"Can you think of a better place?"

She could. Sure—the scenery was unbeatable and the solitude a nice change, but after years of dealing with the public, Toni was nothing if not a social being, and she needed the interchange on every level that only a business could bring. She answered, "Not for Monsieur Henri Sevrier. I should imagine that he is a man who values his privacy."

Her eyes moved from the village, which was perhaps seven or eight miles away, to a narrow secondary road and finally to the dirt track that wound up the mountain to the chalet. There wasn't a tree in sight. "Who is he, by the way? A real person or fictional?" She turned to Payson.

His head had gone back, but he was smiling, assessing her. "Real. He was a Konstanz attorney I shared digs with in university here. The people who knew us called us the twins. Died, the poor fellow, a few years back, leaving nobody. No wife, no family. Even his parents were dead. I don't think he'd mind at all my reviving his name to a purpose."

Died when and how? Toni wondered. And for what purpose? "But won't you be lonely here?"

Payson pulled himself out of the low chair and joined her at the window. "Think about my life and who I am, or at least what I've become. I have known books, periodicals, journals, libraries, and study. If I wasn't to begin with, I've become a kind of recluse. Then, if I get cabin fever, there's always Bern right over there." He pointed to an array of lights that they could just see in the distance.

"And finally, loneliness is something a person like you could amend. Now that you know this much about me, perhaps you should get to know the rest?"

Toni smiled slightly. What was she hearing? Was he

merely flirting with her, or making a backhanded offer? "Like what, in particular?"

"Well—we could share a drink first. And then perhaps a little sauna and some whirlpool. It'll do wonders for you, you'll see."

Toni turned her head and looked at him. "Are you serious?"

"Couldn't be more so."

She regarded him: his pale blue eyes and long, thin face with the aquiline nose; the square line of his shoulders; the challenge in his slight smile. "A sauna and a whirlpool and then what?"

"Whatever you like."

She turned back to the scene presented in the window. Below them and to the right, a ski resort had switched on its floodlights, streaking the mountain with silver. "Bruce—I don't know what you have in mind, but I hope you can appreciate that I don't really feel very much like sex now."

"Who said anything about sex? I hope you don't think I'm that easy. And then tomorrow we've got to climb. I wouldn't want to wear you out."

"Climb what?"

He jerked a thumb over his shoulder to indicate the mountain in back of them. "The Finsteraarhorn."

"You mean that giant thing I saw when we arrived? It's got to be thousands of feet tall."

"Over four, very vertical thousands, if you must know, though we'll go around it."

Toni had already noted that Bruce Payson was well preserved, but in the sauna she saw that his muscles had the sort of rigid definition that only daily, vigorous exercise and a close attention to diet could create.

He had narrow hips and a flat stomach that was marked by the tan line of swim trunks, perhaps from their stay on St. Maarten two weeks or so before. His chest, while not large, was well formed and set off by wide, if thin, shoulders. And his arms were taut and sinewy, like his thighs and calves. In all, he made her feel self-conscious about her battered and scarred body, and she was glad she had not as yet removed her towel.

She was sitting and he standing, and he had his towel in his hand. "I see nudity is not a problem with you."

"Should it be?" He laughed and sat beside her on the bottom-most of the three tiers. "Do this much?"

"Nearly every morning after work."

"Feel good? I mean, now with your—" He glanced down at her upper chest. "Why don't you take that thing off and lie on the top shelf? I'll give you a rub with this special emollient that's made in Bern for people who've taken especially bad falls on the slopes."

"Something like Ben-Gay?" she asked, her eyes flicking up to his.

"No—more like Ben Not-So-Gay. It's really wonderful, in this heat."

She hadn't planned to flirt. There was too much at stake, and it was best to keep things on a business basis. Then, from what Lucca Furco had implied the day she'd gone fishing with him on his boat, orders had been given to work on Jack and ensnare him in debt and her in the situation in which she now found herself. Why? Just so they could bank money in her name? She found it hard to believe.

And orders given by whom, Payson? Looking at him now—his distinguished-looking face, which was creased in a smile; his body that belied any bad habits; his clear blue eyes in which there was a plea—she couldn't believe that either.

As though sensing her confusion, Payson now opened her towel. "You get up there. I'll go get the stuff."

The touch of the liniment on her back was like a deep-probing heat that warmed her to the bone. Payson's hands were strong and sure, and he carefully avoided the stitches, working her arms, the sides of her neck and shoulders, the muscles of her back, and around her kidneys. But slowly, so that her body moved in a swirl on the towel below her, and she began to feel at once tired and relaxed but aware of every glide and stroke.

"Bruce?" she asked.

"Ms. Spina?"

"How about 'fessing up?"

"About what?"

"About what all of this is about."

"All of what?"

"The whole thing—why Jack and I were set up, why I'm here, and what you're up to. If this is to continue, as you've said, wouldn't it be better to let me in on the entire script, rather than just handing me—" she searched for the appropriate word "—scenes?"

His hands stopped moving. "Have you ever considered that knowing the entire script might be dangerous? To me *and* to you?"

She had, but knowing only what she suspicioned made her feel vulnerable. She decided on another tack. "Then we'll keep it general. How about what we discussed there in Bern, before we went to the bank—you know, about your being one thing but admiring and, I assume, wanting to retreat here to another. Isn't your position . . . anomalous?"

"A leading question, if I ever heard one. I'll let you guess how I'll answer it."

"Evasively."

"No, elliptically." His hands began moving again. While he spoke, he massaged her hips and the flat area near the base of her spine, her buttocks—lightly and gingerly—and the backs of her thighs, her calves and feet, even the bottoms, which he kneaded for so long that she nearly fell asleep.

He told her about having been an undergraduate at Harvard on what a classmate, whose father was the attorney for the southern district of New York, told everybody was a "Mafia scholarship." From then on it didn't matter that he was near the top of his class and captain-elect of the crew or, "you know, good company, I was branded. A girl I'd been dating at Radcliffe put it best: 'First it was your name'—which was then Henrico B. dePasquale—'I could have gotten over that. But this—is it true?'

"I can remember looking into her big, blue, WASPy eyes and saying to myself, I could spend the rest of my life fighting who I am. Or I could embrace it. Then, history was my major, and if I'd gotten anything out of all the reading I'd been doing, it was the realization of how difficult and often futile it was to try to change somebody or something, once that person or thing was set on its course."

And so he'd decided to become a Mafioso, after his

fashion, Toni concluded. "But isn't this a similar situation? Aren't you now choosing the other option?"

"You mean, Bern?"

And the chalet, anonymity, and whatever huge amounts they were banking.

"I see it as a reward."

"For having won."

When he said nothing, she went on, "Then the prize is to inhabit order and rectitude and law and tradition. All the values that you or your cohorts violated. Somehow I see that as anomalous."

Did Payson actually laugh? Toni thought he did. "You do? Well, you haven't thought about it very hard. Order, rectitude, law, and so forth are the 'values' that the haves embrace to keep the have-nots in their place. And in a chaotic and purposeless universe, perhaps it's Bern and Switzerland that are the anomaly. For how long, who can tell? But I'll be the first to admit that I want to live here where things are regular and money has been—"

"Enshrined," she supplied.

"Thank you. And will continue to be, at least in my lifetime. Do you blame me?"

Toni didn't know where to start, and decided not to.

"Why don't you turn over?"

She did, and she saw that he was erect.

"Can't help it. You're beautiful and I'm only human. And then, we were discussing my favorite subject."

"Money?"

"No—metaphysics."

She smiled and closed her eyes. Again he began at her neck and shoulders and worked down her body, avoiding those places—the ends of her breasts, her nipples—that were most obviously injured. The cold-hot-stinging-soothing ointment on her lower stomach and the insides of her thighs that he touched feathery and soft made her flinch and then smile more completely.

In the whirlpool, which was immense, like a Jacuzzi the size of a small, circular, swimming pool, the cool water against the ointment made her whole body tingle.

"Are you ready?" Payson asked her.

"For what?"

"For the whirling part of the pool."

As far as Toni was concerned, it was whirling fast enough for her and felt wonderful with the effect of the liniment, like the water was passing right through her body and purging it of all the pain.

But when he reached up and turned the dial, it felt like a tidal wave struck her, and though still holding onto the rope—a kind of lifeline—that was strung through hoops around the side, she was pushed and swirled around and around until Payson took her in his arms and they were swirled together, around and around.

It was like dancing but better, and at some point when she felt him still hard between her thighs, she pulled back her neck and looked into his eyes. For all the mystery of what he or somebody associated with him had done to her, he seemed at the very least an intelligent, capable, and interesting man whose attraction to her was also physical.

But after Jack and her long abstinence from men, she now reserved the right to choose and also to name the ground rules, and one "affair"—if she could so call her involvement with Colin Ross—was quite enough. "I think I'll get dressed now."

"But why? We've only just begun. We haven't yet cracked the champagne, and think of the long, enlightening discussion we could have in my eiderdown. The view from my bed surveys half of Europe and all of the northern heavens."

"No—really. Don't think I'm not flattered. I'm sure Monsieur Sevrier has little trouble finding companions to scan the skies."

"So that's it." His grip relaxed for a moment, and she spun away. But his hand darted out and caught her wrist. "You're afraid I'm a roue."

"No, I'm *sure* you're a roue. It's just that I'm not rouable. Is that a word?" Years ago she had learned that there was nothing that angered men more than saying no absolutely, and then—who knew?—there might be hope. "At least, not tonight. I hope Dom told you *all* of what happened in the parking lot?"

His expression changed, and a glaze suddenly filmed his eyes. He pulled her closer to him, holding her shoulders. "What if I were to insist?"

She tried to look unfazed and to hold his stare. "But you wouldn't."

"Why not?"

"First, you're a gentleman, and that's beneath you. Second, you're intelligent and in your own way compassionate, and you know that I'm injured. When I resist, which I will, I'll probably injure myself more. That'll only destroy the good feeling between us, and perhaps ruin the climb you've planned for tomorrow. Third, I know you like me, I can feel it—" she smiled slightly "—and I like you. But not tonight."

Their eyes remained fixed on each other's for a few moments, until he smiled and held her out at arm's length. "Well—you're something, really. You've got . . ." His eyes roamed her face and shoulders and hair. He shook his head. ". . . just what I chose you for."

"Which is?"

But he ignored her. In spite of his smile, he was serious, she now realized. "Has it ever occurred to you that your perceptions might be wrong?"

She nodded. "Would I be here if they weren't?" She meant her mistakes with Jack and his gambling debt and with Furco at the restaurant and however she had gotten herself into her present position.

He loosed his grip on her shoulders, and the surging water sent her tumbling down the length of the pool, where she smacked her head on the side wall and nearly blacked out. Gasping, she pulled water into her lungs and felt the pain intensify at the top of her head.

Standing on the walkway beside the pool, Payson had seized her by the hair and now directed her into the shallows, where she began coughing. The water burned through her chest and throat.

"Call that proof," he observed when she had quieted. "I'll be by the windows, if you care to talk."

"Who's Giancarla Marchetti?" she asked from the doorway to the kitchen, where she had gotten herself a glass of water for the pills in her hand. Painkillers, they had been given to her by the doctor in Atlantic City. They made her groggy, and she didn't want that. But the throbbing was intense now.

After a while, Payson said, "Go to bed. You'll need to be fresh in the morning. We'll start at first light." He turned his head to the sweep of glass that now presented the panoply of stars.

They began at daybreak and climbed for hours up a road that became a trace, a narrow trail, and finally a barely discernible path along the margin of a glacier. They climbed through mist so wet they had to don slickers and PVC-coated trousers from the packs that Payson and Dom carried. In places it was so thick that each lost sight of the person in front and voices were muffled, making conversation impossible.

Toni could hardly speak anyway. The air rapidly became so thin that she thought her chest, which was still raw from the pool water of the night before, would burst just trying to pull in enough to go on. But then they broke suddenly into brilliant sunlight and a wind so cold that the wet slickers immediately froze stiff.

It was there at 3,200 feet that they came upon the cache that Dom and Payson had dug into a slope near the trail and then concealed with boulders. In it she saw what looked like rifles in pouchy bags, jugs of water, and boxes, when they opened it to store the slickers.

"We might need them again sometime in an emergency," Payson explained. "We can always get more for the chalet." But he also stored the suit that Toni had worn, as though in that emergency she would be traveling with them.

Even there the mountains towered, like three white, speckled teeth above them: the Wetterhorn and Eiger now behind them, the Finsteraarhorn off to the right.

But they had finished their climbing, and after a rough transit through a glacial valley that grew so narrow that it ended in a heap of fractured plates of ice that they had to squeeze through and scramble over, they came out upon a cliff that seemed to present them with the vista of a new world.

In this valley there were no clouds, and the sun was radiant and suddenly warm. As though contained within an ice bowl with towering, snow-peaked mountains all around, lay an oval swath of green punctuated by four small communities. The mountains across the valley were not quite as tall, and beyond them—so far below that it looked like another country—lay a sea of brilliant green.

Said Payson, *"Au-delà des Alpes est l'Italie."*

"Do you feel like Napoleon?" she asked.

He seemed surprised that she had recognized the quote. "Not really. And then, Napoleon was only paraphrasing Livy. But it *is* another country that offers another sort of freedom."

"Like what?"

"Oh, different laws. Different customs. In some ways greater license. It depends on the individual. For you, it means ownership of your aptly named restaurant, which it might be argued is a type of freedom." He pulled up the shoulder straps of his sack and started down the steep, narrow trail, the teeth of his ice cleats biting into the slippery, melting spring ice.

In the village—Münster by name—they had a late supper at twilight, and only when it was fully dark did Dom go for the car that Toni assumed Payson kept somewhere in town. There was no mention of a rental, and Payson handed him the key. Using a back door of the inn, Payson and Toni met him in an alley.

It was a gray Porsche with a jump seat into which Dom, over Toni's objections, squeezed himself.

And Payson, driving at speed, careened around mountain curves that Toni was thankful she could not see now at night. From time to time glancing in the rearview mirror, he said, "You can't be too careful."

About what? Toni wondered. The IRS or some other U.S. government agency? She doubted it. Given the way they had left Bern and climbed up through clouds, nobody even in an airplane or a helicopter could have followed them. And *would* they? If what Payson and Pasqual, the banker, had told her about Swiss financial arrangements was true, then anything but a paper pursuit through courts and government channels would be fruitless.

Then who?

On a straightaway uphill, the Porsche's speedometer quavered past 120 mph. Toni closed her eyes.

18

Joe "The Bear" Scarpone didn't know what to think, but in his hospital room at U. of Penn. Hospital in Philly, he felt hunted and trapped, even with the cop on the door.

They'd been trying to keep the papers from him, his family, saying the doctors said no, you got to rest. Then they pulled the TV, but too late.

As if in a trance, keeping still, the bed sheet pulled up over his fucked teeth and mouth right to his nose and moving nothing but his eyes, Scarpone had watched while the news showed Tiny's midnight black Gran Prix, ". . . riddled with bullets," they said. They also said the corpse was all cut up and some cop had guessed he bled to death. There was no sign of anybody else being out there, except for maybe some footsteps down to the ocean. But the place was so windy and empty this time of year, all trace of his killer or killers had been blown away.

Killer, Scarpone thought. He had flicked the remote from channel to channel, almost memorizing the words, his eyes fixed on the car every time, until one news guy said some other cop guessed the damage was made by automatic weapons fire. It backed up what Scarpone had been thinking: a fucking Saturn 2-22 that put out so many slugs so fast—

That was when they took the tube away, and the cop came on the door—protection. The state of New Jersey wanted to extradite him for their probe of the murders on the beach across from Barnegat. Scarpone had seen them on the tube, too. Every wheel he knew had been iced, and even the heat didn't know how. Furco? He hadn't been there and he stood to gain. The whole fucking dry and most of the other action in South Jersey had fallen into his lap. They showed him leaving the state police barracks in Toms River with his lawyer, quiet-cocky. They looked like two fucking guys from Wall Street about to make some fucking deal.

Lap. Scarpone's own was a mess of tubes and stitches and drains. The knife the guy had cut him with had been full of shrimp guts and shit. He couldn't move, and his right hand where it'd been caught in the door was broken all across the fingers and in a cast. Scarpone was right-handed and he couldn't do much without it.

Then his ribs were broken from the nigger pounding on them, all the small ones both sides, and it hurt just to breathe. His nose was busted so bad they'd have to reconstruct, but it'd have to wait until he was off the drugs they were giving him for blood clots. Last and what hurt the most was his front teeth. Just touching his tongue to them made him jump, and because of the nose he had to breathe through his mouth.

But Dino had come through for him, like he knew he would. "Care package, from your mother. I suppose everybody's got to have a mother," the dumb fucking cop had said after going through the box out in the hall. Scarpone had watched him, and after he put it down on the bed, Scarpone'd asked him to close the door.

"Why?"

"Because I'm gonna play with myself. Why you think?"

"In your condition? Way I hear it, you're lucky your voice ain't high." The cop had laughed at that, laughed like hell. But he shut the door, and Scarpone had examined the box.

It was a big box and even had a bow and some ribbons on it, though the cop'd had to break them to get in. Then the Maz musta splashed it all with perfume or something, because it stunk. Inside was a mess of sports mags and paperbacks and newspapers from everyplace with more details about Tiny. The *Star-Ledger* said he had been opened up right down the back. The sentence had been underlined in red and then everyplace Furco's name was printed in all of the papers. It was like Dino was trying to tell him to watch out. And he'd sent more.

The box had smaller boxes. Boxes of cookies and candies—"Hey, cop! Cop!" the Bear had called out until the asshole came into the room. "Everybody's mother make fuckin' cookies like fuckin' this?"—though he knew where Dino had got them. In some bakery. They were perfect, like the ones all stacked up behind glass near the register and pie case at the restaurant.

But one box, wrapped up in cellophane with a big bow around, was heavier than the rest, and in it Scarpone found a Ruger GP-100, like Tiny'd had, and enough loads to blow away half the hospital. Note said, "Furco come in there blow his fucking head off. Dino."

Furco waited until night, just before visiting hours were over when there'd be hardly anybody else on the floor, and with a big bouquet of thirty-six long-stemmed roses that had cost $125 and was guaranteed to knock the eyes out of any nurse at a desk, he stopped at reception.

He had a new taupe Pierre Cardin topcoat hooked over the shoulders of a suit by the same designer. It was dark brown like his hair and eyes and set off by an off-white silk tie and pocket hanky on a taupe silk shirt. He'd had his hair styled and been shaved close by his cousin in South Philly, who was a barber. The nurse looked from the roses that he nearly stuck in her face to him and back again. She then took another look at the suit.

"I'm sorry, sir, but visiting hours are over."

"Yeah? Gee—I tried to get here in time. Once I heard, I drove flat out all the way from A.C. I'm Luke Furco." He slid her a card, so she wouldn't forget. He started talking like a gangster in some movie. "Guy I'm here to see works for me. Couple, three days now, no Joe Scarpone. I figure he met somebody special, somebody—" Furco let his eyes eat her up "—like you, and—hey—let the guy have his fun.

"But this afternoon, I go to my secretary, I go, 'Dottie, where's Joe Scarpone? Where's he at? I mean, two days, three, I can see. But what's with this week stuff?' She goes,

'Haven't you heard, Mr. Furco? Nobody tol' you? Joe had an accident, and he's in U. of Penn. Hospital,' and she gave me his room numbah.''

Speaking with his hands, using his shoulders and eyes and face like he never did, Furco now had her attention. ''This guy, he's key. Without him— Look, lemme just pop up there and drop these off. If I'm not down in—'' he checked his watch ''—fifteen—''

Her eyes widened.

''—no, five. *Five* minutes, you send a cop after me. Really. All right?''

''Well . . .'' She glanced down the corridor into the hospital, and then slid him a pass.

Furco started away from the desk, but he quickly turned back. From the bouquet he pulled six roses and placed them in front of her. ''You're nice. You're beautiful. If I was a couple years younger, I could go for you.''

The way her head moved as she wiggled her legs under the desk, the way her teeth snapped on the gum she was chewing and she looked at him and not the roses said she could go for him, twenty years or no.

It was enough, he thought, turning to the elevators. She'd cough it all up when the cops asked her, especially when she found out who Luke Furco was.

Mafioso. Kingpin. All the shit they were calling him in the papers. Furco still didn't know who had done the Babe and Grisanti and the others on the beach, but nobody else—guys from Vegas and Florida and New England, who had tried before—was moving in, and after all the years Furco knew at least this much: you could do anything you wanted from a position of strength. If you were weak when, like now, things were up for grabs, it was usually you who got grabbed.

Even the federal cops had treated him with a kind of respect. They gave him that look where they tilted back their heads and their eyes sparkled as if to say, So, this is the guy who pulled it off, the one we'll have to go after now. Admiring but sizing him up, too, but like always Furco gave them nothing: no smile, no long stares, no words. Not even an acknowledgment when they kept questioning him more, it seemed, about Solieri's disappearance and Toni's absence than about the thing on the beach.

227

Toni? At first he'd figured that after what had happened to her she just got in her car and took off, but Tina and the old lady were still in Cherry Hill—he'd checked through a police contact—and that bothered him. If she'd gone anywhere, she would've taken them, and would the Toni he knew just up and leave the restaurant? Furco didn't think so. She had too much stick.

And then there was the matter of the other guy who'd been there who must've taken care of Solieri's body after he stuffed it in the trunk. That got Furco, too, who didn't know who he could be. Cop? Nah—if the cops knew, why would they be asking him? Payson's guy? It was a possibility.

Then, could Payson have been the one who done the Babe and the others on the beach? Cheech? Furco almost hoped it was him, just to teach all the assholes who'd called Payson that and underestimated him a lesson. But, again—where was he, why wasn't he picking up all their action, if it had been him?

"*Toni,*" he said aloud as he stepped out of the elevator and followed the arrow toward the low-number 500 rooms. He was missing her bad, and she worried him.

He could see what room it was because of the cop who was sitting in a chair there in the hall, watching a little portable television in his lap. The wire ran into the room— 514—and the door was a little ajar, which was good. Furco wanted Scarpone to hear him before he saw him and be ready.

It took the cop a while to look up from the screen. "Yeah?"

"I'm here to see Joe Scarpone. I got something for him."

The cop was old, close to retirement, with pouchy, tired blue eyes and skin you could see red veins through. He had a big nose and a double chin that said "Irish." Furco had always hated Irish cops. They were judge, jury, and executioner, all in a stare, and Furco only hoped the sonofabitch had done more cop work in his life than parking his ass outside hospital room doors.

"Leave it. I'll see that he gets 'em." He looked down at the floor, like Furco was supposed to put the flowers there.

"You don't seem to understand, asshole—I wanna fuckin' see fuckin' Joe Scarpone, and I want you to stand up and fuckin' frisk me like you're s'pozed to. *Now*." It was the way you talked to Irish cops, if you were somebody, and Furco was now a big somebody. The only thing Irish cops respected was authority—somebody who could make their personal lives shit—and it didn't matter what side the authority was on. All they wanted was an eight-hour skate, no hassles, no problems, and the less they did the better.

"Who the fuck are you?"

Furco blinked. He had a smart one here, had to be, since he'd hit himself an Irish cop home run: hospital door, a television, and a chair. All that was missing was a fucking beer.

"Luke Furco."

The tired blue eyes worked down Furco's face to his clothes and roses and back.

Furco could hear movement inside the room. Covers being pulled back, a bed squeaking, a box opening.

Still the cop didn't move. "*Mr.* Furco, I don't like being talked to like that."

It was time for Furco to ease off. "Officer Dowling," he read from the plastic tag on the man's pocket, "I'm not used to being treated like this."

He blinked. There wouldn't be any problem this shift if he just got off his ass. With a sigh, he lowered the television to the floor and pulled himself up. "You got five minutes. Raise your hands." He frisked Furco quickly.

"Aren't you going to check my topcoat?"

"Why?"

"I could have a weapon there."

The cop's head went back. What, more trouble with this greaseball guinea? At this point the cop was getting mad, and he didn't care how big a wheel Furco was.

"Tell you what—I'll just leave it here." Furco draped it over the chair. "And my jacket. I don't want them getting messy. Also, I'm going to show you my garters, you know, my ankles, so you know there's nothing down there where you didn't check." Furco pulled up each trouser leg, and then, raising his arms again, he turned in a circle. "I want you to be absolutely sure I got nothing on me before I go in that room. Are you sure?''

The cop was wary now, and his eyes professionally scanned Furco, whose tailored shirt and trousers fit him so perfectly that there was no way he could be packing a piece.

"Now I'm going in there." With his hand on the door, he added, "I'd take that clip off your revolver." He waited.

"Why?"

"Fucker's crazy. And he's got a gun. His mother sent it to him, believe that? You know, in that big box a' cookies and shit." Holding the roses in front of his face, Furco opened the door and stepped into the room.

Scarpone had raised the Ruger in his left hand and was trying to steady it with the cast on his right, and he only had to see Furco bob his head from behind the bouquet before he squeezed the trigger.

The blast was huge in the small room. But Furco had put a blank in the chamber, and he'd bet that Scarpone wouldn't check any gun sent him by his buddy, Dino Mazullo.

He reached for the door handle, pulled it back, and dove into the hall.

The closing door caught the next shot and the next and the next and the next, the low-power, 125-grain loads Furco had placed in the .357 magnum flowering wide, ugly holes in the regulation hospital fire door but thwacking harmlessly into the concrete wall on the other side of the hallway where people now were screaming.

"Wait," Furco said to the cop, who with his gun out was crouching by the wall near the door. "It's a revolver. He's got one more shot before he has to reload." And all of them duds, he didn't add.

Furco pulled open the door and waved a hand at Scarpone.

The sixth bullet smacked into the door and caromed bits of metal and paint into the hall.

"Now!" Furco shouted, and shoved the cop into the room.

Dowling emptied his service revolver into Scarpone.

With his foot, Furco shoved the roses aside. He then brushed the paint flakes and metal pieces off his suit coat and fitted it on. He sat in the chair and draped the topcoat over his thighs.

Nurses now were approaching cautiously, hands to their mouths or eyes.

In some other room, an old woman was crying.

Furco would wait until the other cops arrived. He didn't want Dowling to screw up his story.

19

Again Toni slept. It had taken five hours of tortuous driving to reach San Marino. They had taken back roads and had weaved in and out of traffic, passing long, lumbering trucks only to have to brake suddenly for the farm vehicles that seemed to be creaking along every good stretch of highway. Tar surfaces suddenly turned *bianco,* which meant rutted dirt, and even at Payson's speeds, which were extreme, they were passed twice, once by a man who stuck an arm out the window and jerked his hand skyward.

Said Payson, "Maybe I should buy a Lamborghini with some of your money."

Then at the Excelsior, a large modern hotel, he'd pulled the car into a parking lot in back and announced that they would complete their business here on the following day and then continue on to Rome to "relax," as they had on St. Maarten. They would enter the hotel, however, one at a time and register separately, Toni yet again using the Giancarla Marchetti passport. In the morning he would contact her. If she awoke first, she was not to attempt to reach him. He would initiate any contact, and she was to stay put.

But there was no chance of her leaving the bed. After the long day's climb from the chalet at Grindelwald through the pass to Münster and the car ride here, it held her in its soft, seductive grip until finally street noises woke her: a car horn, the slap of leather soles on pavement as children ran home from school, a firewood vendor crying, *"Fagotti! Legna da ardere! Fagotti!"*

Sun, streaming through glass doors, was baking her face, and she opened her eyes into a burst of light so brilliant that at first she thought she was blinded.

In a closet she discovered that the very same bags that she had found at the Schweizerhof in Bern had arrived here, and a summer wardrobe had been unpacked and hung up. Selecting a Paquin robe of burnished silk, Toni moved directly to the balcony that looked out from an enormous height over a wide valley striped with vibrant green. Directly below her, she peered down a long, granite-block street bounded on one side by a fortress wall that led to a castle and by canopied shops on the other. And she remembered Payson saying that the entire country, "all twenty-four square miles of it," had been built on three mountain peaks linked by a road and bounded by a wall.

But unlike Switzerland, where the vistas were long and the country rugged and harsh, here the valley seemed a pleasant expanse, knowable even at its farthest reach and quilted everywhere with farm fields. Here, too, the earth was not silver or white or even delicately green. Instead it was an abiding brown that was ribbed neatly with the deep green of row crops or laced with luxuriant vines or bordered by bounding hedgerows or avenues of limber poplars and tall, full-bowled cypresses. And from the heights of San Marino even the white walls and red terra-cotta roofs that appeared through protective trees seemed orderly and controlled and not intimidating like the glacierscapes that she had viewed on the day before. Raising her face, Toni closed her eyes and again let the sun have its way with her.

Until a voice said, *"Open my heart, and you will see/ Graved inside of it, 'Italy.' "* Startled, she looked up at Payson, who was sitting with Dom on another balcony that had been set higher and off on an L of the building so that it looked directly out on the street and not at the valley that she was seeing. And it struck her, turning back to look into her room, that with the doors open, both of them sitting at the table on their balcony had been able to see her in bed.

"Can you join us for coffee? We just ordered a fresh pot. But dress for business and try to hurry. I took the liberty of putting out a dress for you—the yellow one with the full skirt and big black polka dots. Wear the black hat, too. We really must try to finish things up today."

How long had they been watching her? Had they seen her toss off the covers and stretch in the sun as she awoke? Feeling violated at this breach of privacy, Toni turned away from the scene and moved into the shadows.

Payson was still on the balcony of the other room when Dom opened the door and invited Toni in. He pointed to the castlelike fortification with Tuscan arches that they could see at the end of the street.

It, too, was bathed in sunlight and had flags and pennants flying from its turrets. "Right across from the entrance to the *fortezza* you'll see a narrow doorway leading upstairs to a landing with four doors. The fourth is lettered with the advisory *Privata*. Knock and then proceed as we did in Panama and St. Maarten and Bern. You're expected, so there won't be any problem. Engage nobody in conversation and say as little as possible. Get receipts for everything. We'll be waiting here.

"Oh, and let me have your handbag. I have another for you. Everything that Signor DeCroce will ask you for is in here, including your Spina passport, which, of course, you'll need."

"But my compact. My purse."

"You'll not be gone that long. If you need anything, come back here or step out into the street"—his eyes moved toward the castle—"we'll be watching."

"Now?" Thinking only too late of the card that the Bern banker, Pasqual, had given her, Toni reluctantly handed him her handbag and received another exactly like it.

"You'd better hurry. They won't open specially, no matter the amount."

Standing, Toni took another sip from her coffee and turned toward the door where Dom was positioned.

"And don't come back here. Go straight to your room and remain there until we contact you."

Out on the street Toni felt like running, fleeing, but to where? In the elevator on the way down she had looked in the purse and found nothing but documents in Italian and her passport, no money. She didn't even have credit cards, and she felt helpless and trapped.

She didn't look into the sun-drenched shops she was passing, nor at the diners who were sitting in the awninged shade of sidewalk cafés near the fortress, and the view of the valley no longer held her interest. Something had changed, and she didn't know what and that was the problem. She just didn't know enough about what she was doing and what Payson actually intended for her.

The hallway was deep in shadow and felt damp, and the stairs were worn and netted with cobwebs and snags of dust.

She knocked and knocked again and knocked a third time. Though the translucent glass was dim, she could hear from somewhere beyond a din, as of typewriters clacking and people speaking into telephones. Finally using the heel of her palm, she banged on the wooden panel of the door, which rattled in its jamb and made a racket. A light then went on beyond the glass and the door opened.

"*Si?*" a middle-aged man in shirtsleeves asked.

"*Voglio parlare al signore DeCroce.*"

Brusquely the man asked who she was, his eyes scanning her yellow dress, her black stockings and shoes. She removed her sunglasses and told him who she was, and he said, "*Aspetta qui,*" and closed the door on her.

After a wait of several minutes, a younger man with a head of black hair so thick and dark it looked like a wig opened the door and leaned his body out. "Ms. Spina, pardon us. Please come in." He, too, was in shirtsleeves, and she followed him back into the building through two wide storerooms that contained boxes of business forms and abandoned, dusty business machines. Opening a third door, he ushered her into an office crowded with desks and file cabinets and computer terminals. There were people everywhere, it seemed, and far too many for the size of the room. Everybody seemed to be on a phone, and she caught snatches of conversation in at least four languages before they entered a tiny cubicle.

He closed the door behind her and motioned to a seat, which he watched her take before sitting behind the desk. "I'm Michele DeCroce. Excuse our informality. It's just that we're not accustomed to dealing directly with anybody, even shareholders. Has Monsieur Sevrier told you about us?"

Toni did not know how to answer, but she decided a yes would more probably close off conversation. "No."

But she was wrong. Looking at her even more closely, now taking in her new watch, he said, "Well, then—shall we get down to business? Passport, please." He held out a hand, and she abandoned the idea of asking for an explanation. This man was different from the old banker in Bern, or at least he didn't perceive any advantage in making small talk.

"Documents?"

"What?"

The hand was out again. He even shook it. "The packet of documents I sent you by post to complete."

Toni handed him all else.

As DeCroce's eyes ran down the documents, he asked, "And how is Monsieur Sevrier?"

"Fine. Last time we spoke."

"You're fortunate to have him advising you. I admire him greatly. Please sign everyplace you see an X."

Toni looked down at the documents, which were in Italian, and, pretending to search them for the place to sign, tried to understand what they meant. Having been sent them "by post," obviously she would already have read them, and she couldn't take too much time. But she hadn't read Italian in ages, and nowhere could she find any figures except a phrase that said, ". . . a million shares at market price of around 26,000 It. lire." The name of the firm was La Banca di Monte Titano di San Marino.

"*Why* do you admire Monsieur Sevrier?" she asked, picking up the pen that he had slid across to her.

The man seemed to blush. "Well—I've never actually met the man, but over the years we've spoken countless times on the phone, and his acumen, his foresight in investments, and his obvious qualities of leadership—" He looked away, as though embarrassed. "We started with nothing here, and suddenly—" His eyes returned to her. "Since he's your advisor, you must know all of this yourself."

At least something else, she decided: that, unlike the

arrangement with the bank in Bern, here Payson was boss and some sort of distant, disguised owner or partner. And she was glad she had not chanced more than she had.

Finished with the signatures, she handed him back the papers, which he examined. "Well—" He stood.

But Toni remained seated. "Receipts, please." At least she would leave with something that, in the dark stairwell before stepping out into the street where she could be seen, she could examine.

"Oh, yes—I forgot the receipt."

She wondered if he thought she would actually forget proof of purchase of a million shares of anything, even a penny stock. Toni had no idea of the value of the lira. When she was a student more than fifteen years before, it had all seemed like so much play money, with little bills in bright colors and some of the large denominations the size of small flags.

But, receipt duly completed, DeCroce accompanied her out through the busy office and storeroom and down the stairs into the street.

"*Mille grazie, signora.*" He offered his hand, but Toni only smiled wanly and walked out into the street that was now thronged with traffic and pedestrians.

Turning to the hotel, she saw two figures on the balcony of Payson's room and caught the glint of whatever it was that one of them—Payson himself—was holding to his eyes. Binoculars, she guessed.

And she decided that it was probably her last chance to be alone with some hard evidence of what they had been about, and she would take it.

Stopping suddenly, she turned to the *fortezza* and the Tuscan arches. As though wanting to examine them more closely, she touched a hand to her sunglasses and, changing direction, advanced upon them.

"What's she doing now?" Dom asked.

"I don't know. She's over looking at the *fortezza*." Payson lowered the glasses. "She's probably just sight-seeing, and—" Let her enjoy herself, he thought, considering what lay ahead. "But maybe you better check it out." They hadn't come this far to blow it on sentimentality.

"What if she's doing somethin' stupid?"

Payson shook his head. "We can't have it happen down there. Get her back here. She's got to have all the clothes on and the bags and the car for a positive ID. And for sure we don't want it to be here where she's banked. It would spoil everything."

Toni paused in the castle entry, which was crowded with a tour group whose guide was speaking French. There she removed her wide-brimmed black hat and scanned the street. Which direction would be better—forward toward the hotel or away from it?

Again she remembered how resourceless she was. Her purse contained nothing useful but her passport, not even enough money to make a telephone call.

But the thought now gave her an idea, and she stepped out into the crowd and across the street under the shop awnings, which would at least conceal her from view. She could always say that, after having been attracted by the castle, she'd decided to return to the hotel by some other route, if only to see the sights.

Would he send Dom after her? Only if he thought it an emergency. They had arrived in the dead of night and registered separately—those two under aliases, she did not doubt—because they did not want to be seen in San Marino. And she had been dispatched alone to the bank for the very same reason. Anonymity. No matter how skilled he was, with only one man looking for her, she would have some time to herself.

At last she found what she was looking for: a small sign outside a café that pictured a telephone. She could use the excuse that she just had to call her daughter. Or her business. Payson, as a man, might buy that.

The café was fortunately the Italian archetype with a metal-topped bar crowded with men who after work had stopped in for coffee or a drink. It was loud and filled with smoke, and had a kind of dining room in back that was nearly empty. The phone booth was in between.

Only a few stopped their conversations as she passed, and she had to wait a long minute for the booth to be vacated. It, too, was filled with smoke, but the light bulb on its tiny ceiling was strong enough to read by, and she pored over the documents. Her Italian was rusty, and she skipped over or guessed at legal and technical terms that she did not know.

The first page appeared to be an affidavit swearing to her ownership of the account in the St. Maarten Bank of Commerce, N.A., and the second a transfer order sending the funds to La Banca di Monte Titano di San Marino. The third was a telex communiqué from the St. Maarten bank certifying the funds available for transfer, the transfer fee, and the rates and charges for converting the deposit from Panamanian dollars to Dutch guilders, the form in which they had been kept in St. Maarten, and finally into Italian lire, which was the currency of San Marino. The final two sheets were a bank form authorizing the payment of a banking transaction tax to the San Marino government and the tax form itself.

What did it tell her that was new? Nothing, really. In fact, it corroborated all he had told her of what they had been about from the first time he spoke with her to the present moment—transferring funds from one bank to another using her name.

And it occurred to her what this second European deposit was—Payson's insurance, the cache he would come to and what he would have if for any reason the Bern funds were frozen or if somebody came after him. It explained the long night of evasive maneuvers after the banking in Bern, the isolated mountain chalet and his identity as Henri Sevrier, and the escape route over the mountains to the fast car that he kept in Münster.

It also accounted for why he did not want to show himself in San Marino, where, from what DeCroce had implied, he had some years ago established a sort of bank so inconspicuously that its resident director had never met him personally.

Had she misjudged Payson? It appeared so, and she was about to leave the booth when she remembered that at last she had seen some figures about the amount—or a part of the amount—that she had deposited but without understanding what it meant in dollars.

Glancing out the glass door of the booth, she noticed a rack of newspapers, the bottom one of which was the *Daily American,* which was published in Rome.

At the counter she placed a paper on the bar. "I'd also like a glass of your best white wine." Turning her head slightly, she met and held the gaze of the man beside her until, intimidated by her mien, he looked away.

When the glass was set before her, she said, "I have no money. I came out without funds. Take this for security." She pulled the BVLGARI off her wrist and handed it to the barman, then picked up the glass and the paper and returned to the booth.

There she snapped open the paper and quickly turned to the back, where she found the exchange rates. The lira was currently 1,235 to the dollar, which made the price of a single share in the Banca di Monte Titano—in the dust of the shelf on which she'd placed the wineglass she worked it out—five cents over $21 a share. That would make a million shares . . . No, she'd done something wrong, and craning back her head she checked her figures.

What—$21,050,000? It couldn't be. But it was.

As *insurance?*

Then how much was in Bern? And she remembered what the old banker, Pasqual, had said about the "fortune" it was. The "magnificent sum." And how he had even risked Payson's displeasure trying to persuade her to employ him and not Payson as her investment advisor.

Could Payson himself possess such wealth? she wondered. Was it his money alone? And if it was, why had he chosen to work for whoever it was who controlled things there in South Jersey or Philly or New York? Because of what he had revealed to her about his undergraduate experience at Harvard? No. A figure like $21,000,000 more than made up for any slight, real or imagined, that he had received as a young man. He could always go back for a reunion to understand how truly successful such a sum could make him feel.

And then she herself had had personal contact with the people whom Payson had served. Nobody of his caliber would willingly consent to serve that . . . ilk with that kind of money in hand.

But what if it wasn't *his* money? What if it was *theirs,* and she had been engaged in an elaborate international—was *theft* the proper term? If the banks maintained their vaunted confidentiality and Payson had schemed well enough, then only three persons actually knew where the funds had been deposited: Payson, who knew everything; Dom, who would know at least something; and the gullible, trusting Toni Spina, who now knew too much.

She reached for the glass of wine and thought of Lucca Furco saying, "There's only so much you can set a person up." Furco. He was fairly senior in the Mob, but she could also remember the questions he'd asked her about Cheech. He appeared to know little more than the nickname.

Still, she had not yet once caught Payson in a lie. Everything he had told her had been the truth. And everything that he had told her in regard to herself seemed to depend, as she believed it always had, on his assurance that in the future he would need her for withdrawals. Certainly that appeared to be the case here in San Marino. There was nothing in any of the documents to suggest that anybody but Toni Spina owned any part of the shares that had just been purchased. Payson, as Henri Sevrier, could have founded the bank as a holding company for Mob funds. Would he have retained control? Yes, but understandably.

Perhaps she had been selected to be a kind of Mafia queen—a front lady—and that's why they had taken so much time and effort to set her up. She had heard of such people before.

But it was then, in closing the newspaper and folding it back in two, that something caught Toni's eye: a photo at the bottom of the front page. It was of a woman wearing dark glasses and a head scarf who looked familiar until Toni turned back and realized that it was because the woman looked like her.

The caption said, "Giancarla Marchetti, daughter of slain mobster boss Sal 'The Babe' Infantino, leaving JFK Airport for Rome." The story detailed federal and New Jersey state police inquiries into the deaths of nine men at Island Beach State Park in Seaside Heights three days ago. Even Furco's name was mentioned. With his lawyer present, he had been questioned. It said no more.

Rome: where Payson said they were heading to "relax." Pushing open the door of the telephone booth, she said to a man who was waiting to make a call, "I'm not through, and

I won't be for a while. If the phone rings now, it's for me."
It was a stratagem, of course, but as a student she had spent
too many hours waiting for Italians to quit *telefono a get-tone.*

"Ma signora, è essenziale a mia moglie telefonare."

"Go home to her. She'll appreciate you more." Toni had
never cared for the word *moglie,* which meant "wife." Its
very sound—"mole-ee-ay"—was laden with contempt.

At the counter she said, "Now I wish to make a credit-card telephone call. A token, please."

The man's eyes fell to her body, as though she would have
to surrender something else to get the token.

She slapped her hand on the counter. "Token. Now, please."

Back in the booth, she dialed the operator and said she'd
like to make a credit-card call to Bern, but she did not know
the number.

The operator took her credit-card number, which by use
Toni had long since committed to memory, and connected
her to Bern information. The number for Die Nydegg Finanz
Gaselltschaft was soon found and the call put through.

After a long wait, Pasqual himself answered. They exchanged greetings, and he said, "You're lucky to catch me
here. Everybody else has left. What can I do for you,
signora? Have you considered what I said?"

"That will take a bit more thought and consultation, and
I'll call you back sometime next week. What I'd like you to
review for me now is the process of withdrawing funds. I've
run into a lovely villa here in San Marino, which I'm thinking
of buying."

"A good choice. An exquisite little place, and then God
isn't going to make any more San Marinos—He's a depositor
here, if you didn't know, and has confided that information
to me personally. San Marino can only become more valuable."

Toni glanced out the glass door of the booth, not at the
man who was still waiting for the phone but rather out into
the café. How long would it take Dom to find her? Not long,
if he began checking the possibility that she had made
directly for the nearest phone.

"As for withdrawals, it's the simplest thing in the world.

We Swiss, you know, have kept pace with changing banking practices in spite of our reputation as traditionalists. I admit we don't as yet have those little machines that in the dead of night you can place a plastic card in and get instant money, but our method is probably even simpler, if not as convenient.

"As you know, in order to maintain the secrecy that Signor Payson has told me you require, we send out no periodic reports or account statements. We limit all communications to telex or, like this, telephone—preferably an untraceable pay phone. You have your code, which is your account number."

"Three seventy-one," she said.

"Exactly. And in this bank, account-holders with deposits as sizable as yours deal only with top officials. Nobody else has access to your file. What is your daughter, Christina's, birthday, may I ask?"

"November twenty-first."

"Right. And where was she born?"

"Beth Israel in New York."

"And the name of the attending physician?"

"Burnstein."

"And the name of your neighbor Jane Wallace's cat?"

"Ted. Where did you get all this information?"

"From you, of course. It's all here in this file." Toni had not spoken to Payson about any of that. He must have gotten the information himself. What must it have taken in terms of man-hours and expense?

"Deposits, of course, are always made by cashier's check in amounts under ten thousand U.S. dollars. Never, *ever* write us a personal check, or you might trigger an audit by your Internal Revenue Service. Hasn't Signor Payson told you all of this?"

"Signor Pasqual," she interrupted. Dom had just entered the bar. He paused to look around. She stood and, burning her fingers, twisted out the bulb on the ceiling of the phone booth. "Who is Giancarla Marchetti?"

There was a pause, and then with what sounded like a smile in his voice, he said, "Well—I don't know if I should relate this. But then, I suppose it is you and not Signor Payson who is our depositor. You realize, of course, he has been a bachelor for many years. Giancarla Marchetti is a friend of his. A very good friend, and I was astonished by how much you two look alike. In fact, at first I thought he was trying to pass Giancarla off as one Antonina Alexandra Spina, which, of course, we could not allow. Under the 1972 Treaty on Mutual Assistance in Criminal Matters, Swiss banks must provide access to financial information for investigations of organized crime, and both Giancarla Marchetti's husband and her father were involved in what some call La Cosa Nostra or the Mafia. In short, organized crime.

"It's unfair, but if only to remain above reproach and avoid a possible investigation of all our depositors, we could not accept her money, no matter the sum."

"*Were* involved?"

"Yes, tragically. Both are dead, having been murdered. The husband several years ago. The father only a few days ago. Perhaps you saw it in the Italian newspapers, which are full of it. His name was unlikely for a man with his pursuits—Infantino."

Dom now noticed the man who was waiting outside the phone booth, and he began pushing through the crowd toward her.

"Now for your withdrawal. How much do you require and where would you like it sent?"

Toni thought for a moment that she would tell Pasqual the real source of the money she and Payson had deposited in his bank and make a plea for his help. But how could he help her from Switzerland?

It explained, however, what Payson had been up to all along: for banking purposes, Giancarla Marchetti, her look-alike, would become Toni Spina, and in death—she now did not doubt—Toni Spina would become Giancarla Marchetti. That way Monsieur and Madame Henri Sevrier could establish an eminently comfortable retirement in the mountain fastness of Grindelwald, secure in the knowledge that the fortune they had stolen from her father and the two other men like him was equally safe in the name of an obscure American *restauratrice*.

It also explained the expensive clothes with the name tags and the sable coat and the jewelry, which, she supposed, she would have to don again before they dispatched her in Rome or on the way.

She thought that, if she was going to die, she should tell Pasqual to send a couple of million to her personal account in her bank in Cherry Hill. At least that way Tina would have a legacy that would launch her in life.

But Toni was not ready to die, and Dom now pulled open the door of the booth and tried to take the phone from her hand.

"Please," she objected, "I'm speaking to my maître d'."

He grabbed her wrist and wrenched the receiver out of her hand. "Hello—who's this? Hello? Hello?" He hung up. "Who was that?"

"Muñoz, my maître d' at my restaurant in Hammonton. The Borghese."

He still had her wrist, and he pulled her roughly from the booth.

"Let go of me."

With his face close to hers, he said, "Think of Cherry Hill. Your daughter and mother-in-law. Make you a bet?"

She stared into his dark eyes. His widow's peak was repeated by the line of his eyebrows. He said, "I can make things happen there first."

Toni looked away, and he relaxed his grip.

Most of the men in the bar were now watching them.

"You all right now?" he asked.

She nodded and straightened the wide belt of the yellow dress.

"Your hat and newspaper?"

"Only the hat. It took me some time to get through to the restaurant and I've read it."

The picture of Giancarla Marchetti was staring face up at him, but Dom retrieved only the hat.

"I've got to pay. I've given him my watch as security." And you'll need that, she thought.

"Signor?" the barman asked.

"*Orologio*," Dom said in a small voice.

"*Che? Che dice?*" the man snapped, looking down the bar as though his other customers required his attention. In his mid-thirties, he was a tall man with a good build. He was

245

balding and had his hands on his hips, as though expecting trouble.

Dom moved closer and repeated the word.

"Clock? Are you trying to say the word for clock?"

"No—*orologio da polso.*" Dom tapped the crystal of his own wristwatch.

"Aha, now I know what you're getting at. I'm sorry, but we don't sell wristwatches here. If you want a wristwatch, you'll have to go to a jeweler. There's one down the street by the hotel where you're obviously staying."

The others in the bar began laughing, until Dom's hands shot out and grabbed the tall barman by the knot of his tie and the back of his neck and in one motion pulled him across the bar and threw him on the floor by his feet. Glasses and cups crashed everywhere, and before any of the others could move, Dom had a shoe on the man's throat.

In clipped Sicilian Italian, Dom said to the other man behind the counter, "Get the lady's wristwatch. *Sprigati!*"

The breathing of the man on the floor was loud and troubled, and the watch was quickly produced from a well of the cash register.

"How much do you owe?" Dom asked Toni in English.

"For a glass of wine and a phone token."

"How 'bout the paper?"

"It's old. I don't want it."

Dom tossed a few bills down on the man on the floor. His eyes were bulging. "Get your hands off my ankle." The man removed his hands. "Hold them out." He held them out.

Dom slowly removed his foot. "You wanna take us down, show us the jeweler? Or you too bashful now?"

The other men made way for them.

In the hotel room, Payson had spread the contents of Toni's purse over the top of the dresser.

Pasqual's business card was in his hand. He tossed it at her. "Make any withdrawals?"

Toni said nothing, only looked down at her driver's license, her credit cards, her compact, her little sewing kit, the keys to her house and business, Solly's knife, which she had picked up the night he was murdered.

"She was on the phone," Dom said.

"Who to?"

"The restaurant, she said. They hung up."

Thank God, Toni thought. Maybe she could talk her way out of it, at least for a while. They wouldn't kill her here where she had banked and been seen, here where he had at least $20,000,000 and whatever other shares he needed to control the strange little bank. And then, once back in the car with them she stood no chance. None whatsoever.

She glanced at her watch. Twenty minutes had elapsed since she'd hung up the phone. "Look, what's the problem? Why're you getting so uptight? I did what you wanted—your business—and then I took care of my own back in Hammonton. You never said I couldn't or shouldn't. You want me to make my phone calls in front of you from now on, I'll make them. You want my credit card number to check the calls I've made on this trip, you've got it." Toni moved toward the dresser and her credit cards.

"That thing?" She pointed to the business card on the floor. "Your old *friend* gave it to me because he thinks he and his firm can manage *my* money better than you, a lawyer. When you were out of the room, he insisted I take it."

"Why didn't you tell me that then?"

"I didn't think it was worth mentioning, since you and I both know it's *your* money, not mine."

"But you kept the card?"

"I *forgot* the card. If you remember, after we left there we began that exodus that took all night before we got to your chalet."

"And the number on the back of the card?"

Toni decided that she should tell him at least part of the truth so he'd believe her. "It's the account number. Your account. He wrote it on the back. He said, just in case I forgot, which he thought was some kind of joke."

Payson's head bent as he retrieved the card, and she noticed through his silver hair that he was balding. It made him seem suddenly elderly and vulnerable, and she wondered if she had the courage to strike first, if she got a chance. She had never in her life consciously physically injured another person, but something like that would have to happen if she were to get out of this alive. She thought of her daughter and her mother-in-law—certainly innocent parties. Would they be allowed to live to complain that their mother and daughter-in-law was missing? Not for $20,000,000 and whatever other sum they had deposited in the bank in Bern. There wasn't a chance.

Payson was staring down at the number on the back of the card, which she had copied exactly as she had seen it on the banking document. It was perhaps the only time in her life that she had drawn a line through a seven.

"My card," she said, extending her AT&T credit card toward him. It would take at least a week to get a printout of her charges, so it was worth the bluff.

Payson's smile came on slowly. "It's just that we have much at stake here, Toni." Glancing up, he nodded at Dom, who then left the room.

Toni's heart suddenly began beating in her throat. Where would Dom be going? To check them out and get the car. Would he be back for bags? Yes. He had been out looking for her. And then she would have to dress up in all the Giancarla Marchetti stuff.

As though reading her mind, Payson tossed the credit card back on the dresser. "You should have been a lawyer, you argue so well." He smiled. "Get yourself all dolled up now. Put on the best that you have—jewelry, the sable coat, the works. We'll be traveling up over the Apennines and it can get cold."

Toni pretended to reach for the zipper on the yellow dress. If she could be injured for sex, she could use sex as a weapon, too, she decided. "Could you help me with this?"

"But of course." He moved toward her. "I can help you with everything, but why don't we begin with your stockings? Can I admit that I've always loved ladies' stockings?"

Sure, she thought. You can admit anything you want to a dead woman. But, no. Knowing what she did now—how he had planned all along to destroy not just her marriage and her business but everything about her, her daughter included—she couldn't let him touch her. For all his pretensions, he was no different from Mazullo, Dino, the little one whose voice she could still hear shouting in her ear, "You know snuff? Bear likes snuff." Over and over again.

It was what Payson here intended, after his fashion. He'd

fuck her and then he'd kill her. An hour in between. Or two. For convenience' sake.

He now had his hands out but held low, as though he would reach down to raise her dress. He was smiling slightly, and his smile was both smug and libidinous, as he peered over the top of the half-glasses that were balanced on the bridge of his nose.

Reaching behind her, Toni moved her fingertips over the dresser until they found the worn wooden handle of Solly's filleting knife.

Payson had raised her dress and now lowered himself to his knees.

Pretending to relax for what would now transpire, Toni leaned back against the dresser and, bending farther still, eased the hand with the knife back along the veneer surface as far as she could.

His hands were fumbling with her garters. "Black. I've always had a weakness for black lace."

She felt the rough surface of his shaved cheek graze her thigh, and she made herself think, This man kneeling before me will kill my daughter and my mother-in-law. He'll have to, to tie up loose ends.

Suddenly her left hand, as if acting on its own, grabbed up a handful of his gray hair and jerked back his head. And, whipping her body and right arm with all her force, she plunged the filleting knife straight through his throat, which popped and made a gurgling sound.

His blue eyes were wide in surprise, but his hands jumped and seized Toni's fist on the knife, and he pulled them to their feet. As though trying to speak, his lips began moving, but he did not go down.

Instead they staggered together, like in a dance or a whirlpool, Toni trying to pull the knife out to stab him again and again and again, to cut him to ribbons, now that she had begun, and Payson—it seemed—trying to pull them toward the sliding glass door and the balcony. With each breath, air whistled over the blade of the knife, then coated Toni's face with a fine spray of blood.

Dom. Could he already be up on the balcony of the other room on the next floor watching them?

Payson jerked his body toward the bed, and in trying to

pull him back, Toni's hand suddenly came free along with the knife. Payson tripped over the edge of the bed, fell to one knee, and then—pulling himself up with a desperate effort—staggered backward toward the balcony. He fell into a stuffed chair beside the glass doors.

Toni did not know what to do, whether to leave him like that or to—she looked around the room—to hit him with something heavy. She dropped the knife. The moment had passed, and she couldn't stab him again. His chest was heaving, and every breath sounded like the wail of some small, dying thing.

And his eyes. They were open and staring at her. Blood and spittle had trickled down on his chin and were spilling in clots onto the front of his shirt.

She noticed his half-glasses on the rug. She picked them up and carried them over to the chair, as if to hand them to him. Glancing up, she was nearly transfixed by the figure of Dom standing on the balcony above, hands clasped behind his back, looking down at them.

Sitting in the chair like that, Payson's back was to Dom. Toni pretended to hand Payson the glasses, but instead dropped them in his lap and moved away.

At the dresser she stuffed her personal effects into her purse and added the banking documents and passport from the other bag. She had her credit cards, her checkbook, and maybe $250 in cash, and she hadn't the slightest idea where she could get the quickest flight back to the States—in Milan or Rome or back in Switzerland—or how to get there. All she could think of was her daughter, and how Dom had said—

The Porsche. With that she could at least get out of San Marino before Payson was discovered. That, too, would take mobility away from Dom, at least for a short while, and maybe Payson was carrying cash. But how to get it without Dom seeing?

She looked over at Payson. His eyes were open and on her, and they gave her an idea.

Quickly she slipped out of the conspicuous yellow dress. She would have to change anyway. The dress was simply too impractical for her escape. In her underwear, which, like the stockings, was black, she moved to the chair and—

slowing her pace and steeling herself—eased herself onto the edge of the chair.

Payson's breathing was erratic, and the flowing blood had transformed his face into a garish mask. Bending toward him as though bestowing a caress, she reached into the jacket of his linen suit and found his wallet, which she also dropped in his lap. In the opposite pocket was a small-caliber automatic pistol and nothing else. That, too, she added to the items in his lap.

As though intending to become more intimate with him, Toni swung herself around in front of the chair and knelt between his legs. Out of the corner of her eyes she could see Dom still watching them, and she could feel but could not reach her fingers into the pocket to touch the keys in his trousers. Even unbuckling the belt and zipping down his fly, she couldn't get a finger in the key ring that she could feel through the material. And how to get them without Payson standing up?

But that was it—to stand up. She did and, walking toward the glass doors of the balcony, looked up and stared directly at Dom, as though angry that he was still watching them.

But the moment that she touched the cord of the curtain, he spun around and rushed off the balcony.

Back beside Payson, Toni still couldn't reach into his pocket because of the tall arms of the chair and his upright position. Suddenly an arm snapped up and seized her wrist and twisted her down into the carpet. Trying to turn his body out of the chair, Payson drew his face toward hers. His pupils were shallow pinpricks, his eyes glazed and bluer than she had ever seen them. Brilliant and horrifying.

But he fell back against an arm of the chair. As though trying to say something, he coughed a ball of dark blood that rolled heavily down the front of his linen jacket like oil. His body then slumped from the chair, and she dug for the keys.

How much time had she?

Dom's room was on another floor in another wing, and—God—she had to dress.

The hiking clothes that she had worn on the passage over the mountains were on a chair near the bathroom, and she pulled on the turtleneck sweater and insulated trousers. She stuffed her feet into the sturdy boots and drew her arms through the sleeves of the down jacket.

A fist pounded at the door. Again and again. "Bruce? Bruce—you all right?"

There was the small-caliber gun, and Toni was experienced with guns. She had carried a gun to make early-morning bank deposits after busy nights, and she had practiced at a firing range so she would know how to use it.

But instead she stuffed it and Payson's wallet and the keys into her purse and ran.

"Bruce! Bruce—open up!"

The sound of guns firing—hers and surely his—would bring the authorities, and all Toni wanted was to get out of there fast and back home to her daughter and whatever safety she could find.

The balcony. There she threw her purse over onto the adjoining balcony four feet away. Committed now, she climbed up onto the narrow concrete rail and tried not to look down.

Dom was throwing his body against the door now.

Taking two quick steps, she more fell than jumped across the gap and landed on her stomach on top of the wall of the other balcony. She heard wood splintering behind her as she tumbled onto the balcony out of sight.

"What?" Dom roared. *"What the fuck!"*

Toni scrambled up, grabbed her purse, and pulled open the sliding glass door and stepped in, closing the panel and throwing the small metal lever to lock it behind her. She pulled the curtains and turned to find a bare-chested man sitting up in bed.

"Che? Che cosa vuole?"

She put a finger to her lips. *"Per favore.* It's a matter of life or death."

"Bruce," she heard through the wall, "where the hell is she? And the numbah! If you're gonna screw up like this, at least give me the fuckin' numbah!"

Pulling open the purse, Toni couldn't at first find the handgun. She came up with Solly's knife. Next she found Payson's wallet, which she stuffed in a pocket of the jacket, and finally the gun.

The man gasped. "No, please—"

But Toni shook her head and again held a finger to her lips. "No—*silencio, per favore.* That man is a killer, a murderer. Understand?"

The man's eyes were wide with fright, and he watched her pull the San Marino banking agreement and Pasqual's card from her purse. Unable to find a pencil, she dumped the purse upside down on the carpet by her feet and, finding a pen, searched through the documents until she found the San Marino account number. She noted both numbers on the new cowhide of the underside of her belt and hitched it back up.

In a wide ashtray on a coffee table, she then lit the San Marino documents with the new BVLGARI lighter and added the Swiss banker's business card. If Dom, whatever he was—henchman, coconspirator, killer—was going to snuff her out, she would not yield him her only advantage. As the pyre flared, they heard a thud on the balcony and saw a shadow and then a form in the space where the curtains did not quite meet.

By then Toni had the handgun out and pointed at the door, and when the man began to make noises, pushing himself into a corner of the bed, she waved a hand at him to be quiet.

"Hey," Dom shouted. *"Polizia.* Open up! *Aprire!"*

But then as suddenly they saw the shadow depart, over the balconies to the one on the other side of Toni's room, she guessed, hearing him call out again.

It was her chance—she could leave now, but go where? The car, the Porsche. She didn't know if it was still in the parking lot and how difficult it might be to get it out. Had there been a gate? Yes, she now remembered, there was a kiosk with a wooden bar that an attendant had raised. Would she have to sign out of the hotel and present a receipt to get it? What if the car wasn't there and Dom caught her in the parking lot?

Then, she didn't know the roads or if there was a local airport with connecting flights to Rome or Milan. And even if there was, she'd probably have to wait, and Dom was good at all of that. She'd seen for herself in Atlantic City.

She despaired. The odds were against her, and she'd learned the hard way never to buck the odds, especially with a heavy bet. And what if a miracle happened and she managed to get out? What then? What would life be like, living in fear that some professional killer might snatch her daughter for the number or kill all of them to get even?

There was no point in running, not when it was she who knew where he was, and not the other way around.

Out in the hall she squatted down opposite the room where Payson was, and raised the gun in both hands, just as Dom was coming out.

The gun was small and light, and the first five shots—fired as quickly as she could pull the trigger—caught him in the chest. The force of the slugs and the surprise knocked him back. The sixth struck his right thigh and, as he fell back into the room, the seventh passed through a muscle on one side of his neck.

Rushing in on him, Toni held the Baretta to the back of his head and squeezed the trigger. Nothing. She squeezed again and again.

A hand, sweeping out, nearly caught her ankle, and she only just made the door before a slug splintered the door beside her face. Another shot smacked into the wall and showered her with bits of concrete and paint as she ran.

The Porsche was where they had left it, and the man at the kiosk opened the gate for a 5,000 lire note. Painted on a wall across the street were arrow signs pointing the directions to Rimini, Roma, Bologna, Venezia, and Milano. Another arrow said, "Aeroporto di Miramare, 5 km."

After Dom had stopped the bleeding in his neck and leg, he opened his shirt and examined the Webley combat vest that he always wore on the day of a hit. The skin of his chest was bruised, but the .22 slugs had fallen harmlessly into the shirt. He dropped them into the toilet, one by one.

He'd been careless, and she'd surprised him. She wouldn't again. After all, he had a pile here, if he played it right. His neck and his thigh? If she thought a peashooter like that could stop him, she was wrong. Dom had studied everything he could about wounds and knew how to handle them. It had been part of survival, all those months behind enemy lines in Vietnam.

He got the room cleaned up, and he dumped the clothes

from a bag and stuffed Payson in it. Broads—Dom made it a point to stay away from them. Totally. They made you vulnerable, which was the lesson in Payson, he thought as he closed the door to the room and moved down the hall.

Payson had probably been the most careful person he knew, outside of himself, and there he was dead. Why? Because he thought he needed Giancarla, and therefore the other bitch as cover.

But this Toni had her soft spot, too. She'd go back for her kid, and, if she knew how to use the money that was in her name, he'd have a hell of a time finding her. But he would. Dom was confident. He was a guy who had proved his talent, time and again.

His leg was already stiffening up, and his neck hurt like hell. But he found a turtleneck in Payson's bag and put it on, and at the reception desk in the lobby, where he settled up the bill, he managed to smile. He also rented a car. "The biggest you got. There's a whole gang of us. We're going to Rome, and Mr. Payson ain't feelin' too good.

"And here—this is for the door and the damage. We had a little party. Things got kinda rough." With deliberation he placed five crisp one-hundred-dollar bills on the marble counter. He added two more. "That's a little tip. All around." Slowly he turned his head and smiled at the two bellhops who had come over when he appeared at the desk. Somebody had probably complained, and Dom had learned long ago never to hurry when dealing with people. Speed always tipped them off.

Back up in the room, he made a few calls and waited maybe an hour before boosting the bag with Payson onto his good shoulder and taking him down the back stairs to the car in the parking lot. No buddy of his got whacked without Dom putting him down deep where the dogs couldn't get at him. He meant all the cops and pathologists who made a mess of a person.

He'd have to wait until dark, but he knew just the place. Top of a little mountain with a view of the sea. Bruce had always liked being up high where he could look down and see what was coming at him.

* * *

At the airport, Toni called her father and asked him to collect Tina and her mother-in-law at Jane's and take them to a hotel. "Anywhere. Just do it now and don't tell me where. But it's got to be fast."

"What's wrong? You in trouble?"

"Pop, it's a long story. I'll tell you sometime. Just make sure they're safe." She thought for a moment. She needed a way to get in touch with him that would be quick and secure and safe for her. "You know the old black man who works at the parking garage in Harrah's? Billy, his name is. Billy—"

"Miller. Sure, most of my life."

"Do you trust him?"

"I would. With my life."

Good—they would have to. She could pull into the garage in a car, speak to him quickly to collect or leave a message, and pull out, she explained to her father. And then she remembered how he had looked down at Furco's card with a kind of veiled contempt. Furco who had worked for Grisanti who had worked for Infantino whose money Payson had stolen.

"When will that be? Where are you? Did everything go right?"

Toni hung up. The small plane for Milan was about to leave.

PART
V

20

One thing Lucca Furco had was runners. He'd been a junior partner to Frank Grisanti and now that the Griz was gone, Furco had an army of them.

But they didn't seem to do much good. He'd put a team on Dino Mazullo's house, another on the funeral home where his old man—or what was left of him after the hit on the beach—was being mourned, and another on Dino's sister's townhouse on Rittenhouse Square in Philly, but still nothing.

It made Mazullo more like a rat, far as Furco was concerned: able to vanish like that but still be in the area. Mazullo proved it a couple, three times a day with hit-and-run phone calls to Furco's answering machine and messages he left at the joint and even an hour-long talk with Carmella, Furco's wife out in Longport. Mazullo told her Furco had a thing for this glorified waitress who was balling coons regular. Carmella loved it, she wanted *details*. She told him to speak louder and slower, and she taped it and then called Furco up and tried to play it back. But he'd already heard it.

Said Mazullo, "Nothin' but nigger pussy, Luck. Take a look at the guy—hey, don't he work for you in the kitchen of your joint? (Laughing here.) Didn't last week. Came and applied as a waiter, but she'd met him before at the Plaza. They made it for a weekend, all on you. And there now he's in your kitchen. She just had to have him. Hey, Luck? Every

259

time you see him, see her sucking his dick. You ever kiss her deep, Luck? How's that big nigger taste? *Asshole*."

At first Furco thought Mazullo was making it up, trying to fuck his mind the way Furco had psyched out Scarpone in the hospital with the newspapers and the box of cookies and shit. But then he talked to the guy himself, the cook or waiter or whatever he was, and something was off. Furco didn't like niggers, never had, and he wasn't used to dealing with them—what they said, the way they used their hands and eyes and never looked at you straight.

Furco tried to tell himself he was letting Mazullo get to him, but the way the guy mumbled or looked sneaky or was too good with the answers . . . Furco didn't know. And there was a look in his eyes he didn't go for neither, like the guy was sizing him up. A few days later, Furco found out he'd been right.

Way it happened was Furco thought he'd burn Mazullo a bit, so he sent two big baskets of flowers—funeral sprays, they called them—one to the funeral parlor and the other right to the Mazullo house. The cards said, "From Lucca Furco with deepest regrets," and no more.

But Dino himself ran the one at the house out the front door and down the lawn and threw it into the street where it got run over by traffic. And he was gone by the time Furco got there maybe ten minutes later. "How'd he get away? Weren't you guys watching? You working for him or me?" he said to the runners he'd put there.

Then Furco had walked right into the house and looked around, Dino's mother saying, "Don't mind Dean, Mr. Furco. He's a good boy, but respec', he never had none. Not for his father even. All the time they just fought and fought, and look what it got them. I'm not blaming you." She had raised both hands, but whether to the mantel where a photo of Freddo was wreathed in black silk or to Furco himself, he couldn't guess. But it was plain she, like everybody else, thought Furco had done him and the others on the beach, and now wanted the son to make things neat.

That last part was right. But when Furco got back to the restaurant, he found Mazullo had already been there and dropped off the other wreath from the funeral home, where again Furco's guys saw him too late. In Mazullo's childish hand, the card said, "TO THE NIGGER IN THE KITCHEN. ONE OF THESE DAYS WHEN I WAKE UP YOU'LL NEED THIS NIGGER." He signed it, "Lucca Furco, Gangster." And that's all it took for the guy to split. He was gone, and Furco couldn't even find an application.

It was now a full week since Toni had gone. Lucca Furco put his feet up on her desk and wondered where she was. Or why he should care, but he did.

In Cherry Hill, a block away from her house in a third-floor office he'd rented in a Route 41 office building that looked over her neighborhood, Mazullo decided something was up. It was afternoon, and the school bus he'd been timing had dropped the kid off twenty-five minutes ago. Right after that, a big older car in good shape—something like a Pontiac or a Buick—had pulled into the driveway, but the two old guys who got out had gone straight to the neighbor's where the kid was staying.

Then the door opened, like they were expected, and Mazullo decided he'd wait. He'd made the runners Furco had put on the place the first day they showed up. Guys had run for him, too, and would again, when he worked things out.

Who was Furco anyways? A nobody, a nothing asshole, and it pissed Mazullo off that the papers were saying Furco stood to "inherit" all of South Jersey. A guy only inherited what he could hold. Mazullo didn't know if Furco had done his old man, and it didn't matter much anyhow. The thing between them had been deep enough as it was, and who else was there now who had the contacts and knew the dry good enough to run it? Only Furco and him, and what Mazullo had going for him was smarts and nothing to lose.

The broad? The way she had messed up his life was something else, and knowing—like he'd known from the start—that doing her would touch Furco off would make it even better. And then, she was a witness to the murder of the chef in the parking lot.

"I got nothing to lose," he said aloud, and everything to gain. Hey—he was twenty-five fucking years old, and if he could put himself in the driver's seat now, he'd be fucking rich by thirty, who knows what by forty, and maybe head of the whole goddamn show by fifty.

To the west the sun had begun to sink behind a bank of dark storm clouds. It would rain before morning.

"Let it fuckin' *rain!*" His voice echoed around the empty room. He had nothing there but a chair and binoculars. And an assault rifle he could score with from 500 yards. Who needed close? Mazullo just needed dead.

Furco had already gotten the call.

Who could it be? Two old guys in a big old car. "How old?"

"I don't know. Old. 'Bout a block long. Looks like something from the sixties."

"What they look like?"

"Two old guys, like I said. One big. No, both big. Tall. But one of 'em with bulk."

"Dark, bald, hats—what?" Furco couldn't think who they could be. Cops? Why two old cops? Old cops were in offices. Why the old car? Cops were given nothing else except cars and they got them changed every couple of years, and old cops drove new cars when they drove.

"One guy's got a big, red face I seen somewheres, I know it. The other guy's thin, dark, dark moustache, maybe sixty-five, a little older. Sharp dresser. Least, everything goes and fits him good. They didn't have to knock. The old lady opened the door."

Then it had to be somebody the old lady knew well and trusted. From what Furco knew of her, she was cut off. She had had nobody but Jack. No husband, no relatives, no other family.

But what about Toni's family? She had a brother who was older and her father, Abe Sammasian, who used to run a little game in the back of his tailor shop. Craps. Furco had never met him, but he was willing to bet he'd be dark and the way he was described fit the picture.

Then, if he had showed up in Cherry Hill, it was because Toni had sent him. As far as Tina was concerned, Toni called all the shots.

"Any sign of our friend?"

"Nothin'."

Furco hung up and called the number in Toni's desk register that had "Jane" before it.

"Hello?" a young woman's voice answered.

"Put Abe on. Tell him it's Luke Furco, and I want to speak to him. Please."

"But nobody's—"

"I know he's there. His car's parked in Toni's driveway. I also know he's been talkin' to Toni, and I want to speak to him."

A hand went over the phone, and not long after a deep voice said, "Hello."

"This is Luke Furco, Mr. Sammasian. I'm Toni's partner out at the Borghese. I know you probably been speaking to her, otherwise you wouldn't be there, and I wanna know how she is, where she is, and what gives."

Sammasian said nothing, and Furco went on, "Look— maybe things didn't start out this way, but now Toni and me are partners *and* friends, believe me."

Did he hear the guy snort? Furco thought he did, and he shoved himself in close to the desk and closed his eyes to concentrate. When he wanted to be persuasive, he could be very persuasive.

"You with me, Mr. S.?"

"I'm with you, but that's not what I've heard."

"From who?"

"From Toni herself."

"When?"

The guy didn't answer right away, so Furco said, "The other night and what happened in the parking lot of the restaurant—?" It was habit with Furco not to give details over the phone. "That wasn't me and I think you know it. The guys that did that thing—" He waited, then asked, "You with me, Mr. S.? You read the papers?"

Abe Sammasian read the papers, all right, and he knew who Luke Furco was or had become. And he knew all about the night in the parking lot firsthand from Toni.

"Well, they're wrong about one thing—I don't let nobody clean up for me. Some of my guys mess up, I handle it. I didn't hear you say you read the papers, Mr. S. You know what I'm getting at?"

Sammasian grunted. He knew what Furco was getting at,

but it didn't make him like him or what had happened to Toni any better.

"Then—how you think I know you're there?"

It had already occurred to Sammasian that they'd hardly gotten their hats off when the phone had rung.

"I've had—" Furco searched for a word that was not "runners," which he considered too technical "—two guys on that house 'round the clock since what happened. My people, just to make sure who's left won't—" He broke off; he was saying too much. "You following me, Mr. S.?"

Sammasian was. But he was also wondering how Toni had gotten involved with a man like him. Sure, she had told him about Jack, but still—even Furco's voice, his words, how he spoke, was offensive.

And what faced Sammasian now was in no way palatable. He, an old man and a tailor, and his longtime friend Gene Heffernan, who at least was a retired A.C. detective, were going to try to move his granddaughter and her grandmother away from some person or persons whom the man on the phone was enough concerned about that he had placed a double guard on the house, twenty-four hours a day for a week now, if he could be believed.

"And lemme add this. I—" Was "love" too strong? No, it wasn't, but it wasn't right either, said here like this to him and not her. "—admire and respect your daughter very much, and once we're outta this you'll see things'll change for her, and that's a promise."

Furco let that sink in before he asked, "So now—what gives?"

Sammasian glanced over at Heffernan, who'd agreed without hesitation to help him help his daughter who was in a jam, but whose eyes said he was retired and enough was enough. And how could two old men, one of them a guy who'd never had as much as a fistfight in his life, protect two people, one of them a child, from somebody like this man on the phone who'd obviously been in situations like this much of his life?

"Look—am I saying trust me? Yeah—very definitely I'm saying trust me. I'd be hurt if you didn't."

Was that a threat? Sammasian wondered.

"You still there, Mr. S.?"

Sammasian made a sound.

"Way I read it is you heard from Toni and she's worried about Tina and Gabriela."

That was a nice touch, Furco thought, remembering the old gal's name. But then, he remembered everything connected with Toni, and he now fought to keep thoughts of the nigger and what Mazullo had said out of his mind.

Mazullo, that little rat bastard. Concentrate on him.

Furco went on, "So she said move them. She thinks something might happen and she don't think they can be protected there. Or she don't want Jane dragged into this. Or all of that, right?"

"Munh," said Sammasian noncommittally, but to Furco it was a yes.

"Where was she when she called?"

Nothing.

"Look, Mr. S., I'm trying to help you help her, and I can't without your cooperation." Furco could hear this whole conversation being played back in a year or two in some RICO lynch trial, and he chose his words carefully. "Things with us—you know, *us,* Mr. S.?—things are all goofed up, what happened. How it comes down is things *I* do *I* got control of, but, like a puzzle, there's a lot of pieces out there that need rounding up. Know what I'm saying, Mr. S.?"

"Yes." In his mind Sammasian went over Toni saying that she couldn't understand what had happened, that she and Tina and the mother-in-law had had such a good time on Furco's boat and he'd been so much the gentleman, only to have the other three . . . And now two of them were dead, one of them with Furco almost being present in the room.

"You're moving them, then?"

"Yes."

"Got a place in mind?"

"Yes."

"Can I make a suggestion?"

Sammasian waited.

"Know the Ramada Inn on the pike Toni stays in weekends?"

Sammasian did. Several times he had come out and visited her there.

"I own that place, and the people there are mine. It's big, it's open, it's public—I can put a couple people in rooms either side, somebody out in the parking lot, guy in the hall. You and your buddy—makes you feel any better—right across the hall or in the room. Don't matter to me. Then, I won't allow nobody else on that whole floor till it's ovah. This thing. Sound all right to you?"

It did, but Sammasian wondered what Toni would say. On the phone she told him not to say anything to anybody. "I'm going to trust you because"—you convinced me: I'm an old man and tired and I know nothing about killers and violence— "my daughter has told me you're a gentleman, or at least now you treat her like a gentleman."

Furco's head went back. He looked at the wall where all Toni's diplomas were and pictures of her at the Claridge with people like the Chairman and Frankie Valli, and Furco glowed. "Really?"

"Yes. And I want your word as a gentleman that this is on the up and up."

"You got it, Mr. S. I done a lot of stuff in my time, but nothing as up and up as this. Now, don't do nothing—don't move—till I call you back."

When he did, Furco told him where to place the car alongside Jane's house and how to let the Town Car that was parked down the street lead and make sure he didn't run no lights so the green Chevy he'd see behind him wouldn't get stuck. At the Ramada he was to pull up to the marquee. People would be there to take charge.

Before Furco hung up, he asked, "You know, you ever hear Toni talk of a guy name of Ross?"

"No."

"Big guy. Black. He's a cook and a waiter."

There was a pause, but Sammasian said, "No, I've never heard her mention that name."

Furco stayed at the desk for a while, thinking; it didn't mean much. Furco himself hadn't known the guy's name until three days ago and, like Mazullo said, there he was working for him.

Then, was that something you'd tell your father who as a Jew was probably particular about his daughter? Furco had once dated a Jewish girl whose father had hated his guts.

Furco shook his head. How he wanted, *needed* that little rat-fuck who had hurt Toni.

Mazullo, in the now-dark, empty office that he had rented on Route 41, was congratulating himself for his patience, for waiting.

Furco was moving them, why? Because the house with the other family in it, with only two cars out on the street and the back exposed at night and the front with big windows like a department store, wasn't secure? Maybe. Or because Mazullo himself, with the messages on the phone and sending the wreath to the nigger in the restaurant, had turned up the heat? He didn't think so.

No. Something had happened, something that had nothing to do with him, and whoever was calling the shots had decided a change was in order.

Furco? Slipping down the stairs and into the little Escort he'd rented only that morning, Mazullo let the caravan of Town Car, heap, and some kind of nothing Chevy move past him to the stoplight before he eased out into traffic. He didn't think it was Furco either. Far as the kid was concerned, the only person in control was the bitch herself, and that meant she was coming back from wherever she took off to. After what had happened, she'd be a little edgy, and the house in Cherry Hill, so far away from what she knew—the joint, the nigger—just didn't cut it.

And when he saw where they stopped, at the fucking Ramada, Mazullo nearly shit. What a combination—the joint, the nigger, Furco, and now the Ramada, which could be had from the roof of the building across the street, the marquee of the motel next door, and maybe even the storm sewer. Mazullo had once worked for a Holiday Inn, and, when he'd been sent down to clean out the storm sewer, he'd seen how the whole thing connected up in the court-yard.

But would she come there herself, the bitch? Not first. First she'd still be scared, and she wouldn't want to lead nobody to her kid. Furco, then? Nah—maybe she still didn't know about him. After all, she probably thought Mazullo himself and the other two were part of Furco. The police? She was in too deep for the police, and the police—at least the ones she knew—were in Furco's pocket. And one thing about her, she wasn't dumb.

Then who would she go to? Probably the nigger.

Pulling out of the real estate agency parking lot across the pike from the Ramada and into heavy shift-change traffic from A.C., Mazullo congratulated himself. Now he had two places to whack Furco or, better, to get somebody else to whack Furco like Furco'd whacked Scarpone. The Ramada and the nigger's place. When she showed up there, he'd put Furco wise and see what happened. Furco wouldn't be able to help himself. He'd roar right out there armed to the fuckin' teeth, and that nigger? Mazullo had confidence in that nigger and whatever he was: cop, ex-cop, or just plain tough mother.

See, Mazullo thought, gearing the Escort up until its little engine almost burst, the big advantage he had was smarts. Smarts made him better than the others. Trick was to put himself in the other guy's shoes. Ask himself what was so important to them it was worth more than money.

First it was Furco. What would *eat on his guts like acid?* The nigger and the bitch. Now he would try on her shoes, and hey—he wiggled his toes, he let out a little shriek—he liked how they fit. For her it was kid, kid, kid, and he knew where the kid could be had. And what did the kid need? "Se-curity!" he shouted. And who could provide that security, far as she knew? That mean, mother-humpin' nigger and nobody else.

It had become one of those rainy spring nights that reminded Mazullo of summer. It was raining, but it was hot really, with soft winds in the pines and crickets and bugs and tree frogs croaking up a storm near where he parked the Escort. It was deep in cover, but he could see the driveway to the nigger's place, and he wasn't taking any chances this time.

A joint? He had one, but instead he reached for the thermos at his feet.

Coffee. He'd drunk enough to float his kidneys the past couple days, but it was nice, too, staying sharp and staying alive. Picking and choosing. Being in charge.

21

Colin Ross knew Mazullo was there almost from the moment he arrived. Through night-seeing, infrared binoculars the Escort was picked off stopping at Ross's mailbox, turning, and then backing down the narrow sandy track across the street.

"He's going deep into the pines. Hundred yards now. One-fifty," was shouted down the attic stairs to Ross.

Running scared, thought Ross, who was in the kitchen fixing them something to eat. Putting himself way back in the kitchen where he wouldn't be seen in the house by anybody or perhaps fatally by Luke Furco.

Ross had heard Mazullo's phone calls to Furco, at least those placed to the answering machine in Furco's condo and the house Furco's wife lived in in Longport. The judge they'd petitioned wouldn't go any further and allow them to tap the phones at the Hammonton restaurant or the house in Cherry Hill, since A. A. Spina had no criminal record and no proven record of links to organized crime.

Ross, however, had known that his time as waiter/chef at the Borghese was short. Sure, he had spoken with Furco, gone through the charade of wide-eyed ignorance—no, he didn't know "Miz Spina" in that way; "Hell, we only talked twice, once where I was working, the other time here"—but when the wreath arrived at the restaurant addressed "TO THE NIGGER IN THE KITCHEN," it was time to bow

269

out of at least that aspect of the investigation. Anybody who stayed after that would have to be a cop, and talk among the personnel would only get in the way.

Mazullo. Ross almost wished he could have a second crack at him or had done him right the week before. But Mazullo was a catalyst and had set things off. He was drawing out Luke Furco, and with the murders on the beach and the power vacuum that now obtained in South Jersey, Luke Furco himself was potentially a much bigger bust than for just his dry.

Ross had finished making the tuna salad sandwiches, and he opened the door of the fridge for some pickles and two cans of beer. It was nearly seven o'clock, and he had a portable television on for the evening news but low, so he could hear the voice from the attic. It was hot in the kitchen and the blustery winds of the storm outside might have cooled things off, had Ross opened a window or a door. But open anything made talk between them impossible, and it was now their third day of waiting.

Carrying the sandwiches on one plate with a second empty plate beneath it, Ross moved through the living room toward the dark stairs that led to the attic. Tucked in the front of his belt, the second beer felt so cold on his belly it almost stung and made the 9mm Taurus, which was concealed by the shirttail, bind against the small of his back. He carried the other beer in his right hand.

He had to wait to accustom his eyes to the darkness of the attic before approaching Williams at the window. The binoculars were bulky and large, and he couldn't see past the other man's head and wide shoulders.

"Getting out now to take a piss. They all like that?"

"What d'you mean, *they?*"

"The new order of the ancient and revered organization known familiarly as Our Thing: Cosa Nostra. It's better than My Thing or The Thing. People might get the wrong idea."

"No, no—you got it wrong. It's La Cosa Nostra. The proper literal translation is 'the thing that is ours.' "

"Well—at least he's got it right."

"Who?" Ross transferred a sandwich to the empty plate and then pulled the second beer from under his belt.

"The heir unapparent. He's a skinny suck, but he's hung like a stallion."

"Now you're puttin' me on."

"Wish I was—you know, a genetic as well as a mental inferior—but I guess he's neither."

Ross eased himself down on the attic floorboards, which were hot and smelled as sweet and dry as old dust. "The important point is, does it bend left or right?" He popped the tops of both cans.

"Right."

"What hand's he holding it in?"

"Right."

"That proves it then, what I been saying all along. *Fucker's warped*," they said together, and laughed. Over the past five and a half years they had watched so many marks take leaks that they had the routine down pat.

Williams lowered the binoculars and handed them to Ross, who waited for the other man to duck under the eaves, before moving carefully to the small window.

He watched Mazullo spit and get back into the little Ford. "What d'you think?"

Williams forked the fingers of both hands through his Afro before picking up his beer and nearly draining it. "Me?" he asked in a voice made small from the tingling beer. "I think that mother gets heavy after a couple of hours. Ain't there supposed to be a tripod goes with that thing? I keep picturing it with a tripod all set up there in front of the window; every once in a while I see a car out there, I touch my eyes to it. This way it's more like weight lifting than surveillance."

"Well—least nobody sends you flowers."

"Or asks me to dance till the dawn's early light. You think she's back?"

Ross thought for a moment: when she'd spoken to him on the phone from wherever she was, she had been careful and sounded scared, but of whom? Furco, who everybody was saying had taken out Mazullo's father and the others on the beach and had then placed an around-the-clock guard on her house? Or Mazullo, who was obviously going for Furco and was trying to get to him through her?

Either way, where else would she turn—a single woman

271

with a child and an elderly mother-in-law to take care of—than to a guy she knew and had an inkling was a cop?

Said Ross, "Mazullo's an asshole, but he's a sneaky, smart, warped asshole, and he's here because he sees or he's trying to find some advantage."

"Could be easier than that. Could be he just wants you because of how you messed them up."

Ross saw a cigarette lighter flare, and he studied Mazullo's long face and nervous gestures as he held the flame to the end of a butt. "He's too smart for that. By now he's got to know it was a big mistake. Spur of the moment. No thought. Could he take it back, I bet he would."

"Maybe he thinks you whacked his friends and—"

"Not him—Falci was nothing but beef to him, utility grade, when that. Scarpone? At least he was muscle, but—" Ross didn't have to add that Scarpone's death had been more like a public execution administered by Luke Furco than justified homicide. The cop was being called a hero, not a fool, since nobody else'd got hurt.

But *why* Scarpone like that, so people would know?

Asked Williams, "Anybody related to Scarpone on that beach?"

"Not as far as we know now." Ross had spent much of the afternoon on the phone with Washington, which had told him to stay there, that no matter the reason, if Mazullo thought he could get to Furco through the woman, then she was centrally involved in whatever was being worked out there, and Ross and Williams should remain on the scene.

Concluded Williams, "Well, what can we know for sure—that obviously Scarpone and less obviously Falci and maybe that asshole out there did something grievous to offend Mr. Luke Furco. And, as the preacher says, they is payin' for it bodily, here in this hell which is earth."

"Whoops," Ross said as a car turned into the driveway and its headlights swung through the pines and flashed on the house. "We got company."

Williams scrambled up, nearly spilling Ross's beer. "You drinking this stuff or just trying to tease me? There you'll be down in company with an icebox full of beer, and me up here—"

But Ross was raising himself up to follow the car down the driveway. "It's a Seville. And guess what?"

"She's got a girlfriend for me. A blonde about six feet five inches tall and—"

"Mazullo's leaving."

"*Leaving?*" Williams scrambled to his feet. "You mean, he ain't comin' in? I don't get to have no fun on this job. Where's he leaving to? Lemme see."

"Hell if I know."

"We need more people. I hope you told them that. Push over."

"Can't get but one man in this slot."

"And you're needed downstairs."

With the binoculars to his nose, Williams watched Mazullo pull the Escort out of the sand across the road and turn south, back toward Hammonton.

In Milan Toni had had a three-hour wait for her flight to JFK, and in an airport boutique she had changed into slacks and a comfortable sweater and shoes, not boots. She had also bought a stylish coat in case it was cold when she got back to Kennedy.

In the dressing room she'd discovered that Payson's pocket secretary had been stuffed with thousand-dollar bills, ten to a banded pack and $60,000 in all. In another compartment of the leather organizer was a blank money order for $100,000 drawn on Chemical Bank. More insurance? Toni wondered.

Whatever it was, the sums were fantastic, and before leaving Kennedy, Toni purchased a tin of Balkan Sobranie pipe tobacco and dumped the contents in a wastebasket in a ladies' room. She then used it to mail the money order and almost all of the cash to her father, who would know what to do with it if anything happened to her. She figured $5,000 was enough escape money for her.

"Hi," Ross said, opening the front door of the house. "You look terrific. After the phone call, I was worried about you."

Toni looked around the room, not knowing what to expect. The phone call in which he had virtually admitted to being some sort of cop had changed him for her, but maybe for

273

the better. Without a doubt he had been assigned the task of getting involved with her on some basis—gambler, waiter, they couldn't have supposed lover—and the craps table set off from the other action on the floor of the Plaza had been part of the ruse. Now, however, she could use his help and perhaps even his official status, whatever that was.

"I'm alone. Well, sort of. My partner's in the attic, watching. We saw you come in."

Toni pulled off her raincoat and tossed her bag on top of it. "What—no work tonight?" She pushed up the sleeves of her sweater and smiled.

Ross, who needed information, decided he would be honest with her. It was all he had to trade on, that and the fact that she had come to him. "I sort of got fired from the Borghese. Or run out. This came with a big bunch of flowers." He reached down to the coffee table and picked up the card that had come with the bouquet. "Like a beer?"

"Love one. You mean a bouquet? Who sent it?"

"Mazullo, though I think it was sent more to Furco than to me."

She had followed him out to the kitchen. "I don't understand."

Ross explained: Mazullo's telephone calls to Furco's condo, Furco's house in Longport where his wife lived, the restaurant; what he knew of the deaths of the nine men on the beach and the murder of Falci and then Scarpone; and finally, whatever was happening between Furco and Mazullo, which seemed territorial but— "Maybe you can help me with some of this."

Her eyes fixed his and glittered, before she said, "Let's back up to what was implied in our conversation on the phone the other day. Just exactly who *are* you that you should be so interested in all of this and me? You can begin with how we met."

Ross tugged on the beer, and then explained further: he and the man upstairs were DEA agents—"lawyers, actually"—and for years they had wanted but had been constrained by administrative fiat from going after what would hurt the drug dealers most: their profits.

"The thinking was the IRS would take care of that, that we should concentrate on product. But around '86 things changed, with all the publicity RICO investigations and Giuliani were getting, and the guys who run our show decided the hell with procedures, we needed results."

With the most successful dry in the country, Grisanti and Furco were likely targets. For 3 percent they were cleaning money. For 5 percent they were sending it to any destination of choice. For 7 percent off the top and 2 percent per year, they were making it disappear into investments that were yielding a guaranteed 9 percent—"That's *after* their cut"— in havens so secure they were also promising 100 percent refunds for any amount confiscated or sequestered by the IRS or any other governmental agency.

It was easy to understand but difficult to expunge the laundering end of their business, with their dozens of runners, their little banks in different areas of the country, their shell corporations and no-show employees and pension funds and legitimate cash businesses through which they funneled bags of ten- and twenty-dollar bills, all gained from the illicit street drug trade. Every time one element was eliminated, like a hydra, another and usually new and creative method sprouted up.

"Charter flights of Panamanian nationals returning for a little *vacación*, each carrying a duffel bag stuffed with U.S. currency. Single-payment life insurance policies written on key dealers. By increasing the death benefit, they could add whole hundreds of thousands at a shot and collect 8 to 10 percent interest in addition to the jackpot that would be dumped on their heirs if they caught some spare lead. Even under the new tax law, 'investments' in life insurance are not reported to the federal government, and you can turn around and borrow your paid-in cash values at a nominal charge."

Ross drained the beer and opened the fridge for another. "But how two guys like Grisanti and Furco, who hardly ever set foot on foreign soil and were watched twenty-four hours a day when they did, were managing the 'financial services' end of the business was what we really wanted to know. It was what was attracting the big money and their own money, Mob money. And we decided we'd go for that.

"You?" He hunched his wide shoulders and tried out a smile but let it fall. "This investigation is, as I said, about three years old. We began where Grisanti and Furco's runners were most conspicuous. The casinos. It didn't take us long to pick up on your husband."

"Jack?"

Ross nodded. "He was doing anything he could for them, but mainly looking the other way. Other gaming managers made them adhere to the $10,000 limit, made them file a statement if they tried to go over. Not Jack. He made sure his office handled that and, whenever he was on duty, he himself."

Three years ago was before Toni had any knowledge of Jack's problems. "You watched them set him up?"

Ross shrugged. He was leaning on the refrigerator now. "It didn't look like that at first. Looked only like he was out for a buck. Then after hours they kept coming by for him, taking him other places. Buddying up. Schmoozing with him. Making sure there was always a little"—Ross raised his eyebrows and cocked his head—"action for him, and that's the truth."

There was a question in her expression.

"Yeah—women, too, but mainly a game. Sometimes cards, other times dice; we bugged a room at Resorts when they even had a wheel. Coke. You name it. They did it right."

Toni's nostrils flared. She pulled in a deep breath and let it out. She raised the beer to her mouth and drank. She didn't like beer, but she hoped it would help. It was having been such a fool that hurt most of all.

"Most games were nothing but shills and guys like Grisanti and Furco, who never drank. They were working, and Jack was their product. It got us to wondering what they could want him for—his knowledge of the casinos he had worked for before you two opened the restaurant? But that wasn't their action, and with things stacked like that, they soon had him—as you know—body and soul.

"So, we stuck with him. And when he disappeared, we concentrated on you, never suspecting until recently that it was you they were after all along. Why?"

Toni stared down at the shiny top of the beer can. "I don't believe you're finished yet. Tell me about the Plaza and that table. The craps table. The one where we gambled."

"We got tired of following you around, is all. Weekend in, weekend out. We thought maybe we were wrong, that they set you up just for your restaurant and nothing else. But, far as we could tell, beyond a little phony heist with Furco picking up the insurance money from the insurance company owned by the pension fund that Grisanti and Mazullo senior controlled, they weren't messing with your operation. And that was just an attempt to put more pressure on you.

"My part was to make contact, just a hello, how are you; what better way than when two people are winning? Later I'd show up looking for a job. You could hardly refuse if you'd made a few bucks, and who among the ones who were hanging out at your place would have guessed? They looked at me, all they'd see was nigger.

"But—" Ross waved the beer can "—I guess the chemistry was right, but it was wrong, too. Lemme say I only wish we'd met in some other way, but . . ."

Toni let the silence carry his ellipsis, while she scanned the rounded features of his broad face, his wide nose, his expectant eyes.

"Your turn," he said.

Toni finished the beer, and while he got her another, she tried to decide how much she should tell him. After all, he was a cop, and no matter the reason, she had knowingly helped Furco and Payson break tax laws. Then, all that money, the source of which Ross had just explained, was in her own personal name for other reasons that would be difficult, if not impossible, to explain without Payson. And finally, she was not about to admit that she—Toni Spina— and not Giancarla Marchetti had murdered Payson, yet again for a very good reason that would be difficult to explain.

But she now told him about what had happened to her and Solly at the restaurant after her date with Furco. She also told him who she suspected had murdered the nine men on the beach. "His name is H. Bruce Payson. He owns—" Did she know this? No. "—or at least he lives in a townhouse on Beekman Place in New York. I believe with a woman. Giancarla Marchetti. They, the others, called him—"

"Cheech," Ross supplied. "Giancarla Marchetti was— is—Sal Infantino's daughter."

Toni nodded.

"But *why* did he kill them if he didn't plan to take over? Far as we know, Furco is in the driver's seat here. He working for Payson?"

Toni toyed with the idea of telling him that Payson simply wanted to quit and they wouldn't let him. But she doubted if Ross would believe anything like that, and it now occurred to her that at least part of the truth might help her more in the long run. "No. There was sympathy between Payson and Furco, but that was it. All Payson wanted was their money—the money they'd entrusted to him on the guaranteed 9 percent plan, I think. Payson had worked it out how he could—" Toni shook her head "—murder them and then disappear in Europe."

"Where in Europe?"

She didn't want to seem coy, but every question was important, and she did not want to knowingly inculpate herself. Her daughter needed a mother who would be there for her in every way with her self-respect and reputation in some semblance of order. "Ah, c'mon—*where* in Europe?"

"Switzerland."

"*Where* in Switzerland?" Ross's tone was suddenly sharp.

"Bern."

"He have any partners?"

"One. His name is Dom, that's all I know about him. He acted as Payson's chauffeur and manservant, but the relationship was much closer. I think they grew up together in Brooklyn and were brought along by the man you just named. Infantino. Infantino put Payson through Harvard and then sent him to Bern to study law."

"And then Payson murdered him?"

"I'm sure it made eminent good sense."

"To Payson."

Toni thought of her conversation with Payson about perceptions, the one in the whirlpool, and how then he had cast her adrift. "To all of them. To Payson and Infantino. And Giancarla Marchetti, his daughter. And Dom." Raising her eyes to Ross, she added, "Dom is a killer."

Ross nodded once. "So it would seem. But just exactly *why* are they after you?"

"Because I'm supposed to die, preferably over there someplace where people who know me won't inquire. I—I mean—Jack and I were set up because I look almost exactly like Giancarla Marchetti. We're the same height and nearly the same weight. We have the same coloring and facially we could be sisters. Then, I own a cash business that might generate unreported profits that might require the types of accounts that Payson needed to hide the money. I understand that many Swiss banks don't accept just any deposits anymore. They're particular.''

"Especially any bank that somebody like this Payson would pick out."

Toni said nothing, and she held his gaze. She wouldn't divulge more than was wise.

"In your name and not Giancarla Marchetti's."

She nodded. "It was his plan. He told me it was because I have no ties to organized crime. No criminal record."

"Giancarla Marchetti would become Toni Spina, and Toni Spina would become dead?"

She nodded.

Ross again raised his beer can, and when he lowered it he smiled and shook his head. His eyes then flashed at hers. "You put this together before or after you killed him?"

Toni blinked, which was a giveaway, but he was a lawyer and a cop and obviously a good one. "I had the chance. The opportunity."

"Where and when?"

She would say no more.

"Just before, I bet. He probably laid it all out or laid out enough of it that what you'd been suspecting began to click. And when you saw your chance—bingo. He had to be close enough for you to whack him on the head or''—Ross snatched up a knife on the counter and feinted at Toni— "you stuck him."

She flinched. One of her hands had gone up, and she now turned her head aside and looked away.

"Girl—don't matter a damn to me. Man like that, they should give you a prize." He thought of reaching out for her, but it wouldn't be professional, now. In fact, he wondered how much of anything she'd ever told him would be usable in a court of law, given their differences and what had gone on between them. "What about this Dom? He the guy who took care of Solieri's corpse?"

She nodded.

"And the helicopter or whatever it was—he fly that?"

"I don't know, but I'd suspect so."

"When's he coming by?"

She hunched her shoulders. She thought of telling Ross that she'd shot him, but the bullets hadn't seemed to do much more than stun him. She decided it wasn't important. "Soon, I imagine. He seems to be"—ubiquitous? No, that was an overstatement—"able to get around, and—"

"And what? You look tired. I want you to get some rest." Ross moved toward a door off the kitchen. "You take the bed in here. There's a phone there if you should need it, but remember, all calls are monitored, so don't say anything incriminating." He smiled and, as she passed by him, they embraced fleetingly.

"Colin—Dom is no ordinary—" What was the word? Killer? Murderer? Hit man?

"You leave that to us. We're no ordinary Feds either, my partner and me. Hell, we trained maybe a dozen years to get ourselves here. Combat training in the bureaucratic jungles of Washington, than which there is none fiercer," he added before closing the door.

In the attic, Williams was wishing that either he'd drunk only one of the beers, or his actual field experience had been more intensive. True, he was forty-four years old and had spent an equal amount of time since his graduation from Howard in the tiny, cramped cubicles that he thought of as torture chambers and on stakeouts like this. First it had been for the Treasury Department and later—beginning in '81—for the DEA, trying to bust what he *knew* was the most pernicious evil to confront the young and disadvantaged in his lifetime. The yuppies and corporate types who snorted coke in washrooms and smoked reefer in the backseats of their Mercedes, Williams had no problem with. Let them fuck themselves up good and make way for some people who would appreciate what they had.

But Williams's problem now was he wasn't sure what he'd been seeing for the past few minutes. First a car—a light-colored Toyota—had gone by at forty-five miles an hour. Then maybe five minutes later it had gone by again, somewhat slower. Five minutes after that, there it was again, only creeping. It turned in the driveway with its brights on, only to back out onto the road and proceed off toward the lights of the three highways that were paling the night sky off to the south.

Okay—somebody was lost and was looking for a certain mailbox or driveway. They had driven past and back again, slowly and then slower still, turning around in the one driveway along an entire stretch of five or so miles that had a new mailbox. But then a few minutes after last seeing the car, Williams began seeing and hearing things. A figure—or at least, what he thought was a figure for the second or two he saw it—out near the road, but moving in under the cover of the pines and toward the house.

The beers, he thought, when he didn't see anything more, and the hours and the days of monotony. On one stake once he'd dreamed up names and histories for maybe twenty different regular customers who went in and out of a convenience store on the south side of Youngstown, Ohio, day in and day out. When they busted them, he'd felt personally sorry and during processing got the facts he dreamed up so confused with the actual facts that Ross'd had to take over.

And now he was hearing things—nothing like a twig snapping or a footfall, but just a kind of change. It was warm, almost hot, and to get a good view out the narrow attic window, Williams had removed the side stops and slid both top and bottom windows out. Late spring like this, the mosquitoes and sand flies and biting gnats—what Ross called the "New Jersey Air Force"—weren't real bad yet, and the open window let in more air. More important, he could hear things like tires hissing on the wet road maybe a mile off.

But now in the rain that was still falling steadily through the mild night that Williams thought of as foggy but not gloomy, he began to hear (or, rather, not to hear) "holes" in the audio pattern that he'd come to know here at the window.

First there were the crickets or tree frogs in the grove of mature pines that lined the driveway on the house side. They stopped for a while. And then the rainwater that was falling from the roof off to the left didn't actually stop, but suddenly for a while there just seemed to be a gap in it before it began again.

Then he heard a kind of squeak, like the lid of the garbage can near the back door was being lifted off. He tried to stick his head out the window to see if Ross was down there, but the angle was sharp, and the roof blinded his line of sight to the back door, and it was raining too hard. When he pulled himself back in, even his shoulders were wet. It was probably Ross or a raccoon. The Pine Barrens were lousy with them, he'd heard.

Williams pulled off his shirt and dried his face and head. He checked his watch: 8:18. Forty-two minutes and he'd have himself a couple more beers and sack out. Four on and four off. It was how they were doing things, just like when he'd been in the navy.

22

Dom Cafaro's hitches in the service had been far different. When they'd found he could put 98 of every 100 shots in the center of a bull's-eye time after time and could drop or disarm any drill instructor who challenged him at hand-to-hand, they told him to return to barracks and wait there. Somebody would be by to see him.

Couple weeks later the somebody showed up and was a colonel who said he was putting together a special force that would learn survivalist skills, hand-to-hand combat techniques, assassination procedures 'specially with silent weapons like eight different kinds of knives and two garrotes. Dom would be dropped behind enemy lines in the jungles of Vietnam with nothing but those weapons and some survival tools, and he'd stay there for up to six months at a time, *if* he could get out on a regular basis.

He'd have to live in the trunks of hollowed-out trees or up in the leaf canopy with the snakes and monkeys. He'd have to hunt for his food silently, setting traps and maintaining a system of trip-wire security checks in his area. He would learn tracking and scenting and how to kill so that his victim would not utter a sound.

Anything else he might need he'd simply take from the Vietcong, but all bodies would have to be disposed of. His victims would just disappear. The purpose? Reconnaissance and assassination. He would be given a list of V.C. leaders,

American deserters, and defectors that he should eliminate. Whenever he could he would sabotage key supply bases, but his main mission was death.

Said Dom, "I already know that shit." And done all the hard parts working for Sal Infantino, he might have added. But when the colonel took him outside and knocked him on his ass three times out of five and took away a knife he'd tossed him, Dom was convinced he could learn, which was why he had joined up.

The hardest part, though, was coming home. He'd spent a year and a half on his own in the jungle, eating raw monkey meat and learning how to move like a snake. When he got to Saigon, they gave him a shower and some fresh clothes with top sergeant's chevrons, shiny boots, and a fucking cap and put him on a commercial airplane with stewardesses and martinis. He felt like jumping out. Stewardess put her hand on his shoulder, he almost broke it off. Food tasted like cardboard, the water like it was chemicals.

In New York it was worse. He couldn't hear anything for all the noise; he couldn't see the things that might kill him. There were too many distractions. And too many people and too many places to die everywhere—elevators, subways, buses with assholes opening windows somebody could toss a grenade in. When a bunch of smart-ass kids complained about Dom's closing one and tried to mug him, he ended up in jail for attempted manslaughter.

Sal got him out, but a couple days later at the San Gennaro Festival he'd got caught in a crowd with some drunks who were pushing and shoving, and an hour or two later he found himself in a car that was not his with a dead man in the trunk whom he did not know, driving to Washington State, where his brother had told him a lot of trip-wire "Nammies" were living out on their own.

It wasn't a jungle, but the climate was wet, game abounded, and there were vast stretches of open mountain and range that led into three other states. "Wilderness," his brother had said, and Dom had kept the word in his mind all the way out. When he got there, he just parked the car and walked into the woods, with only a light windbreaker and the pair of city shoes he had been wearing when the crisis struck him.

It was nearly five years later when his boyhood friend Rick dePasquale showed up. In all that time Dom had spoken to only one other "outsider": a park ranger who'd told him he had no business there, he had to pack his shit and get the hell out. Stripping down and burying the ranger's truck had been the hard part. And when, three years after that, a "task force" was organized to drive Dom and his friends from the woods and provide them with psychiatric care, he decided that sooner or later he and those like him would have to find another refuge that was *secure*, this time, which would take money.

Said Payson, "What if you could own and defend your *own* land? Wouldn't that be the solution?"

"How much land?"

"It would depend where, of course, but with the money I envision you sharing—a hundred square miles of Brazil or Venezuela. Indonesia or the Philippines would be some other choices."

"How long will it take?"

"About four years. You'll have to learn to be with people again, and to drive. I'd also like you to learn to fly a helicopter."

To Dom the helicopter was the ultimate escape vehicle, and he had one waiting for him at the Atlantic City Airport, rented on a Payson credit card and now expendable.

He parked the Toyota deep in a grove so thick with scrub pine he didn't think even a tow truck could get it out. There Dom stripped to a pair of marine-issue combat-training shorts and nothing else, no shirt, no socks, no shoes. There was a tight bandage where she'd shot him in the leg and another patch on his neck, which bothered him when he had to bend or stretch. Otherwise it felt great to finally peel off all those layers and get down to skin. It was the way he preferred to live—close to the land.

At the garbage cans of the bungalow, where he went first, he discovered there were two cops in addition to the woman, Toni, who had just arrived. When they had to cook for themselves, cops, like park rangers, ate stuff that was easy to prepare and didn't mess up pots or pans—cheese sandwiches, soup, luncheon meats—and there were too many beer cans for just one guy who had to stay sharp.

Then Dom could see the hood of the Seville that Toni drove parked near the black cop's Buick. He hadn't made him as a cop then, but he had followed Toni here one night a couple weeks back when she'd come out after work to visit the guy. He'd also seen Dino Mazullo, parked out in the pines and watching them; maybe if he'd dealt with Mazullo then, none of the other mistakes would have happened. Problem was, her rape and the murder of the chef had made them rush. They had invested too much time in her to have to start over, and then, as Payson had said, she was perfect to do the banking.

Passing a hand over the hood of the Seville, which was still hot, Dom nearly smiled. Too perfect, as it turned out, but maybe he could make the whole thing work for himself alone. Dom had this technique of putting his nose alongside the top of a car door and smelling what was inside. Her perfume was fresh, and somebody had just smoked a menthol cigarette. Kools was her brand.

Back at the side of the house, he worked himself along until he could see into the kitchen, where the black guy was cleaning up and watching the tube. He'd known she'd come here. She wouldn't go to the kid and the old lady for fear of giving them away, and who else was there? Furco? Far as she knew, Furco worked for Payson. And she had what Dom needed—access to the money. If she didn't cut a deal, he'd make sure nobody would have it, not even the daughter.

But the woman wasn't in the kitchen or the dining room, the little he could see from outside. The next room, which was the living room or parlor, was surrounded by a screened porch that was dark. Dom didn't want to risk the rusty screen door or the old porch boards. Instead he lifted a piece of loose lattice and crawled into the dry, dusty sand underneath the porch, pulling the piece to behind him.

There he saw what he needed—a window leading into a cellar—but he didn't move toward it, which would be against everything he'd learned or taught himself. He'd seen the way the guy upstairs in the kitchen had messed up the punks in Mazullo's car that night, and he wasn't taking any chances. Procedure was all-important. Procedure left you whole and made you clean *after* the hit. It was the best lesson he'd brought home from the marines.

Instead he worked himself over to the far end of the porch and tested the lattice until he found another loose piece. Before he pulled it off, he listened, which took at least two minutes of accustoming himself to the sounds underneath the porch. When finally he was ready, he placed an ear against a facing board of the house and concentrated. From deep within, maybe at the other end of the house, he heard the sound of water running through pipes and somebody moving around heavy. The big guy. He had to go 240 at least. But Dom heard nothing else.

Only then did he pry off the sheet of lattice. He scanned the side yard before moving out. Replacing the lattice, he inched his way down that side of the building, again hugging the wet clapboards and dipping well under every window. Slowly. He knew she was here, right? Where was the rush?

At two-foot intervals he stopped and pushed his ear against the clapboards, and more and more as he progressed toward the back of the house he picked up two other sets of sounds: steady, rhythmical breathing, like somebody sleeping, and sounds from above. He located the sleeping sounds, in the room just off the kitchen, and the general vicinity of the moving around—in the attic at the far end of the house.

Back under the porch, Dom tried the cellar window and found it locked with a hook-and-eye catch. Unscrewing the handle of the knife that he kept in a sheath in the waist of the combat shorts, he drew out a length of thin, high-tensile-strength steel, like the kind used for a feeler gauge. He slipped it between the window and its frame. With a flick of his wrist, the hook popped out and the window swung free.

It was cool, almost cold, in the cellar, and Dom eased himself down the wall, feeling gingerly with his bare feet for anything he might knock over. Yet again he made it take forever, whole minutes that seemed hours. He wanted that woman and what she could do for him: make all that money and what it meant for Dom—land and sanctuary—secure. But he could only get her and it, he kept telling himself, if he followed procedure.

At the bottom of the wall, he squatted in the deepest shadow and waited until his eyes were fully adjusted. Two more minutes. Immediately in front of him were some boxes, an old bicycle, and a baby carriage. He picked out the square shape of the oil burner and the cylinder of the water heater. The oil tank. Set-tubs. Laundry lines and the stairs with a band of light spilling in under the door.

He listened carefully as he moved into the cellar toward the stairs; the guy was still in the kitchen. He scraped back a chair before sitting, and the TV was still on. He popped a beer can.

Raising a length of wood that he found and carefully touching it to the floor, Dom placed his ear to the other end. After a while he picked out the sound of breathing again, a woman's light breathing, like he'd heard at night through the thin walls of the hootches in 'Nam. Family. Kids. One time it had made him so lonely, he'd killed everybody but the woman, and he didn't eat for two weeks. The stink of her on his body was so strong he couldn't get within a half mile of a monkey, and, her scared like that with the garrote around her neck, it was like fucking an ice cube.

The stairs: Dom took them on his belly, spreading his weight, feeling the boards—how loose, any cracks—before moving up. And then at the landing by the band of light under the door, he could see as far as the kitchen and the legs of a table there, the bottom of a refrigerator beyond. In the living room was a sofa, a stuffed chair, some tables, but no human legs. And he could smell. His nose told him there were no human beings in that room. And no key in the lock.

But still he stayed on his belly to try the handle. A latch, a through bolt? His luck was with him. Nothing. The guy was expecting more Mazullos, more frontal assaults, more of what he knew himself and nothing different, nobody like Dom. He now brought himself to his knees so he could open the door bit by bit and support its weight should it begin to squeak.

But the moment he opened the door, something unexpected happened. Though Dom hadn't seen one, there had to be a window open someplace in the house, and a draft, driven by the storm outside, blew in through the cellar window, which Dom had left open for escape, up the stairs, and into the house, nearly taking the door handle out of his hands.

Dom froze for a moment. When he heard a chair in the kitchen scrape over the floor, he stepped back onto the landing and pulled the door closed. From the sheath at the back of the shorts, he drew the seven-inch utility knife that he'd been using since that afternoon with the U.S. Park Service ranger, and waited. He assumed the cop in the kitchen had some sort of handgun, and once Dom had that, he'd know where the other cop was coming from and the whole thing would be easy.

But it'd alert the woman, and she might have Payson's peashooter or something else by now. He needed her alive and well enough to tell him that number. In Payson's effects he'd found a three-and-a-half-inch computer disk, and he knew what was on it: all the details about Toni Spina that Payson had given those banks. Dom could always get himself a broad to call in. He'd make her learn the stuff cold, everything but who to call. He'd do the dialing himself.

But the cop only walked by the door to the stairs that led up to the attic. "You there, Ray?"

"Yeah. I'm there."

"Long as you're not here."

It was some kind of cop joke.

"You feel what I felt?"

The other cop laughed. "Maybe in six minutes. Right now, all I can feel is me."

"That burst of air, like a door opening?"

"Man—don't you know there's a full-blown storm out-side, or you too absorbed?"

For a moment Ross considered checking the doors, both of which led out onto the porch. But he could see that they were closed and locked. Passing back to the kitchen and the TV show that he wanted to see the end of, he glanced at the cellar door. Nah, he thought, he'd done his wash down there dozens of times and often kept the door open to hear the machine. Opening the cellar door never created a draft.

Moving down the cellar stairs again the way he'd come up, Dom passed quickly to the cellar window and slipped the hook in its eye. Then, back at the door, he again checked out the living room before opening the door and stepping through.

Six minutes, the guy in the attic had said. Six minutes

until what? Until he could feel. Feel what? The woman, of course. It was another joke, but it meant that in six minutes they'd change their perimeter watch, and Dom had to hurry.

He took the stairs up to the attic two at a time, not concerned if either cop heard. One would think it the other, and if he kept in the shadows—

"I wouldn't care if *you* took pity and gave me a break," the man at the binoculars said, hearing Dom move across the dusty floorboards toward him, "but I'd be forever grateful if she gave me"—he raised his watch to his eyes—"four minutes of her time." He was also a splib, about thirty-five or forty. Six feet, with a good build and still in shape. "Wouldn't take me that long by half."

They heard tires hissing on the wet road, and suddenly headlights sprayed the pines and bounced, as a car came to a sudden stop at the end of the drive.

Williams lowered his eyes toward the binoculars, and Dom reached for the neater of the two garrotes he carried.

Lucca Furco had got Mazullo's call maybe a half hour earlier, but he kept getting lost. It had always been like that for him in the Barrens. The pines grew so fast and so totally everywhere, everything looked the same and he kept flying by corners he should've turned down.

What scorched him, though, was that Mazullo knew and had even told him he'd get lost. Furco had let him talk, and there'd been that same laugh—the one that said no respect—in his voice that had always pissed him off. "Luck, you there? Lucky, you want the proof you need that broad is bangin' that coon? You got it, if you're fast. The Maz, he supplies.

"Now, listen close. I know you ain't too smart 'bout things like this. Well—you just ain't too smart, but that ain't your fault. No. You were *born* like that." He then laughed.

"Know that road to Maxwell, the one you take when you go through Egg Harbor . . ."

Furco took down the directions, and asked, "You gonna be there, macho man?"

"Me? Nah—not me. I'm not gonna be *there*." He hung up.

And Furco jumped, even though he knew he was being set

up. But for what? He had the little girl covered and the old lady and even her father and his retired cop buddy at the Ramada he owned. Seven guys, which he thought should be enough. Being set up like he'd set Scarpone up, for what he knew was his weakness: his pride and his temper.

But still he couldn't help himself, and, parking the BMW across the driveway of the house out in the Pine Barrens so anybody leaving would have to go through him, he only hoped he could get out of there without a Murder One charge on his head.

This isn't me, he told himself, opening the back door and reaching under the seat for the case that contained the Model 41, but he had to find out. If she'd been fucking that nigger, he didn't know what he'd do.

He pulled off his jacket and threw it across the seat. He left the silencer in the car. This wouldn't be no hit—he'd want to hear that gun go off.

He walked straight down the driveway, and even before he got to the house he saw her car.

Bitch, he thought. Grisanti had been right. Any of them, all of them'd make it with baboons if they had half a chance.

In the kitchen Ross had heard a thump overhead, then another. And then a bang like something falling, probably the binoculars. It was maybe the fifth time Williams or he had knocked them over, trying to fit themselves under the narrow eaves of the attic, and they really needed a tripod.

Anyhow—he glanced at the clock over the refrigerator—it was just about time, and the show was ending, and he knew how it'd turn out—happy, of course, and not at all like life.

Ross paused to peer into the darkened bedroom off the kitchen to see if she was sleeping. She had looked beat to him, and when she was rested and feeling better and he got talking to her about the chances she'd obviously taken, he'd learn more.

She was curled up in her clothes with just the edge of the covers over her feet, and she looked beautiful. Yeah, Ross decided, he could press it with her, if there wasn't the difference. And that, too, was life. How it was.

At the stove he stopped to pour himself a cup of fresh

291

coffee, and he dug another can of beer out of the fridge for Williams. The man liked his beer, but on a stake like this where Williams was the "silent partner," what else was there for him?

In the living room, Ross kept his eyes on the cup, trying not to spill any coffee on the new rug. True, it was government property, but there was no reason to ruin it. Ross was careful with things. He had a respect for life, which meant the people and things that he knew were good. It was the reason he had become a cop and later transferred to the DEA.

Above in the attic, Dom had Williams's body stuffed out of sight in the shadows of the eaves, and now he was waiting near the stairs.

The second cop was big. Once the garrote was on his neck, he'd slip off the stairs or stumble and be powerless to fight it off. He'd hang, *if* Dom could just hold on.

Dom squatted down, braced his back against a riser, and gripped his heels on the frame of a weather door somebody had installed to keep the heat in the living room from drifting up into the attic.

The garrote itself would help things along. It was the second one Dom carried and used only at times like this, when a mess didn't matter. Like razor wire, its braided cord was woven with bits of surgical steel that could sever a jugular with even the slightest movement.

When Dom saw the cop's shadow on the stairs with him carrying something in either hand, he smiled. The guy had his hands busy, and his eyes were down.

Dom drew in a deep breath that he would hold until he made the snatch.

The first step. The second. The guy was on the third step and the top of his head was just level with the floor of the attic when he stopped suddenly, swearing under his breath as the coffee lapped over the rim of the mug.

Dom, too, had heard the sound—the slap of the screen door on the porch—and now somebody banged on the door, and the head was gone.

* * *

NEON CAESAR

Furco hadn't tried to scope things out window to window, or make a tour of the house. He was afraid of what he'd see. If he found them together in the sack, he'd probably kill both of them, when it was only the splib he wanted. To think of him—a waiter, a cook, a jigaboo—putting horns on him like that so everybody knew was more than he could stand.

He hit the door again with his fist and saw a curtain go back in the window of a dark room on the porch. "That's right, nigger, it's me. Open the fuckin' door!"

Ross let the curtain fall back in place. So, Mazullo had called Furco and told him they were together, and Furco had reacted like Mazullo had pushed a button. Ross shook his head. It was always a mistake to mix women and business, be it crime like Furco or anticrime like himself. But then, she hadn't chosen Furco, nor had Ross chosen her.

With one hand up under the back of his sport shirt, he opened the door. Ross wasn't about to let any hood intimidate a potential witness in his presence, and he was tired of all the "niggers" that had been dropped.

"Yeah?"

Furco had the screen door open, and he now tried to step in. "Where she at? I wanna see her."

"Beg pardon?"

"Outta my way. She's in here, and I wanna speak to her." He tried to push past Ross, who swirled a shoulder and put him back out on the porch.

"She don't wanna speak to you."

Furco stepped away and only now noticed Ross's hand behind his back. "She say that?" He knew he'd make mistakes. The first was in coming at all. "What she doing?" He tried to see past the broad shoulders, but he could only get a glimpse of a piece of wall and a door leading into a kitchen.

Could he take him? Furco asked himself. Maybe someplace where there was more room, but not if the guy got his hands on him. Furco looked around.

"She's sleeping."

"Here?"

Ross hunched his shoulders and smiled a bit, his hand still under the shirt. "Friends all around. Good a place as any."

One thing Furco knew, he was quicker. No guy that big

293

could be as quick as he was, since he hadn't met a guy his own size who was. All he needed was some distraction, and the point was to keep him talking.

Ross said, "I'm sure you'd like to talk to her, but I don't let cheap punks or assholes in my house. Get the picture?" He smiled.

This wasn't the cook he'd talked to in the kitchen speaking, this was somebody else. And then it hit Furco how banged up Mazullo's Trans-Am was the night of the rape and murder in the parking lot of the Borghese. Philly, the sous chef, had told him the car had looked bad and the three of them worse. Had this nigger laid them out?

"Lemme ask you somethin'—two Monday nights ago, some guys come by to see you? Mazullo, Scarpone, and Falci?"

Ross nodded.

"What they want?"

"Same as you."

"But she wasn't here. She was with me."

"Same as I told them. Out on the *Bark-a-Roll,* fishing for blues." He smiled. "With her little girl, Tina. And the mother-in-law, Gabriela. It was nice of you, Mr. F."

Furco now studied Ross more closely. "Who are you anyway?" He took another step back. The barrel of the Model 41 was seven inches long, but Furco could snatch it out in about a second.

In the bedroom off the kitchen, Toni had awakened first to thumping sounds overhead and the crash of something falling. But she had dozed off again, until the sound of a familiar voice, not Ross's, and another noise startled her awake. It was as if somebody had jumped off the roof and landed right beside the window of the bedroom. She sat up in the bed.

Was it Luke Furco? Here and angry? Why? She remembered suddenly what Ross had told her about the bouquet of flowers and the card Mazullo had sent to the restaurant, and what Furco had said once when she'd asked him how he felt about blacks. She was sick of trouble and violence, and by the sound of Furco's voice, there would be more.

Pulling on her shoes quickly, she snatched up her bag and

raincoat and moved out into the kitchen, trying to determine where they were. The front porch. Good.

She'd go out the back, get in her car, and get out of there. By now her father would have left word with Billy Miller, and—Dom or no Dom—she would pick up her daughter and mother-in-law and just leave. Go someplace where nobody, not him or Ross or Furco, would find her. There had to be someplace, and she would find it.

But he was waiting for her in the shadows at the bottom of the back stairs. He clasped a hand over her mouth and then looped something over her head that bit into her throat.

"That's razor wire. You know razor wire? You tug, you move, you turn your head, it'll slice your throat.

"Now, walk toward your car. Steady pace. Don't make a sound. Not with your mouth or your feet. You call to those bastards at the front of the house—I don't give a fuck—you're dead first."

In the doorway Ross was saying, "—tired of you. You get your skinny, white ass—" when Furco saw something move over Ross's shoulder in the kitchen and, following the shape with his eyes, caused Ross to turn slightly.

It was all Furco needed. He snatched the target pistol from the back of his trousers and pressed the long barrel to the cop's forehead. "Gotcha, nigger. Now, bring that hand up slow and empty and move back. Quick, quick—keep moving back toward the kitchen."

Furco let the screen door slap shut. Ross only hoped Williams had been picking up on all of this. He let his eyes slide toward the attic stairs as Furco shoved him through the living room. Where was Williams?

Toni wasn't in the bedroom, and when Furco pivoted suddenly and rushed to the kitchen door and out into the yard, Ross pulled his own weapon.

They caught them nearly at the door of the Seville, both Furco and Ross now with guns raised and pointed at Dom.

"I'm good with this, and she'll be dead in a second if you do anything. She's got something of mine, is all. She tells me, I let her go, but not here. And don't tail me; I don't like being tailed."

"*What* of yours?" Ross asked.

The guy only drew Toni toward the car like he was going to get in the driver's side first and make her drive. Blood was seeping from beneath the cord on her neck. Both of his fists were gripped tight on the handles of the garrote.

They weren't going nowhere, Furco thought, keeping the target pistol pointed at what he could see of the guy's head. Furco's BMW was parked across the drive. It was locked and the wheels were locked and he had the keys. He thought of turning now and sprinting back into the pines that lined the drive, where he could conceal himself and, when the car went by, bounce up and get off two, maybe three quick shots through the windshield and side window. Furco was a good shot. Where he practiced regularly with two former mid-atlantic states champs, he was the best.

But the glass might deflect the rounds, and the guy, if he was smart, would by then be in the backseat.

Or maybe he would wait by the BMW. Sooner or later the guy would have to get out, and he'd pop him then. But could he get all the way down there by then? Not if she drove fast, and the guy would make her drive fast.

Instead he reached out and shoved Ross's hip, telling him to fade out to one side while he himself took the other, which would let him look in the door, once it was open.

Keeping himself as fully behind her as he could, Dom moved them quickly to the car. Transferring both handles of the garrote to one fist, he opened the door. But they couldn't get in together, and he had to position them perfectly so he could crouch into the car without exposing himself or losing her, which meant keeping tension on the garrote all the time.

Still, there'd be that second when he dropped down to the seat where he'd have to ease up on it or risk cutting her throat. He decided they wouldn't chance shooting him, and he had no choice. He made his move.

It was then she reached up with her hands and tried to pull the cord away from her neck. He jerked it back, and she cried out in pain, twisting, trying to wriggle free, pulling it up so she could get it over her face and head.

The first hollow-tipped slug smacked through his left cheek. It exploded in his mouth and blew out his tongue, his teeth and the right side of his jaw, that cheek, and most of his right ear.

He still had hold of the garrote, but she bucked and lunged and fell away.

All she saw next were Ross's feet by her face and Furco's beside the door. Their guns exploded above her, riddling Dom's body, which was driven, twitching and hopping, into the small space on the floor beneath the passenger seat.

Furco reached in and picked the garrote off the seat of the car. He had never seen one like that before.

Toni scrambled up, and she now ran until she stumbled and fell. Like her throat, her hands were hot and felt sticky, but she picked herself up again and ran some more, thinking only of her daughter and escape. They'd just get in a car, any car, and drive off into the night until they found some-place safe to hide. There had to be a place.

But Furco quickly caught up to her. "We gotta get you to a doctor. My car's at the end of the drive there." He pointed to a shape in the distance. "And I know where Tina is."

Suddenly headlights were snapped on in a car at the end of the drive.

What, Furco thought, his own car? No, he had parked his car *across* the drive. Bullets then splashed in the driveway, spraying wet sand into their faces. Through the rain the carbine sounded like harsh clacking.

Toni stumbled. She went down and the clacking stopped. Furco threw himself down by her side.

"You hit?"

"No, it's just my eyes—the sand. And my hands." She tried to look down at her bloody palms. They were caked with sand.

"Roll over. Quick, now—into the pines, and when you get out of the lights, run. It's me he's after.

"Ready?"

She nodded, and when she got to her hands and knees, he pushed her off the shoulder of the driveway down into the young pines that had sprouted up there. Furco then lunged to the left, breaking through the lights to the other side. At the top of the drive the gun was clacking again, and Furco heard its rounds biting through and hitting the pines above his head.

But mindless of his hands and forearms and face, Furco darted through the trees, flanking Mazullo. The rat bastard—

he'd show him quick and sneaky. He'd show him what thinking was all about.

Mazullo was having trouble with the Colt AR-15 he'd bought a couple years ago when him and the Bear and Tiny got heavy into guns. He'd paid two bills for it hot, but a full yard for the Ciener belt-feeder—a kind of cannister thing that fit under the stock—that could jack out 200 rounds as fast as you could pull the trigger.

The trouble was when he did, the goddamn thing nearly jumped out of his hands. He had pulled the little Escort rent-a-car into the driveway as much as he could and then lugged the Colt around to the roof of Furco's BMW, which was parked across it. He thought he'd prop the sucker on the top of the car and get a better shot, if the bastard made it away from the house alive. And then the BMW would shield him from anything fired back.

But the damn thing was heavy, and every time he squeezed the trigger it tried to take off. Jerking it back, he fired again and pinched the heel of his palm between the pistol-grip stock near the trigger guard and the roof of the car.

"Mothah*fuck!*" Mazullo roared, pulling the Colt off the car and running around the hood of the BMW so he could get a clear shot at them.

It was heavy, and the bitch—Toni—rolled off the side of the road into the trees and out of the lights. And then Furco picked himself up and dived the other way, plowing right through the trees like it didn't matter.

By then it was like the gun had a life of its own, and with all them rounds stuffed in the belt-feeder, Mazullo had to pull it down from where it was firing up into the cloudy night sky. His arms were aching, his ears ringing, and he wished he had Scarpone and Falci or somebody like them with him.

The whole place seemed empty now, and the rain was coming down in sheets. Mazullo was drenched. He'd thought at first that at least he'd hit the bitch. He should've practiced with the thing, but how could he have with Furco on his ass and his old man buying it like that, and then Tiny and Rik? Anyplace he knew of to shoot there'd be guys who knew Furco.

Furco.

He knew he should do something quick—throw away the fucking piece of shit in his hands, pull the Erma 9mm out from where he'd stuck it in his belt, and get his ass in the car and the fuck away from there. But it was like he was frozen, fixed, couldn't move. Nothing had worked right. Nothing had gone off the way he'd imagined. How had Furco got out of there in one piece? And together with the bitch? Could Furco really be better than the nigger? And how had he himself missed them like that? They were running right at him. Shit.

Here he stood, not behind nothing, not moving away from where Furco would think he'd be, not getting the hell out of there to plan his next move. What if Furco *did* have a gun? He'd pick his ass off good. Mazullo'd once seen the sonofabitch run an afternoon of clay pigeons without missing one. Not one.

Gone was the up he'd felt planning the thing out. Now he couldn't see himself handling what he had before him, to say nothing of whacking out Furco and taking things over. All he wished he could do was find someplace, anyplace, to hide. But where? He liked it here around A.C. where he knew people and what was what.

Pivoting suddenly, he snapped up the AR-15 and began firing into the BMW—the grille shattered, the tires almost exploded and hissed out, the hood, the windshield. Like a madman, he ran around it, pulling the trigger as fast as he could. The bullets made the sheet metal whine. They bucked through the car and right out the doors and windows on the other side. With the butt of the thing, he smashed at the glass again and again until he broke right through. Standing some five feet away from the gas tank and not giving a shit, he just fired and fired and fired and fired.

Even that satisfaction was denied him. It wouldn't go up, and exhausted now and uttering a cry of frustration that scared him, it sounded so much like a kid, he spun around and threw the carbine out into the dark trees and made for the Escort, fast now. It was over, he had spent his anger, and he just wanted to get away from there.

He walked through the lights, tripped, and nearly fell into the ditch where the driveway met the road. He grabbed the door and slid into the little car. Furco, pulling himself up from the shadows of the backseat, caught him around the neck with the barbed garrote and drew him back to where he could see his face in the rearview mirror.

"Say, 'I am a little rat bastard.' *Say it!*"

"I am a little rat bastard. Luke, look—Jesus—I was wrong. I could never have taken ovah. Nevah!" The thing was biting his neck, it hurt, he could feel his own blood running down his neck.

"Look," Mazullo went on, "I'll work for you for the rest of my life." His eyes tried to meet Furco's, but he couldn't look at what he saw in them. Hatred. The fucking guy *hated* him all the way, and there was nothing he could say or do. "Honest. Anything you want, no questions asked. You tell me to jump, I jump."

"Say it."

"I am a little rat bastard."

"*Again!*"

"I am a little rat bastard."

"*Louder!*"

"*I am a little rat bastard! Little rat bastard! Rat bastard! Rat bastard!*"

With a sawing motion, Furco flexed his fists back and forth once, then pulled the garrote away. Blood from Mazullo's neck spurted over the steering wheel, the window, the door. Looking down, he tried to stop it with his hand. His eyes moved up to Furco's. "Ma," he croaked. "Ah, Mama—look what he done to me."

Ross found Williams in the attic, sprawled on the floor near where the binoculars had fallen.

For the longest time Ross only stared at the body. In the thin light through the open window, the line of the garrote looked blue, like some narrow necklace. His head was bent off to the side, and his eyes were open, as if staring up at the stormy sky.

Ross thought of how they'd been hired together and trained together and even assigned together. After a while, some racist at the agency began calling them "the tar babies," which passed from slur into general use, and helped them get known and—Ross believed—promoted. "Tar Baby 1" and "Tar Baby 2" had been inseparable, until now.

Ross also thought of how over the years he had gotten to know Williams, who had been in some ways childlike and simple, in others street-wise and sharp. And what he knew— Williams's basic kindness and honesty and his outrage at what they saw going down out there in the world—Ross had liked, or, rather, loved.

Finally, Ross thought of Williams's wife and family, and what he would or could say.

Nothing and nobody was worth that.

23

A week later Toni Spina and Lucca Furco found themselves sitting together in the corner booth of the bar at the Borghese. Furco had just finished a satisfying lunch before he left to undergo another long afternoon of questioning or, rather, being questioned. He had become so used to the process of question/no-answer that it no longer bothered him. Content with how things were working out, he drew on a long Macanudo, then reached for the espresso by his right hand.

Toni herself had been interviewed by local, state, and Ross's federal authorities. She had not seen him again, which was good. She felt used by Ross, and she now said she could remember no part of the conversation they had had in the kitchen of the Maxwell house after her return from Europe. She had been distraught and in fear of her life for reasons that subsequent events proved to be entirely justified. Her lawyer, whom Furco had found for her, took over from there. And personally, Toni didn't see how anything she might say could serve the best interests of anybody she knew, which was how she now viewed things.

This afternoon she planned to drive up to Manhattan on "a little personal business," she had told Furco.

"You sure I can't take you? How you gonna drive with those hands?"

"Do you think I *walked* here?" She had taken to wearing

gloves at least until the stitches were removed, and today they matched the white suit and wide-brimmed straw hat that she had put on especially for New York.

Beekman Place was a fashionable address, and she did not want to appear out of place. Only the blouse with the high collar seemed unusual, but the surgeon had assured her that after her neck wounds had completely healed, she would have nothing but a few hairline scars.

She eased herself out of the booth. "This is something I have to take care of myself."

"Well—how long are you going to be gone?"

"As I said, I really don't know, but I'll be back as quickly as I can. Two or three days. I just have to satisfy my curiosity."

She had explained it to him before, but he still didn't like it.

"You keep an eye on Tina." A gloved hand touched the back of his hand and their eyes met, and she was gone.

It had turned hot, summery, and Toni had trouble finding anyplace to park. Finally she decided she would risk a ticket and parked right in front of the townhouse.

Then she had trouble with the keys, not knowing which one of the dozen or so on Payson's ring might fit the front door. But there was no mail in the letter box on the back of the door, nor did the house have that unlived-in stuffiness that even a few weeks could bring.

She found the woman where she knew she would: in Payson's study, sitting in his ladder-back rocker before the computer.

And truly the resemblance was astonishing. They had the same nose and cheekbones, the same chin and forehead. Only their eyes—which now searched each other's—were different, and their hair.

"I know what you want," said the other woman, raising a computer disk. "You know what I want. My money."

Toni glanced around the room to make certain they were alone. "And you think I have your money?"

"I know you do."

So, she *had* tried to get it out. Toni wondered with what expression of dismay Signor Pasqual had turned her out.

And DeCroce? Had he shown her the door? Toni said, "I'm interested in knowing how you think it's your money and why I should give it to you. You, who conspired to destroy my marriage and me. You would have murdered my child, had you thought it necessary."

"It's not too late." The woman brought up her other hand. In it was a shiny handgun.

Toni didn't hesitate. She walked right toward her. "You won't use that, you don't have the courage. If you had, Bruce wouldn't have needed me. He had all the information he needed in there." She pointed to the computer. "A passport no different from the one I had home. Social security card. Jersey driver's license. Credit cards. And certainly a half-decent beautician could have made you appear sufficiently different to fool Signor Pasqual." She seized the woman's wrist and pried the gun from her hand. The woman shrieked and tried to bite her, but her muscles were weak. The floppy disk fell to the floor, and Toni snatched that up, too.

Tears gushed from the woman's eyes. "I'll go to the police. I'll turn you in."

"Certainly not for patricide. Or is that a word you've dropped from your vocabulary these days?"

"But where will I go? What will I do? I have nothing."

Looking down on her, Toni decided that they didn't look a bit alike after all: Giancarla Marchetti's face was too narrow, her chin weak, her eyes, which were darker than Toni's, lacked character. That was it. "My hat's off to your father, then. He wasn't as bad a judge of character as events would suggest." By that she meant Payson.

Glancing at the rows of shelved books and filing cabinets, she only hoped the woman had enough command of her environment to attempt to trade the proper disk for all that money. Toni did not want to have to plow through a lifetime of research.

"Now—get out of my chair. I want to use the machine."

"*Your* chair?"

Toni waited until the woman's watery eyes swung up to hers. "I'm sure Signor Pasqual also informed you that A. A. Spina through Dei Nydegg Finanz Gaselltschaft now owns this building."

The woman blinked but said nothing.

"And the chalet."

She blinked again.

"But I have nowhere else," she said, rising from the seat. "I've spent most of my adult life here. All my possessions—" her eyes flickered over at Toni "—are here."

Toni sat and put her purse on the table. The Borghese's payroll, ledger, and accounts had been placed on computer, and she knew at least something about using one. She switched on the machine and accessed the directory. When she saw her name, she typed that in and hit the return key.

The woman had passed to a window, where she was sobbing, and while the computer was bringing up the file, Toni asked her to leave the room.

"But don't you have any pity, any compassion?"

Toni only looked down at the screen. The woman had made her choices and now she had to live with them.

And Toni was amazed at the specificity of the information that Payson had compiled about her. Somehow he had gotten hold of all her credit-card transactions, her bank statements, and the records of her mortgage payments on the Borghese, her first house (and the person to whom she'd sold it with the price and terms), the second house in Cherry Hill.

He had her IRS Schedule C forms reporting her business profits, her personal tax forms, the record of payment of property taxes in Hammonton and Cherry Hill. Automobile purchases and terms, a list of Borghese employees, bank accounts with amounts of deposits and withdrawals—everything was there, along with a list of Jack's addresses since he'd left the area nearly three years earlier: one in Florida, another in Texas, and the most recent in a town in Georgia she had never heard of.

Reaching for a pen in a holder on the desk, Toni heard the sounds of something heavy being dragged across the hall and a cry of frustration. At the open front door, she found the woman trying to tug a large suitcase out the open door. She had obviously packed before Toni had arrived; there were several others in the hall. Out on the sidewalk a cabbie was standing with his hands in his pockets and a fat cigar in the middle of his mouth.

"You fucking *bitch!*" the woman hissed at her, her face

pinched with emotion. She placed a thumbnail under her front teeth and flicked it at Toni. "I'll get you for this."

"Will you? Then you should understand that I know how and by whom and for what reason your father and those other men were murdered there on the beach. More important, I have proof." It was a bluff. Payson had been careful, and Toni had nothing more than what she suspected.

But when the woman looked away, Toni turned to the cabbie and pointed to the bags.

He threw out his hands and spoke through the cigar, "Well—at last somebody says something. What I look like, a robot? How 'bout a please."

"Please!" the woman screamed.

Toni left them. At the computer she copied down the address, then dialed information for Georgia. When she dialed the number she was given, Jack answered, and Toni hung up. She closed her eyes and bowed her head. Her face was flushed—with shame and guilt and anger—but tears did not come. Too much had happened for crying. "Why guilt, for crissakes?" she asked the amber-colored screen. "What do I have to be guilty about?"

It was a sleepy southern town. The paved main highway led her past some gas stations and a farm-supply store into a square with a courthouse. There was a railroad crossing, a barbershop, a bank, and a restaurant before the road ran right back out into pines that were different from the Barrens only in their height. Even the ground was the same: flat and sandy.

Jack's street was nondescript, a beige track with rows of tall pines bordering patchy lawns and modest one-family homes, all of which seemed low and squat. Jack's in particular.

It was a kind of bungalow with a porch that seemed too wide for the building. The side yard was fenced and contained a sandbox and bright-colored plastic toys.

Toni drifted by in the Continental that she had rented at the airport in Atlanta, and she drove around the block, hoping to see the house from the back.

A young woman—how old? Twenty-five? No older than that—was hanging clothes on a line near a narrow garage, and there was a long vegetable garden running to the border of the next yard.

Like Jack, the woman was a natural blonde with good square shoulders and erect posture. Toni could not see her face from that distance, but she imagined she was pretty, if slight and small. No more than five feet. Five-one, tops.

At her feet were two little towheaded tots, one in blue, the other in pink, who were trying to help her by handing her the clothes. And she kept up with them, her movements quick and sure. Finished, they helped drag the yellow plastic wash bin toward the house, and disappeared inside.

It was three o'clock, and there was no shade where she was parked. And then she did not want to appear too conspicuous in the neighborhood. In town she found a restaurant that claimed notoriety for its barbecue sandwiches, the spicy-hot pork of which she found delicious. She also drank several glasses of unsweetened iced tea that took some doing to prepare. "Most folks hereabouts like it sugared," the waitress told her.

But by six o'clock she returned to the street behind the house and had just lit a second cigarette when Jack appeared in a beat-up pickup truck with the logo of a logging company on the door.

The woman and the children came out to greet him, and he picked up the two tots and swung them around, turning his head from one to the other, his smile complete. He looked good, better than Toni could remember seeing him since their early days in the casinos. After carrying them into the house, he stepped back outside with a can of beer and moved to the garden. There he pulled off his shirt and began working down the rows with a hoe.

His hair was lighter—blonder, or it had begun to turn white—and he had lost weight and added muscle. He had always been a big man, but now his tanned neck and shoulders and arms looked formidable. He worked steadily until the woman appeared again, carrying dinner out to a picnic table near the garden. He then helped her with a crib and the two babies, and they sat down and ate, the woman serving and fussing over him and pointing once at the Continental as though she had noticed it earlier and was now surprised that it had returned. Jack hardly looked up from his plate.

With the car idling and the air conditioner pushing cool billows at her face so that her tears felt cold, Toni cried and cried and cried and cried, until the front of her suit was wet.

Was this what he had always really wanted, and not the high life and chances that he said he loved? Had Payson actually paid him to disappear, or had the threat been enough? It didn't matter now, but why hadn't he ever spoken to her of this? Perhaps he hadn't known himself.

She blotted her eyes and tried to wipe the tears from her face. Could she have provided it for him? She looked back over at the picnic table and Jack bent over his meal and the woman talking to him volubly and happily, twisting a hand on a thin wrist as she spoke.

No. Toni could never be happy here or anywhere like it. It just wasn't her. She had to have activity, details, people, business. She had to take chances over which she had some control: the Borghese, a little light recreational gambling, the track, the market. All that was in her blood; the thought of having to wait for another person to bring home a paycheck that would have to be stretched just to make them comfortable was a deathly prospect to her, no matter how much she might love him.

Then, *should* she help Jack? Watching the woman's thin dress sway as she moved into the house with some empty dishes and quickly returned with another beer, she decided that they certainly could use the money; there were two kids and Jack was some sort of manual worker. And he had always so much enjoyed a big car and the nice clothes that looked so good on him.

Toni found a dry hanky in her purse and blew her nose. She drew in a deep breath and looked at them again.

But who was *she* to disturb *that?* And then, no matter the duress, Jack had chosen. He had picked his chips off the table, and when the cubes were rolled, he had nothing down, which was life.

On a hot afternoon a few days later, *Bark-a-Roll* was taking the moderate swells with an easy rolling motion that was putting Toni to sleep. She was lounging on the upper deck, and the sun was so hot and the breeze so gentle that she thought she had slipped out of her body and merged with the elements and all that remained was her consciousness. And if she could only lose that—

"Got a question for you," said Furco, who was in the chair beside her. Tina was below on the afterdeck with Jane's two children and Lou, the mate. Gabriela was taking a nap.

"No more words, please. My mind is a big red-sunny blank."

Furco had been doing a crossword—"Practice for stir," he had said—but he now put it aside. "This has been buggin' me, and I wanna get it out in the open. That guy—Ross. What was he to you, anyhow?"

Toni tried to open her eyes, but the sun was in them, and she reached for her sunglasses. She looked over at him. "You're serious now, aren't you?"

He just stared.

"Well . . ." She pushed herself up on her elbows and let the breeze cool her body. It was the most perfect day she could remember. There wasn't a cloud in the sky. "I was embattled, beset, under attack from Payson and Dom and you, if I remember correctly. Then there was Mazullo and Falci and Scarpone. They raped me and killed my good friend and chef. Payson and Dom tried to kill me in Europe. I had good reason to believe they would try to kill me here. As far as I knew, Mazullo and his friends worked for you, and you worked either for some other recently murdered men, whom the papers were suggesting you might have killed, or for Payson, who had already proved he wanted me dead. By then I'd realized that Ross was a cop. I thought he could help me at least stay alive."

"When you talked to him on the phone from Switzerland?"

"From Europe." She nodded.

Furco thought about that and watched the gulls work the chum line off the stern of the vessel. "But before. Before you left with Payson. What'd you do with him *then?*"

"I met him at the boardwalk where, by your orders, I was

to gamble. We gambled together. We won. He had a routine
of wanting me to kiss the dice and kiss him before he rolled.''

"And you *did?*"

Toni nodded.

"But later—what happened later?"

"Later I had work to do, remember? Your work with the
valises, and my debt, which we really must discuss.''

He waved her off, and she watched the smooth features of
his tanned face: his long, thin nose and definite chin. His
cheekbones were a little too high, but he was a handsome
man. "How you feel about him now?"

She hunched her shoulders. How did she feel about somebody who had known her husband had been set up, her
marriage ruined, her business virtually bankrupted, but had
said nothing? Or who had suspected she was in danger and,
instead of warning or protecting her, had instead used her as
an expendable shill to further his own ends? Or who, finally,
had exploited her emotions in a scheme to get close to her,
again for a reason that had nothing to do with who they were
as human beings? Not very good.

But she said, "Personally, I think he wants to put both of
us in jail.''

Furco agreed. "Like we had something to do with his
partner. I hadn't come by, he woulda got done, too.''

They had no way of knowing that, but why quibble? Toni
waited, and when he asked nothing more, she lowered
herself back into the lounger.

Some minutes later, he said, "And that Dom—what was
it you had that he said he wanted?"

"Information,'' she replied without opening her eyes. She
believed that the sun was penetrating her flesh and had now
begun to warm her bones.

" 'Bout what?"

"Something in Europe. Did you ever let Payson do any
investing for you?"

"Me?" He laughed. "I probably should've. The guy was
good. You should hear what he made for the others, but I
got this thing. I can't. I gotta know where my dough is and
what it's doing or not doing. Otherwise I don't sleep, which
is worth something.''

Toni laughed. "Mr. Furco—you're really a very conservative guy."

He looked away. "In some ways."

Still later, after they had had a drink and shifted the chairs into the shade, he asked her what she was going to do, now that things seemed to be evening out for her. "I mean, you got nothing to worry about. What can they get you on—carrying imaginary money around some foreign countries?—if you don't tell them nothing?"

"I think I'll expand."

"Yeah?" Furco made a point of glancing at her stomach.

"*And* redecorate." She sipped from her second margarita. It was tangy, and the alcohol went straight to her head. She could feel a light-headed sense of well-being seeping all through her.

She turned her face to his and smiled.

"Sounds like you're suddenly flush."

"Me?" She felt a tautness in her palm as she touched her fingers to her upper chest. The stitches had been removed the day before. "I don't need to be flush. Not with a rich partner who's also—what was that headline?" With her foot she toed over the *Philadelphia Inquirer* until she found the page. It featured an article describing a press conference at which state police officials had said there was not enough evidence to bring crime boss Lucca Furco to trial. Even the target pistol he'd used to defend his business partner (Toni was named) was licensed to him, and a DEA agent had witnessed the shooting.

She read the line she was looking for, " '—Lucca Furco, who some call the "Neon Caesar" of South Jersey.' "

Furco smiled and shook his head. "The stuff they come up with." He looked off at the line of buildings they could just see beyond the taffrail to the west. "Point is—we all know what happened to Caesar. It wasn't pretty."

"You can always abdicate."

"But then what? What do I do for, you know, money?"

Toni nearly choked on her drink. "C'mon, Lucca—you're talking to me, Toni. Your partner. How much is enough?" She took another sip and looked out to sea. "And then I got the feeling we're going to make a bundle after we expand. Tax-free profits." She smiled.

There was a long pause before Furco asked, "You really want me for your partner?"

She turned her head to him. Did she want, did she need protection? Had he—he alone, nobody else—protected her for no other reason than his affection for her? And did she believe, she now asked herself for the first time, that he loved her? "Yes. Absolutely."

Furco's smile broke slowly. He shook his head. He looked away and, as if talking to a third party, asked, "What she saying to me? Could I be hearing right? Is this the time to pop the big question? Go ahead, Lucca. She can't blame you for asking." Furco took in a big breath and turned to her histrionically. "I wonder if I can take you to dinner?"

Toni flicked down the sunglasses so he could see her eyes. "With you, I'll go to dinner. You name the day."

FROM THE BESTSELLING AUTHOR OF
ALICE IN LA LA LAND

ROBERT CAMPBELL

From Edgar Award-Winning author Robert Campbell come big time crime novels with a brilliant kaleidoscope of characters.

☐ *ALICE IN LA LA LAND* ....66931/$3.95

☐ *RED CENT* ....64364/$3.50

☐ *PLUGGED NICKEL* ....64363/$3.50

JUICE
**COMING IN JANUARY
FROM POCKET BOOKS**

POCKET
BOOKS